GUS

Martin Vlain

outskirtspress
DENVER, COLORADO

Outskirts Press, Inc.
http://www.outskirtspress.com

Paperback ISBN: 978-1-4787-0298-6
Hardback ISBN: 978-1-4787-0205-4

PRINTED IN THE UNITED STATES OF AMERICA

Introduction

Call me Gus.

That isn't my name. It's an acronym. Officially, I'm Gregory Ulysses Stern the Third. But only in official places like school do I own up to it. I can't stand Gregory. And Ulysses I hate. Long ago, I suppose, these were great names given to great men. But now they seem fit only for sissies.

What you're about to read are my memoirs. Memoirs are something like an autobiography. Only they're better because dull stuff like unimportant facts can be left out. Usually only old or famous people write memoirs. When they do, I think they lie. They recall far too many of the heroic things they neither thought nor said nor did. They present descriptions of their earlier days through the prism of forgetful and embellished memory. They color the truth to paint themselves as kind, brave, decent, generous and wise.

Maybe some of them really were so.

In this book I haven't tried to color the truth. I haven't hidden the fact that at times I've been cowardly and rotten. I merely have sought to describe with accuracy and honesty what I was experiencing as a boy living mostly in Brooklyn but briefly too in Tennessee during the Depression and World War II.

Gregory Ulysses Stern III
Freeport, N.Y. 1 January 1949

Chapter 1

A Rotten Kid

One morning the W.P.A. shows up on my block. In starting their project the workers seem to make more noise hollering at each other than they ever do while working. They come in two trucks. One brings equipment; the other, tools and six laborers. As soon as everyone and everything is unloaded, the drivers leave with the vehicles.

Running even with the sidewalk about a third of the way into the street are guard rails put up by the work crew. The men call these horses. A better name would be zebras for they are made of wood which has been painted white with black stripes. The forty foot length of the work area which the horses fence off reaches from the edge of our property to Stinky's house.

As Charlie, Stinky and I watch the workers swing their picks and scoop up rock and dirt with their shovels, we think they're having great fun. The job looks important too. Charlie asks one of the men what they're building. The fellow ignores him. Charlie asks him again. A different laborer replies, "A grave in which to bury nosey brats like you."

A shiver of dread passes through me. Then Charlie who is more dopey than daring calls the man a doo-doo. The worker looks like he's going to slug my friend but when the others laugh, he merely makes a threatening swipe at Charlie and tells us to shove off.

We decide to do that.

In the tree in my yard we begin playing Tarzan. From our perches in the branches, we can watch the workers. However, we don't pay them much mind. We have better things to think about.

After all, with apes as our only allies in the jungle, we're engulfed in a fight against all of the world's lions and tigers.

In the middle of the afternoon the W.P.A. trucks return. They bring kerosene lamps. The workers light them and hang them on the horses. Then they pile their tools and themselves on board the vehicles and leave.

In the work area a shallow trench has been dug by the workers. Dirt and rock from it has been heaped up along its length. It looks like a great place in which to play war. The only trouble is that it's in the street. I'm not allowed out there. Nor are Charlie and Stinky. Nonetheless, the trench is too inviting a play area to pass up. I say, "The guard rails make this trench the same as the sidewalk. The troops need us. Let's go to war."

I rush forward and leap into the trench. My friends follow.

The combat in France in 1918 could not have been more impressive than ours twenty years later on East 47th Street. We're blasting the Germans to bits. Of course, our rifles and machine guns exist solely in our imagination. Our grenades and cannon shells, however, are more substantial since we can toss rocks and clumps of dirt to mimic them.

Suddenly the shrill squeaky voices of Andy and Andrea, the six year old twins from across the street, begin scolding us and ordering us out of our trench. It's obvious they're jealous of us and of our good fortune in having the W.P.A. do their digging on our side of the block.

"Mind your own business, unless you want to get clunked by this grenade," I shout as I clench a clump of earth in my hand and wave it threateningly at them.

"Yea, mind your own business," echoes Stinky.

"You're not supposed to be in the street. I'm going to tell your mothers," nags Andrea.

"They're Germans. They're enemies. Let 'em have it," orders Charlie.

He's already winging his second grenade before I heave my first.

His miss. Mine doesn't. I aim my clod of clay straight at Andy's kisser but my throw goes wild and I clobber Andrea instead. She runs home crying.

I start to worry but when Charlie looks at me approvingly and shouts, "Good hit," I feel like a hero. With eager enthusiasm I peg my second and third throws at Andy but they fall far short of him as he retreats to his house.

We never have time to celebrate our victory. The twins' mother comes rushing out of her house shouting insults at us. Threatened by such an overwhelming and imposing force, we do the sensible thing: we panic and flee.

Andrea's mother keeps screaming at us to stop. No one does. My friends dart for their homes. I avoid mine. I hightail it through my yard and Charlie's and hide behind his neighbor's hedges.

Andrea's mother crosses the street and goes directly to Stinky's house. She visits there for maybe a minute or two. Then she leaves and hurries over to mine.

In a short while I hear my mother calling me. I know that if I answer, I'll have to go home immediately and be beaten. If I don't she'd lay it into me later. Faced with this choice, I stay silent.

Even though Mother can't see me, she knows I'm within earshot. She issues what she calls her last and final warning to Gregory Ulysses Stern the Third to stop hiding and to come home at once.

No one needs to tell me I'm in Dutch up to my ears. But knowing that there's no way things could possibly get worse, I stay put.

After re-issuing her last and final warning a few more times, she gives up. Andrea's mother leaves her and returns home.

Most of the time while I'm hiding behind the hedges, I'm too worried to think. Now that the crisis has passed, I begin to wonder why Andrea's mother had gone first to Stinky's instead of directly to my place. I think maybe she's forgotten where I live. Then again maybe she hasn't.

Perhaps, she went right off to Stinky's because she wasn't sure it wasn't him who had beaned Andrea. If neither of the twins had seen me toss the grenade, they wouldn't have known it wasn't thrown by one of my playmates.

All of a sudden, I realize why Andrea's mother had gone to my house but hadn't bothered to go to Charlie's. She must have learned from Stinky that I was the culprit. The rat has squealed on me.

I make my way along the hedges to the back of Charlie's neighbor's yard. There I climb over a fence and land on the property of people from around the block. Then I blaze a trail to the house behind Stinky's. By wedging myself through some shrubbery, I enter the squealer's yard and post myself below his window. It's held partially open by a small slide screen.

"Hey Stinky," I call in a loud whisper.

There's no answer.

"Stinky," I repeat a little louder.

He comes to the window.

"What happened?" I ask in a continuing low voice.

"I've got to stay in my room till supper."

"Why?"

"Cause I was playing with you in the street."

"What happened with Andrea's mother?"

"Nothing. Nothing much."

"You told on me."

"I had to."

"Baloney."

"I had to. I didn't want to get spanked for something I didn't do. It was your fault. You were to blame."

"Some friend you are."

"Tough. Anyway, you shouldn't have hit a girl."

"So?"

"So, you're a bully, Gus."

"I am not."

"You are too."

"Am not."

"Are too."

"Am not, am not."

"Are too, are too, are too."

Our voices have been rising steadily in intensity. Now, mine ceases as I'm much too mad to carry on shouting. I show him my fist.

He puts his thumb to his nose and begins making faces.

I holler, "Tattle tale, tattle tale," and give him a few faces of my own.

It soon becomes evident that I'm out of my league in mugging. He crosses his eyes, thumbs his ears and wiggles his fingers while he cocks his noggin' and gives me a Bronx cheer.

That does it. That's the straw that breaks the camel's back.

Exasperated and in a rage, I pick up a jagged rock and try to bean him with it. The missile sails true but because Stinky does a side step, it misses him but not his window. As glass shatters and crashes down, Stinky's mother arrives at his side. Out of what is left of the window, she sees me and shouts, "You, you delinquent, wait. Wait there for me."

I'm sure it doesn't take her two shakes of a lamb's tail to get outside to nab me. But it's a hopeless effort. Within one shake, I'm gone. I flee up the street to the lot on the corner. There I hide in the tall grass.

I'm exhausted. The running has left my right side burning in pain. My throat feels like a choke collar is squeezing it. My chest aches for air.

Lying on my back with my knees bent upwards, I rest and wait to recover my breath. Overhead, ever so slowly, cotton-puff clouds drift and gradually change shape. The sky is indifferent to my troubles. It doesn't care that I'm doomed. Its disinterest is contagious. I lie there gazing at the heavens and forget my problems. I relax and fall off to sleep.

It's twilight when I awake. As soon as I recover from the shock of waking and not finding myself in my own bed, I wonder whether it's dawn or evening. Nearby, I hear voices. I sit up and peer through the tall grass for their source. On the sidewalk edging the lot a teenaged couple hurries along. They show obvious concern for something which has been happening down the block. I rise, take a quick leak and move off to follow them. In the distance I can hear a trolley and traffic. Down the block, I see a small crowd gathered by a Police car. It's parked next to the W.P.A. trench and under the street lamp in front of our property. By the time I get near the scene, it's dark out.

My mother and father stand in the center of the crowd talking to a cop. I look up at my house and see Gram and Gwen watching everything from a window. I move back to stay out of their sight.

Suddenly it dawns on me that with everyone's attention riveted on the street, I have a golden opportunity to circle around to the back door and sneak into the house. It's risky but somehow, I manage it. I even get to raid a few biscuits out of the bread box before I tiptoe into my room. With my belly full, I undress and crawl into bed.

It must be around midnight when I'm awakened by a piercing shriek. I sit up in terror. My brother does the same. He lets it be known that he's scared by crying.

The light snaps on. Before me is my mother.

"Where have you been?" she demands.

I don't answer.

Matthew's crying shifts down to sobbing. I want to look over at him but I don't dare. I expect my mother to take a swing at me and when it comes I need to be prepared to duck.

My dad enters and says, "So there you are. You had us worried."

My mother adds, "We've had the Police out looking for you."

"Will I get the chair?" I ask.

"What?" says Mother as she moves over to comfort Matthew.

"Will they fry me?"

Mother announces that I've taken leave of my senses.

My Dad tells her, "He doesn't realize why we've had the Police looking for him. I think he believes they're out to capture him and punish him with electrocution for his wrongdoing."

"They should," she insists. Then turning to me she questions, "Is that what you think?"

I nod yes.

I don't know what I expect to happen next but I do know that what happens isn't what I expect. She tells me, "We'll talk about this in the morning. Now go back to sleep."

With Matthew quiet and tucked in, she turns off the light and leaves with my dad.

Next morning I make it a point to mind my P's and Q's. I have no wish to draw attention to myself. I remain as quiet as possible. I even do my best to eat my corn flakes without crunching.

My dad as usual has gotten up late. As I finish my cereal he steps into the kitchen for a quick swig of coffee. He's in a rush to leave. I ask to be excused from the table. Mother says, "Stay where you are. We haven't dealt with you yet for yesterday's escapades."

Because he has to run, the old man begs off of punishing me. He kisses us good-by and leaves.

My dad's quick exit does nothing to temper my mother's ire. She turns on me and snaps, "Have you any idea of how much your rottenness is going to cost us?"

Even if I knew the answer, which I don't, I know I'm not supposed to say it.

When she's in a mood, lots of her questions aren't really questions. They're announcements. Usually they warn you that unless you're looking to be slammed silly, you'd better keep silent and act contrite. But sometimes they're introductions to a tirade.

So the real question isn't whether I know how much my rottenness is going to cost us. Rather it is whether she's going to remain calm or whether she'll work herself up into a furor and beat me.

In five minutes I have the answer. Mercifully, I'm sentenced to spend the morning standing in a corner. There I'm expected to reflect upon my wickedness.

When I go to take up my customary position in the kitchen corner, Mother orders me to carry out the punishment in the dining room. Of late I've been spending so much time in the kitchen corner pressing my forehead against the converging walls that I've begun to soil them and to thin their paint. She's sending me elsewhere to relieve the problem. I don't say anything but I think that this is silly: soon instead of having to paint in just one room, she'll have to paint in two.

After breakfast Gwen goes off to visit a friend. Matthew is put in his playpen and told not to climb out of it. My mother cleans most of the house. Gram washes and dries the morning dishes.

Around ten-thirty Gwen returns. In the kitchen the women sit down to have coffee. I hope they'll talk about something interesting. I don't normally eavesdrop but staring at nothing has left me too bored not to give it a shot. Besides, my punishment is a waste of time. It isn't making me want to do good. Rather it's doubling my desire to get revenge on Andrea and Stinky. I hate them both.

The table talk begins with a discussion regarding the need for a new light bulb in Gram's bedroom lamp. Then it passes through some more dull stuff like grocery needs and should Mother's ironing be put off until tomorrow. Just when I'm ready to give up on the gossip, Gram starts talking about her recent visit with Carolina Wren.

Carolina and Gram have been friends ever since Prohibition when both used to work as waitresses in a speakeasy. Carolina has what Gram claims are the feminine ingredients for success, namely, a good shape and total contempt for men.

Carolina has made a career out of marrying amply insured old men and collecting on their policies when they've died. These arrangements though shady have been thoroughly legitimate. From the moment each husband took to his marriage bed until the day he gave up the ghost, Carolina treated him to the time of his life. Her first three mates succumbed to happy heart attacks. Her fourth had been a problem. It seemed he was impotent. He had married Carolina only for show. He wanted his friends to think he was a he-man. At first, Carolina was furious and considered divorcing him. She feared that without her regular doses of mad passionate love, the old bastard could live forever. But when he regaled her with a more than generous spending allowance and offered no objection to her seeing other men so long as the affairs were kept discreet, she kind of got to hoping that he'd outlast Methuselah.

For a year and a half everything went along fine. Then Carolina got pregnant. To her surprise, the old man didn't mind. In fact, he thought it was great. For month after month he bragged to one and all that his kid was on the way. But when it arrived and turned out to be a six pound six ounce negro, he was mortified. Humbled, heartbroken and humiliated, he quit caring about everyone and everything. Within a few weeks, he died.

Carolina had deep six-ed him.

Gram reveals that Carolina currently is keeping company with three men. The first has brawn but no brains. The second has brains but no brawn. The third has hemorrhoids. What this last one also has to make him especially attractive to her is an advanced age, a heart condition and life insurance. Carolina has been trying to stampede him into marriage. She has a dreadful fear that the old boy will give out his last grunt crapping as a bachelor instead of humping as her husband.

Gram has confided to Carolina that she feels a special attraction to the fellow with brawn. Carolina graciously volunteers to step aside and give Gram a clear path to him. She tells Gram that as long as there's still six miles of cock available in Flatlands, she isn't about to deprive a sisterly friend of her right to have a mere six inches of it.

At this point Mother must have remembered that I'm nearby. Carrying on in a conversational tone she asks, "Gus, are you listening."

"No," I answer.

After lunch Mother and I go shopping. Besides groceries she buys presents: a set of jacks for Andrea and a toy police car with a siren for Stinky. She also purchases wrapping paper and a ribbon. When we return home Stinky and Charlie are taunting the W.P.A. men. They're chanting, "W.P.A., we pick apples."

Before I can even think to comment on this scene, Mother warns me never to let her catch me saying such vile things.

We go indoors. There I'm forced to wash and to change into my Sunday clothes. I can't figure out why I must dress up. I'm wise enough not to ask. Mother begins combing my hair with barber's gunk. I'm certain now that we're headed to church.

I speak up saying, "Going to church on a weekday makes no sense. Not even the minister is there. He's either at a funeral or else he's visiting sick people in a hospital."

"That's true. Now stick out your tongue," she says as she straightens my tie.

I do as told. She moistens her handkerchief by dabbing it on my tongue and rubs some dirt or grime off of my cheek. I hate it when she does that. Even though it's my spit cleaning my cheek, it's unsanitary. My uncle, Ernie, has told me this and he knows what he's talking about.

I'm waiting for an explanation of why we're going to church. When none comes, I say, "Isn't it foolish to go to church when no one is there?"

"Not necessarily. Some people take comfort just sitting there. Some find solace in prayer. What is foolish is this conversation. Why must you bother me with talk of church now?"

"Isn't that where we're going?"

She pauses and replies, "Just because you put on good clothes doesn't mean you're going to church. I want you to look nice when you go now to apologize to Andrea and to Stanley for your terrible behavior."

"Geez, I can't do that."

"You can and you will," she snaps back. After a pause she adds, "And you'll remember when you get to Stanley's to call him Stanley and not Stinky."

"Heck!"

"Heck nothing," she insists as she hands me Andrea's present already wrapped.

We go downstairs and cross the street. Mother waits a house away as I walk slowly up to Andrea's stoop. I look back at her. She waves me forward. I go up the stoop but at the top I hesitate to ring the bell. If Andrea's mother answers, I could get killed.

On the other hand maybe I'd only get screamed at.

Out of the corner of my eye I see I'm still being watched. I'm between a rock and a hard place.

There's a saying that says when you're faced with a devil that you know and one that you don't, it's better to stay with the one that you know. Whoever coined that bit of advice was nuts or didn't have a mother like mine.

I opt for the unknown devil. I ring Andrea's bell.

Her mother answers.

Before she can light into me, I put forth the present and say, "I'm sorry I hurt Andrea. I've come to tell her that and give her this."

"You look very nice, Gus, like a little gentleman. I'm sure Andrea forgives you. Wait while I go get her."

Because it takes Andrea over a minute to come to the door, I figure she must have been in the bathroom. Either that or her mother had to use up a lot of time convincing her to see me.

"Hi Andrea," I say, "I'm sorry I hit you. I was aiming for Andy but my throw went wild. Anyway, here's a gift."

"Thank you. Your apology is accepted," she says as she takes the present.

We say good-by. She goes back inside and I return down the stoop.

Mother comes forward, "That wasn't so bad, was it? Now do the same at Stanley's"

We recross the street. She waits at the edge of our property as I go past our neighbor's place to Stinky's. I go up his stoop and ring the bell.

When the door opens, Stinky's mother takes one look at me and yells, "You! You disgusting, horrible roughneck! You belong in a Reform School. You shouldn't be allowed in the company of decent people."

"I've come to apologize. I've got a present for Stinky."

"His name is Stanley. It is not Stinky. It's Stanley. And Stanley doesn't want your present and he doesn't accept your apology. Now leave. And don't ever set foot on our property again."

I start to leave. Then she orders me to wait. In less than a half of a minute she returns and hands me a dollar and a quarter. "Give this to your parents. It's their change. Tell them the glazier's bill was three seventy five."

She slams the door.

I leave.

Fifty feet away I hand my mother the money and the rejected gift. She says nothing. We return home.

After I've changed back into my regular clothes, Mother hands me Stinky's police car as a present. She says I've earned it for my good behavior in apologizing to Andrea and for trying to do the same with Stanley.

As I roll the toy on the floor and marvel at its siren, I think about these last two days: I played in the street. I urged and led my friends to do the same. I beaned a girl. I willfully ignored and disobeyed my mother's calls to come home at once. I tried with all of my might to injure a friend. I smashed his window. I hid out. By so doing I made the cops stop chasing crooks and waste their time looking for me. I sneaked home. I stole biscuits. I lied about eavesdropping.

I did all of these wicked things. I was a rotten kid and though I didn't quite get off Scot-free, I'm now rewarded with a toy.

Who can figure it? I can't. I won't. I'm not dumb enough to look a gift horse in the mouth.

Chapter 2
Family History

To understand why I am the way I am, it's necessary to know why my folks are the way they are. After all, I'm the product of their genes and their upbringing almost as much as I am the product of my own. So to bring to you, the reader, knowledge of the important things I've learned over the years about my family, I going now to pause in these memoirs and devote a chapter to family history. I should apologize for this but because my relatives have had interesting pasts, I'm hesitant to do so. After all, this chapter may prove to be the best in the book. If so, it doesn't seem sane to say I'm sorry it's here.

I suppose if I were a better writer I would manage to get all the stuff about my kin across without interrupting the flow of my story. Mark Twain could do that. However, I'm not him. I'm me. To quote a phrase coined by my dad. "I'm shortchanged in the currency of genius." So I'm going to write what I have to write in the best way I'm know how and ask you, my reader, to tolerate my literary faults.

This said, get set now to forget about me for a while and read on. You're in for a treat. I'm going to entertain you by letting you in on some of the secrets and high points which marked the lives of the Hamiltons and the Sterns who happened to arrive on Mother Earth a generation or two before me.

I can't remember when I began to fear my father. But from stories I've been told, I'm sure it dates from the cradle.

During my babyhood, the old man used to lift me up to face his face. He'd fix his features in a scowl and in a voice heavy with menace, he'd snarl, "I love you, you little stinker."

I'd scream with terror. He'd laugh. Then he'd kiss me and put me down.

His humor made everyone laugh except me.

Daddy wasn't sadistic. Usually he was very kind. He seldom raised his voice. He rarely gave orders. Never once in my life did he hit me. He generally smiled. He loved to tell stories and to make people laugh at his jokes. Humor was his way. But often it sailed over people's heads. And sometimes it wasn't appreciated. He taught my brother Matt and me to call him "the old man" and our mother "the old lady." She didn't take kindly to that. She was twenty-three and he, twenty-six when this began. I was five and Matt was two.

Come to think of it, the old lady seldom drew any satisfaction from Daddy's humor. She regarded it as his shield against success. She knew it could charm the stuffing out of people. Hadn't she, herself, been dazzled by it? She knew the old man also overflowed with talent, wit, intelligence and personality. She felt, moreover, that with his blond, blue-eyed, boy next door, all-American, good looks he should have been overcoming whatever obstacles to fame and fortune lay in his path. Her assessment was correct. The only trouble was that all of my Dad's obstacles were internal rather than external. He just wasn't the succeeding type. He was more the failing, lazy slob type.

There was a time when Dad was ambitious. In high school his heart was set on going to Cornell to study journalism. He had always been super in English. In fact, he was brilliant in all of his subjects. But writing was his passion. He had over a dozen poems published in newspapers and magazines before he went off to college.

Perhaps, Dad's lack of ambition could be traced to his having suffered success and recognition too early in life. His high school days were a run of glory. Every year he was elected to a class office. He was a member of the Arista, a letterman for three years in track, a reporter for the school paper and the editor of both the school magazine and the yearbook. As a junior he ran for school President and missed election by a handful of votes. As a senior he tried again and won in a five to one landslide.

Dad has said the milk of human approval like that of human kindness trickles from a dry tit and leaves a sour aftertaste. The more popular he became in high school, the more he inspired envy. No longer was he able to be a nice kid bent on being nothing more than a nice kid. Suddenly he'd become a symbol or an image. Like President Roosevelt he learned that a fellow can be damned and adored for the same thing. He knew he was supposed to personify the dreams of his public. But he felt he'd become the living embodiment of their nightmares. When he graduated, he welcomed his return to anonymity.

Dad's desire for a career in journalism faded with his graduation. His father had turned thumbs down on letting him attend Cornell. Pop wanted his son to be a lawyer. Furthermore, he insisted upon an Irish catholic education for Dad at either Fordham or St. John's. There he'd pal around with the right crowd and make influential connections. In my grandfather's eyes and in those of his political colleagues these universities stood head and shoulders above the Ivy League.

My Dad should have stood up to Pop. But as a well mannered seventeen year old boy trained always to say "Yes, sir" to his father, Dad said, "Yes, sir" and enrolled in St John's.

Although Pop in a saloon was always a "Hail Fellow, Well Met," generous treater and spendthrift, at home he was a penny pincher. He told Dad, "Work builds character." So to make sure my Dad would not be shortchanged in character, he got him a job as a clerk by day in a title insurance company so that he could attend school at night and study on the weekends. My Dad obliged. Yet somehow in the midst of this busy schedule, he found time for play. He knocked up my mother. In 1931 on the Saturday between Good Friday and Easter, they were married by a Justice of the Peace. Seven months later, I arrived.

Under circumstances as trying as these a man's character often is revealed:some men rise, some fall. My Dad did neither. He just continued working and going to school. With a quarter of the country drowning in unemployment and the other three-fourths barely able to stay economically afloat, his decision to keep treading water at the title insurance company made sense. For a twenty-one year old with a wife and kid to support, no other responsible option was available.

In 1932, Dad graduated, passed the bar and rejected the practice of law. It was a profession he despised.

Meanwhile my mother was finding that her life was becoming one long succession of disappointments. It hadn't always been that way. While her father had lived, fortune had favored her. Her dad had been a linotype operator in Ontario and later an editor of newspapers in the United States. Every two years, he moved to a bigger city and a better job. My grandmother had met and married him in 1911 in Parkhill. She gave birth to my mother in 1913 in Parry Sound. She added a son, Billy, in 1915 in London. Unfortunately, a year later, the little fellow died of the flu. Shortly afterwards the family moved to Toronto. In 1922 they entered the U.S.A.

In Detroit in 1924 Gwen was born. She was not the first Hamilton to be born on American soil. She was merely the first in 150 years. Before, during and after the American Revolution our family's colonial ancestors had been Tories. Unlike their rebellious countrymen who claimed until 1776 to be fighting for their rights as Englishmen, my forefathers fought merely for their right to remain Englishmen. Such loyalty and devotion to the Crown did not go unrecognized. The victors allowed my folks a choice of staying in America to be scorned, persecuted and perhaps hanged or of fleeing and being fleeced of their property. Fortunately, for me, the family opted wisely and took off without delay for Canada. There they set about the business of begetting Hamiltons, who begot more Hamiltons until eventually, the begotten had gotten to be my grandfather, my mother and me.

In 1926, my mother's dad contracted typhoid fever and died while working as an editor for the Brooklyn Eagle. The circumstances of his departure were unusual. He had been brought to Kingston Hospital and put to bed in a third floor room possessing a door opening to an outside balcony. According to the people at the hospital, my grandfather while delirious with fever got out of bed, went out onto the balcony and leaped to his death.

As telephones were sparse and as Postal Telegraph and Western Union were unreliable in their swift delivery of telegrams, the notification which came of my grandfather's passing was neither immediate nor considerate. He had died in the morning. About four in the afternoon a couple of truckmen knocked on my grandmother's front door. My mother, then a girl of twelve, answered. The men told her they were from the hospital and were delivering the corpse of one Reginald Cornelius Hamilton. In shock my mother went to the rear of the flat and knocked on my grandmother's bedroom door.

"Go away," ordered Gram.

"Some men from the hospital are here," said Mother.

"Find out what they want."

"They've brought Daddy's body. He's dead."

"S---," said Gram.

Rumbling could be heard through the door as she and her boyfriend tumbled out of bed and fished about for their clothes.

My mother returned to the front room. The delivery men brought in a wicker casket containing the body. Gram came out and tipped them a quarter.They left.

Six years after my grandfather's death Gram and Warren LaGrange, the fellow she'd been in bed with on that afternoon got married.

Mother hated Warren. So did I. He was one of those too well groomed, slick, pompous, viper-like fellows who slither through life as snidely as Nazis. He was good only for one thing: making people miserable. Whatever my grandmother saw in him beyond a roll in the hay puzzled all who knew her. Gram really had a touch of class even if she was hot pussy. Warren was all image and no mettle.

After their marriage Warren took regularly to belittling Gram and to having affairs with all of her friends. That wasn't anything new. That was his modus operandi. When my grandfather died Warren had been doing the same with his first wife. Indeed, in his whole life, the only person he ever treated with even a trace of kindness was Gwen. But only on and off. Normally, he referred to her as his whore child. It was a figure of speech but Gwen, I think, believed it. My Dad wondered about it too. I overheard him say once that the real reason R. Cornelius Hamilton moved so much was because of Gram's biennial infidelities. When I heard that I rushed to the dictionary. With mixed feelings I found out that biennial wasn't a synonym for sodomizing.

Grandfather Hamilton had always made a decent salary. As long as he breathed his family had not wanted for anything. He was what you'd call a good provider. Yet he liked to go out on the town.

He used to drink and gamble a lot. When my mother was still in her high chair, he came home one wintry night with a snoot full and gave Gram ten dollars for house money for the week.

"What's this?" scolded Gram.

"House money," he said as he flopped into a chair by their potbellied stove.

"Where's the other ten dollars?"

"I lost it gambling."

"How did you do that?"

"Look, Jenny, when I win as I almost always do, you don't complain. You're as happy as can be to celebrate and spend the winnings with me."

"Of course, but what in hell does that have to do with my house money?"

"Damn, let's drop it. I'll make it up to you next week."

"No you won't," said Gram as she opened the iron door of the stove and threw the money into the fire.

My grandfather looked on in disbelief, "That's ten dollars you've burned," he said.

"It is indeed," answered Gram, "and I'll continue to burn everything you give me if it's short of what I expect."

The following night he brought home her twenty dollars.

Because my grandfather spent money as fast as he made it, Gram had to go into debt to bury him. Yet overnight his funeral bills got paid. My grandfather really had good friends. The fellows on the Eagle and his lodge brothers in the Masons managed between them to collect a few hundred dollars for Gram. Because the burial expenses had been less, Dad wisecracked, "Gram felt sad for a day and euphoric for a month." Even I, however, knew that he was being unfair. No one cut off from a steady income smiles--especially not a widow with two young daughters.

Gram soon found work as a manicurist in a ritzy Manhattan hotel. Although her income from tips was adequate, it was not enough to sustain her former style of living. So when her elder daughter graduated from eighth grade, Gram insisted that she attend Girl's Commercial High School where she could learn a trade. Mother studied to become a seamstress. Because she was always a straight A student, she excelled as expected at sewing. Just after her fourteenth birthday, she was withdrawn from school and ordered by Gram to go out and get a job. Mother obeyed. By day she was overworked and underpaid in a sweat shop. By night she was shafted at home. She had to care for her sister, keep the kitchen and help at house cleaning. Gram overcharged her for her room and board and clothing. All my poor mother had to spend on herself each week was a half of a dollar.

My grandmother, meanwhile, continued to live comfortably. She spent most of her nights and all of her Sundays drinking in the corner bar with Warren. Gwen was fed lunch by Gram before she went to work and left in the care of a neighboring family for fifteen cents a day until evening. Then my mother returned from work and collected her.

When the sisters had finished dinner and had cleaned and put away the dishes, they went out in nice weather for a walk or sat on the stoop and talked with friends. When it rained or was cold or dark, Mother would turn on a lamp and read Gwen stories or tell her of the happy days when their father lived.

In 1930 the Sterns moved onto the block. They took the downstairs apartment in a brownstone next door to the family with which Gwen had stayed every afternoon. Now that my aunt was in school there was no need for a baby sitter. However, Gwen continued to play with the children of the people who had cared for her.

On Saturdays whenever my dad took a break from studying his law books, he'd step outside and watch the activity in the street. He used to like to watch the children play. Dad had always liked kids and began entertaining Gwen and her playmates by reciting fairy tales to them. None of the children had ever heard anyone tell stories as cleverly as my dad. If he did Goldilocks and the three bears, he would give every character a personality. Goldie might sound and act like Butterfly McQueen. Mama Bear would have a Yiddish accent and she'd behave like Mollie Goldberg. Poppa Bear would be a double for Andy Brown of Amos 'n' Andy. As for Baby Bear, he'd be a London cockney. Dad would be doing pantomime and mimicry of all the characters. He'd also toss in lots of jokes, puns and plays on words. As though all of this were not enough of a treat, Dad would whip out his harmonica and add background music and comic themes for the characters. He'd play an Irish Jig as the theme for Momma Goldberg Bear and Dixie for the cockney Baby Bear. What was funnier was his ability to make music sound as he pleased. His favorite trick was to play an Irish Jig and make it sound Jewish. Once I heard him do about fifteen minutes of variations on "My Country 'tis of Thee." It came across as more Hungarian than a Czardas, more Chinese than Chopsticks and more Hindu than "They don't wear pants on the southern side of France."

Gwen lost no time in telling her Mother and sister about her discovery of Dad and of how she was the only one who sat on his lap as he told the stories. Neither, however, cared. My mother was involved with a discovery of her own. She had started to keep company with a college freshman named Phil Napier. It was a short lived romance. It ended just before Christmas when Phil told Mother he had decided to become a priest. He confessed that while he liked her, he had stronger feelings for boys.

It was Mother's first encounter with a homosexual. It could have been tragic: imagine what it must be like for a young girl to have her first romance collapse that way. Fortunately no damage was done. Mother never had much more than brotherly feelings for Phil. So with genuine compassion she wished him well and wondered where and when she'd find another suitor.

When St John's closed for the Christmas vacation, Dad got a couple of weeks of partial rest. He was able to come home directly from work. Otherwise he'd have been running his usual routine of rushing to the Automat for a fast dinner followed by a quick dash to class. On the second of his vacation free evenings, he happened to be strolling down his block as Mother came walking up it with Gwen. The child got excited. Bolting away from her sister, the six year old charged towards my dad and leaped into his arms. He hugged her and kissed the top of her head. As he was putting her down, my distraught mother arrived. Before she could utter a word, Gwen began tugging on her coat sleeve and on my Dad's. The kid babbled out an introduction while jumping up and down. She couldn't contain the joy she felt over the happy circumstance of having two of her three favorite people meet. My parents behavior was less rational. With proper formality they exchanged subdued "hellos." Yet internally both were erupting with passion.

Nature took its course. By New Year's Gram realized a serious romance was underway. It inspired mixed feelings within her. She wanted to see her daughter happy but she didn't want to lose a baby sitter. In her left-handed way, Gram truly desired the best for her daughter. Although she had been hard on my mother, especially since my grandfather's death, she'd been doing it for the kid's good. Gram didn't want either of her girls to grow up and be too much like herself. She was proud of my mother for being bright, pretty, honest, responsible, virtuous, hardworking, modest and caring. Because among these traits only beauty and intelligence were attributes of her own, Gram felt good for her daughter but better for herself. As she often said, "Goodness isn't necessarily good for a good life."

Even as a youngster Gram was wonderfully wicked. She used to pinch her baby sister, Alice, while the kid was in the cradle. When the child cried, Great Grandma would come and relieve Gram of the baby sitting chore and force it on another. Using similar tricks of pluck, guile and rottenness, Gram passed through a pleasant and carefree childhood. As she matured, she became even more adept at sidestepping unwanted duties. Because she was so disarmingly frank in admitting to her shortcomings, everyone forgave her faults. She was charming, interesting and likeable.

On a Sunday in late February or early March of 1931 as my mother was sprucing up to go out with my Dad, Gram shocked her by asking, "How far have you and Greg gone?"

"Mama!" exclaimed Mother.

"Don't 'Mama' me," needled Gram, "just answer the question."

"Oh Mama, you're terrible. You know I can't answer such a question."

"I don't see why not. All you have to do is tell me: talk, tit or twat?"

"Mama, you're impossible."

"Naturally."

For a moment, Mother thought of not answering. She suspected that Gram was enjoying giving her the third degree. So to shake the old lady up, Mother sighed and said casually, "He's had all three."

"What?"

The ploy had worked. Mother was surprised by the simplicity of the power switch. Gram, however, was too much in shock to notice or to care who was dominating the conversation.

"Are you telling me the truth?" asked Gram.

"Don't I usually?"

"Don't be flip with me, young lady. Remember I'm your mother."

"I'm sorry," said Mother, "but I didn't start this. What takes place between Greg and me is personal and private. I refuse to let gutter talk besmirch it."

"You've been to bed with him! Merciful Jesus, you're as dumb as your father."

A hot argument now began in earnest. My mother's crazy button had been pressed. My grandfather in death had become for her a figure more perfect than the Savior. Gram knew this. She hadn't intended to belittle or to besmirch either her daughter or her late husband when she labeled them as dumb. The truth just slipped out as it usually does when the sentinel of tact isn't on hand to guard it with lies. Gram immediately would have backed off and apologized but Mother had exploded and now was calling her a vile, wicked old lady.

Vile and wicked were modifiers Gram could abide but old was a cut which stabbed her where she lived. She stormed back discharging a fusillade of her own insults. But it was fury fired in vain. Mother had left the reach of reason, harm or hearing. She was off in the Jerusalem of her own mind strewing palm fronds and maple leaves before the feet of her sainted father.

The doorbell rang. It was my dad. Immediately anger abdicated and sweetness reigned. Company manners had accomplished the impossible. Mother and daughter acted again like the loving portrait of a mother and daughter that we see depicted regularly on the cover of the Saturday Evening Post.

Once the young couple had left Gram got to pondering over

what had happened. She didn't know whether or not my mother was a virgin. She decided it didn't matter. The important thing was to get the kid out of town. Nip the romance in the bud! Seventeen was too young an age for a girl to become seriously involved with a man. Especially one who still didn't need to shave.

When Mother returned home from her date she found Gram busy packing. Gram said that her sister Alice in Detroit had become seriously ill and needed someone to take care of her. As no one in Ontario could come to her aid, they had called Gram. They asked her please to send Cynthia to attend to the emergency. There was an early train she could catch in the morning. Although it hadn't been decided yet who would meet her at the terminal in Detroit, someone from the family would be present to greet her and take her to Alice's.

Mother, of course, agreed to go. She finished the packing and told Gram to inform the sweat shop in the morning of the emergency trip and to ask them please to hold her job open for her when she returned. She also asked Gram to advise my dad of all that occurred and to tell him that she would write to him.

To Gram's great relief, Mother left home at 6 a.m. with her packed suitcase, four cheese sandwiches, a writing pad, five envelopes and enough money to buy a one way coach ticket to Detroit and still have a dollar left.

Gram then sent a wire on ahead to Detroit for someone to meet the train. When Mother arrived in Michigan after a journey of sixteen hours, she was greeted at the station by a healthy Aunt Alice who had not been ill at all and who was delighted to see my mother and thankful she had not come a week earlier. Had Gram carted her off then, Mother would have arrived in Detroit and have been stranded with no place to go for Alice had been away in Parkhill visiting for the last ten days.

Mother, of course, was furious with Gram. In the telegram my grandmother had asked her sister to put her daughter up for a month.

Alice was delighted to do so. Under less deceitful terms my mother would have been equally pleased. Now, however, she felt she was in a condition only to be angry and bitter. But there was another more potent condition plaguing her: she was pregnant.

In a few weeks when it was clear to Gram that there was no longer any question about my mother's state, she wired her train fare. My mother returned home and became Mrs. Stern.

Seven months later, I arrived. There was nothing auspicious about my birth. However, for my Dad it helped him to solve a vexing problem. He never knew what to call his mother-in-law. He had been getting around this difficulty by never initiating a conversation. He called Gram "you" or nothing at all. When I showed up he ended this awkwardness by calling her "Granny." She was thirty-eight but in face and figure a striking twenty-five. She would have preferred having him call her "Jenny." But she also felt awkward and didn't tell him this.So when Dad called her "Granny," she just smiled and hated him.

In a fairy tale the story ends when Prince Charming finds the Princess. They marry and live happily ever after.

According to my Dad in real life this play of time and happiness is reversed. The golden days precede marriage. The ones filled with ogres, horrors, trials and tribulations come afterwards.

My parents wedding in 1931 came during a year of spiritual as well as economic depression. Hope had vanished. People who believed conditions couldn't get worse were seen as rosy-eyed optimists. Rosy-eyed optimists were synonymous with fools.

A good part of my parents marital troubles could be traced to the economic conditions of their time. However, more of their problems stemmed from their irreconcilable views of time. Mother lived in the past and in the future. Dad dwelt only in the present.

My mother thought nothing of the plight of the world at large. For her the Depression hadn't begun on Black Tuesday but on the day her father died. She saw news events mainly as incidental backdrops or settings for the drama of her life. She was living in a three act play. Act one, she would have subtitled "Before the Fall." It dealt with the days of her parent's marriage when life for her was mostly a happily ever after time marred only by the tragedy of her infant brother's death. Act two, she would have dubbed "The Dark Ages." It was supposed to have spanned the years between her Dad's death and her marriage to my Dad. However, Act Two was spilling over into Act Three, "The Return to Eden."

It was disappointing for her not to see her marriage get off to a story book start. But that was okay since it was the happily ever after ending which counted. A splendid tomorrow was coming and when it dawned, she was sure we'd all be transported back into the happiness of her past.

To my dad my mother's memories and dreams were but mirages in a desert of reality. Neither the past nor the future mattered. Nor as a matter of fact did the present. Like God, my father lived outside of time. His motto could have been, "Procrastinate and if that doesn't solve the problem, sleep on it." For him, yesterday like Humpty Dumpty couldn't be put back together again. So it was best forgotten. Tomorrow, too, wasn't worth waiting for. The promises it tendered were Fascism, Communism, War or worse. The only sane thing a man could do was to make the most of his moments by filling each with kindness, compassion, understanding and humor. Dad said his outlook was old stuff. It was voiced two thousand years ago by a heretic who claimed that "Sufficient to the day is the evil thereof."

Chapter 3

A Second Rater in the First Grade

First grade is something close to a disaster for me. I don't impress anyone with my brilliance. I do just the opposite.

One day, about three weeks into the term, our teacher, Mrs. Adams, slowly begins counting up to twenty. When she's done she asks if anyone else can do this. Three kids raise their hands. One by one she calls on them. Each recites the numbers perfectly. In fact they all rattle them off faster than she had. This delights her. Then looking at the rest of us she says, "Tomorrow, I want every child without exception to be able to count to twenty when he comes to class."

Perhaps if I had known Mrs. Adams was going to say this, I'd have paid better attention to her and to the kids as they counted. I didn't realize that what she and they were doing was important. I thought she was playing a game. I assumed that the numbers were just things she was inventing off the top of her head. I never expected her to ask us to memorize them. I never imagined she would want us to recite them in their exact order.

I guess I must have figured as she was counting that her aim in doing this was to impress us with her ability to say big numbers like 11, 13 and 17. Heck, if on her way from one to twenty she had thrown in an 82 and a 101, I would have been equally up in the air and not have known that anything was out of place.

Of course when she called for volunteers to repeat her feat, I quickly grasped that all of the numbers had to be recited in order. Yet I saw no sense in this. It didn't seem to be a sequence guided by reasoning as in the ABCs. It seemed rather to have a kind of tongue twisting ordering as in "Peter Piper picked a peck of pickled peppers" or perhaps an amusing ordering as in the strange words to a dumb song like "Bei mir bist du schoen" or "Hut sut ralston on the rilla rock and a brawla brawla suet."

As the trio of my classmates had blitzed through their reciting, I had been rooting in turn for each to say every number correctly. They did this. Yet only by watching Mrs. Adams and seeing her nodding with approval could I and my peers tell that everything was proceeding according to Hoyle.

When we're told that tomorrow all of us will be expected to count to twenty too, I don't think that I'm alone in my surprise.

At home that afternoon and evening, I say nothing about the assignment. Nor do I mention anything else about my class. This isn't unusual. I never broach the subject of school at home. I figure it's taboo. Bad news manages always to upset Mother.

If I were to bring something to her attention that was minor in its annoyance and didn't disturb her unduly, I'd get off with a scolding. If it were major and irritating, she'd lose her temper. Then if I didn't disappear fast, I could be in for a clobbering. More likely, however, she'd order me to stand in a corner for a quarter of an hour. So for the benefit of us both, I would never inform her of my troubles at school.

Of course, ignoring a problem isn't going to make it go away. When we return to class the next day we're asked individually to count up to twenty. The four kids who are called on before me rattle off the numbers almost as rapidly as bullets fired by a machine gun. I try to follow what they're saying but all I hear is "one two-three four-five-six seven-night-time then-zoom-zoom zoom-zoom zoom-zoom zoom-teen-twenty."

Suddenly it's my turn to count. In fear and trepidation, I begin, "One, two, three."

I pause. Everything's going well.

I proceed, "four, five, six."

All around me people seemed to be hanging on my every word.

I'm surviving. However, like the fellow who says as he passes the thirtieth floor after leaping off of the Empire State building, "So far, so good,"I know I'm in for trouble.

I utter, "seven."

I realize then that my head is in the noose. From this point on my being is in the hands of Divine Providence.

Several seconds elapse.

"Well, go on Gregory," says Mrs. Adams.

I can see she's losing patience. She's got the same look on her face, my mother has when she's ready to erupt with anger. I make a stab, "eleventy."

"ELEVENTY! Did I hear you say eleventy?"

I know that question has no need of an answer.

I watch her. She flushes red. Then speaking in a serious voice and making no effort to conceal her displeasure, she declares, "There is no such number as eleventy! You didn't do your assignment. You were told to learn how to count to twenty by the time you came to class this morning. I'm terribly disappointed and annoyed with you."

I'm on the verge of tears. The whole class is watching. I'm certain that the next words out of her mouth will be, "You've been a bad boy. Go stand in a corner."

I know this will start my tears flowing. I'll be blubbering like a baby. My embarrassment will be endless. Even if the sum of my days were to double Methuselah's, I'd never be able to live down my shame.

Mercifully, she says instead, "If by tomorrow you haven't learned to count to twenty, you are to bring your mother with you to school. We'll need to straighten the both of you out once and for all on the importance of obeying my instructions."

"Yes Ma'am," I answer and take my seat.

I'm feeling devastated but I'm not crying.

Mrs. Adams calls on the girl behind me and the rat-a-tat-tat incoherence of the counting ritual proceeds. Wrapped up in my own personal misery, I barely listen. I'm too mortified to do so.

After about four kids have their say, Mrs. Adams calls on Sally. She's a girl who speaks with a voice so unique that you automatically stop whatever you're doing to allow yourself to listen to it. Sally recites her numbers slowly and clearly. I'm able to hear her say a distinct eight after she had said seven. Then I catch the nine and ten that follows.

When she sits down I begin to listen intently to those who follow in turn. Most, but not all, lose me with their mumbling.

By the time the last kid has his say, I'm able to count up to fifteen.

In the playground after lunch, I see Gwen and ask her to help me to go from fifteen to twenty. She obliges.

When school resumes at one o'clock, I announce as we are lining up to put our coats away in the wardrobe that I can count all of the numbers up to twenty.

"Can you now?" asks Mrs. Adams in a doubting tone.

I respond by reciting every last one of them in perfect order.

"Very good, Gregory," she says and adds, "I'm pleased. Now it won't be necessary for you to bring your mother to school with you tomorrow."

"Yes, Ma'am," I reply. Then with feelings of pride and relief I proceed to the rear of the room and hang up my jacket.

I don't remember much about any other of my days in the 1A.

I wasn't among the brighter kids in that class. I was just the opposite. I stunk up the place. Not however, in the same embarrassing way as Herby van't Hoff who for obvious reasons was nicknamed Messy Pants. I think my trouble at P.S. 207 stemmed from the fact that while my body remained in the classroom, my mind drifted elsewhere. Always I seemed to be either unaware of what was going around me or not interested in it. I never had the feeling I was lost or dumb. I just felt that there were better things to think about than what was going on in class. From 9 in the morning till 3 in the afternoon New

York State had the legal right to keep me confined in its boy prison. It could place me under the thumb of Mrs. Adams, a woman only slightly less tyrannical than my mother. It couldn't, however, stop me from daydreaming. Its power stopped where my brain began. I had a choice. I could be an attentive inmate and endure days of endless, educational torment or I could ignore the process and roam freely in the more interesting world of my own imaginings. I opted for the latter.

This daydreaming, nevertheless, comes at a costly price.

At the close of term I'm not promoted. I'm left back.

When I hand my report card to Mother, she reads it and goes into shock. When she recovers she begins to cry. She tells me that I've disgraced her and every member of our family. In the long history of both the Hamiltons and the Sterns no one ever has been left back. I've scuttled our family pride. Mother estimates that it will take a thousand years for us to live down my shame.

That evening when my Dad comes home, Mother gets off of my back and lands on his. He learns that my failing was definitely his fault.

Throughout dinner he listens to her. When we get up from the table, he puts on his hat and coat. He's leaving for his lodge meeting. This really annoys Mother. She screams at him, "Go to your damn lodge meeting. Be one of the boys. Ignore your family. Ignore the calamity. Ignore the shame."

In a calm voice he says, "I'll attend to the crisis in the morning. Don't wait up. I'll be home late."

He closes the door. She fumes. I sneak out of sight.

The next day, or perhaps it's a day or two later, Dad and I go over to the school. No classes are going on. It's an intercession holiday for us kids. It's an in-service day for the teachers.

Dad has me lead him to my classroom. Mrs. Adams is there working at her desk.

Dad knocks on the open door and when Mrs. Adams turns to look at us, he introduces himself. He tells her he does not mean to intrude upon her work. He realizes that she is a busy woman but if she has a few moments to spare, he'd like to thank her for doing such an excellent job as my teacher. He says that he realizes that I hadn't quite risen up to the standard for promotion. Nonetheless, he has witnessed a remarkable progress in my development. For this, he and my mother are grateful for they know my improvement can only be attributed to my teacher's excellence.

An initial look of seriousness and of fearful concern on the face of Mrs. Adams recedes and gives way to a smile. Here is this charming, warm, friendly, blue-eyed, 27-year old blond version of Joseph Cotten complimenting the living hell out of her.

A half of an hour passes. They talk. They laugh. They discover they share mutual acquaintances. They learn that they're in agreement on a whole host of subjects not the least of which is the splendid way she has inspired within me a will to learn.

They carry on this way for another quarter of an hour.

I sit aside and pay them little attention. I know from experience that any grownup talk on which I'm allowed to eavesdrop can rarely be worth hearing. This conversation doesn't show signs of becoming an exception. So I ignore it and daydream. As a consequence, I miss out on quite a bit of the chatter. But it doesn't matter because the long and short of their gabbing is that when it comes time for us to leave, Mrs. Adams is pleading with my dad to allow her to promote me into the 1B. She insists that during the end of the term rush to turn in her grades she hadn't been able to give my case the consideration due it. She acknowledges that overall I have been a borderline pupil whose grades were slightly under standard. However, there is this mitigating circumstance of noticeable improvement in my performance during the last six weeks. In averaging my grades this betterment should have borne a greater weight than the feeble marks that I compiled before her teaching began to bear fruit. She assures Dad that it would be a terrible injustice not to promote me.

With grace and gratitude my Dad agrees with her assessment and accedes to her wishes.

We go with Mrs. Adams to the principal's office. There in a matter of minutes my records are revised. Dad thanks both the principal and Mrs. Adams for their kindness, their cordiality and their caring concern. Everyone smiles, even me.

My tenure in the IB is less eventful. I've come to realize that I have a responsibility to meet at least the minimum standard in class. I make certain I do so. I want no part in another calamity.

About the only memorable thing that does happen to me in the 1B occurs when we're obliged to read "This is the House that Jack Built." Now in case anyone has forgotten, let me remind him that there's a line in this story that goes "This is the cock that crows in the morn." Naturally, no one wants to be called on to read that sentence aloud. But as luck would have it, I get stuck with the job.

When I'm called upon I stand up beside my desk, take the reader in my hand and pause. Then I clear my throat.

"Gregory Stern, we're waiting," says Mrs. Adams.

Again I clear my throat.

I begin reading. Around me an undercurrent of subdued snickering and giggling is audible. "This is the.,, This is the... This is the...."

"This is the what?" asks Mrs. Adams.

"This is the rooster that crows in..."

"Rooster?" she interrupts. Then over the giggles of my classmates she says, "I don't see the word rooster. I see cock. Now please read it right."

Everyone around me is in stitches and doing his best to squelch his laughter. To me this is no joke. I'm beet red with embarrassment and covered with sweat.

"This is the cock that grows in the morn," I recite.

"Crows, not grows," said Mrs. Adams. Then she adds, "Now read the line again and this time get it right."

"Yes Ma'am," I reply.

As I get set to do my re-reading, I hear Benny Hailey, the class clown, whispering, "Gus, if your cock grows in the morn, pee and it'll shrink back to normal."

All the boys nearby are laughing. The girls, of course, wear their feigned looks of innocence. They aren't kidding anyone. They know what's going on.

Mrs. Adams becomes furious.

She has me take my seat. Then she bawls out the whole class for its childishness. Finally, to punish us she has us copy twenty times the sentence, "This is the cock that crows in the morn."

I'm glad when that school day ends. But for about two weeks afterwards I remain a sort of living reminder of the events that took place that morning. Every time my classmates would see me, they'd kid me. They'd tuck their thumbs under their armpits and flap their elbows like wings as they'd call out to me, "Rooster- doodle-do."

Chapter 4

The Beggar of Borough Hall

I've just passed my seventh birthday when I awake one night suffering with pains in the bones above and below the knee of my right leg. I wait a while to see if the hurt will ease. When it becomes clear it won't, I call my parents. They come to my bedside and ask what's wrong. I tell them my leg feels as if it were a rope being stretched in a tug-of-war. Mother asks if the pain is sharp and piercing. I answer, "No, it's more like an ear ache. It stays the same and doesn't let you forget it's there, not even for a moment."

Dad advises me not to worry. My trouble is temporary. I'm merely going through the natural process of having growing pains.

Years ago when he was a boy, he occasionally had suffered from them too.

Soon, he assures me, the ache will let up. After that, in all probability, it will never return.

Surely enough, in about a quarter of an hour the growing pains vanish. I put them out of my mind and fall back to sleep.

The next night and many nights thereafter the same thing happens. I try to be brave and to take the growing pains in stride. I can't. Not only has the hurt been worsening but it also has spread to the other leg. As if this weren't trouble enough, the growing pains begin coming upon me during the daytime. The only consolation is that they're irregular. Sometimes a day or two passes without a trace of them.

Luckily for me, Ernie stops by and although he isn't a doctor yet, he examines me. He tells my folks he thinks it would be a good idea if I went and visited Uncle Istvan with him. We do this. Uncle Istvan has a cardiology practice in Manhattan but lives in Greenpoint. Although he isn't an expert on growing pains, he's qualified as an M.D. to treat me. He gives me an examination. Then he has me admitted to Greenpoint Hospital for further tests and observation. He suspects that I have osteomyelitis, a disease of the bone.

Ernie expects Uncle Istvan's diagnosis to be confirmed. It isn't. The physicians at Greenpoint are confused themselves by my condition. The chief resident claims I have a rare form of gout. The pathologist isn't sure I have anything. Most of the others on the staff think I have arthritis. All of them recommend that if the growing pains don't clear up in a couple of weeks on their own, I should be brought back for additional tests and evaluations.

Uncle Istvan and Ernie thank the physicians for their services and bring me home. Because Uncle Istvan is convinced that I have osteomyelitis, he begins to treat me for it with injections of two or three different kinds of sera. Usually because he's busy with his practice, he writes the prescriptions and lets Ernie come over to my house to give me the shots. Because Ernie can't always attend to this, my mother is trained too to administer the injections. Every other day I'm given one or two c.c. treatment. A couple of times each month I receive a 5 c.c. dose. Those hurt. Furthermore, they do not seem to be any more effective in easing the growing pains than were the smaller dosages. Still on any day that Ernie comes, I find the shots and the aching easier to bear than when he doesn't.

My mother's technique with the needle is very businesslike. On me it has a negative side effect. When she treats me the growing pains generally get worse instead of better. When Ernie gives me the shots, everything works positively. Even before I become aware of this, Dad notices it. He tells mother she lacks a bedside manner. She doesn't want to hear that. You can almost see smoke coming out of her ears when she replies to his accusation, "You're right. You need not contend with it. You can sleep on the couch."

A month after my Greenpoint stay, Uncle Istvan has me admitted to the Post Graduate Medical Center in New York. There again I undergo extensive tests. For a week I say "Ah" too many times a day to an army of interns and physicians. They keep sticking tongue depressors down my throat to learn something about my legs. I also contend with a lot of nurses who handle syringes like bayonets. Even worse, they deny me the dignity of having my temperature taken orally.

Of the two hospitals Post Graduate has been less likable than Greenpoint. At the latter only the care and service were poor. I was fed breakfast before dawn, lunch before noon and dinner before five. If at night nature called and led me to ring for a bed pan, the ward nurse allowed me to suffer for an extra five minutes while she finished another page or two in her reading of Gone with the Wind. If my bowels impelled me to ring again, she'd wouldn't put the book down until the end of a chapter. Eventually she'd come and give me hell and a sermon for my impatience. Frankly, she didn't give a damn whether we patients were enduring diarrhea, dysentery or death. We still had to wait on her while she waited on Scarlett and Rhett.

Post Graduate should be heaven in contrast with Greenpoint. For the same number of patients it has twice as many nurses, three times the attendants and lots more physicians. Its services are excellent. Moreover, all of the patients in our ward are boys of ages six through thirteen. Anyone would think that during a stay here, a fellow would make lots of friends and enjoy a vacation away from school.

The truth, however, is that the Post Graduate Hospital makes me miserable. Every other day they put a new kid into the bed to my left. Because I was, and still am, slow to make friends, I barely get to say much to any of them. After meeting the first one who introduces himself to me as Wally, I really don't care to meet the others. I fear they'll be like him.

Wally had been cheerful and friendly when I arrived but the next morning he was quiet and distant. Shortly before noon, he was removed for an operation. His leg was amputated. Along with everyone else, I felt sorry for him. But I was glad it was his leg they removed and not mine.

We neither saw nor heard from Wally again. Our ward assumed he did his convalescing on another floor.

The kid in the bed to my right is named Don. I don't care for him. He isn't friendly. Seldom does he smile or engage in small talk. He prefers being serious.

Don used to make lots of speeches. He thought he was talking to the ward. We thought he was talking to the wall. Everyone kept hoping he'd be transferred to another floor or sent home.

Don is only thirteen but he looks older. He's tall and muscular. With his big pointed nose and his way of staring past people as though they don't exist, he puts me in mind of a hawk, I'd seen in the zoo. From the angry and bitter way he acts, I can never tell whether he's doped up, nuts, mean or some combination of all three. I have no desire to discover which. Because it's clear to me that he's dangerous, I spend my days avoiding him by never looking to my right. Similarly, the guy on his right spends his time never looking to his left. That's an uncomfortable and awkward way for us to live. But it is necessary if we're to safeguard ourselves against being verbally mauled or bored to death by someone we regard as a goon.

Everyday until the late afternoon there's so much activity in the ward that we patients have little time for conversation. As soon as we awake we're allowed to urinate and then a nurse takes our temperatures and blood pressures. Soon an attendant brings breakfast. Another comes by to see if we'd eaten everything they've served. This infuriates me because everyday they give us Farina. To me that has to taste worse than the slop farmers feed to pigs. So I leave it untouched on my plate. The nurse whose job it is to spy on us puts a little check mark next to my name indicating that I lack an appetite and have an attitude. After this a colored orderly comes and removes our trays. Then we're given bed pans and bed baths. Next, the linen is changed, our temperatures and blood pressures are retaken and the floor is mopped. When the doctors, interns and medical students follow, their visits seem more a ritual than a routine. Like priests with crucifixes, all wear stethoscopes and adhere to a well rehearsed litany in their questions to us. The scene in the ward reminds me of communion in a cathedral where the bishop and his holy helpers move in a gang from one faceless communicant to another.

In a left handed example of symmetry the final visitors we receive before lunch are the ministers, rabbis and priests. They're less organized than the physicians and surgeons. They tend to straggle in one at a time. Half appear to be rum pots. I understand why. Visiting sick people and comforting bereaved families must drain the spirit out of them. Whiskey is a way to put some of it back. No doubt alcohol spices up their lackluster lives as much as the occasional trysts some of them undoubtedly have had with hero worshiping women seeking to climb into bed with God. In a mysterious turn around we patients sense it to be our duty to comfort the clergymen. I smile with genuine affection and said "hi" to each. Most answer in kind.

Among these men of the cloth there's one magnificent screwball who calls himself the Reverend Brother Bessel. He's a fundamentalist who neither looks old enough to be out of high school nor acts wise enough to get into one. His enthusiasm for his work is limitless but ridiculous. His clothes too are outrageous. The first time I see him, he enters the ward wearing a purple and yellow plaid jacket. Under it he dons a purple shirt with a matching yellow poker dot tie. His daily attire while not this loud comes close. In serving God I think he's missed his calling. He should have been in burlesque as a comedian. On entering our ward of all boys his routine or act goes like this:

"Brothers and Sisters, have you heard the news?"

"What news, Reverend Brother?" replies the ward in unison.

"The news that because Christ died for our sins, we're all going to heaven."

"I'd rather go to Coney Island," says some wag.

"Little Christians, believe on the Lord Jesus Christ and the truth shall set you free. Believe on Him, our Holy Savior, and anything is possible."

On the day they're moving Wally out of his bed and onto the stretcher to take him into surgery, Brother Bessel comes over to him and asks, "Can I do something for you son?"

"No one can do anything for me," answers Wally.

"God can. God can do anything."

"God can't give him back the cancerous leg he's having amputated," speaks out my angry neighbor, Don. "God can't do a goddamned thing for him or for any of us because God doesn't exist. If He did and He allowed tragedies like this to happen, He'd be no damned different from the devil."

"You're wrong son," returns the Reverend, "You're wrong. God sees and cares for even the least of us."

"Take your God, your sick slogans and yourself, take it all and shove it."

As the orderlies wheel Wally out of the Ward, Brother Bessel just stands there looking helpless, beaten and lost. A couple of times he seems on the verge of saying something but stops. You can see in his face his inability to find words to undo the tension.

After a long pause the Reverend says with quiet dignity, "I'll pray for Wallace and I'll be back tomorrow. God bless you all."

No one replies.

Brother Bessel moves off towards the entrance to the ward.

Although I understand Don's anger and the silence of the ward, my heart is bleeding for the preacher. He's trying to help us bear the invisible but real burden of our anguish.

"Reverend," I hear a voice call after him.

I recognize it to be my own.

Brother Bessel turns to look back.

"See you tomorrow," I say and then add, "Thanks for coming and remembering us."

He smiles, waves and goes his way.

Lunch at Post Graduate offers food as bland as Bickford's. That's okay with me. I've never cared for fancy cooking. I've always felt that if something is good, it shouldn't be messed up with spices, sauces or creamy disguises. If it's devoid of flavor or tastes rotten, there has never been a valid reason to eat it in the first place. Anyway the noon meals at the hospital are filling. They leave me sleepy and ready for my required afternoon nap.

An hour later my forty winks end. The voices of visitors or of nearby patients wake me. Except on the weekends very few of us get afternoon company. I use this time to do school work, to write letters, to read or to talk with the latest fellow occupying Wally's bed.

Wednesday afternoons, however, are different. An arts and crafts lady shows up with two wicker baskets filled with materials for making the kinds of hobbylike things which Indians on reservations sell. During my stay at the hospital I thread beads to make necklaces for Mother, Mom and Gram. I braid a leather belt for Dad. I almost have another one finished for Ernie when the hospital discharges me. I ask to be allowed to take it with me. The Arts and Crafts lady refuses saying, "No. Rules are rules. If you can't finish it here, you can't finish it elsewhere."

After the afternoon visiting hours end, our temperatures and blood pressures are taken for the third or fourth time since sun up. Then at a quarter of five the evening meal is wheeled in. Although it's never much different from the noon one, it doesn't make us sleepy. I figure this is because the noon milk is doctored with Mickey Finns. However, it's possible that the anticipation and excitement of having visitors in the evening hours keeps us alert. When I tell Ernie of this, he suggests another cause as an explanation. He says the rhythms of the human body just naturally make us drowsy after lunch.

That's asinine. To spare his feelings, I don't tell him so. In Spain and in the countries south of our border where siestas are popular, Latins sleep on the sidewalks in the afternoon not because a nap is natural but because they're lazy bastards. If they ever tried to live that way in a great country like ours, the bosses would fire them, the police would jail them and the Department of Immigration would deport them.

When you're a little kid you spend so much time learning the ways of the world, you never think to question whether they make sense. At first, at Post Graduate, I'm like that. I accept all the activity in the ward as necessary and natural. That unseen hands are guiding events in the ward never occurs to me until Don complains one day that "All this goddamned hubbub is planned. Except for feeding us and letting us piss and crap, they could finish the day's routines in an hour. Everything, however, is stretched out on purpose to distract us. It's against the laws of medicine to let us suffer our sicknesses in peace. They go out of their way to force on us routines to take our minds off our misery, as if our ills would vanish if only we would ignore them. If they believe in their medicines there's no reason not to let us take our pills and shots at home and be cured there. Instead we lie here like zombies. We're hypnotized by the traffic of the ward. It's a sideshow. It's as ludicrous as the voodoo dances that witch doctors do to mesmerize their patients back to health."

An hour later he harangues us once again: "Everyone knows the body either cures itself or it doesn't. When it does, the doctor claims credit whether he's dressed in sanitized whites in New York or feathers and beads in New Guinea. When it doesn't, it doesn't matter whether it's the surgeon or the shaman who sends you home crippled. Either way the bill is doubled and you're told the lie that without his expert care you'd be far worse off."

As this outburst ends, any lingering doubt I have about Don's sanity vanishes. I know he's beyond hope. Although he's only half as nuts as Brother Bessel, he's twice as dangerous. We ridicule and laugh at the Reverend for telling us the source of disease is sin. But no one even smirks when Don suggests that the doctors treating us are quacks and con men. I'd be happy to see him moved to a bed in a different ward where the windows have bars of iron and the walls, padding.

Towards the end of my first week at Post Graduate some interns and medical students come through the ward. They stop as one of them picks up the clipboard containing the health chart posted as the foot of my bed. He studies it for a minute. Without ever looking at me, he turns to the others and says, "This is the boy who's to have both of his legs amputated."

The others nod. The clipboard is returned to place. They move on.

I suppose this sent me immediately into a state of shock. It must have because I remained calm and unruffled.

Both of my legs the intern had said. His quiet, indifferent manner and his matter of fact tone cemented the belief in my mind that he'd spoken the truth. Both legs! It was so outlandish and unbelievable, it had to be true. A heartless prankster would have settled for one leg. Only someone stating facts could have defied imagination and called for the amputation of two.

I begin wondering what life will be like without legs. I see myself aging. With leathery, wrinkled skin I'm becoming a duplicate of a beggar whom I've seen at Borough Hall. His body, butt and leg stubs sit on a square skateboard as he proffers pencils in one hand while he jiggles a couple of coins in a metal cup for begging in the other. I remember watching him once when with oven mittens on his hands he paddled his skateboard along on the sidewalk to a new begging site by A&S.

The sight of him filled me with pity, sympathy, sadness and sorrow. But even stronger were my feelings of revulsion. I couldn't take my eyes off of him. As he stopped his skateboard and backed himself into place against the building, I felt I was looking at a living gargoyle. On his tiny, grimy, wooden pedestal he looked as if he had just ridden a volcano up from the netherworld and now awaited marching orders from Satan, himself.

Guilt overwhelmed me. Surely the poor fellow wasn't born this way. For all I knew, he could have lost his legs in the war. As a doughboy both his limbs perhaps were shot out from under him as he led a charge against the Germans. At one time he must have been young, healthy and handsome. At one time he probably had a lovely girl friend and plans for marriage and children. Now what was he? An ogre. Now what was there for him? Averted looks and horrified staring. And worst of all, a life of unending begging.

I sensed in him hatred for the whole planet. It was filled with healthy, undeformed people. I felt he begged not just to survive but also to wreak revenge. He knew that the mere sight of him instilled uneasiness, fear and guilt in people. He was aware that most of the money he received was not charity but superstitious bribes paid to ward off the evils betokened by his presence. I imagined further that he enjoyed the discomfort his mutilated appearance caused. His inner being had become a reflection of his outer self. He was vile beyond redemption and ugly beyond repulsion. He was, I now realized, a present portrait of the future me.

I envision this grotesque, pitiful half-man living life as a loner. Neither family nor friends can stomach his company. Yet as any man he still needs companionship and still craves the warmth of human touch. These everyday pleasures can be his only at a price for only prostitutes are callous enough to provide them.

Of course, at the age of seven, I don't think these things in the words I've written. For the most part I don't think these things in words at all. Like a dog or cat lacking a vocabulary, I sense them far more poignantly and powerfully in images or pictures. Moreover, I respond to these scenes with vital, visceral feelings rather than with unemotional language.

As a fifteen year old I now think mainly in words. Still, however, I do a lot of daydreaming. In these fantasies the things I imagine are the things I see. I've heard tell of only children who, when starved for companionship, invent invisible friends for themselves. I don't buy their invisibility. These strange playmates may not be present to onlookers but to the lonely kids they're visible and they're real. Whether these figments behave sensibly or foolishly, whether or not they have blue hair and green freckles, we'd be silly not to accept them as really being seen as they're described. The trouble with adults is their lack of memory and imagination. Grown-ups foolishly insist that words are needed for thought when all around them in their infant children and in their pets, thinking in images is the only thought in evidence.

All that day after the intern's pronouncement I stay depressed. When lunch is brought in, I skip it. When dinner comes, I ignore that too. The nurse who checks my trays asks why I won't eat. I ignore her. She gives me a nasty look and orders me to answer. I pay her no mind. As far as I'm concerned she is just another smug, church-going do-gooder confident of her own salvation and oblivious to the damnation that now is mine. I have nothing to say to her or to any other butcher's helper.

Terror wells within me as I wait for the evening visiting hours and the arrival of my folks. I want to bolt out of there but lacking clothes, I can't. Yet even if I could dress, it wouldn't help. I'm in Manhattan without even a nickel for the subway. No one here would hide and protect me. Only in Brooklyn would escape and help be possible. My situation is as hopeless as a Jew's in Germany. I have to face facts--amputation is inevitable.

When my folks arrive for visiting hours, I start to give them the silent treatment too. They keep prodding me to speak. Finally I yield saying, "I don't want them to cut my legs off. I want to go home."

I suppose they're taken aback by my directness. For a few seconds they stare at me with puzzled looks. Then Dad said, "No one is going to cut your legs off."

Borrowing a line from the movies I say, "You needn't color the truth. I'm not a child. I heard it from the doctors, themselves."

"Nonsense," declares Mother. "No one is going to cut your legs off."

"Then take me home now so they can't."

"This is ridiculous. This is nonsense. No one is going to do a thing to harm you. I don't know where you got this preposterous idea from. It simply isn't true."

From my right, I hear Don's voice saying, "He got the idea from the interns. I heard, it myself. They said he was to have both of his legs amputated."

Mother is upset. She gets up and leaves the ward. Dad takes off after her. I call for them to return. Dad looks back and says he'll be with me in a moment.

Ten minutes go by.

I figure they have left because they are embarrassed to be caught in a lie. I look over at Don. I want to scream at him, "I wish you'd mind your own business and keep your fat mouth shut." I don't. It would be useless to do so. It wouldn't bring my parents back. About the only thing it would do is prompt the maniac to climb out of his bed and beat the hell out of me. I have trouble enough without that.

Suddenly in a moment of revelation I realize I've been abandoned. For my parents the prospect of having to care for a basket case must have been too much for them to contend with. They've bowed to the inevitable. They've deserted me. Now nothing, not even hope, remains. My future has arrived. The surgeons will cut off my legs. The hobby lady will give me a skateboard, some pencils and a metal cup. The orderlies will roll me out of the hospital and leave me in a doorway on a strange Manhattan street to beg for the rest of my life.

Before my imagination can paint this picture darker, my mother and father return accompanied by a physician and a nurse. They all assure me that my legs will not be amputated.

I tell them I don't care anymore. All I want is not to be abandoned and not to have to spend the rest of my life on the street selling pencils as a beggar on a skateboard.

After a few more days of tests and x-rays, my growing pains are confirmed to be osteomyelitis. I'm released from the hospital and treated at home as before with shots administered to me by Uncle Istvan, Ernie or Mother.

Of that final week at Post Graduate few memories have remained. I did become friendlier with Don. However, I still considered him to be a grade A nut. His continuing wacky ideas and belligerent attitude remained difficult to take.

Now when I realize that he had been bedridden most of the preceding two years and was undergoing treatments which never worked, I grow more understanding and forgiving of him. Anyone, whose health has been as troublesome as his, is bound to be irritable. Yet, there's more to it than that. Being a pain in the ass I think was Don's way of fighting for his health.

If at Post Graduate, they really would have come to cut off my legs, I probably would have submitted without uttering a word of protest. If they would have dared to try to do this with Don, not only would he have unleashed a tirade of objections but also he'd have fought them with his fists. He'd have behaved like a cornered rat. In the end, however, he'd have fought in vain. It makes no difference whether you have Don's courage or my cowardice. In a confrontation with authority, you lose.

Before I went to Post Graduate I was, I think, a standard, run of the mill, seven year old. When I was released, I may have looked the same but inside, I think I was different. I think I had learned something about compassion and the importance of worrying less about what others do to me than what I do to others.

For two years after my hospitalization I'm required to wear orthopedic, high leather shoes. Gradually my growing pains disappear. One day Ernie brings me to Greenpoint Hospital for an overnight stay. There I undergo a bunch of medical tests. As I leave the building, I'm pronounced cured. The disease is either in remission or gone. Nevertheless, as a precaution every five years I'm to be rechecked to see that the disease, if present, stays dormant.

Time, it's been said, heals all wounds. The guy who coined that obviously had a wound that could be healed with soap and water and a band aid. Some wounds kill. Other may fester and never heal.

I can't think of the Post Graduate hospital and not feel bitter. While it's possible that the interns and medical students may have been talking about someone else whose legs were to be amputated when they went by my bed, I don't think this was so. I suppose abuse from well educated but inconsiderate people is so common that rarely does anyone question it. In some fields condescension and contempt from those in authority is noticed only when it is absent. Everyone observes this. Everyone is annoyed by it. Yet we cast it as a petty aggravation out of our thoughts and forget or forgive it. This is wise but sad. It is, after all, only through the luck of inherited wealth that one man with useless legs now sits in the White House and another begs for his continued existence by selling pencils at Borough Hall.

Chapter 5
Public School 83

I begin the second grade in P.S. 207 but after about a month into the term our family moves. I have to transfer to P.S. 83. In age, appearance and quality of education these schools differ markedly. P.S. 207 is new and clean. Its curriculum meets all of the latest academic standards. P.S. 83, by contrast, is an ancient dump. Or rather, two ancient dumps for it is housed in two buildings. The older one, in which the lower grades are quartered, looks as if it could have been built about the same time as the Brooklyn Bridge. The add-on may have predated World War I.

The students who attend P.S. 207 are mainly white, middle class and Protestant. There are many Catholic families in Flatlands but their youngsters choose to go to the parochial school at St. Thomas. At P.S. 83 there's less uniformity in everyone's background and appearance. Approximately a fourth of its kids are coloreds. The rest are mostly Italians and Jews.

After we've been living for a year or so in the new neighborhood, I overhear Gram tell Mother that "If Dorothy had ridden the whirlwind over the rainbow and landed at Protestant 207 she'd have said to Toto, 'If we're still in Kansas, this must be Topeka.' If, however, she'd been dropped down among all the guineas, kikes and coons at P.S. 83, she'd have guessed herself to be in Ethiopia."

Of course, as I am just then beginning to cut my second teeth, Gram's slurs go right by me. Because I know guineas are coins in England, I take kikes and coons to be forms of British money too. Ethiopia, however, throws me. It sounds like a medical condition.

However, that makes no sense. No one gets sick when he's in the midst of money. So after giving her words some thought, I realize that either I've misheard her or she has made a slip of the tongue while trying to say "euphoria."

What concerns me when I first come to P.S. 83 is fitting in and learning the ropes. Doing this doesn't take long. Through schoolyard wrestling I find my place among the boys in class. Before two weeks have gone by, I know my schoolmates by name and have become friends with them. Equally as quickly I learn enough of the way that things operate in class to stay out of trouble. The only stuff I don't master quickly is the material taught before my arrival. In particular, I don't know all of their spelling words. Nor am I familiar with the way some of these are pronounced by my teacher, Miss Jacobsen. So on my first spelling test, I don't do very well.

Just before we're let out of class to go home for lunch on the Monday after that exam, Miss Jacobsen tells me that because she is displeased with my showing on the test, I'm to have my mother come by to see her at three o'clock.

Hearing that terrifies me. I'm on the verge of tears. I manage, however, to contain myself. I answer, "Yes, Ma'am."

At home, I wait until lunch is over and I'm putting on my jacket to leave before I tell Mother the bad news.

"Why does your teacher want to see me?" she asks.

"She didn't say exactly. I think I may have failed a spelling test."

"Well, did you?"

"I don't know," I answer. "She didn't return my paper to me."

Of course, this is an evasion but strictly speaking, it isn't a lie. It gets me off of the hot seat and enables me to get away from Mother before she can give me her third degree in full.

At five minutes before three o'clock, when all of the other kids are dressing for dismissal, I'm told to remain in my seat. Miss Jacobsen marches the class out of the building. A minute or two later, she returns.

Back at her desk she sits down and proceeds to thumb through some papers. By ignoring me, she makes me feel as though I've been exiled to limbo. Yet I can handle that. It beats being yelled at.

After about three minutes Mother appears. She knocks on the door. In a voice that betrays nothing of her anxiety, she says, "Miss Jacobsen, I'm Gregory's mother."

Mother has gotten herself all dressed up. She always does that whenever she goes out, even if it's only to go next door to the grocer's. This time, however, she's wearing her Sunday best.

Miss Jacobsen is surprised and taken aback by Mother's youth, beauty and poise. She smiles and says "Come in please. I want to talk with you regarding Gregory's first spelling test."

After they shake hands, Miss Jacobsen pulls a chair over from the side of the room and gives Mother a seat beside her at the desk. She hands her my paper and has her compare it with the key.

After a pause Mother says, "I must apologize. This is very disappointing. Forty percent. Out of these ten not very difficult words he's misspelled so many. I don't understand how he could do so poorly."

Then looking at me she says, "You know how to spell the."

"T-h-e." I answer.

"That's right. Why didn't you spell it that way on this test."

"Because the wasn't on the test."

"How can you say that?" asks Mother in disbelief. She orders me to come up to the desk.

I do as told.

"Button your fly," she says.

I look down. My heart sinks. Two buttons are undone. I'm embarrassed. I'm mortified.

"And how do you spell *a*?" she asks pronouncing *a* as uh.

I finish buttoning and answer "a," saying it as everyone says it when he's reciting his abc's.

"Right again," says Mother, "so why didn't you spell it correctly on your exam?"

"Because it wasn't on the exam," I say in protest.

"Don't try my patience," she says.

"Excuse me," interrupts Miss Jacobsen, "I think I see the problem. I pronounce t-h-e, thee and *a*, not as uh but as a as in hay."

Then looking as me, she says, "Gregory, I'm afraid I've done you an injustice but I'm still troubled by these other four words you missed.

I confess to my inability to spell them and tell her that I can't remember ever having been taught them.

"They are in your speller," she insists as she opens the text to the page that contains them.

I look. They're there all right.

"Well," says Mother, "why didn't you learn them."

"I guess because I never knew they were homework."

Miss. Jacobsen cuts in. "Mrs. Stern, Gregory, has a point. I had assigned those words before he transferred into my class. I suspect that the speller he used in his previous school isn't the same as the one we're using here. Because of this I now see that this wasn't a fair test for him. I won't record this grade."

Then as she proceeds to erase the mark from her grade book, she says to Mother, "However, all of the words his classmates have covered, he'll be responsible for in the future. And that goes for his other subjects as well."

Then for about ten minutes she goes over the stuff that I was supposed to have covered in my reading, spelling and arithmetic texts.

Mother thanks her for the information and promises her that there'll be no more dismal performances from me on future exams. Then she and I leave.

I'm fearful as we exit the building that I'm in for a scolding. Surprisingly, however, Mother is quite calm and not at all in a bad mood. When we leave the school grounds she says to me, "You have catching up to do. We'll begin working on this immediately. I've given Miss Jacobsen my word that you'll be a bright and attentive pupil.

I'm confident that you'll do this for yourself and for me. I know that the last thing you'd ever want to do is bring shame on yourself and disgrace me."

I don't have to respond. She's right. I'm a Stern. As such I would never knowingly disappoint or dishonor any of my kin. Yet more important and powerful to me than family pride is my desire and my need not to disappoint her.

Miss Jacobsen has no further problem with me. I keep up with my lessons and stay out of trouble. Only rarely do I talk or pass a note to a classmate.

Most of my time in school I spend in daydreaming. Seldom for more than a fraction of every hour that I've spent in school have I found it necessary to be focused. Usually, the first half of a teacher's lesson is spent in review. If you were absent yesterday, this becomes the time when you can catch up and learn everything you've missed. For instance, the first thing Miss Jacobsen does in arithmetic is check and correct our homework. Then she has us do another problem or two like yesterday's. After that she introduces new stuff and illustrates it for a few minutes with examples. Lastly, she gives us our assignment. Usually because we've not exhausted the full hour on math, she lets us use the minutes remaining before the start of the reading lesson to begin doing tomorrow's homework. Normally, this is time enough for me to finish it.

When I first arrive at P.S. 83, I'm told to sit in the last seat in the last row. Until the end of the first marking period that's where I remain. Then everyone in class has his seat changed. The kid with the highest average is assigned the first seat in the first row. The next brightest is put into the second seat in the first row. The pattern continues until it ends with the class moron having to occupy the last seat in the last row.

This arrangement means that for the teacher the kids facing to her left are bright. Those to her right are backward.

I detest this seating for a number of reasons. Seymour Lipschitz sits in first row, first seat, and I sit directly behind him. Around us is a sea of middy blouses and skirts. Across the room are all of our friends, the boys.

Every teacher I have at P.S. 83 uses Mrs. Jacobsen's seating system. This means that each woman spends the class time talking and teaching to our side of the room while disciplining the other. Whenever we do flash-card problems in arithmetic, everyone in the first row rattles off his answer and nearly never makes a mistake. Most of the kids in the middle rows respond correctly too but they tend to take longer to do so. Those in the last row take lots of time and make lots of errors. This causes the teacher's patience to wear thin. If the next retard she calls upon doesn't spit out the right result within six seconds, he's certain to receive a tongue lashing.

At first I don't give the seating system a second thought. I'm pleased that I've gotten good grades and delighted that my days as a dummy seem to be behind me. But I'm uncomfortable in the midst of so many girls. It makes me wonder whether the other fellows will now see me as a sissy.

At dinner when Mother asks about my day at school, I tell her of my re-seating. She's pleased. My Dad is less so. He doesn't think the seating system is wise or fair. He asks how a slow child can ever learn if he feels himself to be always under the gun. Even if the kid isn't yelled at, Dad thinks he still faces his teacher's scowl or looks of hopeless resignation whenever his answer isn't right.

The more I think about Dad's words the more certain I become of their wisdom. The seating system does brand people. It tells us that everyone seated in the sixth row except for a newcomer is a dunce. Since the slow kids receive attention only when they're being disciplined, we--their peers--tend to write them off too. We take it for granted that the fate of a girl from row six is to be gang-banged by the football squad before she drops out of high school. As for the boys, we assume that if they don't land up making license plates in the penitentiary, they'll be digging ditches for the W.P.A.

Probably with or without the encouragement of the P. S. 83 seating system we, the bright kids, would size up the situation and become the same smug, callous and snobbish know-it-alls that we now are. Intelligence can do awful things to people. It tends to foster arrogance and to detract from character. If it didn't, Hell wouldn't be so loaded with geniuses.

A sizeable amount of the time when I'm enrolled at P. S. 83 I'm absent. This is due to a variety of causes. Every time a contagious disease comes into our neighborhood, I catch it. In addition to suffering multiple colds and periodic bouts with the flu, my brother and I endure successively the mumps, chicken pox, measles, German measles, diphtheria and scarlet fever. With each of these maladies we have sore throats. Additionally my afflictions are accompanied with ear aches.

It's not necessary to say people die of childhood diseases. We all know that. However, what many of us overlook is that sometimes those who recover don't do so completely. Complications can develop. Nearly everyone knows mumps can bring on sterility and measles, blindness. What too few of us recognize is that there are many other afflictions associated with childhood diseases such as deafness, encephalitis, rheumatic fever, heart trouble and organ damage.

Because of the severity of the scarlet fever infection that I endure, I have to be isolated for two weeks at Kingston hospital. When Mother and Dad come there to visit me, they have to remain outside of my room. I'm a danger to them. We are able to see each other through the glass pane of the door and thanks to the transom above it remaining half open, we can exchange hellos. The doctors tell my parents the disease has me on the verge of death. Fortunately, God or luck stays with me for I recover and never suffer any after effects.

Matthew who had pneumonia in infancy develops a second case

of it in '39. This time it isn't half as bad as before. To try to help him keep from contracting it again, my parents see to it that he undergoes a tonsillectomy. When Matthew leaves for the hospital, Dad tells him that after the operation ends, he can have all of the ice cream, he wants.

It's a cruel joke but when Matthew comes home, Dad makes it up to him by treating him to a banana split.

Always when I come back to class after being out sick or being hospitalized with osteomyelitis, I'm able within a week to make up the school work I've missed. I think that if my attendance had been regular I probably would have skipped a grade or two. A few times I have had report cards with straight A's.

The first thing a fellow notices when he moves into a different neighborhood is its girls. You kind of look around to find the pretty ones. At P.S. 83 you could go blind before one would come into view. There are, however, some knockouts in the neighborhood. Unfortunately they go either to the parochial school or to P.S. 167. One such is Peggy Ryan.

On Park Place, around the corner from my house, there's a king sized johnny pump. We've nick-named it Mount Everest. It stands about three and a half feet high. That's a good dozen inches taller than the other fire hydrants in the neighborhood. These, in comparison with our Himalayan monster, are hardly more than baby Alps.

Now just as scaling the Matterhorn is certain to seal a fellow's status as a somebody in Switzerland, leapfrogging over Mount Everest on Park Place lets everyone in the neighborhood know that you're a kid to be reckoned with. It instantly ends your days as a nobody.

As a rite of passage leapfrogging over Everest is taken very seriously by every boy who plays on Park Place. No one under the age of eleven has ever been able to scale it. Most kids know they'd be lucky to do so before they're fourteen.

One day Mickey Sullivan, a ten year-old who has to be above five feet in height, announces to the gang that he had leapfrogged over

Everest on the previous night. We immediately tell the lying braggart what it is we're sure he's full of. He swears he's done the deed. We say, "Yeah, prove it."

Accepting our challenge, Mickey backs up several feet and asks us to stand clear. We give him a wide path to the pump.

Off he goes. As he reaches the hydrant, he places his hands on its dome. Then he leaps and hoists himself skyward. With what appears to be effortless grace Mickey's body glides forth and after scaling its objective, it lands in glory.

We, the coterie of Doubting Thomases, stare at him in silent awe. We've just witnessed a Park Place record. Mickey Sullivan has accomplished the impossible. He's magnificent. Not even watching the great Cornelius Warmerdam pole vault to a world's record in the Millrose games could be half as exciting and electrifying as seeing Mickey sail over Everest.

Suddenly and spontaneously everyone in the gang breaks out cheering. We rush up to pat our hero on the back and to offer him our congratulations. We feel honored just to be in his presence.

What a kid! What a feat!

Someone then asks Mickey to do it again.

He begs off but says he'll give it another shot in a little while.

Since it's close to five o'clock, we all know why he's waiting. Soon his secret love, the aforementioned Peggy Ryan, the belle of the block, will be walking by. Every afternoon she visits her friend, Angela, who lives one street over on Sterling Place. But as regular as clockwork she always returns home from Angela's about ten minutes before Jack Armstrong comes on the air. She knows that at 5:15 every kid in the gang will be indoors listening to the latest episode of this serial.

Always whenever Peggy comes by, Mickey pretends not to notice her. It's obvious to one and all that she's doing the same to him. The whole neighborhood knows they're secret lovers. The only people not convinced of this are Mickey and Peggy.

That afternoon as soon as Peggy comes around the corner onto Park Place, we clear a path for Mickey to duplicate his feat and to impress Peggy as he has us.

"I think I'm ready now to scale Mount Everest," he says in a voice loud enough to catch his heartthrob's attention. Then he adds, "Someone give me 'ready, set, go.'"

Peggy, of course, pretends not to notice what's happening. But no one, not even Mickey, is taken in by this. We all know her peripheral vision is 20-20. And even if it weren't so, we know she'd still always have an eye focused on Mickey.

Bucky calls out "Ready. Set. Go."

Off to glory races our hero.

On reaching the pump, just as he did earlier, he braces his hands on the hydrant and hoists himself upwards. His execution is proceeding with a grace worthy of an impala. However, at the top of his flight, the crotch of his knickers catches on the giant wrench-nut that caps the dome of Everest. Mickey's groin stays static. The rest of him goes spinning. His head sweeps from 12 o'clock high to 3 o'clock horizontal to 6 o'clock low. Then it slams nose first into the unforgiving iron on the side of Everest. Meanwhile, Mickey's legs are cart-wheeling from 6 to 9 to 12 o'clock. All of this gyration is too much for the fabric of Mickey's pants. Its center cannot hold. The crotch tears off and with it goes most of the material covering Mickey's butt. Finally, the poor kid falls like a limp lump onto the pavement.

The scene looks like something you'd see in a Chaplin film. It's bizarre. It's tragic. It's hilarious.

Mickey's a mess. His nose is bleeding. His face is bruised and scraped. It's obvious to one and all that tomorrow on awakening he's going to possess two world class shiners.

Everyone but Mickey is laughing. Peggy's amusement, however, quickly transforms itself into tears. Mickey, who by all rights has the greatest reason to cry, is too embarrassed to shed a tear. As he rises bloodied and bare-assed before his beloved, it occurs neither to him nor to us to thank God for allowing him to keep his balls intact.

Quickly, the gang clusters around its fallen hero. Like Victorian gentlemen, we feel obliged to spare Peggy a view of Mickey's torn drawers and naked nether parts. So maintaining a rugby-like scrum we proceed to nudge, budge and trudge our wounded warrior down the block to his home.

At P. S. 83 cheating is both blatant and rampant. For most colored kids it's as normal as breathing. For the majority of Italians too, cribbing is a way of life. Although the Jews frown and look down on anyone who doesn't do his own work, there are plenty of them who are two-faced and not above copying to get by.

While I was at P.S. 207 cribbing probably had been going on there too but I think I was too stupid or naive to notice it.

At P.S. 83 I can't be this dumb. As soon as I start getting good grades, Leo Pacelli begins copying from me. After class when I asked him why he's doing this, he tells me I'm asking a stupid question. I guess I am.

Perhaps cribbing is the reason underlying the decision at P. S. 83 to seat us by our grade ranking. Although copying under this arrangement continues, it becomes difficult for a kid to profit from it. He can only get answers from the people around him. Copying from another dumbbell's paper means you would be duplicating his mistakes. That would be a dead giveaway that you've been up to no good.

My morality has never been a match for my mother's or father's. I'm not above cheating. The fact that I haven't been doing it has never meant I wouldn't. So when an opportunity comes for me to break the ice, I break it and do so without any pangs of conscience or guilt. The circumstances of this event are as follows:

Miss Jacobsen tells us one morning that an expert will be coming into our classroom at 10 o'clock to give us a hearing test. Immediately I begin to worry for I have no idea what the questions on a hearing test will be. I can't remember studying about hearing stuff in class. Furthermore, if the topic is in any of my textbooks, I haven't come across it.

I worry that if I fail the hearing test, Mother will think I've slacked off in my school work and shamed her. I know that means trouble, probably another after school conference with her and Miss Jacobsen. While I've been lucky once, I can't count on being so again.

As Miss Jacobsen proceeds through the nine o'clock arithmetic lesson, I ignore the goings-on in class. I can't concentrate on subtraction. I'm too worried thinking about the hearing test. Will it involve big words? Will the expert read to us material from a scholarly tome and then ask us to answer tough questions about the stuff? If she does, will I ever be able to pass?

The more I think about the hearing test, the more ominous it becomes. My fear of it could fill the room with dread and encase the planet in anxiety.

Finally 10 o'clock arrives. The expert enters our classroom. We're surprised to see that he's not a woman. He's a bald headed man wearing a three piece suit. He's pushing a table truck. On it is a big black box that contains electrical stuff as well as ear phones similar to the ones worn by telephone operators.

That an important man like the expert would bring complicated electrical equipment into our classroom tells us this hearing test is extremely serious.

For ten to fifteen minutes we watch him work. He's jacking cables and plugging leads from a wall outlet into a phonograph and then to a distributing contraption which like an octopus puts out enough wires to reach each individual's desk with an a set of ear phones.

When everything is in place, a special four column answer sheet for the test is given to every kid. On a horizontal line at the top everyone writes his name, the date and the number on the set of earphones he's wearing.

Then we're told that we'll be listening to a recording. On it will be the voice of a woman saying numbers. In the first column on our answer sheets we are to list these numbers as they are spoken.

The test begins.

I hear the voice say "foah-whah." I take this to mean four and write the number on the top line in column one.

Then I hear her less audible voice say "the-ree-uh." I figured she's either from the deep South or has a terrible speech impediment. I write 3 underneath the 4. As I do I notice that everyone around me is doing the same.

The expert then lifts the needle off of the record. He asks, "Is there anyone who did not hear the voice?"

No hands are raised.

"If you heard the number four and then the number three, please raise your hand."

Everyone raises his hand.

"Good, Now I'm going to play another recording. You will list the numbers again but this time please put them in the second column. Your first number will be nine. Please write that now on the top line of column 2."

Everyone does as told. The expert and Miss Jacobsen go around to every persons's desk to check and to be sure no one is writing nine in the wrong place.

Satisfied at last that we all know what we're supposed to be doing, he tells us that as the reciting of the numbers continues, they'll become harder to hear. We are not to worry about that. We are to write those that we hear. But we are not to write the first number which was nine since we have already done so.

The recording begins with "nine-ner" which is followed with a rather quiet "fye-yev." The next number "foah-whah," I can barely detect. Then I hear nothing but see that all around me everyone is marking his answer sheet at the same time as everyone else. I peek at the paper being filled out by Theresa Furillo, the girl sitting to my left. She has just written 6. When she and everyone else bends over to write the next number, I script a 6 directly under my 4. Then I continue to copy from Theresa for the rest of the hour. She fills in the rest of the columns completely and I finish one number behind her in each. If she scores a grade of ninety or better, I'll be at least an eighty. Without cheating, I surely would have failed with a mark no higher than forty.

After our papers are collected and all of the equipment is repacked, the expert leaves.

Nothing further is ever mentioned about the hearing test. Because of this we take it for granted that everyone has passed. I'll bet dollars to doughnuts, however, that in my class that morning I wasn't the only kid who was cheating. It makes me wonder whether anyone should believe any statistic or finding furnished by the Board of Education of the City of New York.

Chapter 6

Relatives

When my dad's kid brother entered medical school he met and became friends with a big red-headed fellow whose name was Oscar Riemann. Understandably, everyone called him Red. He was the kind of guy who could fit the saying, "he never knew a stranger." If you saw him only for five minutes, he made you feel as if you and he had been pals since Adam. He had a ready smile, an easy manner and an ability to light up a room with laughter and joy when he entered it.

Red was not merely likeable but also very bright. He had to be. Dopes don't get into Medical School. But somehow, he wasn't getting the best of grades. Because he was lousy at memorizing, anatomy was killing him. In college he seldom had studied. Aside from getting a grade of C in something called Organic Chemistry, he had never received a grade below B in any subject. In the really difficult courses such as physics and mathematics, he got high A's. He was able to do this by paying attention in class and doing the minimum amount of homework. In medical school, he was finding, he needed more than a quick mind. He needed to memorize, memorize and memorize.

Ernie says quite a few medical students share Red's problem. They don't appreciate the Latin proverb, "Repetition is the Mother of Learning." They don't study enough and when they do, they do it poorly. Instead of daily reviewing their notes, they cram.

I suppose because the Medical School professors were once students themselves and may have had Red's trouble in remembering diseases and other doctoring stuff, they've invented a system of using unusual sentences to help them to recall important facts. For instance, to learn the twelve cranial nerves the students say, "Oh, oh, oh to touch and feel a girl's vagina so hot." Then they take the first letter of each word in this sentence and match it with the first letter of a corresponding cranial nerve. According to Red this helps. Without it, he might never be able to remember and to recite olfactory, optic, oculomotor, trochlear, trigeminal, auditory, facial, abducens, glossopharyngeal, vagus, spinal accessory and hypoglossal.

I know these nerves and I know what each one does because Ernie taught them to me long before I met Red.

I'm glad I learned the cranial nerves without the saying because when Red told me the saying, I asked him what a vagina was.

He sort of hemmed and hawed before telling me he'd explain it when I got a little older. I figured he said that because he didn't know or wasn't sure, himself, what it was. Not wanting to embarrass him, I let the matter drop. However, the next day I asked my mother what it was. At first the question upset her but when I told her I heard it from Red when he was talking medical stuff, she calmed down and told me it was a technical term for a girl's wee wee. When I asked her what technical was, she said specialized. When I asked her what specialized was, she lost patience with me.

So as I said, I'm glad I learned the cranial nerves without the saying. It not only would have amounted to an extra thing to memorize but it's also silly and disgusting. After all who would ever want to touch anyone else's wee wee, especially a girl's.

Around four thirty, one Saturday afternoon while I'm staying on an overnight vacation at Mom's, Red comes by to pick up Ernie. The two of them are going to dinner and to a show with a couple of blondes from Bensonhurst. As Red has arrived early, Ernie is just out of the shower and beginning to dress. From his room he calls out "Hi" to Red and tells him to come keep him company as he puts on his shirt and tie.

"Can I come too?" I ask.

"Of course," answers Ernie.

In the bedroom Ernie is trying to decide whether to wear an all white shirt or one that is white with pinstripes. He asks us which one we think would look best on him.

Red gives him the once over and answers, "The one that's easiest for Rita to unbutton."

Ernie smiles and says, "Get serious." Then turning to me he asks, "What's your opinion, Gus? Which one should I wear?"

Although it's flattering to be asked this, I really have no preference. So after a few moments of musing, I decide to play it safe and pass the buck. I say seriously, "If I were you, I'd listen to Red."

Why they laugh at this is beyond me, but since they do, I join them.

As Ernie puts on the white shirt, Red looks at me and says, "You know, kid, from the way that cowlick of yours always sends your hair slanting down over your forehead, you look a lot like Hitler must have at your age.

"Come here for a minute."

As he's standing by the vanity, I walk over. He has me turn and stand before him looking into the mirror. Then reaching around he puts the end of a comb under my nose to simulate Hitler's mustache.

The resemblance between the Fuhrer and me is unmistakable.

"Wait," says Ernie, "I've got an idea."

He goes out to the kitchen, gets a cork, burns the end of it in a flame on the stove and comes back with it into the bedroom. After waiting a bit for the cork to cool, he dabs the charred end of it under my nose to give me a black mustache like Hitler's.

"Now, I want you to imitate me imitating Hitler," he says as he gets out a few pairs of underwear shorts and puts them before us on top of the vanity.

Then with a German accent like Hitler's, he begins speaking in a voice which rises until it thunders with rage, "I haft no more territorial demands. I haft only vunn demand. I gift duh rest of duh verld, twenty-four hours, to get out!"

He has both Red and me laughing. What makes it even funnier is the way he punctuates each pause in the tirade by tossing an undergarment into the air and by ending the oration in a spinning whirl capped with a ridiculous Nazi salute and a "Sieg Heil."

Mom comes into the room to see what the commotion is all about.

I take over and show her. I imitate Ernie and the Fuhrer to a T.

Although to her there is never anything funny about Hitler, this, for her, turns out to be the exception proving the rule.

Ernie and I have identical habits of clearing our throats. Everyone thinks I picked this up from him. That's absurd.

I've always had something called a post nasal drip. Fluid from my sinuses passes down the back of my nose and falls into my throat. Most of it I suppose I swallow. But some of it feels as though it begins to form a curtain of film over my trachea. Soon it is blocking my breathing. I clear my throat only to keep the air passage open. The alternative to this is dying.

When Red got to know me, he came to me one day and said, "Gus, I want you to do me a favor. I want you to promise me that every time you clear your throat, you'll recite the following words: 'Unaccustomed as I am to public speaking, it behooves me on this auspicious occasion to offer a few propitious comments on the propositions of epistemology, eschatology and filial piety.'"

He pauses and asks me if I've gotten it. Embarrassingly I have to admit I haven't. He repeats the spiel a few more times. Finally, I have it memorized.

Then he asks me to swear on a piece of rope which once had been part of the Lone Ranger's lasso that I will always recite this speech every time I clear my throat.

Of course, I agree. Who wouldn't? Why I would have doled out 100 baseball cards just to have had the privilege of touching the lasso of the Lone Ranger. Even without this honor, however, I'd have agreed with Red's request just to please him.

Often when I stay on an overnight vacation at Mom's, she takes me in the late afternoon to the movies at the Astor, a strange kind of theater located next door to Erasmus Hall High School. Always it's double features are of old movies or ones that are so boring that they could only have been made in France. Mom enjoys these films. She calls them cultural. She assures me that in time I will agree with her that no films more interesting and entertaining than these have ever been made.

Fat chance, I say to myself.

After one such double feature, Mom and I go to dinner at her favorite restaurant, Joe's. She has a tab there. We're served as always by her favorite waiter, Stefan. He too is Hungarian. Moreover, in appearance he puts Mom in mind of her brother, Miklos, who still lives in the old country. Stefan feeds Mom his phony line about her having a youthful appearance. He says he can't believe I'm her grandson. I know that's baloney. He's only looking for an extra nickel tip. Mom knows it too. But to her the flattery is pleasing and a nickel is a small price to pay for a moment of grace.

At the table everything goes along well until it comes time for dessert. Mom orders coffee with her pie and hot milk with mine.

"Moment, please," I say doing my Charlie Chan imitation and then I continue, "I can't drink hot milk. It makes me sick."

"This milk won't make you sick. It's from Hungary," answers Mom.

Because almost every time she has said something was Hungarian it turned out to be terrific, I'm hesitant to contradict her. To me the flavor of cold milk is repulsive and warm milk is a hundred times more so. I'm certain that not even a Hungarian cow can do a thing about this. So I say "If I have to have something warm, better order me cocoa. The hot milk will only make me vomit."

"Nonsense. Warm Hungarian milk is good for you. It can't possibly make you sick." Then turning to Stefan she says, "Bring him the warm Hungarian milk."

"Very good, Mrs. Stern," he utters and leaves.

When he returns, I go through my pie like Grant through Richmond. The milk I let stand. It looms before me as white, ugly and ridiculously useless as the Washington Monument.

"Drink up," Mom insists as she moves the glass towards me.

With a sour puss, I sit there.. I've been through this so many times with her, I know it's pointless to argue. She'll never yield to reason. So to make the best of a bad situationI say, "I'll give it a try, if you'll put a couple of teaspoons of coffee into it to tone down the taste."

Agreeing with me that this is an excellent idea, she spoons just enough of her coffee into the milk to turn it from white to a tan-shaded off-white.

In preparation for the inevitable I clear my throat and after mumbling my "Unaccustomed as I am..." spiel, I begin to drink the stuff. It must be like swallowing pigeon doo.I manage to get half of a glass down. I can't handle more.

This satisfies her.

Ten minutes later as we're outside making our way home, the inevitable happens. I step to the curb and puke all over Flatbush Avenue.

At church the next morning when I'm reunited with my family, I'm introduced to my great aunt Alice and her new husband, Doug Jones. They've both been working for the Kodak Corporation upstate in Rochester. Recently Doug has been given a promotion. It requires him to be transferred to the Eastman plant in Kingsport, Tennessee.

Not wanting to part from Alice, Doug asked her to marry him. So on their way south they've taken a detour in order to honeymoon in New York City and to visit us.

I have heard many stories about Alice. Gram describes her as the family snob. She has genealogical charts which trace our ancestral roots all the way back to the village of Wilgersdorf near the city of Siegen in Germany in the year 1590.

Sure enough, Gram is right. Alice is a snob. Almost the first thing she does on meeting me is to take me aside and tell me that our first ancestor to arrive in the New World did so in New York around the year 1712.

By 1800, however, because our distant grandparents had backed the Tories and had fought against George Washington, our forbears had to flee to Canada to survive. There for their loyal service to the Crown not only in the Revolution but also during the War of 1812, they were given a royal grant of land in the vicinity of Parkhill, Ontario. There the family settled and there Gram, Alice and all of their brothers, sisters and cousins were born and raised.

In Gram's family Alice is the fifth of six children. Gram is the third. There's a six year difference in age between them.

This meant that when Alice was a baby, Gram was made to mind her. Of course, this ended quickly for Alice was the tiny sister whom Gram used to pinch and make cry.

A dozen years have elapsed since Gram and Alice had last seen each other. They carry on with so much hugging and crying, you'd think that God had lifted them out from among the dead to be with one another. Almost as mushy is the reunion of Alice and my mother. They haven't seen each other since 1931 when my mother went briefly to live with Alice before returning to Brooklyn to marry my dad.

After church everyone comes home to our house for Sunday dinner. With Ernie and Mom, Alice and Doug, Mother and Dad, and Gram and her new husband, Hans, filling all of places at the big table in the dining room, Gwen, Matt and I are given our dinners at the little one in the kitchen. None of us is happy about this, especially Gwen. She's sixteen. She claims that anyone her age is too old to be treated as a child. After all, her sister's children aren't her peers.

Her aggravation makes mine bearable. In fact, witnessing her misery tickles me pink. "Knock off the complaining," I tell her, "There's only room at the table for eight grownups. Until we can get a high chair in the dining room big enough for a sixteen year old cry baby, you'll just have to stay here in the kitchen and eat with your peers."

This makes her furious. She calls to my mother, "Cynthia, your son is being a brat again."

Mother comes in and lays down the law, "No more. Do you hear? No more. Gwen's in charge here. I don't want either of you to give her any trouble."

I start to ask if I can change my seat so I won't have to look at Gwen. Mother cuts me off saying, "I told you Gwen's in charge. Direct anything you have to say to her."

I look at my aunt. Although she isn't sticking her tongue out at me, her face still radiates with the pleasure she's feeling. I'm in no mood to ask her permission for anything so I let the matter of the seating drop.

A minute or so later dinner is ready. You can tell this meal is important not just by our being relegated to the kitchen but also by the fact that we had to come into the dining room to listen to the saying of grace. We only do that when the minister comes or when it's a special holiday like Christmas, Thanksgiving or Easter.

When we return to the kitchen, I slide my plate to a better place on the table. Then I sit down opposite Matt and go through dinner like the Germans through Poland. I'm finished with dessert before anyone else is even half done.

I want to be excused from the table but I'm not of a mind to ask Gwen for her permission to leave. As I watch Matt and her dilly-dally with their dinners, I begin to think Doomsday will arrive before either of them will finish their meal. While trying to decide what to do, I clear my throat. Automatically I begin reciting, "Unaccustomed as I am..."

"Will you stop this silly nonsense?" demands Gwen.

I pause for a moment. Then in a louder voice, I continue, "to public speaking, it behooves me on this auspicious occasion to offer a few propitious comments..."

"Cynthia," calls Gwen, "Gus is being obnoxious."

"I am not," I lie. Although I hadn't known before what obnoxious meant, I know now.

Suddenly, there's my mother standing next to me. I turn away and brace myself.

A long time passes. Maybe six or seven seconds. That may not seem like a lot of time but when your noggin is an inescapable target for a forthcoming round house right, a wait that long is an eternity.

The blow to my surprise never lands. Instead I hear Mother saying, "There will be no more of this. Do you understand?"

"Yes, Mother," I say.

"Now apologize to Gwen."

"Do I have to?"

Her answer comes swiftly. Wham! A solid slam on my nose. It sends me and my chair sprawling. I land on the back of my head. I guess I see what people call stars but I'd describe them as jagged bursts of silver tinged with technicolor. Anyway, I'm not too concerned about these. My nose is smarting and my eyes are watering.I know too I'm bleeding because as I go to get up blood drips onto my shirt. I expect to get clouted for that. I don't remember much else except that I had double vision and felt dizzy.

I guess I passed out.

A day later I awake in St. Mary's Hospital. I don't feel sick. I just feel starved.

The next day I come home. I'm told I have had a concussion. That means my brain had been squeezed like an accordion inside my skull. I also learn that everyone has been worried about me. A couple of months later I'm told that I could have died or suffered permanent brain damage.

Anyway, at home things have changed. Dad has laid down the law against hitting. Everyone agrees that's a good thing. Nonetheless, I know neither my mother nor I can obey it. Sooner or later, I'll slug Matthew and sooner or later she'll whack me.

Meanwhile my grandmothers haven't been talking to each other. Apparently they've traded harsh words. About what, I'm never told. But I don't think it requires much imagination to know they quarreled over the way I was being disciplined.

Chapter 7
Fair Fare

It's like a Jewish Holiday. Except for the coloreds and the poorest of us poor whites, the school is empty. Our classmates have gone to the World's Fair.

We stay-behinds have been rounded up and herded into the auditorium. There throughout the day we sit in silence two seats apart from each other. The older kids read. I scribble, draw pictures and yawn.

In the afternoon the Principal stops by and gives us a speech. He tells us the World's Fair is something too important to be missed. It's a once in a life time event. He says it makes him sad to know that neither the taxpayers nor our parents have been able to come up with the twenty five cents that the Board of Education requires of every individual taking part in the field trip. He urges us to plead with our folks, when they have money, to take us to the Fair. He ends his talk saying, "Your classmates today are learning how rich in culture our planet is. For you, I hope, today's lesson hasn't been that culture is only for the rich."

At home I never say anything about the do nothing day or the Principal's speech. Experience has taught me that discussing the negative stuff that goes on at school isn't wise. It kindles Mother's anger. Since next to nothing positive ever happens at school, the Principal's talk is a topic easy to avoid.

That evening after supper, my mother and father come outside with Matthew and sit on the stoop. I play before them on the sidewalk.

Seymour Lipschitz, a classmate of mine, comes by.

"You really missed out, Gus," says Seymour. "The Fair was great.

We went inside the Perisphere and saw the world below like we were in heaven. And we saw man made lightning and thunder. And lots more. Why one building, I think it was Italy's, had a waterfall on it!"

"Baloney," I say.

"Baloney nothing," he returns. "It was sensational. The whole school saw it."

"Baloney anyway," I insist.

"It was like the future. Everything looked like Flash Gordon. It was something. Miss Jacobsen said we would never forget this day. I know I won't."

"Then don't."

"You're just a sore head because you were too poor to go."

"Gus," interrupts Mother, "I think you had better come in."

"Jeez, Mother, it's early."

"I know but I want you inside."

"Heck," I complain.

"See you tomorrow," says Seymour.

"Yeah, see you tomorrow," I answer and go in.

After this conversation with Seymour, we seldom say anything at home about the World's Fair. In some mysterious way the family has come to realize that talk about it is taboo. That's okay with me. It isn't anything I give a hoot about. Heck, the Fair is in Flushing Meadows. Maybe that isn't as far away from Brooklyn as the unseen side of the Moon but as far as I'm concerned it is. If Flushing Meadows hadn't been the answer to a joke, (What's the largest plumbing job ever?) the place would have held no more interest for me than Lansing, Michigan,or Wheeling, West Virginia, which incidentally are also answers to silly jokes: (What's the biggest operation and what's the greatest engineering feat?)

A year passes.

Instead of the 1939 New York World's Fair ending as planned, it's extended for another year. Some countries like the Soviet Union and

Argentina choose not to renew their exhibits. Who cares? In attacking Finland the Russians have shown the world they're just a bunch of thugs no different from their Nazi allies. As for Argentina, everyone knows it's filled with fascists. The only thing good that can be said about such people is that there aren't more of them. Anyway, with these nations gone, the Fair has improved and any slack caused by their departures has been taken up by new exhibitors and by increases in the quantity and quality of the amusement rides. Perhaps the best change of all in the second year of the Fair is the lowering of the entrance fee for adults from seventy-five to fifty cents.

One morning late in August of 1940 when the air war over Britain is at its height, Gwen comes over to our house to mind Matthew while Gram, Mother and I go to the Fair. The trip is a surprise. No one has warned me of it. Had I known about it and of the necessity to take a series of trolley rides with transfers to reach Flushing Meadows, I'd have raised so much Cain before hand that they'd have gone without me. Given my history of vomiting on streetcars, it's obvious they've taken leave of their senses in bringing me along.

Surprisingly, the trip passes without incident. I don't get motion sickness. I think that's due mostly to luck. It also helps that I never have to sit sideways.

When we enter the Fair we don't go immediately to the Trylon and Perisphere. We go instead to bathrooms and relieve ourselves. Then we begin walking around to observe things. We're impressed by the magnificent buildings, the grand statues and the well manicured gardens. Most of all we're fascinated by the people. While nine in ten look like normal New Yorkers, one in ten definitely doesn't. Maybe I should have been saying normal *Americans* since as anyone who's been to New York knows there's no such thing as a normal New Yorker. Anyway, out of the thousands of visitors present, hundreds are from foreign lands and are dressed in exotic clothing.

On seeing all of this Gram says, "This fair puts me in mind of the Islamic saying that if Mohammed won't go to the mountain, the mountain will come to him. Only now it should be updated to be, if we don't go abroad to see the world's freaks, the freaks will come here. That wouldn't be bad except for the fact that most of them will never return home. They'll choose instead to stay here and live either as thieves or as bums with their families on Relief."

When Mother and Gram tell me that everything that I'm seeing will be torn down and destroyed or removed within a year, I'm dumbfounded. "Why?" I ask. They answer saying the upkeep to maintain the buildings and grounds would be too costly.

I can't understand this. I would think that when the fair is over everything in it not already owned and controlled by the great industries would be sold or rented to corporations. Companies could establish their headquarters here. A place as elegant and impressive as this should become the business and cultural capital of the world. Tearing it down, strikes me as a sacrilege. Don't these jerks know there's a Depression?

Although the magnificence of the fair is obvious, I soon begin to regard it as tiresome. So many of the buildings charge a fee to enter them. With less than five dollars to spend on the three of us, Gram and Mother have to pinch pennies and to choose carefully which exhibits to see and which to ignore. As almost all the dull stuff like looking at machinery is free, we see lots of it. Most of the good stuff we have to skip because we can't afford the price of admission.

I'm only a little surprised to find that the things that impressed Seymour Lipschitz are the things that impress me. Inside the Perisphere it's awesome to look down on a model city of the future. Yet as neat as that is, it isn't half as magnificent as viewing Con Edison's block long diorama of a city of the future. We watch as a full day of events takes place in it in only 12 minutes. We see the metropolis awake to morning, endure its rush hour, run its elevated trains, survive traffic and undergo a sky darkening thunderstorm. It's fascinating to see the lights go on in the many windows of the tiny skyscrapers. As for the man made lightning and thunder in the GE pavilion, I find the first flashing bolt with its ear shattering sound to be stunning. But after that, just sitting and waiting for the phenomenon to repeat seems stupid and boring.

Unquestionably after the Trylon and Perisphere, the immense waterfall on the front of the Italian Pavilion is the architectural highlight of the fair. I want to go inside the building to examine the pumping system that makes the sixty or seventy foot high cascade possible. Gram nixes that idea. With a twinkle in her eye she says such an investigation would be a disappointing waste of time since all we'd find in there would be a goat and a bunch of greasy guineas singing opera, cooking spaghetti, cutting hair and resoling shoes. When I ask her why they'd have a goat in the building, she says, "Isn't it obvious? There's no backyard here for it."

In the Canadian exhibit we see sensational totem poles and honest-to-God real mounties dressed in red tunics.

We stop in at some of the other national pavilions looking for places to eat but always we leave because their prices are too high. After several such turn arounds we go to an American concession and get hot dogs and cokes. This food is also overpriced but not as outrageously as in the foreign restaurants.

All of this cost comparing leads me to conclude that it's nonsense to call America a rich country. Maybe to the Chinese or to the Bolivians we look prosperous. To the Europeans, I think, we're just a bunch of good natured slobs whose pockets are easy to pick. As the saying goes, "With friends like these, we have no need of enemies."

For reasons that will never make sense to me when evening comes we spend a long time watching a fashion show in the Japanese Pavilion. The colorful kimonos are captivating to Mother and Gram.

They aren't so to me. I think these silky articles of clothing look like shower curtains and undoubtedly when worn are just about as uncomfortable and confining as straight jackets.

Ever since the war-tickets, which my friends and I trade and play with in games for keeps, began printing cards picturing the cruelties inflicted upon the Chinese in the Sino-Japanese war, I've not liked the Nips. They've been at least as rotten as the Germans. So even though I kind of admire the neat little wooden bridge that they had built over the tiny rill that flows through their pavilion, I won't admit to it. To me the only pleasing aspect of the fashion show is that no Japanese men are present. I assume the reason for this is that they are away at war, murdering unarmed and helpless Chinese.

The fair sort of ends at ten o'clock with a fireworks display. Most people have hung around to see it. I wouldn't have. I've been ready to leave since seven. Anyway, after all the rockets red glare and the bombs bursting in air stuff is finished, the only parts of the fair still open are the rides in the amusement area. As we had scouted them earlier, I've had plenty of time to decide on which ride to try. Only the 250 foot high parachute jump has been excluded for the obvious reason that it charges too much. Because I now am tired, I would not be disappointed if Mother's earlier offer to me of a ride were withdrawn. I'm ready to leave and go home. However, when Mother says to hurry up and decide on which ride to take, I know I'd better grab one. It won't do to set a precedent of not caring. That could lead to losing forever another opportunity to have a treat. So I point to the nearest attraction: a fun house with spooks.

When you work your way up past some scary terrors to the top of the fun house an attendant waiting there hands you a little rug to put under yourself as you slide down a long, steep, spiraling tunnel and go sprawling almost into the street to finish the ride. Normally something this childish wouldn't have been my first, second or even fifteenth choice in an amusement park. However, I must admit it was fun and I'm not sorry I picked it.

Instead of using the trolley to return home we ride back on the subway.

Miss Jacobsen had told Seymour, a day at the World's Fair is not a day that anyone is likely ever to forget. She was right.

No one can deny the importance of the World's Fair. It is, indeed, worthwhile, interesting and educational. But unlike a day spent at Ebbets Field watching the Dodgers, my day at the fair isn't one I'd care to repeat. To me it's too much like window shopping on Flatbush Avenue.

Chapter 8

Two Thanksgivings

Every afternoon in 1939 when the kids on the block would begin to round up to head for the candy store, I'd rush home to ask my mother for a penny. But the closer I would come to our door, the less heart I'd have in my mission. My mother is tight with money. Asking her for it often puts her in a foul mood.

"Mother, the gang is going to the candy store. You wouldn't have a penny to give me, would you?"

"Right, I wouldn't."

"Jeez."

"I didn't ask for back talk. Nor did I ask for blasphemy. You know we're poor. You had a penny yesterday. If you're good, maybe you'll get one again tomorrow. Now take this dust cloth and go clean the legs of the furniture."

Just after Armistice Day my teacher, Miss Cantor, asks if anyone in class knows of a poor family.

"We're poor," I answer.

"How do you know that Gregory?"

"My mother says so. She's always saying so. She says we're so poor that it makes her sick every Thursday morning."

"I don't understand."

"It's simple. On Thursday mornings when we have assembly, all the girls must dress in white middy blouses with red scarves. All the boys must wear white shirts and red ties. But a red tie costs a dime. Since we haven't got a dime, I can't dress right. This upsets my mother. So she gets sick every Thursday morning and keeps me home to care for her."

"I see, Gregory. I see."

On the Monday before Thanksgiving we are asked by Miss Cantor to bring food to school for a needy family. I tell Mother this. It upsets her but she hands me a can of soup to give as my donation. By Wednesday afternoon the contributions of the class fill two small bushel baskets.

Miss Cantor is pleased. She tells us that our charity brings tears of joy to the eyes of God. Then she reads to us the tale of the Pilgrims and the Indians celebrating the first Thanksgiving. We end the school day singing, "We Gather Together to Ask the Lord's Blessing."

At dismissal time Miss Cantor asks me to help her carry the baskets of food out to the trunk of her car. I'm happy to do this. I take it to be an honor just like being made an errand boy or being picked to go outside and clap the erasers clean.

When everything has been stowed into her car, she says, "Get in. I'll drive you to your home."

I hesitate to obey her.

"Get inside, Gregory," she repeats.

"I'm sorry I can't. I'm not allowed to take car rides with anyone unless they're members of my family."

"That's a good rule," she agrees. "It shouldn't be broken. So I won't ask you to ride with me. However, I want you to go straight home. I'll meet you there when you arrive. Now tell me, what is your address."

All of this seems very strange but I reply, "192 Schnectady Avenue." Then I leave and head home.

As I reach my block, I see Miss Cantor's car go by. It pulls up and parks in front of my house. When I arrive my teacher is opening the trunk. She calls to me to come and assist her. She asks me to help her carry the baskets of food up to our door. Although I think this to be a strange request, I comply. I figure she wants to show my mother how much stuff our class has collected for a needy family.

When I press the bell, Mother doesn't answer it. We can hear her vacuuming. Because the sound of the machine must be drowning out the sound of our ringing, it takes us three more tries to be heard. The cleaning stops. Mother comes and opens the door.

Before I get a chance to introduce anyone, Miss Cantor speaks up saying, "Good afternoon, Mrs. Stern, I'm Miss Cantor, Gregory's teacher. I'm bringing you a Thanksgiving gift of food from Gregory's classmates and their families."

"There must be some mistake."

"May I come in for a moment?"

Nodding yes, Mother says, "Please do."

Miss Cantor enters bringing with herself one of the baskets. I follow with the other. Miss Cantor then says to Mother, "Mrs. Stern, there is no mistake. You and your family have need of this food."

"I can assure you there is a mistake. We're not poor. Look. You can see we have a vacuum cleaner. We can't be poor."

"Gregory says otherwise. He quotes you as saying you are.

"I'm familiar with children his age. Then don't make things like this up. Please take the groceries. You have need of them."

Mother is upset. Tears fill her eyes. In a voice breaking with embarrassment she sends me outside to play.

In a quarter of an hour Miss Cantor comes out. She is leaving empty handed. She waves to me and calls out, "Happy Thanksgiving, Gregory."

I wave back and wish her the same.

Next day at dinner I'm denied my holiday privilege of saying the family's grace. My father explains, "You can say grace at Christmas. Except for the generosity of your classmates and their families, we don't have too much to be thankful for this Thanksgiving. So I'll say the blessing today. We'll save yours for a truly festive occasion."

He says grace and we eat our eggs and beans in silence.

Over the course of the next year, I seldom hear my mother complain about poverty. She penny pinches as always and by November she has saved up enough money to buy us a turkey. Never, she insists, will she endure again another Thanksgiving like the last. This makes Dad smile. He kisses Mother and tells her he is proud of her frugality.

On the Sunday before Thanksgiving, Pop stops by. He tells us not to buy a turkey. He's won one at church in a raffle. He says he'll be bringing it by in the afternoon on Wednesday.

This news makes everyone's day.

Mother now decides that she can spend the money that she has saved up to get a turkey on other things. We will celebrate the holiday like royalty. So on Monday and Tuesday instead of just buying pumpkin for pies, she also buys currants, mince meat and apples. In addition she purchases three pounds of assorted nuts and plenty of pears and tangerines for extra trimmings. She even gets marshmallows to mix in with the sweet potatoes. Our Thanksgiving is going to have everything--even turnips which I hate. She says this will be a day we'll never forget.

After school on Wednesday as we wait for Pop to arrive with the turkey, I peel green apples and with my brother break bread for stuffing while Mother does the baking. As the afternoon wears on, she grows increasingly nervous. Where's Pop?

At five we set the table. At five fifteen my brother and I go into the living room to listen to my favorite program, Jack Armstrong. A few minutes after it ends, Dad comes home. After he kisses us, he listens to Mother as she expresses her concern about Pop's lateness and the possibility that something has gone wrong.

"Relax," says Dad, "Pop probably stopped off for a shot. He'll get here. Meanwhile the odors coming from the kitchen are making my mouth water. Let's eat."

"It's not yet Thanksgiving," says Mother as we sit down. In no time she proves this. She feeds us our regular Wednesday night pea soup.

After the supper dishes are washed, dried and put away, Mother grows increasingly irritable. She has visions of everyone sitting down to dinner tomorrow and seeing not a turkey but three square feet of empty space in the middle of the table. Dad tries to ease her worry by assuring her that any minute now Pop is bound to come through the door with the bird.

At seven as usual Matt and I sit down in the living room and turn on *The Lone Ranger*. When it ends Dad will take over the radio and catch the last half of WNYC's *The Master work Hour*. He's a regular listener of that and of *Symphony Hall*. Mother is a fan of neither. She likes popular music but always keeps the volume low.

During the commercials of the Lone Ranger Mother lets us know she's very upset with Pop's lateness. When seven-thirty arrives her anxieties get the best of her, She blows her top. She shouts at Dad over the second movement of Beethoven's Fifth, "I don't care how poor we are, we're having turkey tomorrow. I'm not going through another Thanksgiving like the last. I'm sick of this. I'm sick of poverty of pea soup from Wednesday to payday, of scrapple, eggs or fish cakes as main courses. I can't take the guilt. I can't stand the ordeal of having to deny our children the daily penny, their friends get."

Because the old man knows that when she's out of control like this, anything he says will only fuel her fury, he keeps silent.

She turns to me and tells me to put on my coat. She goes into the bedroom to get hers and comes out carrying her most precious possession, her portable electric sewing machine. We then leave and go to a late closing Pawn Shop on Fulton St. With the money she receives for hocking the sewing machine, she buys an 18 lb. turkey in a butcher shop that overcharges. Since it's the only place still open she has no alternative.

When we return home around nine, Pop is there. He's brought us a turkey as promised. So now we have two of them. This aggravates Mother but when Dad made jokes about the absurdity of the situation, she laughs. Pop doesn't need to see the humor to smile. He's already grinning. He's drunk. He gives Matthew and me a nickel each just for being his grandsons.

Because each bird alone can barely fit into the oven, Mother has to get up at five in the morning to begin roasting them one after the other. Somehow, and only God knows how she manages it, both are cooked and hot when they're brought to the table for dinner at one-thirty. My dad takes a snapshot of the scene. It's spectacular. It shows both turkeys. It shows our table filled with so much food that there's barely room for anyone's plate. It shows Mother, Matt and me as well as Gwen, Hans, Gram and Pop seated at the table. Some things such as the pies and the dessert dishes aren't in the photo. They're stacked on the buffet where there's room for them.

Matthew says the grace. Then for the only time in history he, Dad and I each get a drumstick.

By Friday on our block our two turkey dinner is common knowledge. My friends tell me I'm rich. I invite them to come with me to the candy store. There we spend the nickel Pop has given me on jawbreakers and on other two-for-a-penny items. As we eat the candy and glory in my good fortune, I know nothing really has changed. Our family is still poor. Last year when we celebrated the holiday with eggs and beans, my mother's sewing machine wasn't in hock. This year when we do the holiday right, it is. So which Thanksgiving is better? Hands down, my vote is for the 1940's. Not only does it give us a great day but it also provides us with great memories. Moreover, half way to Christmas it makes us feel as one with America as we share in our great national tradition of dining daily on cold turkey sandwiches, hot turkey sandwiches, turkey soup, turkey stew, turkey cakes, turkey salad, turkey hash and turkey pot pies.

Chapter 9

A Fish Story

It's dark and foggy. A chill is in the air. As we leave Pop's house on Ryder St where I've stayed the night and head for Mill Basin, I have harsh feelings towards the sweater I wear. It isn't keeping me warm and it itches.

"Do we have to get bait, Pop?" I ask.

"No they'll have it on board the Hypatia."

"Is she your favorite ship?"

"She's as good as any. She'll do."

I can tell he's wrapped up in his thoughts. I remember my mother's advice, "For God's sake, when you're with your grandfather tomorrow, hold your tongue and allow the man a few moments of peace."

We walk along Avenue U in silence for about five minutes and take a right onto the Flatbush Avenue extension. Although only 50 feet or so of the road ahead can be seen, the stars are clearly visible.

"What causes fog?" I ask.

"The Fog man," he replies.

"Heck Pop, I'm eight. I'm too old to swallow Fog man stuff."

"It's very involved. Suffice it to say, young fellow me lad, a fog is a low flying cloud. It follows, therefore, that what causes clouds causes fogs."

"What is the cause of clouds?"

"The Cloud man," he answers.

"It's too involved to explain to me, huh?"

"It's even too involved to explain to me," he says with a laugh.

The dawn is breaking as we approach the ships. Red, green and white lights shine on the decks. Voices can be heard but due to the fog, there's no telling who it is we're hearing.

In a little while I make out the silhouette of a yacht worthy of Hollywood. We're headed for it. When we reach it, Pop stops and says, "We're here."

Enormous pride swells within me. What a beautiful ship!

Then Pop moves onto the dock and boards a neighboring vessel which looks like a pygmy tugboat built of dilapidated barrel staves.

As I follow Pop on board I say, "I smell vomit."

"That's low tide," corrects Pop.

"Smells just like vomit," I say.

"No vomit's not as bad," advises a seaman who looks like Wallace Beery.

"Morning, Skipper," says Pop.

"Morning, Greg. Who's the landlubber?"

"My grandson, Gus. Gus, meet Captain Eudoxus."

"How do you do, sir?" I say and put out my hand.

The Captain shakes it and scowls, "We'll be gone all day. I don't want any guff from you, mate. There'll be no crying, belly aching or mutinying aboard the Hypatia. Understand?"

"Aye, aye, sir," I answer and salute.

My naval courtesy must have taken him aback. He studies me for a couple of seconds. Then he returns the salute and says, "Good to have you on board."

Pop pays our fares and buys some bait. After he gets his fishing rod and tackle box set up, we sit down.

Within twenty minutes it's daylight. About a dozen more passengers have come on board. Captain Eudoxus starts the motor. A deck hand on shore unties the ropes. Then with a jump, he boards the vessel. We've shoved off. The ship moves slowly along the channel towards the bay and the open sea.

The putt-putt-putt of the motor fascinates me. When an author writes pshaw or ahem, everyone knows the sound he's trying to describe. It's nothing like the spelling. The sound of the motor on the

Hypatia, however, is a faithful duplication of the printed words putt-putt-putt. The putting of the best of beat up jalopies could not have sounded truer.

As we make our way around the land into the open bay, I stay awed by the thought that a few feet beneath me is water.

That a boat floats strikes me as miraculous--a million times more so than any freakish thing in the Bible. If a vessel as ordinary as the Hypatia or as great as the Queen Mary could ever be picked up and placed on land, it would dent the ground. Yet when it's put on water, it floats. The rules for a ship are the opposite of the rules for non-swimmers like me. On land unless I'm on mud or wet sand, I make no impression at all. But put me on water and I sink straight to the bottom. So what's reasonable for a ship, is unreasonable for me and vice versa.

As we pass Breezy Point I notice that the fog has lifted. Coney Island can be seen. Off in the distance, the skyscrapers of New York are visible.

"How far out are we going?" I ask Pop.

"We'll be fishing off of Sandy Hook," he replies.

"Is that near Europe?"

"I'd say closer to New Jersey."

"Aren't we going the wrong way?"

He doesn't respond. I press him saying, "People go on the ocean to get to Europe, not to New Jersey. So isn't the Captain going the wrong way?"

This time he answers. "He would be, if fish acted like people. But they don't. They prefer Sandy Hook. The garbage scows from the city do their dumping there. That attracts fish in much the same way as a landfill draws gulls."

After a while when the Hypatia seems to be nowhere except in the middle of the open sea, the Captain turns off the motor and drops anchor. Like Pop every fisherman picks up his rod and begins to bait his hook. When this is done, each stands at the railing and casts out his line.

"Where's Sandy Hook?" I ask.

"Under us." replies Pop.

"How can you tell?"

"The Captain has a compass in his cabin. He knows where we are."

He flexes his knees to try to reach into the tackle box and then thinks better of it. "Here," he says as he hands his rod to me, "I want you to hold on to this for dear life. If you let go, the day and the trip are ruined and I'll never take you with me anywhere, again."

I grab hold of the rod with both hands just where he wants me to. Before letting go he warns, "You have to hold carefully. You're not to let go if there's a sudden yank caused by a fish taking the bait."

"I won't let go," I assure him.

He opens the tackle box and gets out a line and a hook for me.

After threading and tying the hook, he baits it. Then retaking the rod from me, he says, "Good job, fisherman. Now pick up the line that I've baited and drop it over the side. Feed out enough line so that it sinks fifteen feet or so into the water."

I do as told.

"Good," he praises, "Now stand with one of your feet on the line beneath you to anchor it in case you hook a big one."

"Do you think, I'll catch a big one."

"You never can tell. You may have beginner's luck."

"If I catch a lot of fish, will you get me a rod?" I ask.

"We'll see."

I notice that the water is more green than gray where we are. It's also choppy.

"How come everyone has a cork on his line?" I ask.

"If a fish bites, he'll pull the line and dip the cork. It helps to let the fisherman know that he's got a bite."

"Oh."

Suddenly, I feel nauseous. I've had corn flakes for breakfast. They can't be making me feel queasy. They've never made me sick in the past.

I decide that getting up so early must be what is making me ill. If not that, it has to be the odor of low tide. Its smell is still present even though we're way out to sea.

"Pop," I say, "You'd better hold my line. I'm going to be sick."

"Are you sure."

"Yeah. I'm about to vomit."

"The can is over by the cabin, that door to your left."

I hand him the line and dart to the john. It's a filthy commode housed in a tiny closet. Caked all over the toilet, floor and walls are grime and congealed vomit. The place reeks of low tide.

I reach the commode barely in time. As I bend over it and throw up, half-digested milky corn flakes shoot out of me like fire erupting from the throat of a dragon. When I straighten up after a half of a minute of violent retching, I'm weak, teary-eyed and still nauseous.

I then find out the toilet doesn't flush. I also discover there's no sink. A deck hand raises the rope on a half gallon bucket that he has cast over the side and demonstrates to me how to pour sea water into the commode to flush it. He then shows me where the bucket is to be kept on the deck. It's close by the place where the far end of the bucket's rope is attached to the railing. I'm instructed on how to loop the rope around the bucket when it's not in use. This is important. People could trip or become entangled in a rope left carelessly on deck.

Because there's no sink, I have to swill some sea water in my mouth to remove the taste of vomit. Then I spit it into the sea.

When I return to Pop, he opens a coke for me and tells me to take a few sips. I do.

It's a mistake.

As fast as the coke goes down, it U-turns and races faster coming back up. There's no time to scoot for the john. I puke over the side into the sea.

That becomes another mistake for looking at the green water inspires me to vomit some more. But this time I have enough of a warning to make it back to the john. I retch and heave and go through all the other involuntary motions of vomiting. Nonetheless, nothing comes out.

When I return to my post and tell Pop of my strange ability to vomit nothing but air, he says that I've been suffering something known as the dry heaves. He adds that it's a good sign indicating that my vomiting is about over.

He's wrong.

All morning long I keep right on dry heaving. My shipmates must think I'm out to set a world's record at doing it.

Meanwhile no one is catching any fish.

Finally, around eleven o'clock, one fellow gets a bite. It's a blowfish. I've never seen one. He unhooks it and drops it onto the deck. It looks like it's gasping for air. It swells up like a balloon. After it does this, the man picks it up by its tail and tosses it back into the sea.

"Why did you do that?" I ask. "Don't you want to eat it?"

"Never, son," he answers, "No one eats blowfish. They're poisonous."

If he intends to provide me with a further explanation, he has to forego it. I have to race again to the head.

Incidentally, a head is what seamen call a john.

I can't figure out why I keep vomiting. Pop tells me not to worry. Soon my condition will ease. He says the dry heaves are natural for anyone of English descent: Shakespeare wrote about this in "Much Ado about Nothing."

Towards the end of the morning the deck hand, who had shown me how to use the bucket, begins hauling in fish as fast as he can cast his line into the water. He's doing this up at the port bow. Those close to him begin getting bites too.

I turn to Pop and ask, "Why don't we go up forward and put our lines in where the fish are?"

"That's bad form. We can't do that. We'll just stay where we are."

"Why?"

Because it's the code of the sea. A true fisherman respects another fisherman's rights. He never horns in on the catch."

"If the fish turn our way, will we have to stop fishing because he got to them first?"

"The school is his. But if the fish turn our way, then it will be ours too."

I hear what he says but I'm reluctant to buy it. "If the Captain's hand were a fisherman paying for the trip, what you said would make sense. But his job, like the Captain's, is to take us to where the fish are. So if he finds them, it should be his duty to let us horn in on the school."

"Gus, don't be a pain in the ass. The discussion is over."

I let the matter drop and return to my specialty, dry heaving. When I come back to take my line again from Pop, Captain Eudoxus comes up behind us and says, "A most impressive case of sea sickness, matey."

"Where?" I ask.

"Where?" he says mimicking me.

"Where's the impressive case of sea sickness? I'd like to see that."

"You would, huh?"

"Honestly, I didn't even know the sea could get sick."

"It's not the sea who's sea sick. It's you."

"I'm not sick. I've just got the dry heaves."

He laughs and says, "That's what sea sickness is. And mate you've had one of the best cases on record. I've had my eye on you. You've been taking it like a man. I'm proud of you. Everyone's proud of you. In no time at all, I'm sure you'll get your sea legs and never be sea sick again."

Suddenly feeling lousy doesn't seem bad at all.

The Captain asks me how many times I've vomited. I tell him I haven't bothered to keep count.

Pop breaks into the conversation and says, "It must be up to twenty by now."

I think he exaggerated. I figure it's closer to eighteen.

After this talk I dry heave that day six more times.

Around two o'clock the Captain starts the motor up. I figure it's about time. Pop has caught only one fish, a bass. I've caught none.

"We haven't had much luck here. I hope he's taking us to a better location," I say.

"He's taking us back in," says Pop, "We're through for the day."

The folks around us are laughing, "Haven't you vomited enough?" one of them asks.

"I guess I've vomited enough for us all," I answer.

As soon as the Hypatia stops rocking and begins moving, my sea sickness vanishes. At last I've got my sea legs. The trip back is great. I'm happy to be heading home.

When we get back to shore, the deck hand who has caught at least forty fish begins giving them away to the passengers. Pop and I get six. We wrap them up in a newspaper and head for my house.

We're spared the long walk back to the Utica Avenue trolley. A fellow fisherman gives us a lift in his car to the streetcar barn at Avenue N. Pop and I thank the fellow.

When the fellow drives off, Pop says, "It's early yet. The trolley can wait. Let's cross over to the saloon and whet our whistles."

"Best idea, I've heard today," I say.

We spent about an hour in the saloon. Pop has three or four shots of bourbon with beer chasers. I have two cokes and lots of pretzels. I play shuffle board for keeps with one of the patrons and win a nickel.

Just before five we arrive home. Although I almost always can be counted on to get sick on a trolley, this day I handle the ride from Avenue N to Park Place like a pro. I think having gotten my sea legs has helped. Anyway, Pop and I drop the fish into the kitchen sink and tell Mother that as we've done our part in bringing home the day's catch, she can clean the scales off of them and refrigerate them for dinner tomorrow.

"Nothing doing," says Mother, "You caught them. You clean them."

"I didn't catch any," I say, "Pop only got one. A deck hand gave us the other six."

"Same difference," says Mother.

Pop looks at me and questions, "What do you think?"

"Into the garbage with them," I answer. "I've seen and smelled enough fish. I just want to go out and tell the gang of my world's record of 26 vomits."

Chapter 10

The Bicycle Grief

Every Sunday as I walk to church in the spring of 1941, I pause while passing a second hand store on St. John's Place. In its window on sale for eight dollars is a size twenty bicycle, painted in the Brooklyn Dodger baseball colors of royal blue and white. It's beautiful. It has to have been the property of a rich kid. It's without dents or rust spots.

Owning it is my dream.

I imagine myself peddling the bike down the streets of New York. Everywhere, every eye is focused on the machine and me. Grown-ups watch us with awe. They wonder whether in the midst of a six day bicycle race at Madison Square Garden I've just darted out to pick up a deli sandwich or whether I'm racing on a special mission to deliver an important telegram from President Roosevelt to Mayor LaGuardia. Girls look at me with admiration and swoon. However, like the Lone Ranger I ignore this good stuff and ride on. I'm in search of great deeds to do.

Of course, the great deeds I'm doing are only daydreams. But what daydreams!

It's the bottom of the ninth in the seventh game of the World Series. DiMaggio is coming to bat. The bases are loaded. Two outs and the tying run has a lead off of third. The last of the Dodger pitchers, Hugh Casey, toes the rubber and trembles. A sweating Leo Durocher is at his wit's end. He knows his normally reliable reliever hasn't a Chinaman's chance of throwing one by the Yankee Clipper. The situation seems hopeless.

Suddenly a roar from the Dodger fans thunders through Yankee Stadium. It is answered by an echoing moan from the home team's rooters.

"Time out," Leo hollers to umpire Beans Reardon.

"What's this?" Red Barber asks radio land. "Can it be? Folks, I do believe miracles still occur. Out in the Brooklyn bullpen, baseball's version of the seventh cavalry has just entered the stadium. Once more into the breach, dear friends, it's 'Bicycling Gus' to the rescue."

Above the din of the crowd, the voice on the Public Address System blares the announcement, "Now pitching for Brooklyn, number 86, Stern."

The ballpark erupts into pandemonium. Hilda Chester who has made the trip with the Dodgers up to the Bronx sits in the first row of the box seats between third and home and joyfully rattles her cow bell. Its ringing, however, is lost in the noise of the crowd.

As I reach the mound, Leo puts the ball in my hand and issues his orders, "Take your time, Gus. Go for the corners. Don't give in to him. For God's sake, don't walk him."

As I wing in a curve to complete my eight warm ups, my team mates are relaxed, composed and ready. To borrow Mark Twain's phrase seeing me on the mound has given them each the calm confidence of a Christian with four aces.

Up in the broadcasting booth the old redhead informs the listening faithful that once again our borough's happy band of brothers are sitting in the catbird's seat.

Beans hollers "Play ball!"

DiMaggio steps into the batter's box and carefully plants himself, legs far apart and assumes his intimidating stance.

The stadium quiets. The air becomes electric with tension.

To establish my position as dominant in this match up, I immediately deliver Joltin' Joe a brush back pitch just below his chin.

"Ball," shouts the Ump.

I then drop a fast curve on the outside corner.

With the tension building and the count now at one and one, Pee Wee calls time and comes to the mound to offer me a few words of encouragement. I realize this is a ploy. The excitement just has gotten to be too much for him. “Relax, Pee Wee,” I say, “the worst that can happen is that we’ll lose and have to wait again for next year. But I don’t think that’s in the cards. Even though the greatest player in the world is at bat, I think next year is now.”

A relieved Pee Wee smiles and returns to short.

Mickey Owen, my catcher, flashes me a sign for a change up. I shake him off. It’s time for me to challenge Joe with my Sunday pitch, the old high, hard one.

I wind up and let go.

Crack!

Oh God, no.

I hear the awesome, terrible sound of DiMaggio's swinging bat connecting head first with my heater. The ball as a blur rockets past me, well to my right. It’s headed high up and way out--a sure homer into the third tier.

I plead to the Heavens, “Push it foul, please.”

God comes through. Joe’s “grand slammer” curves and misses being fair by about a foot.

Sweat oozes from my every pore. I’ve been reminded just who it is I’m pitching to.

Mickey Owen calls time. He comes to the mound and chews me out for shaking him off. I tell him to shut his f------ mouth and get his fat ass back behind the plate.

“Good,” says Mickey, “I just needed to be certain that Joe’s shot hasn’t intimidated you.”

“Of course, it intimidated me. Only an imbecile wouldn’t be intimidated by it. He’s never gonna see that pitch from me again.”

Mickey laughs and goes back to his position.

Once again, the Clipper sets himself in the batter’s box and once again I remind him of who’s boss by decking him with my duster. Two and two.

The Yankee fans are booing me. They're shouting "Headhunter" and screaming at Beans to throw me out of the game for engaging in dirty baseball.

I don't blame them. But what the hell else should they expect. This after all is baseball and not some sissy's game like football where you're penalized for playing rough. So casting a cold eye at McCarthy's dugout and sneering at DiMaggio, I reset myself for Mickey's sign.

Do I dare to aim a spot pitch at the black and risk a call of ball three? Certainly not. A full count would put everyone off and running. I'd be inviting a loss on an infield hit. I have to come in with a curve.

I shake off Mickey's call for a fast ball. Then he signals for a knuckler.

Brilliant! But what a risky pitch. Although Joe would never expect my knuckler, there's a terrible chance Mickey would either bobble the delivery or miss catching it entirely. It would be hell to throw strike three and lose the game. Nonetheless, it's a gamble we have to take.

I pump once. Then I pump again and let go. The Clipper lunges into his swing. Too late he realizes that I've floated him a knuckler. He tries to adjust his swing but the ball sails by and drops anchor in Mickey's mitt.

Victory. The Dodgers, at last, are the World Champions.

My team mates and some eager but unruly fans rush to the mound and begin to hug me and to pound my back. I'm carried into the clubhouse on the shoulders of my two favorites, Pete Reiser and Dolph Camilli. As the players pop champagne and celebrate, I slip quietly into my street clothes and leave. Outside by the bullpen gate my secret love, Shirley Temple, meets me and says, "Gus, you were wonderful. I love you." I sweep her up onto the cross bar of my bike and we ride off. New deeds of glory await me.

In the distance church bells have begun to toll. They've dropped a curtain on my daydream.

I've been warned that one more lateness at Sunday School will mean my chance of earning a church attendance medal has vanished. I race there to avoid this.

In Sunday School the lesson this morning is that here in America there are people known as atheists. They claim God is a myth. Our teacher, Mrs. Weierstrass, explains that a myth is a story which most people accept as real even though they know it isn't. She tells us of the little Dutch boy who puts his finger into the dike and saves Holland. That's a myth. So too is the fable of George Washington chopping down the cherry tree and then ratting on himself because he cannot tell a lie.

I'm pleased to hear that the cherry tree story is a myth. Ever since I first heard that tale, I've worried that as a boy the Father of our Country was a fool. If I had been in his place, I'd have blamed the deed on Matthew.

Mrs. Weierstrass rambles on saying most atheists are decent but misguided people. They believe in the golden rule. Like the Christians, they want to do good works. They also desire not to do evil. Because they reject God, however, they're handicapped.

I wonder about them. They sound like Giant fans: good guys but dumb.

Mrs. Weierstrass goes on boring us with more stuff about the atheists. She asks everyone in the class to pray for the conversion of these unfortunate people. We do this. According to her our prayers are like letters to God. He treasures them. He wants us to pray and to ask Him to do us favors. Answering prayers is His business. He's good at this but sometimes when he answers prayers, He doesn't reply in the manner people expect or desire.

"Does God answer the prayers of atheists?" asks one of the girls.

"God answers everyone's prayers," replies Mrs. Weierstrass, "but He can't answer the prayers of atheists because atheists don't pray."

It seems to me that atheists are dumb. If God is willing to give everyone things just for praying, a fellow has to be pretty stupid to pass up that deal.

I don't much care about atheists. I've never seen one. Nor have I ever heard of one. I figure they live in someplace exotic like New Jersey. I'm interested, however, in this prayer business. I have heard my mother say the same things about prayers as Mrs. Weierstrass but I reasoned from my own experience that God didn't necessarily listen. Hearing the same thing now from another source leads me to think that, perhaps, I've been wrong. My mother always has made me say my prayers out loud. If when doing so, I haven't been praying the way she wants, she doesn't hesitate to interrupt and say, "Cancel that God and please forgive this wicked, sinful boy for his disrespect." Then she's warned me to mind my p's and q's or she'd beat the hell out of me. So I've continued to pray as ordered.

Naturally, I've hated praying. I haven't been too fond of God either. When Jesus said, "Suffer the little children to come unto me," He told the truth in spades. While Sunday School hasn't been as unwelcome as a whipping, it's remained a pretty close approximation. That hasn't been just my opinion. I could have backed it up with the testimony of every kid in Brooklyn except the sissies.

Anyway, as I've implied, praying was more punishment than pleasure. Even in Mother's absence when I was able to slip in a request for electric trains or for an erector set, God never heard me or He refused to pay attention. When it came to answering prayers, God was always reliable at getting a fellow underwear and socks. When, however, He was asked for toys, He never failed to be tight-assed. So knowing He was Jewish, I wrote him off as a haberdasher.

At the end of the Sunday School lesson, Mrs. Weierstrass asks if anyone has a question about the day's lesson. I put up my hand.

"Yes, Gregory, what is it?"

"Suppose I were to pray to God for something important and good, something which would help me to do great deeds. Would God hear my prayer and help me?"

"Of course, He would. That's exactly the kind of prayer that pleases

Him the most." Then she begins explaining her "of course." Sometimes these explanations last longer than our minister's sermons and always they're just as dull. Big people are always telling her they admire and respect her for teaching children to come to God. I wonder whether they'd think the same if they had to sit in our seats.

As she rambles on, I dream of the two wheeler in the window of the store on St. John's place. If that isn't something important and good, then nothing is. I want it badly. I can't wait to let God know this. So right then and there in the middle of her explanation of what her "of course" means, I start praying to Him just as I always have--aloud.

"Gregory," she interrupts, "If you must pray now, please do so in silence. God will hear you for He hears your words as clearly as you do when you think them."

That's good news. I keep my hands folded and continue in silence to pray.

Every day for weeks, I say silent prayers. When no one is around I play it safe and say them aloud too. I pray very hard, so hard my knuckles turn red and then white. I know something as expensive as a bike requires plenty of praying and lots of time. God is no fool. He's a Jew and like the rest of His tribe, He gives away nothing for nothing.

For two months, before and after church, I check the window of the Second Hand Store. Always the bike remains in place. No one has bought it. Clearly God has put the machine into a spiritual lay away plan for me. He has heard my prayers. However, in answering them, He's taking His time. Since the bike is valuable that's understandable. Not until He has extracted His money's worth from me in prayers, can He be expected to part with something as wonderful as my two wheeler.

Then one Sunday as I go by the store I don't see the bike in the window. I'm terribly upset. It couldn't have been sold. God wouldn't have permitted that. I figure the shopkeeper has moved it to the back of the store. He probably wants to put on display in its place some faster moving item. I try to enter the store. Its front door is locked. I knock hard on the door's glass pane. After a while a lady in a house coat appears at the door. She hollers at me, "Clost, go hah vay."

"The bike, The blue and white bike," I call.

"Go hah vay," she shouts

"The bike," I persist and point to the empty window.

"Solt. Go hah vay. Ve get da Police. No more the bike, solt."

Grief sweeps over me like a tidal wave and washes me in misery. As I walk away, my eyes flood with tears. My dreams, my great deeds--gone. Sold.

Bitterness, hurt and anger enough to fill the universe now add themselves to my grief and misery. I look to the Heavens and call out to God, "I ain't never praying to you again." Then to let Him know I mean business, I show Him my fist.

That gives me some comfort but not enough. I want to hurt His feelings as He has hurt mine. I shout, "I ain't gonna believe in you no more. You four flusher. Do you hear me? I ain't gonna believe in you no more. I'll show You, You double crossing double dealer. You're supposed to be a good guy. Well, you ain't. You're an atheist. You hear? You're an atheist."

I know that atheist shot lands on target and shakes the s---- out of Him. I must admit too, I'm more than just a little scared as I tell Him off. But I've no choice. I have to let Him know He isn't messing with just any kid off the block. He's taken on Gregory Ulysses Stern the Third, a four square, upright boy who will not kowtow to His two faced, two timing shenanigans.

I guess God knows He deserves the scolding. He could strike me dead with a bolt of lightning but He doesn't. Instead, He shapes up and takes His dressing down like a man. I respect Him for that.

Chapter 11
The Revenger

One afternoon after Easter, my mother sends me out to buy three loaves of bread from the outlet store of the bakery on Pacific Street. On my way there, I happen to see two older colored kids beating the dickens out of my classmate and friend, Seymour Lipschitz. They're robbing him of fifteen cents, stealing the jacket off his back and punching him until blood not only runs out of his nose but also leaks out of his ears. When he falls they kick him and spit on him. Finally one of them speaking with either an impediment or a funny Scottish accent calls him a f---ing Jew and warns him not to tell anyone who it is who has robbed and beaten him.

When I see this going on, I make no effort to rush to Seymour's aid. Instead I duck into the vestibule of the nearest two family brownstone and hide behind a gauzy curtain which covers the glass pane on the front door. I'm able to watch and hear most of what's happening. One of the bullies I recognize. He's the older brother of our classmate, Roosevelt Pearson. The other and more violent one is a stranger.

After the negroes have run off and are out of sight, I go to Seymour's aid. He's lying on the ground, crying and hurting. I help him to his feet. With his arm across my shoulders and my arm about his waist, I begin walking him home.

"Why?" he asks, "Why were they beating me? I gave them my money. Why did they do it? Gus, I don't even know them. Why were they beating me?"

Sobs and sniffles have been punctuating his questions. I give him my handkerchief. That's a mistake. He blows his nose and sends blotches of blood into it."

"We'll soon be at your house," I comment in an effort to change the subject.

"Why me?" he asks.

"Who knows why?" I answer. "Maybe to the coloreds, all white guys look alike. Maybe they mistook you for somebody else."

"Yeah, James Cagney," he wisecracks.

We laugh. Then I say, "Your sense of humor is still intact."

"So's my sense of pain."

I can't keep myself from giggling at his joking.

"Gus, you know what's the worst thing about this?"

"Tell me."

"It's peeing in my pants. When they kicked me I lost control. I couldn't help it. I'm nine years old but with piss in my pants, I feel like I'm two."

"Seymour," I say, "You look like you walked into a spinning aeroplane propeller. With all this blood, who's going to notice your crotch?"

"I'll notice it," he replies.

We hobble along in silence. When we reach his house he takes his arm from my shoulder and asks, "How do I look?"

"Like a sight with sore eyes," I kid.

"I hate to worry my mother. This will upset her. Oh well, I'll just have to make her understand that I'm okay."

"She won't buy that," I assure him.

"Thanks for helping me," he says.

"I just wish I could have done something to have stopped them," I reply.

"So do I," he agrees. Then he smiles and adds, "If my bowels had been as weak as my bladder, they literally would have kicked the s--- out of me."

I laugh.

He tries to return my handkerchief. I tell him to keep it. We say goodbye. He goes into his house. I leave to get the bread that I have been sent out for.

At school the next day Seymour is absent. Because I arrive only a minute or so before the first bell, I don't get a chance to tell anyone about the beating. It doesn't matter. Everyone already knows. Half the class even claims to have been eye witnesses. None, however, can identify the attackers.

After lunch our teacher, Miss Hurwitz, tells us Seymour has been hospitalized. If he does not develop complications, she expects him to be back with us in a week. She urges us to bring her any information we might receive about Seymour's assailants. Then she has us use the rest of the afternoon to write letters to Seymour telling him to get well.

I glance over at Roosevelt. I wonder whether he knows about yesterday. I don't think he does. He's a nice guy. It isn't his fault his brother is a bully and a thief.

Some of my classmates are composing two page letters. I marvel at this. All I can think of to write is "get well."

As I sit there groping for words the image of my battered classmate stays before me. I don't want to write him a trifling letter. I want to send him the severed heads of the bullies.

I decide to help Seymour get even. I get out a separate sheet of paper and on it I print the following:

Dear Roosevelt,

Tell your brother he has only 24 hours left to confess to beating up Seymour. If he doesn't turn himself in, I shall go to the Police. Then he will go to Reform School.

Your friend,
The Revenger

I raise my hand and get permission to sharpen my pencil. On the way back to my seat I pass the open wardrobe. With brilliant nonchalance I slip The Revenger's note into a pocket of Roosevelt's jacket.

I feel very pleased with myself. Thinking up a pen name has been a stroke of genius. I begin daydreaming about the torment and the anguish which the note will bring to Roosevelt's brother. When he realizes that The Revenger has his number, he'll sweat with fear. He'll know he's doomed.

I want to write to Seymour to tell him what I'm doing. I feel a need for an audience and for admiration and applause. I'm performing the part of The Revenger with brilliance. But because I know Miss Hurwitz will be collecting and perhaps, also reading our letters, I have to omit mentioning to him anything about my exploits. I can't chance her finding out about Roosevelt's brother from me. I'd never break the code and be a squealer.

I begin to fantasize a role and a uniform for myself as the Revenger. Like Superman I'll have a cape but with a red, white and blue costume. I'll also ride a fleet-footed horse and swing a pearl-handled sword. With it I'll lop off the heads of bad guys.

In delightful reverie I concoct up dozens of names for both my horse and my sword. I envision a daily fifteen minute radio serial about me and my exploits. It will start with a heroic bugle call and a deep throated announcer saying, "It's time for more of the story of the guardian of good against evil and the protector of widows and their helpless children. It's time for The Revenger, that bravest of heroes who with his trusty steed, Invincible, and his terrible swift-sword, Retribution, sallies forth daily in a never ending search for daring deeds. To defeat wickedness and injustice and to restore righteousness to its royal throne is his never ending mission. All hail The Revenger."

Three o'clock approaches. Miss Hurwitz collects our letters. Mine is the shortest.

The following morning as the classes are about set to enter school, Roosevelt's brother sneaks over to our line and demands to know, "Which of you idiots is The Revenger?"

No one answers.

"You hear. I said, 'Which one of you idiots is The Revenger.'"

My secret love, Cathy, must have thought correctly that he was some kind of nut. "Be quiet and leave," she says.

"Girl, shut up," he warns her. Then he pushes his way over to her and grabbing her by arm asks, "Are you The Revenger?

"Leave me alone, you nut," is her reply.

My admiration for her bravery is matched only by my adoration of her beauty. What a girl!

Suddenly the unbelievable happens. He punches her on her arm. Then he backs away and hurries to his own line which is moving to enter the building.

Cathy is crying. Our whole class feels sorry for her but none more than me.

I hadn't lifted a finger to protect her. I hadn't behaved like The Revenger. I had acted like a coward.

"Roosevelt, your brother stinks," says Alice. "I'm gonna tell your Mama what Jefferson has done."

Roosevelt shrugs his shoulders and offers no reply.

I think highly of Alice. She's colored but she has stuck up for justice against one of her own kind. I also feel Roosevelt is getting a raw deal. Everyone kind of blames him for being brother to a bully.

On Saturday afternoon when I can't wheedle eleven cents out of my mother to go to the movies, I walk up to St. Mary's Hospital to visit Seymour. The nun at the Reception Desk tells me he isn't a patient. She has no record of him.

I walk over to Seymour's house. There are no curtains in the windows. His flat appears to be vacant. I ring his bell. No one answers.

As I'm returning to the street a lady from next door asks in a thick

Yiddish accent what I've been doing. I answer that I've come by to visit my classmate. I tell her he has suffered a bad beating. She informs me that the Lipschitzes have moved away that morning. She also sets me straight on Seymour's hospitalization.

It has never occurred. Seymour's mother had taken him to the nearest Doctor's office where he was attended to. She and her husband were so distressed with what had happened, they willingly paid an extra month's rent to break their lease and leave.

I thank her for the news and leave.

I realize that what I have long heard from some of my classmates is true: little by little P.S. 83 is becoming a colored school.

A year ago almost all of my classmates were white.

Now almost half aren't. Jews and Protestants have been fleeing to allow their kids to attend better schools in nicer neighborhoods. Most of the Catholics are staying put. That isn't because they're democratic but because they're poor and can't afford to move. Most of these at P.S. 83 are Italians and Poles. Their families still have hopes of getting them into the Parochial school at St. Matthew's. But anyone with half of a brain knows that won't happen. St. Matthew's always caters to and cares for the Irish first. As they've always bred faster than fleas, a Mediterranean or East European Catholic has about as much chance of entering his local Catholic School as I have of becoming the Pope.

I feel bitter and angry with the turn of events. Evil has been triumphing. No one seems to care. Jefferson Pearson and his rotten friend are Nazis. Someone has to punish them. Someone has to stop them.

It's one thing to know something should be done. It's quite another to do it. I'm not dumb enough to try to make my fantasies as The Revenger come true. Heck, I couldn't even afford the price of hay and oats for the trusty steed, Invincible.

Although I know that The Revenger stuff is nonsense, Jefferson

Pearson doesn't. He's annoyed or troubled enough by it to punch an innocent girl. Maybe if I were to play my cards right, I could not only annoy and trouble him some more but also fill his life with fear and misery. I decide to give it a try.

On Monday, I try but am not able to sneak a Revenger note into Roosevelt's possession. The best I can do is write on the Boys' Bathroom wall F--- Jefferson Pearson.

I would have signed it, The Revenger, but I had to stop short as kids from other classes were coming in to do their Recess peeing.

That afternoon I tail Roosevelt and find out where he lives on Atlantic Avenue. When I get home I compose and print the following letter:

Everyday 1941
Dear Bully Jefferson,

You and your cowardly friend are going to pay for robbing and beating up Roosevelt's classmate. You are going to pay for punching a girl. But most of all you are going to pay for for something you didn't know I know. You have been watched. You are being watched. You shall be thoroughly and unmercifully punished. All in my good time..

Your friend,
The Revenger

Because I can't get my hands on three cents for a stamp until Mom and Ernie visit on Tuesday evening, I have to wait until Wednesday to mail it. When I do, I address the envelope to Jefferson Pearson but on the line immediately below his name I write Thief, Bully and Girl Beater.

At school on Thursday I can't concentrate on a thing. I know that in the morning drop the letter will arrive at Roosevelt's home. When his mother sees the envelope, he'll have a lot of explaining to do. He'd be in Dutch up to his chin.

At lunchtime I run home, eat in record time and get back to the school yard almost a half of an hour before the bell. Neither of the Pearson boys are there. Only a dozen or so kids are on hand. One is my classmate, Alice Carmichael. I stroll over and tell her how impressed I was with her and that even if she hadn't ratted on Jefferson for punching Cathy, she had shown guts to threaten it.

"Shucks," she says, "that wasn't nothing. I ain't afraid of that no account Jefferson. And I ain't afraid of that Samuel Borel bum that he hangs around with. Neither of them would dare mess with me. My daddy'd kill them."

"Is your daddy a cop?"

"Of course not."

"A prize fighter?"

"My daddy's a preacher. My daddy's a great man. He's the Reverend Calvin Wesley Carmichael, Minister of the African Methodist Episcopal Church and Spiritual Father of the neighborhhod."

"Wow!"

Alice is obviously delighted with the impression she's making. She asks me if my dad is a great man. I answer that I think so but I'm not sure. I tell her he's an usher and Sunday school teacher at church.

"My daddy bosses people like your daddy around."

"I know," I answer.

"What church do you go to?"

"St. Charles' Episcopal. It's not around here. It's pretty far away."

"We're the same religion," she says and adds, "I'm Episcopal too."

"Wow!"

"It's a small world, isn't it?"

"Sure is," I agree.

A couple of her girlfriends come over and ask her to jump rope with them. She can hardly refuse as she's the best jumper below the seventh grade in school. No one, not even the older girls can match her at Double Dutch.

I look at the school yard. It's filling up. I look around for the Pearsons. They haven't arrived.

Soon the bell rings. We gather on line. The second bell rings. We go upstairs.

Roosevelt and his rotten brother must be playing hookey. I feel cheated. I wonder why at least one of the many truant officers on the city's payroll isn't earning his pay by hauling the Pearsons in handcuffs back into their classrooms.

When the Pearsons cut school on Friday, it's clear to me that they've done so to avoid a run in with the Revenger. Only an idiot would believe they're home sick in bed. Most likely they're with Samuel Borel robbing someone helpless and beating up on the weak.

In the school yard that afternoon in another talk with Alice and her girlfriend, Julia, I learn quite a bit about Samuel Borel. Julia tells me he's mean but bright. He's come to the U.S.A. from Jamaica but before that he spent most of his days in Trinidad.

I interrupt to set her straight. "Jamaica is in Queens. Anyone who comes from there doesn't immigrate. He's already a citizen."

"Silly," replies Julia, "everyone knows there's a Jamaica in Queens. But there's a whole country, Jamaica, in the West Indies. That's the one Samuel's from."

"Oh, I didn't know," I admit with obvious embarrassment.

"If you ever hear his Calypso accent, you'll not make that mistake again," says Alice.

"Kablixo accident? What's that?" I ask.

"Kablixo accident!" she repeats in a tone of disbelief.

Then both girls start laughing. I smile helplessly and would laugh too but they're making such a big deal out of my ignorance, I can't.

"What's so funny?" I ask defensively, "Isn't that what you said?"

"No mahn, that not what she said," says Julia, speaking in a strange rhythmical way which sounds like she's doing a bad imitation of Harry Lauder. She continues, "She said Calypso accent. A Calypso accent, mahn, is speaking English like I'm doing now."

"People really talk that way?" I ask in disbelief.

"Samuel does and so does everyone else in his family," replies Alice in a normal voice.

I'm not certain that Calypso is the same as the British accent that I had heard from the fellow who had beaten Seymour and called him a f---ing Jew. I suspect, however, that it is.

With gentle prodding, I learn from the girls that Samuel lives above Feynman's Pharmacy on Fulton Street. They reveal further that Samuel is a political nut but not the usual Republican or Democratic kind. He's of the Black Supremacist kind.

I nod knowingly figuring Black Supremacists are followers of Mussolini and wear black shirts like the fascists in Italy. However, as the girls ramble on, I see I'm wrong. Samuel is a follower of Marcus Garvey, a Jamaican colored man who was kicked out of America for saying negroes are better than white people.

Hearing that throws me.

I've always believed that the only people who could be thrown out of America are either spies or crooks like Al Capone. I tell the girls this. They say I'm right but only partly so.

Marcus Garvey has been tried and convicted as a crook. But everyone knows that the evidence against him was manufactured. Garvey has been framed and has been given the boot unjustly.

I can't argue against this. I know nothing about such stuff.

But I feel I have to defend America so I say, "When the G-men couldn't get Capone for being a gangster, they got him for not paying his income taxes. Maybe in sort of the same way, they did this to Garvey. After all, he was crazy."

"How so?" asks Julia as Alice nods in agreement with her.

"Well, when he said coloreds were better than whites, he proved it. After all, no one in his right mind could possibly believe that."

"I believe it." says Alice.

"So do I," agrees Julia. Then she adds, "And so too does every negro I know."

I'm not dumb. I see that this is a touchy subject. I've waded into something that is way over my head and the wisest thing I can now do is not to tread water but to beat a swift retreat. The girls are giving me an education. However, it isn't about stuff that would ever appear in textbooks. I'm discovering that to the coloreds, America is a different nation from the one I know. They see this country as a land run by whites for nobody's benefit who isn't white.

I tell the girls that since Joe Louis is the world's champion, they and Marcus Garvey could be right. But I'm just being tactful. In all creation the only instance I can think of where something dark can top something white is on a sundae of hot chocolate poured over vanilla ice cream.

On Saturday I decide it's time to put the fear of God into Samuel Borel. I'll mail him a Revenger letter. But there's a problem. He'll never get it until I get three cents for a postage stamp.

I compose the letter anyway. It reads much like the one I had sent to Jefferson. I put it in an envelope. Then I go to Ben's Candy Store to look up the address of Feynman's Pharmacy in the telephone directory. That is no mean feat. I try to find it first under Fineman. When that fails I try Feinman and Fienman. Then I get a flash of brilliance and look it up under P as Phineman, Phienman and Pheinman.

Ben comes over and tells me to stop horsing around with his telephone book. I say I'm not horsing around. I tell him I've been sent to look up the address of Feynman's Pharmacy on Fulton Street. He takes the book from me and immediately finds the listing. When he shows it to me, I don't want to believe it.

"That's Fainman," I reply with phonetical accuracy.

"That's Feynman as in Feynman's Pharmacy on Fulton Street. Now take down the address and leave me in peace."

I thank him and do as told.

I think briefly of delivering my latest Revenger letter to the Borel mailbox myself. Then I remember that on Fulton Street almost everyone is colored. On it I'd stand out like a dark barn in a field of snow. I'd be an irresistible target for any gang of colored hoodlums looking to maul a white guy.

I bring the letter home, stick it in a schoolbook and go back outside to play.

At school, Monday begins as an uneventful day. The Pearsons again are absent. That annoys me. Yet it makes it easy for me to slip my Revenger letter to Samuel Borel into Roosevelt's desk. In fact, I manage to do that right off as we enter the classroom to take our seats.

After our arithmetic lesson the Principal shows up at the classroom door. He motions to Miss Hurwitz to join him out in the hall. She complies. For a minute or so, we sit whispering and wondering what's up.

Miss Hurwitz returns. She has Roosevelt with her. He goes to his seat and opens his desk to put his books away. He sees the Revenger note. He doesn't look happy.

Miss Hurwitz begins talking, telling us how disheartening it has been for us all to lose a fine student like Seymour and to discover to our great sadness that he had been robbed and beaten brutally. It's been a shame that his family had felt compelled to move. Fortunately, however, the culprit has been caught and is being punished. Finally to bring this matter to a close she wants whoever the anonymous Revenger is to stop sneaking harassment notes into Roosevelt's pocket and desk.

Then Roosevelt pipes up, "I think this is another."

"Bring it up here," she instructs.

He does.

Without opening the letter and reading it, she tears it into several pieces and tosses them into the waste basket saying, "As I said, there'll be no more of this. Roosevelt was not the guilty party. He should not be harassed.

"However, there's one thing more. Whoever it is who has been harassing Roosevelt and signing himself as The Revenger, he should cease doing so immediately. His ignorance is on display. I doubt that any such word as Revenger exists. The word he should have used is Avenger, A-V-E-N-G-E-R. I consider it to be disgraceful and a terrible reflection on my teaching, when any pupil of mine employs such feeble English."

I want to leap to my feet and shout, "Screw you, you i-dotting, t-crossing, important document shredding snob. Avenger or Revenger, what in hell is the damned difference? Without my prodding, Jefferson Pearson would never have been nailed. Furthermore, the matter isn't about to end. There's another culprit to catch. And the Revenger won't rest until he's punished."

Of course, I restrain myself and say none of this. As the adage says "Discretion is the better part of valor." I know that protesting will accomplish nothing except to infuriate her. Worse still, it would reveal my identity to potential squealers.

There is no point in antagonizing her and in putting myself in jeopardy of being failed in 4B. Nor does it make sense to call attention to myself and have my head bashed in by Samuel Borel, Jefferson Pearson or any of their thugish confederates.

At lunch time, however, I rewrite the letter to Samuel Borel and at one o'clock when it comes time to hang my sweater in the wardrobe, I stick the copy in a pocket of Roosevelt's jacket.

That afternoon Miss Hurwitz tells us about the battle going on in Crete. I already know about it and about Max Schmeling, the former boxing champion, who was one of the paratroopers for the German invaders. She tells us it will be another dark day in Europe if the English lose again. Then she teaches us two World War songs which soldiers used to sing in France: Pack up your Troubles in your Old Kit Bag and It's a Long Way to Tipperary. Neither sounds much like a war song to me. I'd rather have had us sing Ninety Nine Bottles of Beer on the Wall.

At the close of the school day, when Roosevelt gets his jacket and comes back to his seat, he pulls the Revenger's letter out from his pocket and starts crying. Miss Hurwitz wants to know what's wrong. He hands her the envelope. She opens it and reads the note. Then she waves it in front of us and demands a confession from the pupil who has written it.

After a long silence she announces that no one is going home until she finds out who the Revenger is. Everyone groans. Then Rachel Volterra raises her hand and says that as she has to be at her dentist's office at three thirty, she can't stay.

Miss Hurwitz agrees and excuses her.

The bell rings. We can hear the other classes filing past our door as they made their way out of the building. A couple of the girls begin to cry. Miss Hurwitz repeats her demand. I keep silent.

Hatred, fear, tension and anguish fill the room. Five long, silent minutes go by. Then Anthony Saccheri raises his hand and confesses that he's the Revenger. Miss Hurwitz tells him and us that she's very mad at him. He should not have been writing threatening letters even though it's clear he believed they were penned for a good cause. He also should not have detained the class by taking so long to confess. However, since he has done the honorable thing, she's decided to be generous and forgo giving him or us further punishment.

In two minutes we're out of the building. Everyone is crowding around Anthony. He's being treated as a hero.

I can't figure him out. Why has he confessed to something he hasn't done? I decide he's not too bright. I'm also envious of him. He's getting all of the glory which rightfully is mine. Nevertheless, I have to admit he has behaved bravely. I have to admire him for that.

By the start of the next week, I know that my episode as the Revenger has ended.

On Saturday, Samuel Borel and Jefferson Pearson had gone looking for Anthony. Unhappily for them, they found him. They tried to beat him up on his own block. Each got in about one blow. Then half of the neighborhood must have come to Anthony's rescue. They taught the bullies a lesson. They taught them that it made more sense to try to attack a gorilla in his cage than to attempt to maul an Italian on a block populated with Pisanos.

Whether the coloreds learned their lesson, I cannot say.

I only lived in that neighborhhod until the year's end. During that time although P.S. 83 got more and more coloreds and kept fewer and fewer whites, I never heard of another racial incident of violence.

One last note for Miss Hurwitz: revenger is in the dictionary. It's a perfectly good word. Look it up, if you don't believe me.

Chapter 12

Religious Instruction

A few weeks after I enter the fifth grade an errand boy from the Principal's office comes to our classroom. He gives a bunch of forms along with a note to our teacher, Mrs. Scott. She looks over the stuff. Then she reads aloud from the note:

Any child desiring to participate in the program of released time on Wednesdays for religious instruction must return as soon as possible a copy of the accompanying form filled out and signed by a parent or guardian and by an official of the sponsoring church or synagogue.

She asks if anyone wants a form. The Catholics raise their hands. So too does Herbie Lipschitz. As Mrs. Scott begins handing out the forms she looks at Herbie and says, "Herbert, you weren't in class last week on Rosh Hashannah. You brought a note from your mother. She asked that your absence be excused on religious grounds. You're Jewish, aren't you?"

"Of course."

"Then why do you have your hand in the air?"

"I figure if the Catholics can get away with cutting school for an hour, I ought to give it a try."

"The Catholic children aren't cutting school. Nor are they getting away with anything. During the released time they go to their church. There they're given religious instruction for an hour."

"An hour, my eye. At St. Matthew's all the priests ever do is tell the kids to say three Our Fathers and ten Hail Marys. Then they send them home to play."

As Herbie speaks, a look of surprise flashes across Mrs. Scott's face. Quickly it gives way to aggravation and anger. For a full five seconds after he has stopped talking she gives him an evil stare. Then she says, "What a priest deems proper as religious instruction for his congregation is his business and his parishioners'. It certainly isn't yours. Nor is it mine. If each of us would confine his religious considerations to the concerns of his own faith and would leave those of others to others, we'd all be better off."

"Yes, but," he starts to reply.

With a glare as menacing as my Mother's and with a voice to match, she cuts him off saying, "Herbert Lifschitz, that's it. Not another word from you. Not a peep."

She orders the class to return to doing word problems in arithmetic. Even though none of us can do them, we're happy to oblige.

After lunch when I come back to school, the punch ball game is underway. It's too late for me to get into it. I see Herbie hanging around. I walk over to him. "Hey, Herbie," I say, "I didn't think Mrs. Scott was being fair to you. It wasn't her place to ask you why you wanted a religious instruction form."

"Maybe not, but what does it matter? I was just being a smart aleck."

"Yeah, I guess you were."

"My folks would never sign that form. Rather than let me get out of school for an hour, they'd choose to die. My mother thinks I'm not in school enough. If we had to go to class an extra couple of hours everyday, she'd still complain that the school day was too short."

"Still," I say, "It should be your right to take religious instruction, if that's what you want."

"Listen Gus, I know you mean well but you're so far off track, you're in Africa. I already get religious instruction. In fact, I get too much of it. Three afternoons a week from four to five-thirty I'm in Hebrew School. There I'm fed all the religion anyone can take. Sometimes I'd like to rid myself of it. Sometimes I'd like to shove the Torah up the Creator's ass and the Talmud, up Hitler's. Sometimes I wish I was free to play ball everyday like everybody else."

Even though I'm unsure of what the towel mud is, I think Herbie's destination for it is clever and funny. But I can't laugh. His crack about sticking Theodora up God's ass has terrified me. Whoever Theodora is, it's clear, she doesn't belong up there.

I've never thought of God as someone having an asshole. Yet if people are made in His image, He must always have had one. To suggest that anything other than a thermometer or a tube for an enema should be shoved into it is both disrespectful and insolent. Herbie is begging for punishment. I expect the Angel of Death to appear right away to give it to him. I figure He'll frazzle and fry Herbie down to a disappearing pile of ashes. Either that or he'll turn him into a pillar of salt.

Because I've been standing next to Herbie, I'm anxious about my own safety. There's no telling how mad my classmate's irreverence has made the Almighty. It could be sending Him into a blind rage. God could be getting so worked up that in giving orders to the Angel to murder Herbie, He could foul up the directions and get me killed too.

Pretty soon, however, it dawns on me that nothing terrible is happening. For that, I give God a thought of thanks. But I remain uneasy. Clearly, Herbie is neither a safe nor a sane person to be around. Although he's the smartest kid in class and maybe the brightest fifth grader in all of Brooklyn, he's still a blockhead.

I decide to say to him a polite "so long, Lifschitz," and seek other company.

Without giving me a chance to do this, Herbie jaws on, "Being religious is insane, especially if you're a Jew. If Moses had but half of the brains he's credited with, instead of crossing the Red Sea, he'd have sailed it. With luck the winds would have blown him and his followers off course. All of the twelve tribes could have crossed the Indian Ocean. They could have bypassed Australia and gone on to the South Seas. Then instead of wandering around in the wilderness of Sinai for forty years with nothing to eat but manna, they could have floated around Polynesia living on pineapples, mangoes, coconuts and bananas."

I break in and say, "Good point, Herbie." I'm about to add, "I've got to run; see ya." Before I can, however, he again beats me to the punch as he rambles on saying, "Instead of capturing Jericho they could have taken Tahiti or Hawaii. But they didn't.

"Why not? Why not I ask you?"

Without giving me a chance to answer "Beats me," or "Who cares?" he announces the answer. He says, "It was because in Egypt the children of Israel were given a Moses instead of a Noah. So instead of Jews becoming citizens and rulers over island paradises, they became unwanted, hated and hunted down nobodies. Even here in America where every religion is tolerated, Jews are tolerated the least. You'd think we were niggers."

Now there's no doubt that he's nuts. We're surrounded by coloreds. Throughout the school yard they're everywhere. Fortunately, the only person paying attention to Herbie is me. Otherwise he might have been beaten to death.

He stops to catch his breath. Or maybe he's only pausing to admire his thought. Whatever the reason, I welcome the result. Opportunity isn't going to get by me again. I say to the fruitcake, "I've got to go. See ya." As I speak, however, the school bell rings and drowns out my words. When it stops, we have to be silent and to go get on line. As we head for our places Herbie says under his breath, "Nice talking to you, Gus."

I whisper back, "Nice talking to you, Herbie," but I don't mean it. I'm only being polite.

What Herbie has said about God, Moses and Noah annoyed and disturbs me. He sure doesn't talk like a normal kid. I put his words out of my thoughts. Nonetheless, they sneak back in. Over the next few days this continues. Against my will something within me is prodding and forcing me, as it must have prodded and forced Herbie, to question whether God knows how to do his job.

After school as I walk home, I begin thinking too about Herbie's description of religious instruction: ten Hail Marys and three Our Fathers. In under a dozen minutes anyone, even a stammering idiot, could spit out those prayers. Small wonder then that on Wednesdays when the public schools are just letting out, the Catholics are on the street playing.

Every year our teachers have told us that religious instruction lasts for an hour. Every year I've swallowed this baloney as gospel. It never has dawned on me that they're talking through their hats. After all they're responsible grownups. As the people who know everything, their words have been falling on my ears like a minister's and have been leaving me blind to the truth. Now at last, thanks to Lifschitz, my eyes are opened. I can see religious instruction for what it is--a sham.

Oddly enough it seems, the teachers don't know or don't want to know that religious instruction is a sham. Why they don't is a mystery for this isn't something being guarded as a secret. Every Catholic knows it. Herbie Lifschitz knows it. And any Protestant not as dumb as me knows it All that is needed to know it is to ask how can it be that on Wednesdays at three o'clock, the Catholics could all be in the fourth or fifth inning of a stickball game.

As released time for religious instruction is a sham, its lasting year after year doesn't make sense. Why would any religion want its own children to be given in the public school one hour less of lessons each week than kids of other denominations? The answer can't involve money. The church isn't footing the education bill. The city is.

If released time for religious instruction is, as Catholic haters might think, a plan devised by the Pope to keep Catholics dumb so they'll remain Catholic, he's going to a lot of trouble for nothing. They're already hopeless. Every marking period when report cards are handed out, anyone with half a brain can see that but for some individual exceptions, Jews are smarter than Protestants who are smarter than Catholics. The only ones dumber are the coloreds. Furthermore, released time can't do a thing to make Catholics dumber than the rest of us because on Wednesdays after they leave class, we're never taught anything anyway. I suppose this is because the teachers realize that if they bring up anything new, the next morning they'll just have to repeat it. So during the released time to spare themselves a lot of useless work and to keep us quiet and entertained, the teachers read to us stories from mythology or fables from the brothers Grimm.

The Catholics aren't alone in signing up for released time. Here and there a Protestant does it too. My church, St Charles', runs a Wednesday afternoon program of religious instruction. I've long known about it. But because my church is situated more than a mile away from both my school and my home, I've paid it no mind. Any thought of trekking to church to be bored with some middle of the week Bible study has had less chance of entering into my head than an ice pick.

As I wise up to religious instruction and realize it isn't Bible study, I begin to question whether it might not be such a bad idea for me to get into it. I do some calculating: it would take me about twenty-five minutes to walk from school to the church and around twenty more to get from there to my home. Next I reason that since Episcopalians don't do Hail Marys but do say the longer Lord's prayers, we might get off with just saying ten of these. Probably, however, we'd be forced to do them in unison. That would kill ten minutes. I also figure I'd better write off another quarter of an hour for the time we'd spend milling around while waiting for everyone from the different schools to arrive and for things to get started. In sum, religious instruction would involve about seventy minutes. It figures to put me back home around five minutes later than usual. Viewed this way, released time is clearly what Jimmy Durante would call, "a losing proposition." I'm better off without it. So I decide to go on doing without it.

That evening, or maybe it's the next evening, as my Dad sits by the radio listening to classical music, my mother, Matthew and I are in the dining room playing a board game. It's called Bo Carter. To win in it, your man has to get around a map of the world before any of your opponents' do. On one of Mother's turns as she's moving her piece part way across the Pacific, I look at the board map to see if it shows Polandeastia. It doesn't.

"Can you show me where Polandeastia is?" I ask her.

"Poland is next to Germany, here," she says pointing to it on the board.

"Gee whiz, I know where Poland is. What I don't know is where is Polandeastia?"

"Polandeastia?" she questions. Then she adds, "I never heard of Polandeastia. Are you sure there is such a place?"

"I think so. I think it's somewhere in the Pacific Ocean. I think it's kind of like Australia which isn't Austria here in Europe, but is this upside down America looking place just below the Philippines."

"Greg," she calls to my Dad, "Do you know of a place, perhaps in the Pacific, called Polandeastia?"

"It's not Polandeastia. It's Polynesia," he corrects as he comes into the room smiling. He then says, "It's a geographic term. It refers to several island chains mostly in the South Pacific. However, it does include the Hawaiian Islands."

"Is Tahiti part of it?" I asked.

"That's right," he replies. He goes to the secretary and takes from its first shelf the volume of the encyclopedia, Wonderland of Knowledge, containing the P's. "Are you studying about Polynesia at school?" he asks.

"Naw, it's just something that Herbie Lifschitz mentioned. He said if Moses had his wits about him, he'd have led the Jews there instead of to Palestine."

My Dad grins and says, "He may have a point. Herbie sounds like a very bright boy."

"In some ways, he is. He gets all A's on his report cards. But mostly he's a horse's ass."

"Will you listen to him?" breaks in my mother. Then looking at the old man she nags, "See what happens when you don't watch your language. They pick up every wrong thing you say and repeat it."

Then turning to me, she scolds, "There'll be no more talk like that from you. I won't tolerate it."

"I'm sorry," I apologize.

I can see that this isn't enough. She still seethes. To lessen the tension, I add, "I won't say it again, I promise."

"See that you don't," she replies and with the same stern tone she continues, "and stop making promises to me that you'll never keep."

On the following Sunday as I walk my Dad to his early communion service, he says to me, "Remember the other night when you told me of the boy who thought Moses should have gone to Polynesia instead of to Palestine?"

"You mean Herbie Lifschitz?"

"Right. What got him onto that topic and what else did he say about it?"

I answer by describing the run-in that Herbie had with Mrs. Scott over released time for religious instruction. Then I add the stuff that he told me in the schoolyard about Moses and Noah. During my telling of the parts about shoving towel mud up Hitler's ass and Theodora up God's, my Dad interrupts to clear up some things. He informs me that the Torah is the first few books of the Bible and the Talmud is a sort of companion book to it. It's filled with stories which make you think about good and evil.

"What do you think about Herbie's ideas?" asks my Dad.

"They're troubling."

"Do you think Moses was wrong to cross the Red Sea instead of sailing it?"

"I don't know," I answer.

"When Moses and his people were making their escape from Egypt, Pharaoh and his army were charging after them. They barely had time to get across the Red Sea before the waters closed in and drowned the trailing Egyptians."

"You know your Bible," I say.

"So too do you. I also know you know some geography but do you know whether Egypt and the Sinai have forests?"

"All of Egypt is a desert except around the Nile. All of the Sinai is a desert. There are no forests in either place."

"Excellent. So whatever few trees the Egyptians had, they had to be growing only around the Nile."

"That makes sense." I agree.

"Were the trees valuable?" he asks.

"They weren't as valuable as gold."

"Were they valuable at all?" he persists.

"Well, if they grew fruit, you could make money from them. But other than that, I don't know. It's hot in Egypt. No one would have needed to cut them down to make fire wood."

"I agree," says Dad. "In fact since trees give shade and cool the ground beneath them, the Egyptians might have gotten very angry with anyone who cut a tree down. In fact, I would think there would have been a law against cutting down a tree needlessly. What do you think?"

"I'd guess there would have been a law against that," I answer.

"Are valuable things made out of trees?"

"Yeah, sure, you can make chairs and tables out of them. You can even make houses out of them."

"Like log cabins?" he asks.

"Well, yes. But I was thinking more about regular houses, like the ones in Flatlands."

"Then strictly speaking you meant houses built from the lumber and wood obtained from the trees."

"Right. That's what I meant."

"Were ships made of iron and steel during the time of Moses and the Pharaoh?" he asks.

"Heck no. You know they weren't. Not until the Monitor and the Merrimac fought in the Civil War was there an iron ship. In olden times there were only wooden ships."

"You're right. It's only in the last 100 years that some ships such as ocean going vessels have not been made of wood.

"Now, Gus, I'd like you to put yourself back in time as an Egyptian family man. It's a hot day, a very hot day. Because the sun is so scorching and the heat is so sweltering you and your family sit under a tree. It's a sad day, a very sad day. You've just come back from a funeral. It was for your oldest boy. He died mysteriously in a plague which killed every Egyptian's oldest boy but no first born son of any Hebrew.

"Now imagine some happy Hebrews coming upon you and your family while you're mourning. One of them says to you," and here Dad switches to a Jewish accent and adopts a set of mannerisms to match, "Becking your pardon. Ve must dis tree cut down. Ve need planks for a sheep to make dot vill sail the Red Sea and out from bondage take us."

As he talks, I laugh.

Then dropping the accent he asks, "Do you think if you were this Egyptian, you would say," and here he affects the speech and mannerisms of Ronald Colman, "'Hebrew slaves. Thank you for your courtesy. Please be my guests and cut down our beloved tree. And by the way, give Moses our thanks for the plague which killed our child.'"

"Of course not," I say while laughing.

"What would you say?"

I reply, "I'd say, get lost and don't come back."

"I think I'd say the same.

"Now put yourself in the position of Moses. Along with all the other Hebrews you're fleeing Egypt. Racing after you are Pharaoh and his army. If they catch you they'll either kill you or enslave you. You see them coming. Only a miracle can save you. Suddenly one occurs.

God parts the Red Sea and opens a path to safety. Do you say to God, 'No tanks, Gott, dot's a nice miracle but dot's not the right one. Giff us please annudda miracle vit sheeps to take us to Polynesia."

I'm laughing hard at his mimicking of Moses. When I calm down I say, "With the Egyptians about to overtake me, I wouldn't look a gift horse in the mouth. I'd take whatever miracle God offers and be grateful for it."

"Lastly," my Dad asks, "If you were a Hebrew escaping from Egypt who would you want to lead you: a nice, righteous man, like Noah, who is good at building an ark but can't build one now because there's no wood or would you want a born leader like Moses who has already more than matched wits with the Egyptian king and has convinced him to let the Hebrews go."

"I'd want Moses."

"So would I," says Dad. "We agree. When God needed a man to lead the Exodus, he picked Moses because He knew he was the right man for the job."

"He made the right decision, all right," I say and add, "and He didn't need advice from us nor help from Herbie to do it."

We're about half a block away from the church. The old man puts his hand on my shoulder and says, "Well put, Gus. I don't think Joseph ever could have been more pleased with his son, Jesus, than I am with you."

That Sunday our guests for dinner are Mom, Ernie and our minister, Dr. Wilson, who is given my dad's place at the head of the table when we go into the dining room to eat.

I'm a little afraid of Dr. Wilson. He's a scary figure. Always he dresses in black. At church when he speaks, he sometimes hollers like Hitler. Ernie describes his voice as ten storey-ian. That's an apt description since surely he could be heard over a skyscraper. When, however, he says the grace for us his voice is natural. As he finishes, Matthew--who comes to the table late because he has been made to go and re-wash his hands--says, "Dr. Wilson, you're sitting where my dad sits."

A smile as wide as the Brooklyn bridge breaks out on the minister's face.

"It's okay, Matthew, Dr. Wilson is our guest. We want him to sit at the head of the table," says Mother.

"How come other guests don't get to sit there too?" he asks.

I can see my brother is in his never ending questioning mood and probably will continue to hog the conversation. I know that will not sit well with Mother. So I break in and tell him, "The other guests are just company. Dr. Wilson is special. He's like President Roosevelt or Leo Durocher. He sits in Dad's seat 'cause he honors us when he comes to our house."

"If the two of you cannot be quiet, I can sit you at the kitchen table and let you finish your meal there," warns Mother.

Fortunately, none of the other grownups are upset with us. In fact, Dr. Wilson tells Mother that he thinks we're delightful, well-mannered boys and that he's pleased and proud of her for doing such a magnificent job in bringing us up. This embarrasses her. But anyone can tell, it also pleases her.

Throughout the dinner Matt and I keep pretty quiet. Until dessert, the only time I speak is when I take a piece of celery and have to ask for the salt to be passed. Matt may not have talked at all. Ernie and Dad every now and then tell a joke. This makes the conversation bearable since most of it is about boring, grownup stuff. When briefly they discuss the war, I listen with interest. Everyone is very worried that Russia will fall and that once again the British will be left alone to face the Germans.

As we drink our milk or coffee and eat our cake, Dr. Wilson tells us that he has gotten a kick out of the story my Dad has passed along to him about Herbie and me and the stuff about Moses and Noah. Then he asks me if I think the story of Pharaoh persecuting the Jews has a parallel in the present. After the meaning of parallel is explained to me, I answer that I think Hitler is like Pharaoh and that modern Jews are at his mercy just as ancient Jews were at Pharaoh's.

"Is there a parallel, Gus, for Moses?" he asks.

I think about this for a few moments. Then I say, "If there is, I can't see it. Can you?"

Sadly and slowly he shakes his head to say no. "This time it does appear that the Jews have been abandoned. It has been a great sin. The Christian world has turned its back on them. For so doing, I'm afraid the Lord is going to make civilization pay a terrible price. But I see another parallel with ancient Egypt and maybe for this one, there is a Moses."

I wait for someone to ask him what this parallel is and who is the modern Moses? When no one asks, I do.

Dr. Wilson draws a picture in words of our world of 1941 as a modern version of ancient Egypt. Hitler is Pharaoh. The people in the Axis nations are the Egyptians. The men and women of the democracies are the Hebrews and Winston Churchill is Moses. Here Ernie joking as always, asks "When our Moses, Mr. Churchill, dies, who'll succeed him as Joshua? Harry James or Louie Armstrong?"

Everyone smiles or laughs except Mom. She thinks Ernie has been rude. So making a scene, she tells him so and apologizes for his behavior to Dr. Wilson. She's nuts. Ernie's words if spoken by someone else could be taken for rudeness, but in the good natured way that Ernie has voiced them everyone knows they're just playful.

Mom sometimes has no sense of humor at all. She can be worse than my mother. Nevertheless, in this instance I know we have to forgive her. As someone with brothers and sisters living in the old country, she sees nothing funny about Hitler or his politics. To her he's the anti-Christ and her despite for him is so complete that she refuses even to say his name. She calls him "that terribly wicked, evil man." As most of her friends in New York are Hungarian Jews, she knows their relatives in Europe are in danger of being rounded up like cattle and herded into slums and concentration camps. That, after all, is what the Nazi storm troopers have been doing to the Jews of Poland. Since Mom's people in Hungary are Calvinists, they don't have to endure what the Jews do. If, however, the war lasts into 1942, Mom's brothers and nephews may be drafted into the Hungarian Army. Then they'll be sent to fight and probably die for the unholy German cause in Russia. Her sisters and nieces won't fare much better because sooner or later they'll be bombed out of house and home by the R. A. F.

To take the edge off Mom's anger, Ernie apologizes to her and also to Dr. Wilson. He adds that he hadn't meant to be rude. The minister who has never felt offended thanks him anyway and resumes the discussion about parallels between Ancient Egypt and the present. This lasts for a few more minutes. Then Dr. Wilson gives his compliments again to Mother for the delicious dinner. He also praises her once more for the way she had been bringing up her sons. He says he expects Matt and me to grow up to be replicas of Ernie and Dad whom he sees as gallant soldiers for Christ.

When the big people get up from the table and the men go into the living room, I help Mom and Mother clear the table. Then I'm excused. I change out of my Sunday clothes and go outside to play.

During the next few days my mother is in a good mood. Apparently the Sunday dinner has been for her not a meal but an occasion. She likes and respects Dr. Wilson. Above all she has wanted to see him enjoy himself in our home. He has. So she is pleased. She says that even when things had gone wrong as when Mom had made a scene or when Matt and I had our little to do about Daddy's chair, they went wrong in a positive way.

It's nice being around Mother when she's in a good mood. She can brighten anyone's day when she wants to. With most people she does this. With them she's friendly, forgiving and cheerful. With me, however, she's usually the opposite. She tells me this is because I'm lazy and shiftless. As I have all of the earmarks of becoming a spoiled brat, she has to be strict with me for my own good.

Her most common complaint about me is that I'm self centered. I can't deny this. I'd never been much at seeing the world through the eyes of someone else. If something grabs my fancy, I get concerned about it. If it doesn't, I pay it no mind.

I have never been able to see the point of caring about things that don't interest me. Why give a hoot about the Giants when the Dodgers are so much more interesting? Why tune in a soap opera when Jack Armstrong is on the air? Why read Orphan Annie or Winnie Winkle when Dick Tracy and Smiling Jack have better adventures? Why be a busy bee like my mother and dream up work to make myself miserable when it's way more fun to live like a drone and play?

If I had been born a girl, Mother's notion that I should be devoted to doing household things like dusting, cleaning or vacuuming would make sense. Fortunately, I haven't been born a girl. So I believe it's only natural that I should always be finding ways of not acting like one. When I tell her this, she answers that men have always been experts at women's work. She says that in cooking no woman is the equal of a French chef and in cleaning whether it be of windows, rugs or dishes, the male professionals are unquestionably superior to women. I listen to her because I have to. But we both know that more bulls--- is coming out of her mouth than out of a longhorn's ass.

As life at home is nice when Mother is happy, I want to keep her that way. As the cause of so many of her bad moods, I figure I could also be the cause of some good ones. Many times she has told me that if only I would improve my behavior, she would be proud of me. While I want to gain her approval, I've become resigned to living without it. There's no way that I can change from being me and become the sickeningly sweet, sissified, Little Lord Fauntleroy, she wants me to be. I already have moved about as far in that direction as is possible when I became a choir boy. Anything further is unimaginable. Moreover, I only stay in the choir because every Sunday Mrs. Littlewood gives us each a dime for our services. If ever anything drastic should happen to her, I'd insist on being the first in line to be defrocked.

Watching Mother beam in quiet delight over how well the dinner with Dr. Wilson went leads me to do some serious thinking. An idea takes shape in my mind. Suppose I were to volunteer for religious instruction. One day a week it would cost me five to ten minutes of time away from play. That is its minus. Its plus is that it would please Mother immensely. She would think I've reformed. She'd get off my back and maybe onto Matthew's. Perhaps by sacrificing a handful of good minutes to the Lord, I could get out of having to endure a lot of bad ones. It appears to be a trade off that no one possessing an ounce of intelligence could ever pass up. So I do the sensible thing. I seek and secure permission from my home, my church and my school to take part in the program of religious instruction.

On that mid-October Wednesday afternoon when I first leave school and head for religious instruction at St. Charles', I follow a route that takes me by the St John's Home for Boys. Everyone I know feels sorry for orphans. I can never understand why. It's true that they have lousy Christmases. They receive only one present. But other than that, I know of no drawbacks. They live by rules which are the same for everyone. So everything is fair and everyone has a lot of fun.

Across the street from the orphanage is its block-long, fenced-in playground. It contains a full-sized, all grass football field with goal posts.

A week earlier I had watched a bit of a game that St John's main squad had played against a team from another orphanage. That was almost as impressive as going to a Dodger game. There were real referees who blew whistles and gave penalties. The players wore uniforms. During times out each team had a boy carry a water bucket with a ladle for drinking onto the field. The game was played with a brand new football. This was a luxury that we, the lucky ones on the outside with parents, seldom see.

Our touch tackle "pigskin" is a tied-up roll of folded newspapers. We sandwich our play into the times left open to us by passing cars and horse drawn wagons. In the orphans' huddle the call goes something like, "Hike on three. We'll fake a buck with Willie and I'll lateral to Charlie who'll run off tackle." Ours goes, "Hike on three. I'll hit Gus with a pass as he cuts left at the pile of horse s--- past the sewer."

As I leave the Orphans Home field I decide to cut over to St. John's Place. It's more interesting to walk on a street with stores and people than on blocks without them. I also want to see whether in the window of the second hand store a bike is on sale. None is.

When I get to the Church I go in the downstairs side entrance and see some kids from my Sunday School class standing around. We say, "hi." I learn from them that it will be ten minutes or so before things get started. Because I'm tired from walking I leave the group and take a seat in a comfortable chair outside the minister's office. As I wait four more kids arrive.

Suddenly two women walk in and everyone becomes silent. I stand up. "Are you Gregory?" the elder lady asks.

"Yes, Ma'am," I reply.

"Welcome to our religious instruction class. I'm Mrs. Cartan and I'll be your teacher. Come. Follow me."

The kids break into two groups. Half go with Mrs. Cartan; half, with her counterpart.

Mrs. Cartan introduces me to the class. It's a nice formality but I already know everyone and everyone knows me. Then she has us all stand to say the Lord's Prayer. As I recite it I wonder whether like Catholics we'll be saying three of these. I also am interested in finding out whether we'll substitute the Apostle's Creed for the Hail Marys. But most of all I'm concerned about how long we'll be in Church. If it's ten minutes, I'll be home just about when I've figured I would.

When we say Amen after one Lord's Prayer, Mrs. Cartan has us sit down. As Andy, the acolyte on Sundays, passes out Bibles she reminds everyone that last week our lesson had ended with Moses dying as the Hebrews were at last in view of the Promised Land. She tells us Joshua has been chosen by God to succeed Moses. Joshua is a wise leader. Before he will do battle he wants to know the strengths and weaknesses of his enemy. So he orders two of his spies to cross the River Jordan into Jericho to learn all they can about this city.

Then she asks Andy to begin reading aloud from Joshua, verse two of chapter two.

I've been getting aggravated. This seems like Sunday school. Where are the religious instruction prayers? When will we be saying them so we can leave?

As Andy reads I flip the pages to find Joshua II. 2. It strikes me as odd that we've skipped verse one of chapter two. So I glance at it.

It says, "And Joshua the son of Nun sent out of Shit'tim two men to spy secretly, saying, Go view the land even Jericho."

I don't have to finish that verse to see why she skips it. I scan ahead to find the next mention of Shit'tim. I find it in verse one of chapter three. If she's going to call on other people after Andy to continue reading, I sure hope that when we begin chapter three, it won't be my turn to read.

After Andy reads about six verses she does call on others to continue. When we finish chapter two she has us discuss it. She puts some interesting questions to us: Was Rahab, the harlot, a good woman? Was she a traitor to her people? Can people who betray their own kind be worthy of our esteem? Are there modern parallels? Would we admire a German streetwalker who harbored English spies? Would we admire an English Lady who protected Nazis?

While this stuff is interesting, it's going on and on, on my time. This isn't what I've bargained for. I want the discussion to end. I want to go play.

Well as usual, what I want and what I get are two different things. The lesson drags on and on. It's a quarter after four when I get out of there. The only good thing about the afternoon has been that neither I nor anyone else has had to say Shit'tim.

Back home that evening at dinner I'm asked about how the religious instruction went. I answer that we had been reading about Joshua. I add that Mrs. Cartan asked us good questions. She has made us realize that the stories in the Bible have meaning for what is happening in the world today. My mother and father press me for details. So when I tell them pretty much about everything that went on, they're pleased.

I add that I thought the lesson was too long and maybe it would be best if I withdrew from the program. My mother disagrees. She reminds me that this has been my idea. It's time I began to grow up and to behave accordingly. I should not be a baby like the kids who pester their parents for piano lessons and then quit. I should finish what I start.

I can see she isn't about to listen to reason. I've screwed up. Like Joshua, I should have asked around and done some spying on religious instruction at St. Charles' before going into it. Now I have to pay for my stupidity. I have to have religion rammed down my throat on Wednesdays as well as Sundays. It isn't fair. It isn't fair at all. But what can be done about it? Nothing! Nothing when you're powerless. That has been and probably will continue to be the way of the world. If it's also the will of God, and let's hope it's not, then there's a place for religion. As Herby Lifschitz might put it, "It's with the Torah."

Chapter 13

Pearl Harbor

Late in 1941 around the time of my tenth birthday my mother seems to be growing more irritable than usual. She's always tired. I notice this but I don't pay it much attention. It's her way to be a crank and because home is to me a place to get yelled at, I'm of no mind to hang around it to study her mood. She is, after all, stern in more than name and I'm content not to give her cause to expound on it.

At breakfast on the Saturday after Thanksgiving as Matt and I are shoveling our corn flakes down so we can get outside to play, Mother takes her seat at the table. As she seldom eats breakfast, her behavior in joining us is strange. I brace myself for trouble. I slow my eating before she can declare my cereal crunching a cause for complaint.

Matthew is smiling at her. That's his way. He's really stupid which probably explains why he's always happy. People like him. Even her. She brushes back the hair on his forehead and in a quiet voice says, "Children." Then she pauses.

Aw shucks, I think, there goes my Saturday morning. She has a way of saying children which sounds to me more ominous than her screams.

"Children," she repeats, "I must have a serious discussion with you."

"Yes Mother," says Matthew as though on cue.

I know better than to speak and am careful to look interested.

"Next Thursday," she says, "your mother will be going to a hospital in New York for a week to be examined. Lately, you must have noticed she hasn't been herself."

I wait for Matt to ask her who she's been. He doesn't. She stares past us as if we aren't here. Ten seconds of tense silence passes. It seems longer.

"I'm scared," says my brother.

"There's no need to be frightened now," she replies. "You boys both know that your grandfather died at thirty-three. As your mother is fated to die at the same age, she'll still be with you for another five years. The doctors are merely going to examine her to see whether she has as yet contracted the disease that will kill her."

She pauses to let her words sink in. I hate it when she speaks of herself in the third person. I know from experience that it's a prelude to morbidity. As she recites her tragic lines it becomes the duty of my brother and me to be more than her audience. Like a Greek chorus we're expected to interrupt her on cue with comments that will intensify the dramatics of her scene.

Unhappily I realize that a command performance is now underway and that she's enjoying every miserable minute of it. Whenever she plays this dying act for the old man, he applauds and calls her Sarah, which is short for Sarah Bernhardt. This makes her furious. Every few months she reminds us of her impending death at the age of thirty three. Dad says she's been rehearsing and perfecting the dramatics of dying for so long that when her thirty-third birthday arrives, there'll be no way for her to refuse to give encore performances of her dying for another thirty-three years.

"Will the disease be contagious and maybe kill us too before we're thirty-three," I ask.

"The disease won't be contagious. But I'm sure you'll die at thirty-three. It's our lot as Hamiltons to live only as long as the Savior."

"Maybe I'll live longer because I'm only 50% Hamilton but 100% Stern," I counter.

"No. You've got Hamilton blood in you. You'll die at thirty- three.

I think to myself, Hamilton blood! I'd as soon have s--- squirming through my veins. Who needs such stuff if it's designed to go off like a time bomb and murder a fellow in the middle of his life?

Then a more pleasant thought forms and I say, "Well, if I have to die at thirty-three at least I know Matthew will too."

"I don't wanna die, I don't wanna die," cries Matt going into a panic.

"Quiet!" thunders the old lady, "It's my death we need to be concerned about. Neither of you is going to die for a long, long time. So stop this fretting and pay attention."

She pauses and waits for him to regain his composure. Then she announces, "I've forgotten where we were. Where were we?"

Neither Matt nor I answer.

"Where were we?" she demands to know.

"We're all gonna die at thirty-three," I say.

"Before that," she insists.

"Oh, now I remember," she utters in a calm voice, "I shall be in the hospital for about a week. I'll be subjected to a series of tests for the disease which, of course, will eventually kill me. While I'm gone either your grandmother or Gwendolyn will be coming here to cook your meals. You're to keep your room clean and make no trouble."

After a pause she looks at Matt and continues, "If you wet your bed, you're to put your sheets in the hamper immediately after you awake. Gus, I'll expect you to see that he does this."

"Yes, Mother."

"Any questions?"

She pauses and waits. I can't tell whether I'm supposed to ask something or not.

"Good," she says, "Now finish your breakfast."

I have only one spoonful of cereal left. Poor Matt has half of a soggy bowl.

The next Saturday, Daddy brings Matthew and me to the hospital in New York to visit Mother. She's in a room with three other lady patients on the 7th floor. The view from her window is spectacular. You can see Central Park and beyond it, skyscrapers.

Mother is in bed wearing a white hospital nightgown. We exchange hellos and kiss her. She introduces us to her room mates and to a lady who is a visitor of one of them.

Dad asks Mother how she's feeling. She says fine but bored. She'll be happy when her tests are through and she can come back home. Matt asks her if she got an A on her tests. She explains to him that hospital tests are not like school tests. They're different, like taking your temperature. Her temperature is fine at 98.6. Matt thanks her for the explanation but then the idiot wishes her a one hundred on her next one.

I tell her it's great having Gwen cook for us and that she has made pancakes for us that morning. I add that last night we had fish cakes and spaghetti. Gwen has even let us make home made fudge with her for dessert. I then tell Mother we had saved some of the fudge to bring to her as a gift only I guess I've left it on the subway because I don't have it now.

Dad smiles and says it isn't lost. He takes the little bag of it out of his pocket and gives it to her along with a get well card from Gwen and Gram.

Boy, am I relieved by that.

Matt asks her how she likes looking out of the window. She tells him to come over and stand by her. Then she points at an angle and says, "The tall building with the tower like top is the Empire State Building."

I insist on seeing it too. She motions to me to come over. When I get by her bed and see it, I know it at once. It looks just like it did in King Kong. It's impressive.

Matthew gets bored. Soon I'm too. We stay a long time. When visiting hours end, we say good-bye. Matt starts crying. He doesn't want to leave without her. She also cries. I feel sad. I look up at Dad.

He has lifted Matt up in one arm and has taken my hand with the other. He reminds Mother that Gram and Gwen will be coming to visit her tomorrow afternoon while Mom serves us our Sunday dinner. Then the three of us will return tomorrow evening for the six o'clock visiting hours.

We say our final good-bye and leave.

After church the next day, Dad lets us change out of our Sunday suits so we can go outside and really have fun. We've gotten home very late from St. Charles' because on the first Sunday of the month there's a communion service which always takes at least a half of an hour longer than morning prayer. As far as I'm concerned, morning prayer also takes too long.

Anyway it's 1:30 before I get out of the house onto the street. Immediately, I get into a game of checkers--not the kind of checkers that you play on a checkerboard but the kind that you play on the sidewalk with bottle caps on the third line. To me street checkers has always been an okay game only if you don't have anything more interesting to do. It's similar to marbles but better because no one can afford to buy marbles and even if they could, the nearest dirt on which to play marbles is two hundred yards away on the lot at the corner of Park Place and Troy Avenue. Anyway, just as I'm taking aim with my wax filled shooter, Freckles Thornton rushes up to us and shouts, "The Japs have bombed Pearl Harbor."

"Tough s---," says Bucky Quinn and for emphasis he adds, "Who cares?"

I'd have seconded that but I was too intent on making my shot to speak.

"But you don't understand," says Freckles, "the Japs bombed Pearl Harbor."

"Shut your damned mouth," says Bucky, "can't you see Gus is about to shoot."

I fire and miss.

"Damn you, Freckles," I swear, "Who cares if the Japs bombed a bunch of oysters?"

"Yeah," says Bucky, backing me up.

"You don't even know what Pearl Harbor is," sneers Freckles.

"Who doesn't know?" I shoot back. "Do you think you're the only jackass who's ever seen a Jon Hall picture?"

"Well, where is Pearl Harbor?" he questions.

"In the Pacific south of Pago Pago," I bluff. My voice is so self-assured and certain that I almost believe it myself.

"For your information, smarty, it's in Hawaii and we're at war because the Japs have attacked our Navy and a soldier fort of ours too."

"Up yours, Freckles," says Bucky, "can't you see I'm trying to shoot. Now do you wanna play checkers or do you wanna bulls---."

"It ain't bulls---. It's war. Go home and hear it on the radio."

As he speaks Bucky shoots and knocks the last checker off the line.

"That's it, Bucky. I'm out of checkers. See you guys," I say.

I run around the corner to my house and holler to everyone as I come in the door, "Freckles says we're at war with the Japs. Turn the radio on."

I run to the radio and turn it on myself. When it warms up, it's on a music station. I dial around. All I pick up is more music and religious talk."

"That Freckles, always pulling my leg," I complain.

"Well turn the radio off and go back outside and play. Dinner won't be ready for another hour," says Mom.

I move to do so when the station interrupts its program for a news bulletin to update its listeners on what had been occurring in Hawaii. It backs up what Freckles has said and enlarges upon it.

Dad and Ernie stay glued to the radio. Mom goes back into the kitchen saying, "War or no war, I still have to cook and we still have to eat."

When the announcer stops reporting to bring us a commercial,

Ernie looks at Dad and says, “Although we knew this was going to come sooner or later, it’s still out of the blue. I thought for sure the first blow against us would be from the Germans.”

Dad says, “They’re still the threat to us and to the world. I just hope this attack doesn’t divert the country from the real menace.”

“Three weeks,” I pipe up, “three weeks and we’ll beat the Japs so badly, they’ll never make war again.”

“I’m afraid, Gus, it will take longer than that. It may take us a year,” says Ernie.

“Never,” I assure him. They haven’t got a chance. Let’s see. Three weeks in December brings us to the 28th, almost New Year’s. I’ll make a prediction. We’ll win this one by Christmas.”

“What makes you so cock sure?” asks Dad with a smile as he goes to the secretary to get the Atlas to see where Pearl Harbor is.

“The only country the Japs are good at licking is China. And that’s only because the Chinese don’t have planes and tanks and machine guns. They also haven’t got many cannons and they’re even short of rifles. The Japs in China are an army of bullies beating up on a nation of coolies. Once we drop a few bombs on Japan, their straw houses will go up in flames, their cities will burn down and they’ll be sorry they messed with us. I know about these guys. They’re four eyed, buck toothed, ugly, evil, pint-sized runts. They need a licking and we’re just the right people to give it to them.”

My speech must have made a hit with Dad. He’s grinning from ear to ear. Ernie smiles too and says, “Before you fly off the handle with another speech like that remind yourself first to clear your throat and go into the ‘Unaccustomed as I am routine.”‘ Then he asks me, “Where on earth did you get all of this from?”

“Wait here and I’ll show you,” I reply.

I go into my bedroom and from under the bed I pull out the shoe box which holds my most precious possessions: bottle caps, rubber heels, baseball cards and war tickets. The bottle caps of course are used in the street game of checkers. But they're also a form of currency as are baseball cards and war tickets. We gamble and play for keeps with them in our street games. For example, to get into a game of slap ball might require three bottle caps or two war tickets or a baseball card. Then you play the nine innings. If your team loses, you give your opponents whatever items you've played for. If you win, you take theirs.

The war tickets are sold six for a penny in the stationery stores. They come in what we called a string. Each cardboard ticket in size is about one and a half inches by two. On one side it has a colored picture of some event in either the Spanish Civil War or the Sino-Japanese one. On the reverse side of the ticket in two or three sentences there's a short description of the event depicted on the front. For example, the ticket might show on one side two Japs, one shooting helpless civilians and the other gleefully twisting the arm of a scantily clad, screaming mother holding her baby. On the back of this you read: The Rape of Nanking: Japanese soldiers show no mercy to unarmed and helpless civilians. They rape, pillage and murder tens of thousands during this 1937 atrocity. The six cards are attached to each other with perforations between them much as an interline railway ticket from Baltimore to Savannah would have perforations between the stubs that would be collected respectively by the conductors of the Pennsylvania Railroad, the R.F.& P. and the Seaboard Airline Railway.

When I return to the living room and show my war tickets to Ernie, he reads a few and then asks me, "Is this where you get your news about the war?"

"Only some of it. I read a little bit about it in the newspaper. I also see war in the newsreels and in the pictures in life magazine. I hear about it in school and from Mom and from radio broadcasts. Also because Uncle Ned, Gram's brother, is in the British Eighth Army fighting in Africa, I try to keep up with what's happening there. I know that the Africa Corps is trying to take Tobruk and can't and that the British are holding on to the island of Malta."

"Gus, I'm impressed," says Ernie, "I think you're a walking encyclopedia."

"Well you made him that way," says Dad. "Anyone with a brain trained to be able to soak up the cranial nerves and the five causes of auricular fibrillation ought to be able to keep up with current events."

I really feel good hearing them talk this way about me. So I resolve to do even more to keep up with the wars in Africa, Asia, Europe, and the Pacific. With America now involved in the fighting that won't be hard to do.

I go back onto the street to play. I think I really have impressed Dad and Ernie. I'm convinced I'm a genius.

Three weeks later I have to face facts and admit I'm an idiot. The war is going disastrously. We and the British are losing badly to the Japs. The Germans have also taken up arms against us and are torpedoing lots of our ships. Everywhere the situation is awful. The Nazis are within sight of Moscow. The Japanese are overrunning Southeast Asia and the Pacific. The war appears to be almost over and we not only seem to have lost but also to have been trounced. Still I never doubt we'll rally and win. Nor does anyone else in the free world.

On December 7, in the hospital, Mother is upset. Her stay in the hospital is supposed to be time reserved for her to hold center stage and to furnish us with her rendition of Garbo doing a Camille. Now the damned Japs have ruined everything. They've rained on her parade and by so doing they've earned her enmity and everlasting unforgiveness.

By Monday Mother's tests are complete. She comes home on Tuesday. She really is sick. She has lupus, a chronic disease which in mild form is terrible and in severe form is life threatening. Right now her case is mild.

Once war begins, businesses everywhere begin raising prices. On the radio announcements are made asking people not to hoard things like sugar and coffee. This plea is silly and useless. Most Americans are living from payday to payday. They haven't the money to buy goods to hoard. Those who are well off and can afford to hoard might never think to do so if the blockheads broadcasting on the radio would not keep informing them about the items which are expected soon to be in short supply.

Mom hoards. She goes out and buys sugar and coffee until these products fill half of her pantry. She has been drinking ten cups of sweetened coffee every day of her life since she was sixteen. War or no war, she expects to continue to do this as long as she lives.

Gram reacts to the war differently. She breaks all of her china because it has come from Japan. At first everyone applauds her patriotism but when it becomes apparent that the price of a new set of dishes is beyond her, we feel differently. After eating off pie tins for a couple of days, Gram buys a few cheap place settings in the Five and Ten. When we visit her, we make it a point not to notice the markings, Made in Japan, on the underside of the dishes.

The war brings immediate and severe changes into every American's life but the initial changes in mine seldom distress me. My mother takes her first full time job since girlhood. She goes to work for the Sperry Gyroscope Corporation and quickly gets promotions until she becomes a second class mechanic. That's as high as the defense plant will allow a woman to rise. The pay is forty dollars per week for a five day week of forty hours. She also draws time and a half for overtime. Her salary is way more than my dad's.

Since both of my parents soon are working swing shift hours, my brother and I are only sure to see them at noon. If no company comes, Matt and I are in the house alone four nights each week until one in the morning. This worries Mom and Pop but it thrills me. I can listen to late radio programs and go to bed when I feel like it. Because both of our parents are too tired to be eating with us at breakfast, Mother says that as a consolation prize we can have Wheaties or Wheatena from now on instead of corn flakes or oatmeal. I love this change and pray she's always be too tired in the morning to have breakfast with us.

In the evenings, Matt and I eat at Ray's Diner on Church Avenue next door to the Grenada theater. There Mother has paid in advance to have them serve us chop steak, beans, chocolate milk and a roll. This sure is an improvement on pea soup.

As far as I'm concerned, I've yet to see a better year than 1942. Up until May when we stop the Japs at the Battle of the Coral Sea, the war goes badly. But with our success at Midway in June, Guadalcanal in August and North Africa in November, America has turned the tide of war. The British follow with a magnificent victory at El Alamein in October and the Russians win gloriously at Stalingrad in January of '43. From these times onward, terrible battles will continue to be fought but the ultimate outcome of the war in our favor is assured as long as the allied alliance holds.

Everyone acknowledges that the war is awful for the men in combat and for those who love them. Surely, the world and almost every family in the belligerent nations would have preferred it if peace had prevailed instead of conflict. But any civilian in America who insists that there weren't favorable aspects to the war is a liar or a righteously moral nincompoop.

In 1942 jobs become plentiful and just about everyone's standard of living rises. Feelings of friendship and pride for all of our fighting men and for all of our fellow citizens sweep over all Americans. Anyone in uniform is regarded as a hero, a brother to us all. The rest of us become members of our one great, national family. We care for one another and feel everyday a kinship with all of our fellow citizens. This sense of warmth and unity is something which earlier could be experienced only during the Christmas season.

For the Stern family, the war brings solvency and a good-bye to Schnectady Avenue. We move back to Flatbush where we belong. We're once again members of the Middle Class. We have protein in our diet, change in our pockets and a spare roll of toilet paper in our john.

Chapter 14

A New Friend

I have always found meeting people and making friends to be the most difficult thing about moving into a new neighborhood. I am not like Mickey Rooney. I can't wag my tail and walk up to a bunch of strange kids and say, "Hi everyone, I'm Gus Stern, the new kid on the block. Now that I've arrived we can become organized and go forward and win the state championship." Charming nonsense like that exists nowhere except in movies. In real life nearly every newcomer is quiet, shy and wary. I'm no different. I join in with others only after I've sized them up enough to feel safe and secure in their company.

Linden Boulevard is not like Park Place. On it stickball is unthinkable. It's a wide and busy street with red lights at every corner. It has traffic enough to make crossing in the middle of the block as difficult an adventure as trying to do a buck and wing on a guy wire. As a consequence, two neighborhoods exist on the boulevard. We kids on the south side of the street keep to ourselves. We're no more aware of the kids on the north side than we are of fellows living in Greenpoint.

For the first few days in the new neighborhood I have no chance to meet and to make new friends. It's January. Between the time when school lets out and darkness comes, there's only a little over an hour left for play. Because it's cold, everyone is staying indoors. When I arrive home from school, I park my books atop the radiator inside our front door and go outside to see if any kids are hanging around. None ever are. Soon I grow tired of freezing. I return upstairs to get warm. Every ten or fifteen minutes thereafter I go back outside to recheck the street. Always it's the same story: not a kid in sight.

Sometimes between my trips up and down the stairs, I just hang around in the apartment and do nothing. Other times to kill time I read. As the only material handy is school books, I delve into the P.S. 181 history text.

In my 5A class at P.S. 83 we had been studying New York State history. We had learned about Henry Hudson, New Amsterdam and colonial New York. Although this had been interesting, it was not the kind of stuff anyone ever would have taken out a library card to get.

In 5A at P.S. 181 the history being studied is different. It deals with the New World in the Sixteenth Century. It's about the Spaniards who explored not only Latin America but also immense tracts of territory which later became part of the U.S.A. To accomplish their deeds, these men had to overcome hostile climates, vile diseases and huge armies of disciplined Indians.

Reading about them is inspiring and exciting--much more so than reading comic books about fantasy figures costumed in leotards and capes. The Conquistadors have guts. They're cut from the same cloth as Columbus. They aren't fearless. Rather they're filled with fear but they manage to overcome it. They never lose sight of their mission and they allow nothing to jeopardize it. They succeed because they refuse to fail. They embody the will to win.

Because at my old school I had not studied anything about the discoveries and explorations in New World, my new teacher, Mrs. Bloch, says she does not expect me to pass her history final. She promises to give me a bye on it. However, in the next term I'll have an account to balance. She says that beginning in February, she will demand as much of me as she does any student in the class.

I know she expects me to thank her for this. But all I say is "Yes Ma'am."

On the day of the final she gives me a copy of the test and tells me to look it over and to appreciate how far behind I am. I tell her that if she doesn't mind, I'd like to take the exam now and be treated the same as any other student. She answers, "Suit yourself."

When Mrs. Bloch grades our exams, my paper shocks the s--- out of her. I score a ninety eight. I'm the class leader. The only mistakes I make on the test are minor ones. I rechristen Hernando de Soto, Fernando, and Francisco Pizarro, Pizzaro.

From that point on I continue to excel in history. And on Thursdays when we discuss current events, it's obvious that I know a lot more about what's going on in Europe and North Africa than she does.

When I announce one day in class that I think in giving voice in 1940 to the determination of the British never to knuckle under to the Nazis, Winston Churchill has showed the same kind of courage as Cortes, Mrs. Bloch seems pleased. She has told us repeatedly that people who know history can always find parallels in the past to help them handle the problems of the present. She says when I equate Churchill and Cortes, I've found an excellent example to prove her point. I appreciate the praise. So I say nothing to contradict her. But never for a moment do I think that Churchill in 1940 gave a thought to Cortes in 1519.

After school on the first warm day after a January cold spell breaks I come home, go downstairs and hang around. A boy who looks to be perhaps a year older than me comes out from an apartment house two doors away. A second or two later his kid sister comes after him hollering, "Momma says 'Get milk too.'"

As he turns to say something back to her, he sees me. He pretends he doesn't but I know he does. Of course, I give him the same treatment. Soon he walks by and goes around the corner. In a few minutes he returns carrying groceries. When he gets even with my front walk, he looks over and hollers, "Hey you."

"Hey yourself," I answer.

"You're not very friendly," he says as he stops and looks directly at me.

"So," I answer.

"So did you move in here?"

"Yeah, about ten days ago."

"What's your name?"

"What's yours?"

"Frank Casey. You can call me Frankie."

"I'm Gus. Gus Stern."

"Do you go to one eighty-one, Gus?"

"Yeah, do you?"

"Nah, I go to Holy Cross. I hate it."

"The sisters are strict?"

"Yeah but none of them teach boys. We've got brothers. And most of them are mean pains in the ass."

"All teachers are pains in the ass. I've never yet met one who wasn't."

"Right. Wait here. I've got to bring these groceries inside. I'll be back out in a minute."

As Frankie goes into his apartment, I know I've made a friend. Clearly, he's an all right kid. Of course, he's let me know he's Catholic. That's to be expected: fish eaters who can keep their religion private are, as the saying goes, scarcer than hen's teeth. What impresses me most about this fellow Casey is what he didn't do. He didn't sniff around to see what my religion is. In an Irish Catholic that's class.

Chapter 15
Blacklist

At the start of 1942 the CIO is making a determined effort to unionize the title insurance company for which my dad works. Professional organizers have been sent down from the union's national headquarters to educate my dad and his coworkers about their collective bargaining rights.

Dad is never one to favor unions. However, when he is shown how feebly he and his colleagues are paid by people who themselves are living high on the hog, he joins the union. He believes that belonging to it is a necessary evil. It seems to be the only way an ordinary Joe can get a just wage from a rich employer who lacks a Christian concern for others. My dad is never against anyone amassing great wealth. He just wants to be paid a living wage. So along with two other fellows my old man volunteers to become an agitator for the union and to work tirelessly to try to organize his coworkers.

In 1942 the CIO is loaded with communists. Many of them ask my dad to join their party. He refuses. He wants no part of an organization that has supported Hitler. Moreover, he's convinced that the Reds pay a higher allegiance to the Soviet Union than they do to the United States.

In order to install a closed shop with CIO representation, the union has to win over a majority of the employees in an election supervised by representatives of the federal government. In early February a few days before the formal voting is to occur, an informal canvass is taken to estimate how the workers will vote. The result of this shows that 27 are for union, 8 are against it and 1 is undecided.

When management learns of this, a meeting with the employees is held. Everyone is given a ten cents an hour wage increase. Then the bosses plead with the workers to reject representation. They assure everyone that if they keep the union out, another wage increase will be forthcoming in six months.

A few days later when the election is held, only nine people vote to install the union. Twenty seven reject it.

The following morning my dad is canned. He's the only man fired by the firm.

Getting axed doesn't shock him. Although he has gambled on winning, Dad knows and accepts the consequences of losing. What does surprise him is that his two fellow agitators not only are kept on their jobs but each also is given an extra nickel an hour pay hike. These fellows tell Dad that they attribute their good fortune to having signed up in the Communist Party. The bosses are respectful of Reds.

Immediately my dad begins to apply downtown for work at other title searching firms. Most aren't hiring anybody. Among those who are, not one chooses to employ Dad.

When Dad learns there's no job for him in Brooklyn, he applies for work in Manhattan. The result there is the same. So he tries Queens. This too proves to be a futile effort.

Meanwhile at home troubles are brewing.

For as long as I can remember my parents have been fighting over money. My mother says in her never ending variety of ways that it's my dad's duty as a husband and father to earn more. His only answer is abrupt and to the point: there ain't no more. She begs and bitches, goads and grouses, praises and pleads with him to get off his ass and bring home the bacon. Always he has listened to her with deaf ears until 7p.m. Then he either turns on the radio to hear the Masterwork Hour and Symphony Hall or takes off to attend a Lodge Meeting. This behavior only drives Mother crazier.

I guess there isn't much good that anyone can say of the old man as a husband other than the facts that he neither drinks nor physically abuses my mother. On a scale for rating mates where the letter D stands for failing, my old lady on one of her good days might give my dad a C-. As far as she is concerned, the saying that marriages are made in heaven merely proves that hell is superfluous.

Anyway, after looking for work for over a month, my dad begins to make the rounds again. At one of the more prestigious firms, he and the other applicants are given I.Q. Tests as part of the hiring procedure. A few days later when he drops by to check on his status, he's told by the office manager that the firm will not be hiring him.

My Dad wonders if his I.Q. score had been too low to qualify him for the-job. So he asks if this has been the problem.

A bewildered smile sweeps over the manager's face. Then he says, "Greg, in the three years we've administered this test, we've never had anyone score over 135 until you shocked us with a 157. If I.Q.s have any validity, you've the potential to be an Einstein. The reason you're not being hired has nothing whatever to do with your mind or your qualifications. Your problem is that you've been blacklisted."

"Blacklisted?" utters my dad. Then after a pause he continues, "As an agitator I did nothing unethical or illegal. Although I tried to start a union and failed, I see now that wasn't the reason I was fired. I've been sacked because I wasn't a Communist and wouldn't be one."

"I know that. Everyone working in the Hall of Records knows that. You're trouble was and is that you went to work for a pack of immoral tight asses. Everyone understands that and sympathizes with you. If personnel decisions would be left up to me, you'd have been hired by this firm on the day you were fired. But that isn't the case. I don't make decisions. I merely make recommendations. I'm just an agent for my employer. I don't set the rules. I merely maintain them. You've been blacklisted. As it's the policy of my superiors in this company to honor this evil, you can't be hired. As it's also the policy of every other title insurance firm in New York to follow suit, you're wasting your time by staying in town and looking for work in your trade. You have to look for a job in another city or in another field."

When Dad leaves, he returns home and goes into deep despair.

A job may not define a man but it does give him his identity. Take that away from him and in nine cases out of ten, you destroy him.

There's a Marquis of Queensbury saying: Never kick a man when he's down. It's an admirable thought. In fisticuffs it's usually honored. In all other forums, it's breached. So at our home when Dad reports the events of the day, Mother lights into him saying he'd better be up and about tomorrow morning to take the first job he's offered. She suggests that he should try to find a job in a defense plant. There he could get blue collar work and be paid a salary of over one and a half times his old wages.

My dad responds saying that as a college man he prefers to look for white collar work.

This sets Mother off. She announces that someone has to be the breadwinner in this family. As it sure as hell isn't going to be her poor excuse for a husband, she'll go out tomorrow and get work.

So the next day while the old man goes looking for white collar work, my mother lands a job as a waitress in Schrafft's, a fancy tea room restaurant that caters to junior executives and snobs.

Mother doesn't keep that job very long. The pay is lousy. The women have to rely on tips to obtain a decent income. To get good tips it's necessary to smile and to play up to the horny patrons. The old lady says the job makes her feel like she's in a training program for whores. After a couple of weeks of being ogled at, she quits.

A few days later she answers an ad to work at the Sperry Gyroscope Corporation and is hired. She's assigned to on-the-job training to become a mechanic. The work week is for 48 hours. She's put on the swing shift with Saturday as her day off.

Every afternoon throughout Lent as Mother goes out the door to go to work, she passes Dad who's returning home from his morning of unsuccessful job hunting. It's exasperating for both. Finally, the old man decides to break the pattern. Against his principles on Easter Monday he goes downtown to a protestant employment agency and asks them to help him find white collar work. That afternoon he's sent by them to an interview in Penn Station in Manhattan. There he's hired to be a clerk in the Ticket Receiver's Office of the Pennsylvania Railroad Corporation.

Like my mother, Dad's working hours are from 4p.m. to 12:30a.m. Unlike her, his day off is Tuesday. Most surprising of all is that after my Dad is once again gainfully employed, he's offered piecemeal work by several of the title searching firms that previously wouldn't hire him. Apparently, once it has been established to the satisfaction of his old employer that Dad will never be given permanent work as a title searcher, Dad's blacklisting may be regarded as having been fulfilled. Now nothing stands in the way of other companies commissioning him to do part-time jobs for them.

Chapter 16

Wheels

In February or March of 1942 our Superintendent catches me rummaging through the junk in the basement of our apartment house. In an angry voice he asks, "All right, what the hell are you up to down here?"

"Nothing," I reply.

"Nothing, my ass. What are you up to?"

"I'm just trying to see if we have my brother's old baby carriage down here."

"Well, do you?"

"No, sir."

"You shouldn't be here. What would you want with a baby carriage anyway?"

"I want it's wheels. I'm looking to build a cart."

"You are, huh. Well that beat up baby carriage laying back there in the rear had better not lose its wheels. Do you get me?"

"Yes sir. I wouldn't steal anything."

"You had better not. Now scram."

I scram.

About a week later as I'm coming home from school the Super sees me as I enter our building. He calls out, "Hey 3-C. Do you still want the wheels from my baby carriage?"

"I wasn't going to take them," I protest in self defense.

"Would you want them anyway?"

"Yes, sir."

"Well, I'll make you a deal. I'll trade you the wheels even up if when it snows, you shovel the walk out front."

"Great," I say.

It looks like snow will begin any minute. The weather has been warming up slightly as it usually does just before a snowfall.

"Can I get the wheels now?" I ask.

"No. After it snows and after the walk is shoveled then you can have them."

I go upstairs dejectedly. Ninety-nine times out of a hundred, it would snow on a day like this. But now when it matters, I know it won't. God has it in for me. He only lets it snow when it's pointless.

Inside the apartment I gaze out of the window. The sky is gray and gloomy. It looks as miserable as I feel.

I go downstairs and walk over to Frankie's. He isn't in. So I try Fat's. He isn't home either. After these it's Brother's and then Kevin's--same story.

Jeez, where is everybody?

As I head home, I notice some large, fat flakes of snow beginning to fall. They're wet and heavy – the kind which surely will stick and pile up quickly. Soon the air is filled with them. This snowfall is going to be a six inch beauty. It makes my day. I look up to Heaven and give the Lord thanks for coming through for me. My carriage wheels are as good as gotten. I tell God I'm sorry for thinking He had forsaken me and that if ever I doubt Him again, He's entitled to strike me dead. Then realizing that I'm speaking with too much haste and knowing that nothing is official until I utter an Amen, I tell Him to cancel the never doubting stuff. I figure He ought to build a better record of His coming through with good deeds for me before He's to be entitled to have me put my life on the line for Him. I still remember with undiminished bitterness His slighting of me with the second hand bike on St. John's Place.

As I near my apartment building, I see the gang come around the corner. I wait on them. They're almost as pleased with the snow as I am. They're looking forward to tomorrow when they'll be playing in it.

After dinner I go down and borrow the Super's shovel. The snow is still falling. It's already three inches high. Except where the residents and their guests have walked upon it, the snow is a snap to remove.

By morning when I awake the snowfall has stopped. The radio says eight inches has fallen. When I go outside and see that we do have eight, I'm surprised. Everyone who has ever lived on Linden Boulevard has learned like me that since the Weather Bureau's readings are taken at the Battery, they can't be trusted to be true for Flatbush.

Before I leave for school I have just enough time to clear a narrow path for pedestrians in front of our apartment house. As I work, I wonder why the snow is only one inch lower where I had shoveled last night than where I hadn't. There has been no noticeable wind to cause drifts. By rights I should now have been pushing the blade through a five inch accumulation instead of a seven.

After school I rush home and return to shoveling. Within an hour the job is finished. The Super is satisfied. He has obtained my labor for what he considers to be a worthless piece of trash. And I've gotten half of the basic material I need to become a ten year old entrepreneur. The other half I secure the next afternoon at Tropfke's German Deli on Nostrand Avenue. Inside the store Mrs. Tropfke has me move crates of empty soda bottles down to the cellar and bring full bottles up. For doing this and for sweeping the store and shoveling away slush that has been kicked up by cars onto their sidewalk, I'm given a dime and, more importantly, a large oak box. That evening with the Super's help, I bolt the axles of the carriage wheels onto boards and the boards onto the base of the oak box. Then voila, as the French say, I have myself a sturdy wagon. To steer it I've drilled a hole near each end of the front axle board. By knotting an eight to ten foot piece of rope at its ends through these axle board holes, I'm able by drawing the rope taut to tug and to steer the wagon as I would a snow sled. I'm set now to go into business.

On Friday afternoon, I pull my wagon down to the A&P and line up behind two other kids who also are offering a delivery service to women doing their weekend shopping. For tips we cart their groceries to their homes. I make three trips that day before the store closes at six and earn for myself thirty-five cents. The money gives me a sense of pride and of worth. I feel rich. After all, with this much cash I can go to the movies and see double features on both Saturday and Sunday and have something left over for candy.

Bright and early on Saturday, I'm back at the A&P to resume my business. A few other kids are present and waiting with their carts. One I have seen yesterday.

"Hi," I say as I greet him with a smile.

"Louie ain't going to like you being here," he returns.

Since he isn't friendly, I let the conversation drop. I figured Louie is the manager of the A&P.

The shoppers soon begin coming out. I wait my turn and get a woman who lives three small and two long blocks away. I'm sure as I follow her over that great distance that I'll get at least a dime and maybe fifteen cents for the trip. All she gives me is a nickel.

When I come back to the market there are just two kids with carts out front and another straddling a bike and hanging around as a kibitzer. As I pull into line I know I won't have to wait long for another customer. I just hope she'll be a better tipper than the last one.

The kibitzer speaks up saying, "Gimme a nickel."

He's looking at me.

"What for?" I ask him.

"Don't give me 'what for?' Just gimme a nickel."

"All I got is a nickel."

"Fine that's all I need."

He gets off of his bike and approaches me.

"I ain't giving up my nickel," I say.

He grabs my arm and punches me below the shoulder.

"Are you Louie?" I ask.

"Yeah, I'm Louie. What's it to ya?"

"If I knew what you needed the nickel for, maybe I'd give it to you."

"Look shrimp, I run this goddamn show. No one delivers groceries without my permission. So pay up."

A lady comes out. She needs a carrier. Louie sees her and tells the second guy in line to take her as his customer. Without any objection from the kid in front of him, the second fellow wheels his cart forward and loads the lady's groceries into it. Then he and the woman leave.

Now punk," resumes Louie as he punches me again on the arm, "I'm giving you your last chance to straighten up. I want that nickel. If I don't get it, you'll not only not work here, you'll feel my fat fist in your snoot."

I decide not to risk that. I pull the nickel out of my pocket and give it to him."

"Good," he says as he looks into the store, "for being cooperative, I might let you take the next customer."

I put two and two together and figure if he does, it will be because he knows her to be a lousy tipper.

"Thanks," I say.

"What's your name?" he asks.

"Gus. Gus Stern."

"Are you a Jew?"

"No," I answer.

"Better not be. I don't like Jews. I don't let them work here."

"Are you a devout Catholic?"

"I'm Catholic, I not sure I'm devout" he says.

"Do you know the difference between a Catholic and a devout Catholic?"

He looks at me quizzically. After a brief pause he asks, "Do you?"

"I do," I answer, "A Catholic goes to Mass on Sunday, doesn't eat meat on Friday and hates Jews. A devout Catholic goes to Mass on Sunday, doesn't eat meat on Friday and hates Jews."

A lady comes out. Louie signals for me to take her. I load her packages into my cart. As we walk off, Louie calls after me, "Hey, you. Hey, Gus. I don't see the difference."

I turn, look back and declare, "Neither do I, Louie, neither do I."

During the following weeks my earnings improve. I begin to remember the women who gave me lousy tips. I become very skilled at avoiding them. I also begin to pick up regulars. Some women insist on having me as their delivery boy even if there are five kids lined up and waiting in front of me. On the way to their houses we chit-chat as we walk. Some of these ladies get to calling me Gus. When they do, I'm flattered. I almost always use Ma'am in addressing them. I never would dare to be less formal and polite even if they would permit it. It's wise as well as respectful to be this way with your elders and with your employers. Calling them Ma'am keeps the right amount of social distance between us and assures me of being picked again next week to cart their groceries.

Louie continues to extort nickels on Friday afternoons and on Saturdays from me and from everybody else with a cart. I resent this. Every week my bitterness and my aggravation with the injustice of being robbed grows. I want to beat his brains in with a baseball bat. The trouble is that I'm not dumb enough to try it. Finally I make up my mind never to pay the bully another nickel. I decide to give up going to the A&P. I'll conduct my business blocks away at Bohack's.

On the Saturday morning that I do this, I find Louie there waiting. I can't believe this. Why has he gone so far out of his way to get me?

It turns out he hasn't gone an inch out of his way. When he says to me, "Ante up your nickel, Gus," he doesn't even realize I'm not at my regular place. He's been shaking down every kid operating at Bohack's just as he has those at the A&P. Both places are standard stops for him. When he leaves I ask the other fellows with carts if there's a store anywhere in the vicinity where you can work and not have to pay a nickel to Louie. "Yeah," answers one, "he's not at the A&P on Flatbush Avenue near Caton."

"Then that's where I'll be next Saturday," I say.

"Don't waste your time," the kid responds, "Louie isn't there but Eugene is and he charges a dime."

As the weeks pass my savings grow. I make around a dollar every weekend and bank about half of it. Unhappily my mother makes me tithe a dime to the church. I'm unhappy with that. I raise all kinds of objections. But her wants prevail. I give grudgingly

As far as I'm concerned the church and Louie are two of a kind.

By the time the baseball season is underway, my growing bankroll is making me feel like a hot shot. I offer to treat my Dad to a Dodger game. He smiles at the offer and tells me he'll think about it. I know that means either he'll treat me or we won't go.

When my mother hears of this, she takes my invitation seriously and as usual expands upon it to ruin it. She thinks I should treat Matthew too.

"Not on your life," I declare.

Anger flashes on her face. I realize I'm treading on dangerous ground but I'm determined not to yield. "Matthew doesn't hardly know what baseball's about. He wouldn't appreciate it," I say.

"I'm certain he would. As for his not knowing what baseball's about, well, that's all the more reason for you to take him. Now he'll learn."

I know by her tone that further discussion will be a waste of time. We'll go to Ebbet's Field on Saturday of next week when the Cardinals will be in town. I'll be treating. Doing this for my Dad pleases me. Doing it for my brother makes me pray for a rain out.

On the Friday before the game, I lug groceries as usual. On Saturday I know that if we're to be at the ballpark early enough to get good seats and to watch all of the batting practice, I'll not be able to work more than a couple of hours in the morning. Since Louie will still extract a nickel from me whether I'm on hand for five minutes or for a full day, I decide to take the day off totally.

We get to Ebbet's Field just as it opens. I shell out $3.30 for our three grandstand seats. We get good ones between home and third. We're only one row behind the more expensive reserved seats. We're so close to the field that no poles supporting the upper tier can block our view.

When the Dodgers come out, many of them are accompanied by their sons wearing tailor made Brooklyn uniforms. You can tell whose kid each is by the number he wears on the back of his shirt. Every kid has on his Dad's. Four of the boys are the children of Dolph Camilli, my next favorite Dodger after Pete Reiser. Pistol Pete, of course, as a twenty three year old bachelor has no youngsters of his own. Nonetheless to the delight of everyone in the grandstand, especially me, he proves that he's going to make a wonderful dad when he pitches a one-inning pick up game with all of the kids of the other ball players. They can't play longer because of the time. The Dodger infielders need the diamond for practice as do the Cardinals.

The game itself is a honey. We slaughter the Cardinals 10 to 4. Enos Slaughter, whom Giant fans claim to be the second only to Mel Ott as a right fielder, misjudges a fly ball and drops it at the wall near the 297 foot sign. Brooklyn's Dixie Walker, who anyone with half a brain knows to be the world's greatest right fielder, would have made that a routine catch. The play of the day, however, is made by Reiser on a two out pop fly just behind second. It's a ball that neither Reese nor Herman can reach.

Pistol Pete, however, races in like a blur from Center field and makes a shoe string catch an inch off the ground. Then his forward momentum sends him somersaulting twice onto the infield grass. When he drops the ball on the pitcher's mound and heads for the dugout, everyone, even the Cardinal fans, cheer wildly. We know we'll never see an athletic feat more spectacular than this.

Dad buys each of us a drink, a hot dog and a bag of peanuts. He also takes care of the carfare. On the way home he thanks me for buying the tickets and says he's proud of me. Matthew says the same. I say, "Thanks, it was my pleasure."

It was.

On Friday, when I'm back at the A&P, I decide I've had enough of Louie. When he comes by to collect everyone's nickel, I warn him, "I've told my Dad I've been paying you a nickel every time I work. He said that if I ever pay you a red cent again, he'll beat the hell out of me and he'll run you ass upstate into a Reformatory. He says he'll be by in a patrol car sometime today to get from you all the money you stole from me and these other guys."

"Don't sling me that horse s---. Your old man's no cop. Pay up."

"Louie, it's your funeral. I said I won't pay the nickel and I won't. I'll just sit here and wait. When my dad comes and wants to know why I'm not out there carting groceries, I'll tell him why. Then tomorrow you be packing to go to Mattewan."

"It won't work, Gus. Now cough up your nickel."

"As I hand him the coin, I say, "You can't blame me for trying. In my place, Louie, you'd do the same, wouldn't you?"

Then he looks at me with a smirk worthy of the chief auditor of the IRS and says, "I wouldn't be in your place."

He figures he's gotten the last word in. I don't say anything to make him think otherwise. I just smile inwardly and think "Nor would I ever be in yours."

Chapter 17

The Legionnaires

One summer day shortly after Frankie gets bounced out of the Boy Scouts for being underage, he gathers the gang together and tells us that from now on we're going to be legionnaires.

"What's legionnaires?" asks Kevin.

"Guys that live in desert forts and kill sheiks," answers Fats.

"We're going to be different kinds of legionnaires," says Frankie.

"Of course," agrees Fats, "we ain't got the sand here to be real legionnaires like in *Beau Geste*. And we ain't got real guns either."

"We're going to be Boy Legionnaires. Kind of like Boy Scouts. Only more so," explains Frankie. "We're going to have ranks, too. Owls will be as high as you can go. Since I'm the creator of this organization, I'm an Owl."

"Terrific, Frankie," says Slim. "Can I be an Owl too?"

"Anyone can be an Owl. All you gotta do is pass the tests. But right now, you're all Soft-Hands. That's as low as you can get unless you've got no rank at all."

"What's between Soft-Hands and Owls?" asks Kevin.

"Second Rates, First Rates, Comets and Death Scouts. I mean Legionnaires, Death Legionnaires. Let's see, one of you had better be second in command."

Frankie points at me and says, "Gus, you will be second in command and your rank as of now is Second Rate Legionnaire."

"Gee, thanks Frankie," I reply. What an honor!

"All you guys line up on Gus," he goes on. "I'm going to put some discipline into you."

Frankie then put us in two rows and shows us how to do left face, right face, forward march and halt.

After a while, Fats and Kevin complain. They're bored. They say they don't care any longer to be legionnaires.

"It ain't always going to be like this," says Frankie, "But you've got to learn to drill so you can prove that you can take it."

"Take what?" challenges Kevin.

"It!" thunders Frankie.

"Okay," says Kevin, "don't get your balls in an uproar. All I did was ask cause I didn't hear."

"You hear now?"

"Yeah."

A few days pass. We're shaping up as Legionnaires. But we're awfully bored. Everyone would take French Leave except everyone knows Frankie'll beat the hell out of a quitter. So we just grumble and gripe.

Around the middle of the week Frankie gives the ranks "At Ease" and makes a speech: "You guys look pretty good. You look brave, tough and well-disciplined. You look like Legionnaires. If you wore uniforms everyone in Brooklyn would point at you and say, 'There goes a troop of real Legionnaires.' I don't need to tell you I'm proud of each and every one of you, cause I am. So on Saturday we're going to celebrate the Legion's coming of age by going on a real hike to New Jersey. Everyone will need two nickels for the subway. So save your movie money and show up after lunch with the coins and a can of beans. We'll eat in the field, campfire style. That's it, Legionnaires. Tensh-hut. Dismissed."

We break ranks cheering. What excitement! We're going to cross the Hudson and see America.

On Saturday a little after noon, the Legion begins to assemble. Because it has rained heavily since yesterday and didn't stop until an hour or so ago, I haven't been able to make money delivering groceries. I have neither the nickels for the subway nor any money to buy beans for the hike. I try to borrow two bits from my mother. She refuses me saying if

I had listened to her when she repeatedly warned me to save something for a rainy day, I should not now be coming to her for a quarter. She tells me the overnight rain has been God's way of punishing me for my inability to handle my finances in a responsible manner.

Even though it's ridiculous to suppose that God sends all of New York and the eastern seaboard a 24 hour rain merely to teach me a lesson, I tell her she's right. I've learned my lesson. I'll never be so short sighted again.

"Good," she says.

"Since it won't ever happen again, maybe you could change your mind and lend me a quarter till next week."

"I said 'no' and I meant no. If you have such a pressing need for money, why don't you take your cart to the A&P and earn it? The store will be very busy. Every woman who couldn't get out yesterday or this morning will be doing her shopping this afternoon."

"But I've got to do something with the Legion."

"You no more have got to do something with that Legion of yours than you have got to deliver groceries. The choice is yours. I'm not giving you any money, period. Now go away and stop annoying me."

I go downstairs to the street.

"Where's your beans, Gus?" asks Fats.

"I'll have them when we leave," I lie. I don't want to admit I can't go. It would make me look poor. What's more, I don't want to face a court martial and be reduced in rank to a Soft-Hand for missing the trip. So I pretend everything is okay in order to put off for as long as possible the embarrassment awaiting me.

A few minutes go by.

Dad comes around the corner on his way home from his part-time title searching work. Matthew and his friends run to him to greet him and to get hugged and kissed. I join them.

All of the legionnaires are ready to leave as I return up the block with my dad and the little kids.

"Are you coming, Gus?" they ask.

"Guess I can't, fellows."

"You boys must be going to the movies," says my Dad.

To stay out of trouble, a few of the guys nod 'yes.'

"Have you eaten lunch, Gus?" asks Dad.

"Yeah."

"And Matthew?"

"I just finished it," he answers.

"Then here's a thirty five cents. Take Matthew with you and share a box of candy."

"Gee, thanks," I say as I take the change.

We join the gang.

When we're around the corner on Nostrand Avenue, Fats asks "Where's your beans?"

"Hold on," I say.

I dart across the street to Tropfke's Deli and have two cans of them put on my mother's tab. I then rejoin the gang and we head for the subway.

When we start down the stairs, Matthew begins protesting and crying. He says Dad has given us the money to go to the movie and that's where we should be going.

"Well, we ain't," I tell him and add, "so shut up or I'll really give you something to cry about."

"I want to go to the movie. I'm telling Dad."

I haul off and sock him.

He bawls louder.

I sock him again.

It doesn't help.

Frankie butts in. "Matthew," he says, "you know about the Legionnaires."

"You won't let me be one," he says while continuing to whimper.

"Only on account of your age. But every Legion needs its water boy. Remember Gunga Din. He was a better man than anyone in uniform. He blew his bugle and saved his legion."

"I remember that," says Matthew, "and I remember the snakes."

"Well, I'm appointing you to be our water boy, our Gunga Din. No one else can have that honor. Now let's see. Since you can't carry water cause we ain't got none, you can carry beans.

He turns towards me and orders, "Give him the beans, Gus."

"Nuts to that, he'll drop them and lose them."

"I said he carries the beans. Now give them to him."

Reluctantly I hand the bag with our two cans to Matthew.

He accepts them with a smile and a giggle and follows us down the stairs to the train.

To everyone's surprise in riding the subway, we don't get lost. Mostly this is due to our pestering the other passengers to be sure that the train we're on is the 7th Avenue-Broadway Express to 242nd Street, Van Cortland Park. We're lucky. It is.

Riding this train is no picnic. The IRT is probably the oldest and worst of the city's subways. Its cars are noisy and filthy. The seats are set sideways and woven of hard straw. We sit in the first car. We're there because we had hoped to be able to look out of the front window next to the engineer's and see the path of the train unfolding itself through the dark tunnels. But unlike the BMT, the IRT motorman's cab covers most of the head of the first car and blocks our view. So we sit and wait as stop by stop the train crawls through Brooklyn and lower Manhattan as a local.

An hour drags by.

In New York just beyond Columbia University, the train bursts out of the black and becomes an El. The light of day surprises and cheers us. We stand up on our seats and gaze out of the windows. We're way up. Maybe three floors above the street. The train pulls into and out of a station and goes back underground. Fats jokes saying that it must have seen it shadow which means we'll have six more weeks of no school.

Soon it's 168th Street--our stop. We get out and start up the stairs. They're many and steep. As the station is just a couple of miles beyond the El, we can't figure out how we had gotten down so deep. But on reaching the street, we realize that the train hadn't descended. Instead, we discover that 168th Street is on the top of a very long and very high hill. It's on the same level as the George Washington bridge.

It's a warm, clear, bright, afternoon. We can look across the Hudson and see crags and dents in the Jersey palisades. We marvel at the sight of the river flowing imperceptibly so far below us. Its water isn't colored gray like the Atlantic Ocean. Nor is it blue like in technicolor movies. It's green. An ugly, clouded pea soup shade of green.

A barge passes under the bridge and inches its way down river. In its wake another shade of green appears which makes the Hudson look like it's made of creamy pea soup. We watch in wonder. Our brains tell us the water can't possibly be soup. Our eyes say it can't be anything else.

We cross the street and head for the sidewalk that runs along the north side of the bridge. Far below on a riverside road, cars that appear to be little more than toys move quietly along. Ahead loom the Jersey Palisades. They seem forbidding and ominous. Fats says they look like King Kong's wall. He jokes that their purpose is to keep us, the riff-raff of New York from entering America.

As the Legion advances onto the bridge, we become conscious and fearful of the height. We stay away from the river railing and walk in a line close to traffic. We're scared--especially me. I feel that if I get too near the railing invisible demons will shove me over the side or magnetically draw me to leap to my death.

About half way across the river Kevin says, "I wonder how high up we are?"

"Let's spit and find out." says Frankie. Then turning to me he commands, "Gus, go spit and we'll time our height by counting the seconds till it hits the water."

"My mouth is too dry to spit. Let someone else do it."

"A volunteer," calls Frankie to the Legion.

No one volunteers.

"Are you guys too yellow to spit like legionnaires?"

"It ain't that," returns Kevin, "we just ain't got spit in our mouths. It's probably due to the altitude."

"Horses---," says Frankie. "You're yellow."

A long pause follows.

"You're all chickens," he goes on. "If there was one thing about any member of this legion that I would have sworn to be true, it would have been that he'd spit off of a bridge. Whoever heard of a kid who wouldn't spit off of a bridge? Why it's as natural as hollerin' for an echo in a tunnel or peeing to put out a fire. I never heard of a kid who wouldn't spit off of a bridge. But I've heard of it now."

"That ain't fair," says Kevin, "let's see you spit."

"I will in a minute but first I want one of you to do it to hold up the honor of the legion."

He waits.

No one spits. No one even salivates.

"I'll make a Comet Legionnaire out of the first guy to spit."

"I'll spit," says Matthew.

"Oh no you won't," I butt in. "If you try to spit you'll fall off of the bridge. And Mother will beat me for letting you. If that happens, I'll really give it to you."

"All right," says Frankie. "I'm going to spit and you guys are going to count one Mississippi, two Mississippi, three Mississippi and so on. Fats will give me 'ready, set, go.' Are you ready?"

"Ready," we reply.

"Go ahead Fats," he orders.

"Ready. Set. Go."

"Ptoohey," spits Frankie. He stands by the railing and watches it fall.

"One Mississippi, two Mississippi, three Mississippi, four Mississippi, five Mississippi, six Mississippi," we chant.

"No good," says Frankie. "I didn't get off a powerful enough spit. But even with a hooker I don't think it would have worked. Gimme a can of beans."

We hand him his own.

"Okay Fats. Give me 'ready, set, go' and the rest of you count as before."

"Ready. Set. Go," shouts Fats.

Frankie drops the beans.

"One Mississippi, two Mississippi, three Mississippi, four Mississippi, five," we counted.

"It hit," shouts Frankie. "How high did we get?"

"We were just starting into five Mississippi," answers Brother.

Then five times five and add a zero is two hundred and fifty. That's how many feet high we are. Two hundred and fifty feet."

"Horses---," says Kevin.

"Horses---! What the hell do you mean, horses---?" demands Frankie.

"Horses--- because it doesn't make sense."

"You're stupid, Kevin. You know that? You're stupid! I did it scientific. Something that takes five seconds to fall is up two hundred and fifty feet. The rule is take the number of seconds and multiply it by itself and then add a zero. Five times five is twenty-five and a zero added makes two hundred and fifty feet. That proves it, B.V.D."

"Yeah. Well, if you had dropped a feather instead of the beans, you'd have put us on Mount Everest."

"Up yours, Kevin," I say, "Frankie did it scientific. We're up two hundred and fifty feet."

"Yeah, up yours, Kevin," echoes Matthew.

"I don't know why I bother to argue with a moron," says Frankie.

"I don't know why you asked, 'How high up we are?' if you ain't gonna accept the answer anyway."

Then Frankie looks at the rest of us and says, "Let's get goin'. We're wastin' time."

We resume our march in single file. We stay as far away from the railing and walk as close to traffic as we dare. In ten minutes we set foot on the soil of New Jersey.

We turn north and move along a cindery path next to the highway. Across the road there's nothing but trees. On our right a hundred feet of shrubs, weeds and crabgrass separate us from the edge of the cliffs. The river can't be seen but Manhattan is visible. It looks beautiful. I feel homesick for it and for Brooklyn.

We pass a sign reading Fort Lee. I remember that's where Joe Louis trains. I decide to keep an eye open for him. Just imagine, me running into the Champ.

Soon on the other side of the highway a clearing comes into view. Frankie declares it to be our campsite. When the traffic breaks we rush across the road and occupy it.

This is where we'll build our fire," announces Frankie. "Gus you take Brother and Matthew and rustle up some firewood for fuel. Fats, you stand guard. Slim and Kevin, help me set up the campsite."

In a few minutes we're seated on rocks and on a fallen log around a fire.

"Throw the beans into the fire," orders Frankie.

We toss the cans in and wait.

"This camping scene is boring," says Kevin. "It reminds me of the lousy time I had fishing with my uncle off of the pier at Canarsie."

"Kevin, you're a cluck," responds Frankie. "Fishing is fishing and camping's camping and they ain't got nothin' in common except they're different from street stuff."

"Yeah," says Fats.

"Yeah," agrees the rest of us.

"Let's sing," says Frankie.

"Why?" asks Kevin.

"Cause we got a camp fire and everyone sings by a campfire. You know what? You're stupid. You really are. You don't know nothin'. And every time you open your yap, you prove it."

"What'll we sing?" asks Brother.

"Something we all know," answers Frankie, "like Clementine."

"I don't know it," says Kevin.

"Then shut up or hum."

"Oh my darling," begins Frankie and we chime in, "Oh my darling, Oh my darling, Oh my darling, Clementine.

Oh my darling, Oh my darling, Oh my darling, Clementine."

By the time we repeat this through three choruses even Kevin knows the words.

Suddenly a can pops and blows open. Pop goes another and it hisses too.

We stop singing.

"Why are they doing that?" asks Kevin as he points to the cans in the fire.

"Why shouldn't they?" returns Frankie.

"Yeah, why not?" we echo.

"When my mother cooks beans they don't do that."

"That, stupid, is cause she ain't cooking campfire style."

Another can pops and hisses. Then one blows beans all over the fire.

"They're doing that," continues Frankie, "cause campfire style cooking brings out the true flavor of the food. What you've seen and what you've heard is the farts escaping from the beans. Eat beans cooked the way your mother does and you fart. Cook them the campfire way and they fart their own farts. No one ever got the runs eating beans cooked campfire style."

"Kevin you sure are stupid," says Brother.

"Yeah," I agree. Frankie's brilliance awes me.

After Frankie gets burned and blistered recovering the beans, we sit back and eat them. Mine are half hot, half cold and thoroughly seasoned with ashes and dirt.

"These sure are the best beans I ever ate," says Matthew.

"Mine, too," agrees Fats.

"Yeah," I join in, never realizing I'm not telling the truth.

When we finish the beans, Frankie decides we'd better head back home. It's already past four. We put out the fire and hold a formation. Frankie gives us a speech. Then we pay New Jersey, "Two, four six, eight, who do we appreciate. New Jersey! New Jersey! New Jersey!"

We leave the campsite and retrace our way back onto the bridge. When we're about half way across, Matthew moans that he's tired.

"Keep moving!" I holler.

"I can't," he cries.

I go to hit him. He runs to the railing and screams, "If you hit me, I'll jump."

I'm scared. He'd jump all right. I know that.

Frankie comes over and bends down. He tells Matthew to ride him piggy back. He carries him the rest of the way across the bridge.

That night when we get home, our mother scolds us for staying too long at the movies. Matthew never squeals about where we've been. I keep my mouth shut too.

Then she feeds us a dinner of franks and beans, regular style. We're sent to bed early as punishment for not coming home sooner. We don't mind that. We're tired, anyway.

Chapter 18
The Irish

Until he studies geography no kid in Brooklyn can believe that Ireland isn't the size of Asia. In New York the Irish are everywhere, even in Harlem. Gram says they multiply like bacteria and if in a thousand years the niggers and chinks fail to squeeze us whites off of the planet, it will be only because the Irish do it first. Every neighborhood in the borough teems with them. Irish lads playing ball in the streets are as familiar to the eyes as Irish dads whetting their whistles in the saloons. Our sidewalks are flooded with their kids leap frogging, flipping cards and shooting checkers. Everywhere their girls can be seen skipping rope, playing jacks and spreading gossip. If they're not engaged in these practices, it's a safe bet that they're planning new ways to attract and to torment boys. The older ones manage this by flirting; the youngers, by existing. In every sense in every borough in New York the Irish are a catholic presence. Their culture, their brogues and their bigotry are as common, familiar and unnoticeable to us as is the horse manure in the streets.

Of the many games we kids play, a boring but revealing one is I Declare War. Generally it begins with the toughest kid on the block naming himself America and the second toughest, Ireland. Occasionally it's vice versa. The rest of us then pick countries of our own particular likings or descents. Normally, I'm Canada. For the record, it must be noted that we always have an Italy, often a Poland, seldom a China and never a Palestine.

One day while choosing up countries, a kid bigger than me takes Canada. My next choice, which I would have liked to have been Hungary, is taken.

As always Wally Sejer, the only other Hunky on the block, gets it before me. When my turn comes I make the mistake of naming myself, Great Britain. For an Episcopalian whose mother and other relatives still sing the words of God Save the King to the anthem, My Country 'tis of Thee, this is understanable. But for a streetwise Protestant treading like a tolerated Muslim on the Holy Sod of County Brooklyn, this is insane and suicidal. Needless to say, I spend the day as a target for beaning. Every nation has it in for me. When occasionally one doesn't, it isn't an act of kindness. It's an arrangement forced on a weak kid by a bully who's finagling a way to get an extra shot at me.

Naturally, I try to renounce my identity. I offer to become Holland. I get socked good for that. So like the real British, I stand alone against the evil nations and get blitzed and bombed repeatedly.

As the afternoon wears on, the Irish arms under a league of national guises begin to tire. In any event everyone's throwing becomes as wild as Kirby Higbe's. I'm pleased with that. While getting hit by a hollow rubber Spalding can't be compared with getting zapped by a hardball, it still hurts. It won't break bone but it sure can sting. Anyway, the harder the kids throw at me, the more errant sail their throws. Many are cussing at me for being such a rotten target but more are razzing the missers. As the heckling continues, tempers soar and bitterness builds. Finally the nations become far more furious with each other than they are with me. As usual the game ends in a free-for-all. Finland gets its nose bloodied. Germany's shirt is ripped. France and Sweden cry. Canada leaves with bruises which will evolve by morning into a shiner and a fat lip. Greece, perhaps least fortunate of all, gets punched accidentally in the nuts.

Great Britain, wearing the welts of war, strategically withdraws as at Dunkirk to the safety of home.

My personal feelings towards the Irish are divided. Those I like, I love. Those I don't like, I hate. There's no middle ground. This is because there are no micks in the middle. The Irish always have been either fun loving Errol Flynns or cold nasty Nazis. With their women it's been much the same--especially in beauty. God has made Irish girls either in the image either of Gene Tierney or of wart hogs with freckles.

Once I told my Dad how I envied the Irish. They were so sure of everything whether it was Catholicism as the true faith or Notre Dame as the best university. He smiled. He told me the Irish once were just as positive of the flatness of the Earth and of the existence of leprechauns. The Catholic church, he said, was neither better nor worse than most other churches. Then he went to the secretary and got out some papers and read to me two quotes from the 48th Manual of the Christian Doctrine. It was a kind of catechism for Catholic adults published in 1926. It stated that liberty of conscience, of worship, of speech and of the press was evil.

"Now tell me," says my Dad, "whether a religion which calls upon its followers to condemn almost every freedom in the opening sentence of the Bill of Rights can ever be one which a thoughtful, decent American would convert to?"

Sidestepping the question, I reply that although most of the Catholics that I know are intolerant, I still can't believe they can be against all of the democratic things the catechism deplores.

My Dad confesses that neither can he. Religion, he suggests, hasn't got much to do with reason or sense. Because of cultural beliefs, traditions and emotional needs, people tend to accept authority without question. It takes courage to think for yourself. To refute popular convictions and to oppose those who propound them is risky. Most people are cowards because to be so is safe and sensible. In this Protestants and Catholics don't differ at all. Logic and reason have no place in Catholicism or in Protestantism because both religions when boiled down to their essence are Jewish and each of these branches of Judaism is dedicated to the destruction of all other Jews either through proselytism, forced conversion or annihilation.

Whenever my Dad gets philosophical like this, he loses me. So what I tend to do on such occasions is to agree with him. “Right Dad, gotcha,” I say and then I leave.

Brother Branigan’s real name isn’t Brother. Nor is his sister, Sister Branigan, named, Sister. Brother has been christened Francis Xavier and Sister, Bridgette Bernadette. But as their mother calls them Brother and Sister and as they called each other Brother and Sister, we kids on the block do the same. Their Dad takes a different tack. He calls Brother, “Boy-boy”; Sister, “Girl-girl” and Mrs. Branigan, “Wife of mine.”

In February, when Brother moves onto our block, his dad has just been promoted to sergeant on the Police Force and has just taken over the job as the Police Athletic League (P.A.L.) Director in our neighborhood. Before that he had been pounding a beat in the Bedford Stuyvesant area. That was where so many negroes lived that Brother called it Brooklyn’s answer to Harlem. Anyway while on duty late one night Brother’s dad had shot and killed two unarmed drunken colored guys as they were trying to sneak into a closed saloon through a back yard bathroom window. On the following evening as a protest against the slayings, the people of the community gathered at a local church and held a memorial service. When it ended a group of about one hundred negroes led by the minister of the church marched to the Precinct headquarters. There the minister and a small group of elders went into the station to lodge a formal protest. Meanwhile, the others stayed outside and chanted in unison for the dismissal of Brother’s dad.

According to Brother who overheard his Dad telling his mother what had actually happened, the newspaper story which described the events of that night were part fact but mostly fiction. The reporter, Denny Boyle, who wrote the account that went out over the wire service was never near the scene. He got the story in a call from his brother-in-law, the Desk Sergeant on the scene.

The protest outside of the station lasted nearly a half of an hour.

Flash bulb pictures were taken of it and the negatives were dispatched to Denny Boyle at the paper.

On the following morning all of New York awoke to learn that the protest, which no one in Bedford Stuyvesant knew not to be peaceful, had in fact been a riot. Pictures of the demonstrators filled the front page and center fold of the morning tabloid. All of pages two and three carried details of the non-existing account under Denny Boyle's byline.

Armed with what they assumed to be the sacred truth of the written word, New York's citizenry responded as expected. They rushed to Officer Branigan's defense. As one letter to the editor, typical of the rest, put it:

Dear Editor:

Tom Branigan, a humble, decent and devout officer – loyal to his department, his city and his country--has done his duty. He has fired the shots heard 'round our world. He has upheld law and order.

Now it is up to New York and to New York's Finest to hear and heed the voice of virtue. To requests for Patrolman Branigan's dismissal there can be but one answer, NO. To the shiftless, relief-riding rioters who seek his badge, let Officer Branigan's bravery signal a warning: Obey the Law.

May the good Lord bless Tom Branigan and his family. May the wrath of the Almighty be spewed like scalding vomit onto the heads of the unholy bums and bigots who rioted.

Yours with Christian concern, Terrence P. O'Connor
Jackson Heights

A week after the shootings, Officer Branigan was promoted to sergeant, transferred to Flatbush and made the P.A.L. director of our district. As for Denny Boyle, he collected in 1943 some kind of prize for on the scene reporting.

Brother's dad begins his work as District Director by instituting a new policy for the baseball program. He decides that no P.A.L. sports equipment will ever be used for play. "Baseballs," he tells us, "get bruised, scuffed and grass stained. Occasionally, they even lose their covers. Gloves get soiled, spiked and torn. Bats break--even if you do hit with the labels up. Now if any P.A.L. equipment gets lost, broken, stolen or damaged, it won't be you kids who'll hang for it. It will be me. So as long as I'm responsible for the supplies, they'll be kept in grade A condition. They'll stay permanently locked up in the storage room at the station. When it comes time for an inventory, everything will be ship shape and in good order. My superiors will know that when I take charge of a program, I take charge."

Now odd as it may seem, we kids under Branigan soon had more bats, balls and gloves than we could use. The sergeant managed this by shaking down sporting goods shops and confiscating stolen athletic property. Once a month he'd visit his old beat and when going by a sandlot full of negroes he'd stop and search them for knives, brass knuckles, razors and the like. After pocketing the weapons, he'd tell them there was a report of coloreds having stolen baseball items. It was his duty to confiscate the equipment and bring in the thieves. However, as he was in a good mood, he'd settle just to get the equipment back. Then he'd put his hand on his holster and glare. Because everyone knew he was trigger happy, they gave him their stuff. It didn't matter whether or not they had come by the items honestly. They still surrendered them.

Sergeant Branigan once tried the same tactic on a sandlot filled with Jews. He came back from the encounter with terrific stuff. However, as none of it had been stolen, the Yids' parents paraded to the station and reported the incident. The equipment was returned. After that, Brother said his Dad was more discriminate in whom he discriminated against.

As P.A.L. Director, Sergeant Branigan makes himself the coach of our baseball team. After one practice session he assigns us to our positions. Brother, who has a weak arm, he makes shortstop. Mickey McGonigle, who isn't even respectable as a right fielder, he puts at third. Since I'm the only kid with a first baseman's mitt, he leaves me at first.

A couple of days later we hold our first scrimmage against the kids from Martense Street. As the sergeant makes out the line-up he asks me, "What's your last name, Gus?"

"Stern," I answer.

"How do you spell it?" he asks.

"S--T--E--R--N."

"Right Stern," he says, "I've decided to try an experiment. I'm going to put McGonigle on first. Riley at third and send you to right field."

"But I'm better than Mickey. He can't even catch."

"I know," he agrees, "but you're too small a target. Mickey just needs practice to improve."

By the time we play our first game and lose I'm a sub. By the time we play our third, I'm cut.

That makes Frankie Casey, our pitcher, mad. He tells Sergeant Branigan that there isn't a kid on the diamond without an Irish name. Then he calls him a narrow-back bigot and quits the team.

"And none too soon," shouts Branigan, "I would have cut you anyway. Your pitching stinks. All you know how to do is lose."

That night as we sit around sulking, Frankie says to Brother, "I don't think you're father's too bright."

"He isn't," agrees Brother, "and my mother and sister are daft too."

"Why don't you tell your Dad he's screwing up the works? He's cut good guys and put in worse guys just cause they're Irish."

"Why don't I tell him? Cripes, you're as dumb as him. No one tells my old man anything. No one can talk to him. You either listen to his sermons or you avoid him. I make it my business never to be around him except when I have to be."

"Yeah," says Frankie, "I see your point. fathers, in general, ain't worth dick. Mine's a drunk. He beats me every time he sees me so I avoid him too."

I interrupt to say, "I like my Dad."

"Yeah, everyone does. But he's a fluke," returns Frankie. Then turning to Brother, he adds, "All in all, I think I'm better off than you. I'd rather have a child beating drunk for a father than a sober prick."

"So would I," agrees Brother.

I've never heard anyone speak that way about a parent.

Although what they say is true, to me it seems neither proper nor right.

Frankie and Brother are maturing. They're old enough to have developed some of the qualities of thought that still are denied to me. Only a year and a half of age separates us. I guess that at times like this it shows.

Because we were on the outs with the P.A.L. Frankie decides to join the Flatbush Boys Club (F.B.C.)

"I've heard about that place," says Brother. "To get in you have to let a doctor examine you. He not only looks up your ass but he also jabs a finger up your groin and says, 'Cough.'"

"I ain't joining," I say.

"Me neither," follows Brother.

"Jesus H. Christ! You guys are something. You know that," scolds Frankie, "You really are. Afraid of a medical examination. Hell, all the Doc does is check to see if you're ruptured. It doesn't hurt a bit. In fact it's over in three seconds. Once the physical's done and you're enrolled in the club, you can do anything. It ain't like the P.A.L. The F.B.C. has everything. And it let's you use it. They give out free tickets to Dodger games, to the circus, to the Rodeo and to the Ice Show. They've got a swimming pool, a gym, a game room and a library. They even have an auditorium where they show movies for a nickel on Friday nights. What's more the dues are only a dime for three whole months. It's an unbeatable bargain. You're stupid if you don't join."

"Then I guess I'm stupid because I ain't joining," I say.

"Me neither," adds Brother, "No one is going to poke his finger up my groin."

On Friday night Frankie takes the exam and joins the club. One week later he goes through another exam but this time joins as me. Then a couple of weeks later, he does the same for Brother.

In the fall when we try out for the F.B.C. 90 lb. basketball team, Frankie makes first string. Brother and I have no trouble with the weigh-in but still we're cut. Coach Chebychev tells us to keep playing and learning. He tells us to come out and try again next year. He says he's sure we'll grow bigger and stronger and we'll improve with practice.

Although getting cut hurts, it isn't too bad. The coach has been fair. Only better guys make the team. Unless I'm shooting lay-ups I can't reach the basket.

After Thanksgiving, two starters, the Clancy twins move away. One week later as a result of a fall endured during horseplay in the locker room, our best sub, Roscoe Ryan, breaks his right arm. The team needs replacements. As Brother and I have been playing half court pick-up games daily, Coach C. calls us into his office and says, "Okay, you gym rats, we're playing Grand Street in an hour. You've just made the 90 pound team. Come on downstairs and get your uniforms."

We're each handed a set of F.B.C. blue and whites and given "Congratulations." It's a proud moment. I wear number 19.

Our opponents from Grand Street stink. They haven't a decent shooter. Everything everyone of them throws up from beyond five feet out lacks an arc. Even their foul shots are tossed like darts. We trounce them 46 to 11. In the third quarter with the game safely on ice, Coach puts the scrubs in. Then thanks to Brother's feeds, I get four points and thanks to mine he gets two.

The following week the team goes on an away game. It's at the Jefferson Street Boys Club. There the gym is rimmed with a balcony. On it fans lean against the railing and spit down on us as we drive in for lay-ups. Usually, they miss us. But their saliva makes the court under our basket slick and slimy. Once the ball is dribbled in spit, no one wants to handle it.

Late in the third quarter, Frankie cuts towards the basket on a give-and-go and slips. He falls on his rump and skids off the court until the wall stops him. The fans laugh. Frankie doesn't think it's funny. He rubs his can and cusses at them. They, in turn, cheer mockingly and razz him back. At this, Frankie grows furious. He invites the whole goddamned lot of them to come down and get their asses whipped.

The Ref tells him to calm down.

"F--- you," shouts Frankie.

The ref throws him out of the game.

Even with Frankie gone, our guys hang on and nose out the Jeffersons 23 to 19. It's a great victory. Although neither Brother nor I play, we share in the glory.

After the game Frankie apologizes to the ref. Nonetheless, he draws a ten day suspension and has to miss playing in our next two victories.

In the middle of January 1943, our family moves to 954 East 48th Street. Just before we leave for the new home, Frankie serves out his suspension and is allowed to take part in the last game I play that season for the F.B.C. 90 lb. team. It's an away date on a Sunday against the Grand Street Boys Club. They're the Jewish kids who lost to us by the score of 46 to 11 and who held me to 4 points and Brother to two. We look forward to stomping them again.

Because the game is on a Sunday, only six of us make the trip. Even the coach doesn't come. Mr. Chebychev says he isn't going to give up his day of rest just because the Hebes can't get their calendar straight. So he puts Frankie in charge as player-coach and gave him six dimes to cover our subway fares.

Although it's winter, the day is fairly warm. The trip to Grand Street proves to be long and slow. We have to change trains and go local all the way.

The East side, where Grand Street is located, looks like it belongs to another world. The place teems with tenements and overflows with people. Everywhere you look, the narrow streets are crowded, noisy and filthy. One fellow sets up a portable stand and opens a suitcase filled with neck ties. He begins hawking them for a nickel. As onlookers gather to catch the bargains, they find the five cent price only applies to two chintzy, ugly items. Everything else is much more expensive. When a policeman starts coming towards the sidewalk salesman, he immediately folds up his shop and disappears into the crowd. It's an unreal scene of strange people in strange dress. It doesn't look like New York. It looks like Hollywood depicting the Jewish section of Warsaw.

When we reach the Grand Street Boys Club we find it housed in two adjacent tenements. Although both buildings are four storeys high, their floors are not at the same level. We go into the club, identify ourselves and are given a guide to take us upstairs to the locker room. To get to it we're brought through the gym.

The Grand Street Boys Club Gym is every bit as pathetic as the Grand Street Boys Club itself. Half the basketball court is in one-building. In the other at a level of at least one foot higher is the other half. Because the two ceilings are about ten and eleven feet high respectively, the heights of both baskets are below regulation. At center court a ramp connects the two floors and in fair territory columns are present to hold up the separate roofs.

After changing into our uniforms, we begin practicing our warm up drills. We soon discover that any shot that isn't a lay-up has to be a line drive. Anything aimed with an arc hits the ceiling and bounces down before the goal.

We begin the game with great confidence. In Brooklyn, we've

smeared these guys. However, as play progresses we find ourselves in a tough and even battle. The Grand Streeters know how to exploit their home court advantage. They keep backing us up into the pillars while we keep tumbling up and down the center court ramp. Nearly every pass or shot we fire hits the ceiling. At half time we trail 7 to 5. By the end of the third quarter we've rallied to at 9-9 tie. At the close we lose 13 to 12.

After the game Frankie is furious. In the locker room which we share with the Grand Streeters, he cusses a blue streak. The rest of us stay silent. We know that any comment we'd offer would only cross him.

One of the Grand Streeters, however, speaks up. He tells Frankie that he shouldn't be such a sore head. Basketball is just a game. Winning and losing isn't half as important as winning and losing with grace. Finally, he says we should accept defeat like men. We've been beaten fair and square by a better team.

"Better team, my ass," returns Frankie. "It's this court that won it for you. You guys ran it like rats in a maze. When I think that we left our palace in Brooklyn to come over here to play dart ball in a s--- house, I get sick. Next year when you return to visit us, we'll make you feel at home. Instead of playing in the gym we'll take you on in the latrine and use the toilet bowls for baskets."

Hurt shows on the face of the kid from Grand Street but he answers calmly, "You guys in Flatbush have it rich. There's no question about that. But remember everything is relative. If we haven't got a building as nice as yours for our Boys Club, at least we've got this one. Think of the poor kids in the country. They haven't got anything."

Frankie, for once, is speechless. So too are the rest of us.

It's a long and silent trip home. As the train rumbles along, I wonder what the others guys are thinking: probably sad and bitter thoughts about our losing. Normally that would have been on my mind too. But this time, it isn't.

Chapter 19

Slim Finn

In 6A[1] I catch up with Slim Finn. He has flunked and been left back again. He's now thirteen. Or maybe fourteen. Anyway, he's lots older than the rest of us. Our teacher, Mrs. Zorn, who is only a few years out of college, may be in many respects more his contemporary than we, his classmates.

For a couple of months everyone in the gang had sensed that Slim wasn't behaving like the same old Slim. He had always been a loner. Lately, however, he had become less withdrawn. This allowed his weirdness to become more evident. Still his change in personality had evolved gradually. It had almost escaped notice. Frankie, of course, was the first to spot it. "Slim always was a jerk," he said, "but now he's a jerk-off too."

"True," I agreed, "the jerk's a jerk-off."

One day about three weeks into the school year, Mrs. Zorn marches our class down to the library to give us a free reading period. For five minutes we're allowed to walk around and select books from the shelves. Then we have to take seats at the long library tables. The boys must sit on one side and the girls on the other. A couple of chairs to my left, Slim sits down. Directly across from him is his heartthrob, Mary Lou LaPlace.

Mary Lou isn't a pretty girl. Neither is she ugly. She's what you might call average, except for one exception. She has developed. She has tits.

Anyway, we're ordered to begin reading. Most of my classmates comply. As usual, however, several of us don't. Instead we just pretend to read. Mostly we whisper secrets and pass along notes to each another. Our messages are neither urgent nor important but because they're hushed, they seem so.

Soon our horseplay gets too bold and becomes noticeable. Mrs. Zorn comes over to our table and gives us her evil eye. We all try to look "not guilty." We stare at our open books and sweat.

As soon as Mrs. Zorn is convinced that order has been restored, she leaves. So naturally, we start in again. Slim says something to his neighbor who in turn elbows me and whispers, "Slim says, 'Ain't Mary Lou's tits gorgeous?' Pass it along."

I pass it along.

A minute later, Slim starts another, "Roll me in the grass with Mary Lou LaPlace."

We pass it along.

Across the way, Mary Lou's aware of what's going on. Nonetheless, she tries to look bored, disinterested and nonchalant. She glances to her right, gazes to her left and returns to her reading.

Because she ignores him, Slim grows angry and coins another pass-along: "Her tits sag."

That isn't too original but it gets a rise. "You bore me," whispers Mary Lou in such an exaggerated way that even if you were deaf you could read her lips to know what she's said. Then to emphasize the point she puts her arms up and back and yawns.

The gesture backfires. In stretching, her boobs balloon and became more firm, shapely and prominent. At the sight of them Slim groans with anguish and delight. Then he unbuttons his fly and frees his herman. It's monstrous. Where a cocktail frank hangs on everyone of the rest of us, he sports a knockwurst.

"Wow!" some kid exclaims.

"Wow is right," whispers another, "What a wang!"

It really is unbelievable. As round as a mello-roll and as rigid as steel, it towers to touch the side board under the table top.

Slim puts his hand around it and hunches over to focus a mouth watering stare at Mary Lou's knockers. She does her best to ignore him.

He begins massaging himself.

Across the way the girls know something is up. They have to. We guys have our eyes focused on Slim as though we're his disciples at the Last Supper.

Soon on the other side of the table pens and pencils are being fumbled to the floor. This rash of feminine butterfingering isn't accidental. The girls are taking plenty of time to retrieve their belongings. On rising most wear that look of ladylike innocence which is a dead give away that they've been up to no good. Slim's meat has impressed them.

We boys have been doing our best not to giggle.

Slim strokes his herman like a gambler rattling dice. As he does this, his face grows red. But never redder than his rod. Suddenly he looks like he's having convulsions. Leaning back, he goes rigid as he moans, pants and gasps. Then suddenly he relaxes and goes limp.

I begin laughing. I can't help myself. It's funny. It's scary. It's ridiculous.

Others are now laughing too.

Mrs. Zorn comes towards us. She's on the warpath.

Slim barely has time to force his dong back into his drawers. His fly remains unbuttoned.

The commotion at our table makes Mrs. Zorn furious. With a face colored almost purple with rage, she stands over us screaming. Her anger is intimidating. It terrifies everyone. She is unbelievably mad, so much so that I can smell her wrath. It smells like Chlorox.

Slim's behavior no longer seems funny. Everyone becomes silent. Even though my customary response to terror is to laugh, I manage this time not to do so.

Mrs. Zorn slowly circles our table and glares at me. Menace rather than oxygen seems to be filling the air between us. I'm petrified. It becomes difficult for me to swallow. My tongue feels dry and seems to be swelling like a balloon. I expect it at any moment to cleave to the roof of my mouth and cut off the air going into my lungs. I'm on the verge of panic. Her gaze is making me feel as though I'm a trapped animal about to be skinned alive.

I suppose I have a nervous smile on my face. Looking at me exasperates her. She again screams for silence. When she does, I laugh. I can't help myself. It's an involuntary reflex. It's what happens to me whenever I'm frightened.

"Gregory," she thunders, "stop laughing. Stop laughing this instant."

I try to obey. But I laugh anyway.

She tells me to get up and to follow her.

I do as ordered.

Outside of the library she stops in the hall and grabs me on both arms. She shakes me as she tells me again to stop laughing. When I can't, she backs me to the wall and slaps me as hard as she can. I scream. She slaps me again and drags me by the arm to the outer room of the principal's Office. Meanwhile I keep laughing but I also am crying.

Inside the principal's outer office, she directs me to wait while she goes in to speak with Dr. Polya. I take a seat on the deacon's bench alongside the wall. I feel at home there. It's where I sit whenever I come late to school and have to wait to be given a pass allowing me to get back into class.

While Mrs. Zorn and the principal confer, I get out my hanky, wipe my face, blow my nose and calm down.

In a few minutes my teacher and Dr. Polya come out. She leaves, I suppose, to return to our class in the library. He looks at me and sees that my face is dirty from crying. He sends me off to wash it.

I do as told but take my time in doing so.

When I return, I see Mrs. Zorn is there too. She's talking with Dr. Polya by the entrance to his inside office. I notice too that Slim is seated where I had been on the deacon's bench.

The meeting breaks up as I enter. Mrs. Zorn comes towards me and raises her arm. I flinch. Instead of hitting me, she puts her hand on my shoulder and tells me she's sorry she had yelled at me. Dr. Polya says, "Everything is fine now, Gregory. Return with Mrs. Zorn to class."

He then motions to Slim to come into his office.

As my teacher and I are leaving, I can hear Dr. Polya saying "Slim, I understand you've been playing with your organ."

That's a dirty lie," counters Slim, "I ain't got no organ and even if I did, I still couldn't play it 'cause I don't read music."

Chapter 20
Partners in Crime

There's a distance between Frankie and the rest of us. He's a natural leader. He has admirers but lacks a true friend. Although he inspires trust, we know deep down that he'd use or sacrifice any of us to have his way.

Frankie marches to the beat of a different drummer. Although he has many virtues, Frankie has faults. One of these is that he's a thief.

Whether his thievery is evil or sinful is a judgment I leave to others.

In his stealing Frankie has not been without scruples. He has never robbed individuals nor has he ever broken into anybody's home. Once when he found a lost wallet packed with dollars, he returned it to its owner intact and refused to accept a reward. But in confrontations with corporate businesses, Frankie has had no compunctions. Anything and everything in their possession, he always has regarded as deservedly his for the taking.

The way Frankie approaches a crime leads me to believe he regards thievery as a game as much as a science. Stealing in his eyes requires skill and artistry. To him the object swiped has small significance. The way it's swiped is everything. He never pulls a job on impulse. He cases it first and if necessary, he cases it again. His theory is that crooks get caught not because they're unlucky but because they're stupid and make mistakes. He figures a part of any successful crime involves allowing for the unexpected. There's no room in his thievery for luck because to him only the unlucky believe in luck. An intelligent thief doesn't need it.

Before I joined Frankie as an unwitting partner in crime, he cased me. He assembled the Legion and accused it one day of having in its ranks a thief who had stolen his hunting knife. We each denied being the thief. A few legionnaires looked guilty and none, I suppose, looked it more than me. Frankie saw this but said nothing until we were alone.

"Gus, I know you didn't take my knife. So why did you look guilty?"

"Beats me, Frankie. Some people go through life looking ugly; some, wise; some, happy; some, ordinary. I'm one who does it looking guilty. But tell me, how did you know I didn't steal your knife?"

"Because I never had one. But tomorrow we both will."

The next day we take a walk down Bedford Avenue. As we pass Sears and Roebuck he says, "Let's stop in here."

"I'm not stealing," I warn him.

"Nobody's asking you to," he answers and adds, "Let's go in."

"Inside the store we walk towards the section where the Boy Scout goods are. Half way there Frankie notices one of his classmates from Holy Cross in the store. We take a detour over to see him. Frankie says "hi" to his friend and introduces us. The kid's name is Mad Vinnie Volterra.

As they talk it becomes evident that their meeting has not been accidental. This troubles me. I speak up saying, "If you guys are stealing, I don't want to have anything to do with it."

Mad Vinnie laughs and says, "I ain't never yet seen a kike with guts."

"He ain't no kike," says Frankie, "He's got guts and something better than guts. He's got brains."

Mad Vinnie snickers and walks away. I start to thank Frankie. He says, "Forget it." Then he adds, "Wait here. I want to put that punk in his place."

I watch Frankie walk towards Mad Vinnie who's standing two aisles away and talking to a clerk who suddenly looks at me and hollers, "You, stay where you are."

He starts running towards me. I get scared. I turn and run. The clerk shouts, "Stop thief."

As I flee towards an exit another clerk grabs me. I struggle to get free. He wrestles me to the floor.

The first clerk comes up and stands over me. In a demanding voice he says, "Let's have it."

"Let's have what, you lunatic," I shout. I'm boiling over with both fear and rage. I'm also crying.

"Let's search him," he says to the clerk who is holding me.

I squirm and kick. But together they're too powerful for me. One twists my arm to keep me still while the other searches me.

"Why he doesn't have a thing! Only a handkerchief and a nickel."

"He must have dropped it along the way."

"Dropped what?"

"A hatchet."

"A hatchet? You're out of your mind. If he dropped a hatchet while fleeing, we'd have heard a clunk."

"Well, he had it."

"You saw him with it."

"Well, this other kid did."

"That was Mad Vinnie," I shout, "He's a lunatic who hates me."

"Where's this other kid?" asks the clerk who grabbed me."

"Gone, I guess," says the other, "but what does it matter. This kid here is up to no good. With only a nickel in his pocket, he shouldn't have been in here in the first place."

They let me go and warn me never to come back.

"This is a free country," I shout as I get to the door. "You can't go around beating up and searching people who are innocent. I'll be back. But with my dad who's an attorney and we'll sue you good."

One of them feints as if to rush at me.

I flee and don't stop running until I'm fifty yards away. I look back. Neither clerk is in pursuit. But across the street I spot Frankie. He holds a bag in one hand and waves at me to join him with the other.

We walk towards home. For about a block I relate everything that had happened to me. Then I look over and ask, “What have you got in the bag?”

“Guess?”

“Hunting knives.”

He smiles, reaches into the bag and brings out a beauty with a four inch blade. He says, “Take it. It’s yours.”

“Did mad Vinnie get his?”

“Of course,” he answers as he continues to offer me the knife.

“No thanks,” I say as I wave it away.

“Take it,” he insists.

“Ram it up your ass,” I answer.

“What’s with you? I’m doing you a favor.”

“Like hell you are. I’m a Stern. Like my dad and his dad before him, I’ve a family tradition to uphold. Sterns don’t steal.”

He looks at me as if I’m crazy. Then he puts the knife back into the bag which also contains a hatchet, another knife, a Boy Scout Manual and a compass. As we walk home he does most of the talking.

I continue to play with Frankie but our relationship is never the same. I still respect him but there’s now a chasm between us. He tries a couple of times to bridge it. But all he builds is a bridge to nowhere.

Chapter 21

Dissidents

In the fall of '42 at P.S. 181 anyone who can get back from lunch early gets to play punch ball. I never get back late. Two brothers who manage like me to make every game are the Barrows, Andy and Ed. Andy is a classmate of mine. Ed is a year older. Both are superb athletes. Andy can hit flies off the short center field fence for doubles. Ed can hit them over it for homers. Each is what you'd call a regular guy. Before I discover that they're Quakers, this doesn't surprise me. Afterwards, I'm shocked.

I had pictured Quakers as weird. I didn't know that they lived anywhere except in Pennsylvania. I imagined them all to dress and to look like the Puritan pictured on a box of Quaker Oats. Furthermore, because I had heard they were conscientious objectors and sissified pacifists, I figured they weren't to be trusted. They were reputed to be the kind of people who would rather surrender America to Tojo or Hitler than fight to save it. All they seemed to care about was their religion and their right to say thee and thou.

Although the Barrows are Quakers, they're neither weirdos nor yellow bellies. Like their clothes, their manner and ways seem to be no different from anyone else's. Nor is their speech ever at odds with our own. The boys "you" everyone except each other. When I first notice their mutual thee-ing and thou-ing, I figure they're kidding around. After all who can be told to "go f--- thyself" and take it seriously? While the brothers seldom have run-ins with their friends, they never shy away from scrapping with one another or with a playground bully. I like them both. As far as I'm concerned they have guts enough to be marines. And if all Quakers are like the Barrows, America has a need for a lot more of them.

The Barrows aren't the only kids in the neighborhood with a strange religion. Around Halloween a family of Californians named Heavyside move onto our block. They have a boy, Orville, my age and a girl, Arvella, a year younger. Both kids are characters. Orvie, like his Dad, never wears a necktie. When he first joins our class, he's told by our teacher, Mrs. Zorn, that there's no place for Bolsheviks in the New York City School System. Therefore, he's to go home at lunch time and put on a tie. He's not to reappear in the afternoon without one. At noon he leaves to do as told and doesn't return until the next day. Then once again, he shows up without a tie. Mrs. Zorn hits the roof. When she finally gets a grip on herself she instructs him to return wearing a tie after lunch. He's also ordered to bring a letter from a parent to explain his absence on the previous afternoon.

At one o'clock, there's no compliance. Orvie again has taken the afternoon off. The following morning he comes to class not only without a tie but also without a required letter of excuse. Mrs. Zorn is furious. She informs Orvie she has had it up to here with his absences and with his willful disobedience. She tells him she wants his mother or father to come up to school to see her.

Orvie says that's ridiculous for neither will come.

Instead of telling him to go home again at lunch to get a tie, Mrs. Zorn decides to take him then and there to see the Principal. Before leaving class she gives us a short pointed lecture on why we should sit still and keep silent during her absence.

A few seconds after she and Orvie leave the room, Aaron-the-Cluck Minkowski volunteers to stand watch by the door and to holler "Chickee" when she's returning. Most of us get up from our desks and begin horsing around and having a field day. After a while Stuart Toeplitz, the class clown, gets an idea. He decides to imitate Mrs. Zorn. He calls for a volunteer to play Orvie. Tony Tartaglia obliges.

"Comrade Orvillevitch," says Stu as he picks up an imaginary emery board and files his nails in perfect imitation of Mrs. Zorn, "How dare you come to school wearing a tie? What are you, an imperialist? Don't you know that only criminals, degenerates and New Yorkers wear ties? Are you some sort of pervert?"

"Of course not," answers Tony, "I'm a ballet dancer."

"Well even so, I want you to bring all three of your parents up to school."

"But I'm an orphan."

"Don't try my patience by offering such a feeble excuse. If you"

Stuart never gets to finish his sentence. Mrs. Zorn and Orvie have returned. She stands looking at us by the open door.

Instead of watching for the battle-axe, Aaron-the-Cluck had abandoned his post. He had been laughing with the rest of us at Tony and Stu.

He isn't laughing now.

Nor are we.

Mrs. Zorn just stands there as still and as silent as a live grenade waiting to explode. For an instant so too do we. Then in a kind of mad but understandable burst of pandemonium we scramble for our seats. Within the blink of an eye, order prevails. Mrs. Zorn glares at us and says nothing. She keeps this up for about ten seconds. The tension we feel makes it seem like ten minutes.

Orvie has returned with her. He's wearing an oversized tie which probably belongs to the Principal. Mrs. Zorn motions to him to take his seat. He complies.

Mrs. Zorn is fuming. She informs us that because our behavior has been abominable, she will not begin the morning lesson in arithmetic. She will defer it until eleven o'clock. First she has to deal with our wrongdoing.

She decides to begin our punishment by having us spend the next quarter of an hour in silence. We're to sit with our hands folded at the edges of our desks and contemplate the gravity of our misdeeds. Then we each will be required to write a two page composition on "The

Evils of Disobedience and Talk." After that some of us will be called upon to read our essays aloud for everyone's edification. Although none of us knows what edification means, it doesn't matter. We get the message.

I still have the paper I wrote.

I'm forced to read my composition aloud to the class because as Mrs. Zorn goes walking around the room monitoring us as we write, she says she sees that some of her pupils are missing the point. Later she grades everyone's composition. She only gives me a C for mine. I think I deserve a better grade. My friends agree. Everyone who writes boring stuff and apologizes to her for not behaving like a sissy or a saint gets an A or a B. My paper is different. It makes a hit with everyone except her and the girls. It reads as follows:

P.S. 181 — *Gregory Stern*
6A — *November 4, 1942*

The Evils of Disobedience and Talk

People who disobey rules sooner or later get caught. When that happens, they get spanked or hollered at or sent to jail. Sometimes they are even made to write compositions. After they have suffered enough, they are allowed to be like everyone else: good obeyers.

People who talk always cause trouble. As the war slogan says, "Loose lips sink ships." Girls talk a lot. Because they're sneaky, they don't get caught. They're like politicians. Everyone knows politicians sneak and lie a lot. They're crooks. Because so few of them go to jail, they don't get punished until they die. Then they go to hell.

Dying and going to hell started with Adam and Eve. Until they disobeyed God, they were stupid and happy in Eden. God had wanted them to live that way forever – sort of like white trash in Alabama. But when Adam and Eve didn't do as told, God had no choice. He had to punish them. So He chased them off the property for being smart and sexy and made them work, grow old and die.

When Gary Cooper played Sergeant York, he didn't do much talking. He worked hard at farming but got nowhere and stayed poor. Afterwards, he got good at obeying orders. For killing and capturing over one hundred Germans, he became a hero. In a kind of turn around from Eden, he and his beautiful bride, Joan Leslie, were allowed to live happily ever after in a new house on a farm with good property called bottom land.

On Saturday while the gang is hanging around waiting to decide what we should do, Orvie announces that I had written a terrific composition. His talking about classroom stuff surprises us. No one ever broaches that subject. Whenever anyone speaks about school it's only to gossip about things like Orvie's getting sent home for not having a tie or of our smoking in the john. Only a new kid or a simpleton would bring up the boring business of learning.

"Who cares if Gus is smart?" says Fats.

"Yeah," chimes in Kevin, "Who cares?"

"No one cares. I don't even care," I say.

Actually that's a lie. I'm as pleased as punch by Orvie's outburst. The kid is all right. He may not know how to speak gang stuff but that's because he's from California. In time he'll learn and be one of us. But right here and now he looks rather downcast. I decide to try to raise his spirits. I say to him, "Orvie, we know you meant well. But you kind of broke the code. When you've lived here a while, you'll see there are certain things we never talk about. School work is one of them."

"What's another one?" he asks.

Because I've been speaking off the top of my head, he's got me. I feel like a jerk. If there are any other forbidden topics, I can't think of one. Fortunately, however, Frankie can. "Girls," he says.

"Yeah, girls," echoes Fats.

"Girls are swift pains in the ass--just like school," continues Frankie. Anything that's a pain in the ass, we don't talk about."

I couldn't have put it better.

Frankie's a genius. He always knows exactly the right thing to say. No wonder he's our leader.

"Maybe, you'd better fill me in on the rest," says Orvie. "What's a pain in the ass in California maybe isn't the same as what's one in Brooklyn."

"This conversation's a pain in the ass," says Frankie. "It's time to drop it. Let's do something interesting. Let's go rob Woolworth's."

In the days that follow Orvie and I become good friends. He sort of gets to be a normal Flatbush kid by following my example. In turn, I get wise about California. I already know about its climate, Hollywood, Alcatraz, oranges, the rich valleys, the Mojave desert, Yosemite and the mountains. The stuff I don't know about is Okies and Asians and weird religions. California teems with these. Orvie's views about them reflect his Dad's. Mr. Heavyside is a free thinker. He believes that although America is the best country on Earth, it still isn't living up to its principles as stated in the Declaration of Independence and in the Bill of Rights. He says we as a people have too much respect for people with money and power and too little reverence for those who are poor and powerless. He likes Okies. He says they're like the colonists who came to America looking to better themselves. They've been trying to do that in California. There, however, they're facing persecution. It's even worse for Americans of Japanese ancestry. Their property has been practically stolen from them and they've been thrown into Concentration Camps.

I figure Orvie's Dad is very smart. Maybe even in the same league as my Dad. When I ask him what he does for a living, he tells me he's a professional anarchist. He asks me if I know what that is. I answer, "Of course, Emma Goldman was one."

My answer impresses him. He says he's glad Orvie and I are friends. I wonder if he would have felt the same if I had told him that the only thing I know about Emma Goldman or anarchism is my grandfather's story about his kid brother getting arrested in 1910 at the Labor Temple in New York.

Uncle Istvan had gone there with other medical students to razz Emma Goldman. She was speaking about women's suffrage and sexual freedom. In the middle of her spiel, Uncle Istvan stood up and threw an egg at her. He missed. A direct hit wasn't necessary. The egg landed at her feet and splattered on her. As it did Uncle Istvan shouted, "Hatch that, you anarchistic bitch."

Immediately a pack of thugs began beating the hell out of both him and his friends. He was rescued by the arrival of the cops who were bopping skulls left and right with their billy clubs. They arrested him and about a dozen others. Emma Goldman resumed her rabble rousing talk which legend now holds to have been one of her best.

At the Police Station, the students and the thugs were booked and jailed. Because family or friends came and posted bail for everyone but Uncle Istvan, he was the only one not back out onto the street by morning.

Around midday Uncle Istvan was brought before the Sergeant. The officer told him he was aggravated with him. He said tax money should be spent on better things than putting down unnecessary breaches of the peace. Then he paused to let his words sink in.

Uncle Istvan must have looked properly contrite for unexpectedly the sergeant's tone became brotherly. He asked, "Do you regret your behavior?"

"Yes, sir," replied my great uncle.

"What specifically do you regret?"

"I regret the trouble I've put you and the other fine policemen to.

I regret getting clobbered. I even regret the fellows who clobbered me getting clobbered. But what I regret the most," he added as his eyes sparkled mischievously, "was that I lacked Christy Mathewson's accuracy when I winged the egg at that damned bitch."

Orvie's sister Arvella also takes a liking to me. In fact, too much of a liking. She wants me to be her boyfriend. I tell her to get lost. Anyone would think that would have ended her feeling for me. It hasn't. It has only made matters worse. She tells everyone I'm mean to her because I'm fainthearted and afraid of revealing my true affection.

From then on it doesn't matter what I say. I've been had. Everyone is convinced I love her. If she had hated me and had wanted to get revenge for my indifference to her, she couldn't have planned or gotten it better.

What is strange is that even though Arvella annoys and aggravates the hell out of me, I don't dislike her. I just feel kind of nothing towards her. She isn't ugly. In fact you could say she's pretty in a Bulgarian sort of way. Nonetheless, she isn't my type. So I handle the situation as well as I can by avoiding her.

Just before Christmas Kevin discovers that the Heavysides are atheists. When he stops us in the middle of a touch football game to tell us this, I'm not impressed. Hell, I've figured that out for myself long ago. But Kevin makes out like it's a big deal. He says the Heavysides are weird.

I never knew before how much contempt I have for Kevin. He's plain out obnoxious. He seems to get pleasure only out of being the bearer or the spreader of bad news. You can see by his grin that he's now in seventh heaven. I decide to lower him a level or two.

I say, "You're the one who's weird. No real American gives a damn about another fellow's religion. Who cares whether the Heavysides are atheists? Needle-nosed, narrow-backed, catholic bigots like you aren't good for a damned thing but stirring up trouble where it isn't needed. I thought the only people you felt a calling to hate were Jews. Orvie and his family aren't Jews. So knock this off and play ball."

"Yeah, play ball," says Frankie.

I really appreciate his backing me up. It couldn't have been easy for him as a Catholic to back up a Protestant against one of his own. But that's Frankie. He's got class.

We play on but that isn't the end of the matter. That evening most of the kids tell their folks about our sidewalk run in. The parents respond by ordering their kids to avoid Orvie and Arvella. The Heavysides are to be treated as lepers. Within a few days during this season of brotherly love and homage to the Savior, prejudice prevails. Everyone on the block shuns and razzes the Heavysides.

I never tell my folks about this. I know my Dad. He would ask me to make a special point of playing with the Heavysides. Then I too would be treated as an untouchable. So what I do is what I think all of us do. I raise my voice against my friend, Orvie, and laugh with others at his predicament. And inside of me, I know and feel I'm nothing but pus.

In January, a week before we move to 954 East 48th Street, the Heavysides move. Where to? I don't know. Maybe to a place where the Principal doesn't have to loan Orvie a tie. Maybe back to California where people are less afraid to be different and to show tolerance. Where to? It doesn't much matter. I figure any place is better than Brooklyn.

My thoughts and feelings about my behavior towards the Heavysides will always trouble me. I know that nowhere, not even in a whore house or in Hitler's Third Reich, can there ever be found anyone lower than me. While my friends on Linden Boulevard also behaved as cruds, they deserve forgiveness.

They acted out of ignorance and in accord with their parent's wishes. I had no such excuse.

I think of my great uncle walking into a hall crowded with bomb throwers and tossing an egg at their revered heroine.

He had guts.

It didn't matter that night if he was young and stupid. Razzing Emma Goldman on her territory took courage. That was and is a quality I lack.

At heart, I'm as contemptible as a good German. I know that if I had been raised in Stuttgart, I probably would have Heiled Hitler as loudly as everyone else.

Because I felt contempt for myself for behaving so miserably towards the Heavysides, I began to resent them. Why had they let Kevin know they're atheists? Why couldn't they have been like me and kept their disbelief secret? Why had they gone ahead and invited trouble? Why had they forced me to choose between them and my friends? What right had they to do this to me?

In no time I almost convinced myself that the persecution they endured was of their own doing. I told myself they deserved it. I was mad as hell at them. The more mad I got, the more I hated them. The more I hated them, the less I liked myself.

Much later, I guess I started to grow up. I no longer buy into the self deluding lie that the Heavysides were responsible for what happened to them on Linden Boulevard. My arguments and complaints against them were and are feeble excuses and lies of the same caliber as those employed for centuries by Christians to denigrate Jews.

The Heavysides did nothing to be ashamed of. They were good Americans being true to their consciences.

My shame was and is that I wasn't true to mine.

Chapter 22

Flight Lieutenant Gus

In 1940 there are two battles of Britain--three thousands miles apart. The one that history recalls is fought and won in a few months by the Royal Air Force. The one I'll always remember lasts until 1943. It too gives victory to England. The aerial maneuvers which mark this second Battle of Britain take place in the itchy-bomb trees of Brooklyn and could never have been won without the services of the world's greatest ace, Flight Lieutenant Gregory Ulysses Stern the Third.

I have always been aircraft crazy. My love for flying began sometime after my second birthday when I watched a plane fly over our block. I pointed at it and said, "Bird."

"No, plane," corrected my mother.

"Yes," I agreed, "plane."

So pleased was she by my ability to withstand correction and to string two words together, she decided to buy me flying clothing as a reward. When told of this I guess I swelled with excitement. I envisioned myself bedecked in a suit of feathers. I expected to glide up to the cookie jar or perch on the mantel piece. When reality dawned and I found myself garbed instead in a leather jacket, leather cap and white silk scarf, I suppose I was more startled than disappointed. Although the outfit was what I neither wanted nor expected, it did make a hit with relatives and neighbors. I've been told I took to it as readily and proudly as though it were my first pair of long pants.

My next memory involving aviation occurred a year later.

Dressed again in the jacket, cap and scarf, I stood on the curb of Flatbush Avenue and waved a small American flag at a motorcade featuring the great Wiley Post. He had just set some kind of world's flight record and was being escorted from Floyd Bennett Field to City Hall. Everyone was impressed by his heroics but I seemed to have been less taken with his aerial feat than with his eye patch and the story told to me that he kept his pockets packed with candy.

In later aviation memories I am to be found playing up in a tree which in my imagination is the cockpit of a plane in flight. No longer do I wear the silk scarf and leather jacket and cap. I've outgrown them. Despite being bereft of the proper aviation attire, I remain addicted to flying. This annoys and worries my mother. Because I do not behave as a boy does in the movies, she fears I'm demented. She believes I'm supposed to be like Spanky or Alfalfa in the "Our Gang" comedies. Instead I'm Kid Tarzan roosting on a bough and dreaming he's Charles Lindbergh.

Dad tells Mother I'm quaint rather than crazy. Reminiscing about his own childhood, he confides to her that I'm a lot braver than he was at my age. He tells her he didn't see his first aircraft until he was six.

It came from nowhere roaring like fifty angry lions and it cast a Dracula-like shadow over him and his street. In terror, he filled his pants and fled for home.

When we moved to 192 Schnectady Avenue the street was treeless. The avenue around the corner, Park Place, was also bare except for a few coarsely barked trees standing far off down the block. Their distance from my home tended to limit my passion and my preoccupation with flying. It subsided further as I grew interested and skilled in all the street games that we played. Every now and then I still climbed atop a johnny pump and played "Spitfire" by shooting down the Heinkels which passed disguised as cars. Yet this activity neither rekindled old memories nor stirred new yearnings for aviation. I had to wait until we returned to Flatbush to rediscover the glory of trees and my love for flying.

In 1942, we were back in Flatbush.

By 1943, I've become an expert on the specifications of every major allied or axis plane. No cop has ever known cars nor a bird watcher, birds as well as I know aircraft. My nickname in the neighborhood is Gremlin Gus and I'm revered as a walking encyclopedia on matters regarding aviation. Moreover when we move to East 48th Street I take control of the games on the block and have every kid up in the trees playing R.A.F., Eighth Army Air Force or U.S.S. Hornet with me.

Long before the other kids get interested in the war, I'm addicted to it. My great uncle is in the Canadian Army. He's been serving with the British Eighth Army since 1940 in North Africa. During the actual Battle of Britain I, myself, have tasted real combat when the micks on Park Place beat the living hell out of me for bringing a "Bundle for Britain" to my church. The whipping can't cower me. As strong as the passion of the Irish thugs is for Ireland and the Nazis, mine doubles theirs for Britain.

In 1939 when Hitler invaded Poland, I thought America should have entered the war. To our everlasting shame, we didn't.

In 1940, the R.A.F. not only saved their own nation but ours as well. Had England fallen, sooner or later Hitler would have invaded America. When Churchill said, "Never have so many owed so much to so few," he was talking not only about his people but about ours as well.

Of all the aircraft games we play, R.A.F. is by far my favorite. However, as a Yank, my allegiance is first, last and always to the U.S.A. So in 1943, I go to see King George and the Prime Minister. With a heavy heart I tender to them my resignation from the Royal Air Force. With great reluctance they accept it. They know it's only right and proper that I be allowed to enlist in General Arnold's Eighth Army Air Force as a light colonel. But before I'm allowed to leave the royal presence, I'm awarded my third Victoria Cross. Furthermore, despite my protest, Winston promises to have Parliament pass a resolution thanking me for my four years of gallant service to their king and country.

Perhaps, the major influence in my decision to serve with my countrymen is my desire to be on a B-17 with my boyhood idol, Randy Boole.

I first met Randy in Flatlands when I was a first grader at P.S. 207. He lived on our block and was a classmate of Gwen's. I liked him enormously. He taught me how to play checkers and chess. Under his training I got to be skilled at both games. He didn't play down to me. At first, he could have whipped me with ease but to keep the games interesting and fair, he used to start himself short a few pieces. Then he'd play his heart out. Because, as my mother has observed, I was born with my father's flair for the useless, my game became a challenge to him. He had to start play with all his men on board to beat me. When I played against anyone else, even Dad, I triumphed.

Randy taught me neither to gloat when winning nor to whine when losing. He said a purpose of play is to inspire respect in us for our opponents. He meant it too. Every time I made a clever move, he complimented me. When I did the same to him, he'd crack an enormous smile and reach over and affectionately tap my shoulder or muss my hair. That made me feel as terrific as a Saturday morning.

I'm sure a lot of the attention that Randy gave me was due to Gwen. She was living with us. No doubt he had a school boy's crush on her and in order to be closer to her, he probably played up to me. Yet unlike Gwen's other boyfriends, Randy was nice to me because he was nice to everyone. Aside from my Dad and Ernie, he was the only person I ever knew who always made me feel as though everything I thought, said and felt was important. He was this way with everyone.

After my family moved away from Flatlands, we kind of lost track of Randy. Once in 1940 or 1941 we bumped into him at Riis Park. In 1942, however, he came back into our world and we began seeing him regularly. Early in that year he and Gwen started keeping company. In June they eloped. I think I was as happy about their marriage as they were.

Right after their honeymoon Randy reported for duty with the Army Air Corps and was sent to Hondo, Texas where he was trained to be a navigator. Early in 1943 his B-17 flew to England and he became a member of the Eighth Air Force.

Back on the block on East 48th Street, I tell the kids of Randy and of his assignment to England. I impress upon my friends the need that rookie American airmen like Randy will have of help from experienced fliers like us. So I suggest that they join me in resigning en masse from the R.A.F.

To my surprise half of the fellows aren't too keen on coming over to Eighth Air Force. What shocks me is that two of the dissidents are Irish. However, I quickly regain my poise. I remember that it has been always the custom of the Irish to fill Tommy's ranks when -England has gone to war.

I listen to everyone's reasons for staying in the R.A.F. Then I lay down the law. "Tough s---," I tell the dissenters. "As Americans we have no choice but to fight for Old Glory. Like it or not, we're all in the Eighth Air Force."

Then I give them a pep talk about Happy Arnold, our commanding general, and describe the new bombers we'll fly. The fellows voice their approval of manning the B-17, Flying Fortress, and turn thumbs down on the B-24 and on the smaller B-25 and B-26.

Suddenly my brother, Matt, interrupts us saying, "Knock off the bulls---. Give us our mission and let's get up in the trees and do it."

For his lack of military courtesy, I immediately demote the little son-of-a-bitch to P.F.C.

This action meets with resistance. The fellows begin to razz me but I quell the mutiny by recognizing Matt's outburst as a daring display of initiative which merits him a promotion back to corporal. Then to myself I make a mental note to kick his ass in later.

For an hour or two every non-rainy day throughout April and May, I have the gang with me up in the itchy bomb trees. To us, of course, these aren't trees but aerial vessels for our valor. In them we radio back and forth messages about targets, flak fields and Me-109 attacks. Because our raids give everyone lots to do, Eighth Air Force is a great game. The enlisted men spot and shoot down the Luftwaffe while the officers keep busy piloting, navigating and bombing.

One Saturday early in August after we all return from a movie I get Jimmy Fredholm and Lloyd Cramer to take separate crews up into nearby trees. Then we pull off an around the clock, mass raid on Dortmund. The Heinies never have a chance. We're great. We devastate the place.

Later that evening my grandmother, Mom, learns of our Dortmund bombing. My tail gunner, Cpl. Matthew Stern, has boasted at dinner of his feat of shooting down three 109 Messerschmitts and a Focke- Wulf 190 during the raid.

Matt had a right to brag. He did a hell of a job. Not only did he give us a great display of gunnery but also he told a couple of pestering girls who wanted to play to get lost. His actions merited a medal. So I've put him up for the Distinguished Flying Cross.

Mom who hates war and who has been a pain in the ass as a mother now becomes one as a grandmother. She never let Dad or Ernie play with guns. Now she's out to stop Matt and me. She complains to Mother about our playing "bombing."

"Mom, it's only play," says Mother.

"Play! Tag is play. Baseball is play. Bombing is not play. Bombing is wicked. Even more terrible than wicked is this bombing of Dortmund, the city of their cousins, the city of their forefathers."

Then she turns to Matt and me. Shaking her finger at us, she orders, "No more bombing. No more bombing."

Matt starts to whimper. This makes Mother uneasy. That worries me. Meanwhile Mom continues to rave. Matt's whining increases into bawling. Mother becomes upset and agitated.

I look at Mom and say, "If Dad were here, he'd hand you your hat and coat and tell you to leave."

From out of nowhere Mother slams a slap on my face that not only makes my cheek sting but also sets my nose to running and my eyes to watering. Next she tells me to apologize to my grandmother and to go stand in the corner.

I back away from her in getting off of my chair. When I'm safely out of range, I look over at Mom and say, "I apologize. I didn't mean to offend you. But we both know that what I said is true."

"My God," says Mom.

"Go stand in the corner," Mother screams. Then turning to Mom she says, "Mom, I can't take this. Please."

"I'm sorry, Cynthia," says Mom. "Sometimes I just don't know when to stop. I was going to leave in a few minutes. I think I'll do it now."

She goes and gets her coat.

I'm feeling bad about the way I behaved. It isn't right of me to sass my grandmother. But neither is it right of her to scold my tail gunner. I have to protect him. What kind of a Commander would I have been if I hadn't risen to his defense? Moreover, if it has been demeaning for her to be talked back to, it has been no less humiliating for me and for the military. After all, as General Arnold's right hand man, I should not have been scolded, slammed with a stinging slap and ordered to stand in the corner.

When Mom has her hat and coat on and is ready to leave, Matt is no longer whining. She kisses him and then comes over to my corner. She turns me around and kisses me good-bye while saying, "Colonel Stern, I agree with you that this war must be won by the Allies because the alternative, God forbid, is a return to the Dark Ages. But we must remember, our fight is not with the German people but with the Nazis and with their horrible, evil, wicked dictator, Adolf Hitler."

I'm not sure whether I agree with her about it not being against the Germans too but I'm pleased and proud of the military courtesy she has shown me. To be addressed by rank and to be treated as though

I'm a grown-up is no small thing. I give her a big hug and kiss. Then I do a snappy about face and resume my stance in the corner.

Mom must have forgotten that she has already hugged and kissed Matthew good-bye. She goes back and does it again. Then she says to him, "I'm not telling you not to play and have fun. I just would like it if you would play nice games like punch ball and hide-and-seek. But not bombing, please."

He starts sniffling.

As Mom moves over towards my mother to kiss her good-bye, I sneak a look over at my tail gunner and say to him in a low voice, "Don't cry Corporal. Headquarters has just confirmed your medal. You'll be awarded the D.F.C. tomorrow."

I can tell that pleases him but it starts Mom off again and earns me a verbal reprimand and a terrific wallop on my rear from Mother.

When Mom finally leaves, the old lady says with exasperation and resignation, "The trouble with both your grandmother and you is that neither of you knows when to keep your mouth shut and let someone else have the last word."

Horses---, I think, mothers always have the last word.

For the next couple of days it rains and wets the trees. On 48th Street this keeps the Eighth Air Force grounded. As I can't play, I have lots of time to think.

I consider what Mom has said about Dortmund. Unquestionably our relatives there are much like those here. I realize that although the Americans are the good guys, many individual Americans aren't. As the Germans are the bad guys, no doubt they too have good guys as exceptions. But where?

If a trace of humanity had persisted in Germany, Hitler's legions would have been as mine--harmless figments of a childish imagination. They weren't. They were real, as real as their weapons and their murdering.

I remember the newsreels I had seen of a Nuremberg rally. In these tens of thousands of grown-up Germans dressed up like Boys Scouts are standing at attention and cheering madly as their beloved fuhrer tells them they're the master race.

Some master race! A race of murdering Neanderthals.

Suddenly it dawns on me that if you bomb Germans, it isn't like killing real human beings. Willingly and proudly the Huns have abandoned their humanity and had turned themselves into a nation of cruel and vicious robots. Throughout Europe wherever the krauts have set foot, they have murdered or enslaved people.

They have to be stopped.

When the weather clears and the Eighth Air Force of East 48th Street reassembles, I give them their mission: an around-the-clock drop on Dortmund.

Chapter 23
Marilyn

When it comes to girls, I'm a clod.

I guess I should qualify that. Around a pretty girl, I'm a clod. I lose poise. I try to impress her. I strut. I exaggerate. I put on airs. I behave like someone I wouldn't have a thing to do with. So of course, when I act so outrageously, I doom myself to failure.

Ugly girls and girls in general don't inspire this kind of stupidity in me. Around them I'm pretty much myself. Still, I suspect they too think I'm a clod. So I try never to have time for them and I go out of my way to avoid their company. I find the less I have to do with females, the better it is for everyone. Girls are nothing but trouble.

A pretty girl, however, is something else. A pretty girl is exciting. If she smiles at me or says "hi", it makes my day. If she happens to be my secret love, a smile from her can lift my spirit higher than the spires of heaven. But that happens so seldom, it may not be worth mentioning.

My first and perhaps only true love is Shirley Temple. I get to discover her in the movies. Although we've never met, we will. She's the perfect mate for me. She's got beauty, brains, personality and charm. She's got it all. I'm crazy about her. Somehow I know that fate will see to it that our paths cross. When that happens, we'll live happily ever after.

Unfortunately, there may be a problem with Shirley. She's older than me. I've noticed too that I'm not the only guy with a crush on her. Many other fellows believe that she's fated to be theirs. Now, I've no doubt that God has reserved her for me but while she's in California waiting for me to grow up, she may meet one of these rivals. Since she doesn't know I exist, she may believe I'm only a dream. If so, she may settle for a second choice and make a tragic mess out of my life, her life and the life of the unfortunate fellow who wins her.

Because this could happen, I've been keeping an eye open for a possible replacement. In the motion pictures there are two girls I kind of like. One is Anne Todd; the other, Elizabeth Taylor. If Shirley and I miss out, either of these two would be okay as a consolation prize.

In all of the schools that I've attended so far, I've had a secret love. Some of them haven't been so hot. They just happen to be the best available. One, however, at P.S. 208 is stunning. Her name is Marilyn. Marilyn Maclaurin.

If the truth be told, Marilyn has got Shirley Temple and the other lovely girls in Hollywood beat. She's not as flashy. She doesn't have blonde curls. She's a brunette with deep blue eyes. She's beautiful. She looks like she's a kid sister to Jeanne Crain, Gene Tierney and Hedy Lamarr. Her only drawback is she's Catholic. That doesn't bother me. But it does trouble her.

I think she's a little sweet on me. One day at school she goes out of her way to tell a bunch of us she would never marry anybody who isn't Catholic. She keeps glancing over at me as she says this. I ask her what she would do if she were the last woman on earth and among the guys left to marry, all were colored and Catholic except one who was Protestant and looked like Tyrone Power.

She answers that she'd try to convert Tyrone but if he prized his religion above her, she'd become a nun.

Her answer annoys me. I hate the way she was demanding that another human being change his belief to accommodate hers.

If Catholicism were a religion like any other Christian one, I'd switch to it in a minute for her. But it isn't. It's dogmatic. It spits on other faiths. Its structure is just like Nazi Germany's. The Pope is its fuhrer. The priests are its Gestapo and the faithful make good Germans.

Before I can tell her how annoyed I am, she asks me what I would do if I were the last man on earth and all the women were colored Protestants except for one who was white and Catholic. I tell her I'd marry the Catholic while remaining Protestant. However, I would not sign away my children's rights to pick their own religion.

She's more aggravated with my answer than I am with hers. She calls me a bigot. Because I had never heard that word before, I think she's implying that I'm stubborn. I let it pass. Later when I look it up, I realize she was saying I was prejudiced. That upsets me. It's an insult to my character. But in truth, she's right, at least, racially. I can't ever conceive of myself taking a negro for a mate.

Marilyn is not the kind of girl whose beauty at first glance bowls you over. She has no moles or other discernible flaws. Her looks have a sedate quality. When you see her initially, you say to yourself, "nice." Then you go about your business. When you see her for the second time, you say, "Very nice." Then you hesitate before returning to your business. When you see her the third time you say, "Nuts to the business, just give me Marilyn."

In January of 1943 in 6A at P. S. 208 there are two very pretty girls:Rachel Landau and Marilyn. Rachel is tall and thin with great cheekbones and delicate features. She looks a lot like Ida Lupino in High Sierra. Two thirds of my fellow classmates, the Jews, are in love with her. Rachel has everything: money, looks, charm, poise, personality and intelligence. I might be in love with her myself if she weren't half a head taller than me. Marilyn's height is closer to mine. She only edges me by an inch. That isn't too bad. Every boy in 5A and 5B tops me by at least this much.

I don't remember when I first saw Marilyn. When we move to 954 East 48th Street, she's out sick with the flu. I glance around on this first day to look over the girls. Rachel strikes me as a knockout. The rest look like wallpaper. I figure all of the A's and B's in the vicinity go to the Little Flower Parochial School. I'm wrong. The girls there are just as ugly as the ones I'm viewing.

Because Rachel in her stocking feet can eat peanuts off the top of my head even if I were to be standing on a box, I rule her out as a candidate to be my secret love. I look at the others. The view is pitiful. There's no chance of a secret love for me here. I have to fall back on my old standby: Shirley T. I'm not worried about the situation. I'm getting older and expanding my horizons. I know there are at least a hundred winners my age in Brooklyn and soon I'll start growing and possibly hook up with one.

At P.S. 208 because I'm the new kid, I keep my trap shut and speak only when spoken to. In this way, I avoid arguments and fights. I have no trouble keeping up with my class work. In class I spend most of my time learning to print in the unusual manuscript style that the school requires.

February comes. I'm promoted and become used to my new surroundings. I also become accustomed to being quiet and courteous. I think I'm doing a good job of making myself invisible. But oddly enough, everyone keeps noticing me. I'm becoming popular.

One day shortly after our arrival in the neighborhood, mother sends me to the grocer's to get a loaf of bread and a roll of toilet paper. When I enter the store a few customers are present. Among them is Marilyn with her girlfriend, Joanne. When I spot them watching me, I look the other way. I don't want to start talking with them. I figure they might hang around till I get waited on. If so, they may laugh at me when I ask for toilet paper. So I nonchalantly act as though I'm looking to buy something which isn't on the shelves. Then I stroll out and walk down Avenue D until I find another store in which to make my purchase.

The next day at school I keep glancing at Marilyn and Joanne. I expect them to be making fun of me and telling their girlfriends that I'm so shy and frightened of girls that I walk four blocks out of my way to avoid them.

I have the feeling that when I'm not glancing at Marilyn,

Marilyn's glancing at me. But I haven't spotted her at it. Whenever I see that her gaze is about to catch mine, I turn and look towards the blackboard or the teacher. I really am shy and afraid of her. The longer I look at her, the more devastated I become by her beauty. By the time Valentine's Day arrives, I know there's no girl anywhere whose loveliness can overpower me like hers. Not even Shirley Whats-her-curls.

During the spring Marilyn and I do many of the things that eleven-year-olds do to signal their love. We both manage to find reasons to walk by each other's house. We trade glances and we get into arguments about things as silly as religion or how many kids should there be in an ideal family and what should be their names.

In June just before school lets out, Joanne is to have a birthday party. She invites five of her girlfriends and six boys to attend. I'm one of them. I accept.

A fellow can build up a mountain of anxiety worrying about how he is supposed to behave at his first party with girls. It's easier for a guy to handle this if he's got a sister. If he hasn't and he's like me, he's almost paralyzed with fear.

I think of backing out of Joanne's party but I know Stuart Robinson will be there and I'm of no mind to let that jerk beat my time with Marilyn. I don't like him. He's a sneak and a Momma's boy. I figure him to be a Giant fan. But I've overestimated the punk. He's way worse. He doesn't root for anybody. Not only doesn't he follow baseball but he also doesn't play it. All he ever does is compose love poems and pick flowers for Marilyn. She thinks he's cute and adorable. I think she needs her head examined.

I'm worried because I don't know how to dance. I'm concerned about what would happen if I tried it. Would I have rhythm? Would I step on my partner's feet? Would I get a hard-on? For a guy like me who wears boxer shorts that could be a problem. I've heard older kids, teenagers, talk about the way they get automatic erections whenever a girl stands close to them. "If she penetrates Herman's perimeter, Herman's gonna penetrate her," they brag. I know that's baloney. But I also know that my dick is untrustworthy. It would do something like that. It's always coming up at the wrong time.

Joanne has let it be known that we'll be playing Spin the Bottle and Post Office. I know that can mean trouble. Girls rate guys on how well they kiss. My kisses always end with a smacking sound. Clark Gable and other leading men smooch in silence. Since movies are supposed to imitate life, Clark does his kissing wrongly. But girls want life to imitate the movies. So even though I kiss right, I'm wrong. That's what a fellow has to expect when he messes around with women.

It would be helpful if someone were on hand to advise me in these matters. But the problem for an eldest son is that he's on his own. I can't consult my Dad. I'm afraid he'd think I'm a sissy if I told him of the many fears girls inspire in me. I dare not ask my mother for advice. With her Victorian and Puritanical airs, she'd have sentenced me to a year in the stocks for having a sinful mind.

Girls have it made. From the day they're born their mothers harp on their sexual training. Even before she's trained to use a toilet, a little girl learns to cross her legs. A boy grows up in a different world. He becomes skilled in sports, war, work and other things which don't involve females. Consequently he has no idea of what to expect or what to do with a girl. However, he knows that whatever he's supposed to do, he'd better do it with grace, style, skill and excellence. If he falls short of her expectations, heaven help him.

When Friday arrives I feel miserable. I don't want to go to Joanne's party. I want a whirlwind to whisk away her house, or a flight of Heinkels to fly over and bomb it, or a plague to come to Brooklyn and have it keep us quarantined in our homes. But luck is against me. Nothing this good happens.

After School I walk down to the Five and Ten. There I buy three handkerchiefs with lace around the edges. I also get wrapping paper and a card. The same lady waits on me at the two counters where I make my purchases.

"Are you bringing someone a present?" she asks.

"Yes," I answer.

"Your mother?"

"No, the hankies are for a girl who's having a birthday party tonight."

"How nice! Would you like me to wrap the gift?"

"Would you please?"

"I'd be delighted to," she answers.

She goes and gets a small cardboard box for the hankies. Then I follow her to another counter where ribbon and cord are kept. As she wraps the present she asks about the party. I tell her I don't know much about it except that girls will be there and they will expect us to play Post Office and Spin the Bottle. She asks how I like parties with girls. I answer that I don't know because I've never been to one.

"How exciting! You must be eagerly looking forward to tonight."

"Not on your life," I reply. Then I add, "I'm scared."

She smiles and says, "I think tonight is going to be one of the nicest nights of your life. I'm sure you'll have a pleasant time and cherish the memory of it always."

"Yes ma'am," I lie.

She begins to wrap ribbon around the package. Because I have only eight cents left, I ask her to stop. She says there'll be no charge. It's a present from Woolworth's to me.

I tell her she's very nice and that of all the Five and Tens in which I'd ever shopped, this is the friendliest. She thanks me for saying these things. Then handing me my package she tells me to give my sweetheart a special hug and kiss to make the evening more memorable.

"Never," I say as I pay her.

She grins and I leave feeling a lot less frightened about the party. In fact, I'm kind of looking forward to it.

The party is held in Joanne's finished basement. Her parents stay upstairs. For the first quarter of an hour the girls tend to stay on one side of the room. We boys try not to gawk at them while we wait for someone to break the ice. Joanne is changing records on her phonograph. She looks at us fellows and asks if anyone would like to help her pick out a selection. No one volunteers. In the center of the room a couple of girls are dancing together. Everyone else watches. Then Stuart asks Marilyn to dance. She accepts. With envy and anger I note that they move almost as gracefully as Fred Astaire and Ginger Rogers. Herbie Klein and Rachel join them. When the song ends they switch partners. That eases my anguish.

I sort of feel left out. I decide I have to act. Since I can't dance, I do the next best thing. I ask Joanne to stop the music to allow me to make an announcement. She obliges. "Enough of the preliminaries," I say, "let's start spinning the bottle."

To my surprise everyone, even the dancers, welcome the suggestion. Joanne hands Klein the bottle. We get into a circle and watch Herbie go into a maze of contortions as he humorously winds up and executes the first spin. He does all right. He gets Rachel. As Herbie goes to kiss her Charlie makes everyone laugh by saying he wants to patent that spin.

The game hasn't gone on for more than ten minutes when Joanne's mother interrupts to present her daughter with her birthday cake. When the candles have been blown out and Happy Birthday has been sung, we sit around and have cake and ice cream and soda while Joanne's dad entertains us with magic tricks. Then Joanne opens her presents and says her thanks. The dirty dishes are brought back upstairs by the grown-ups. We resume the game.

Somehow the delay has taken the fun out of the game. Or maybe we've been playing with too many people. Anyway we soon switch to Post Office. For a while that holds our interest. But soon the ten people who aren't doing anything get bored waiting to be one of the lucky two.

Stuart comes up with a great idea. He invents a game. It's called "Lights Out." All of the boys are to sit on one side of the room on the day bed. The girls will be opposite on the couch and easy chairs. Stuart will turn the lights out and each boy is to cross the room, kiss a girl and get back to the day bed before the lights snap back on. Any guy not back has to sit out the next run and work the lights.

Some of the girls begin to object but Stuart switches off the lights and the game is underway. The room is dark but not pitch black. A streetlight sends just enough illumination into the room to allow us to distinguish silhouettes. I start across the room towards Marilyn but half way there I'm clipped accidentally and sent sprawling by a down field block laid on me by Charlie who's dashing to get hold of Rachel. Meanwhile the girls are sort of giggling and screaming. I get back onto my feet. But before I can take a step, I'm body slammed by one of the guys trying to return to the day bed. I'm seeing lights long before Stuart switches them back on. When he does I'm declared the loser. I'm in no condition to disagree.

The girls call a time out. They decide to circle in a huddle until the lights go out. Then they'll scatter. That way the boys can't be certain of who it is they're grabbing. This evens up the odds for the homelier girls and gives them a chance to get kissed.

Still aching from the blind side hits, I stand by the light switch and marvel at the girls. Two minutes ago they were against the game but now they're embellishing it and dictating its rules.

I flip the switch. The charge begins. The girls scatter and scream. Some even yell "rape." There's lots of noise in the room but there's also a sound detectable on the staircase. I flip on the light switch. My action draws annoyed looks from everyone but these vanish instantly as the door is jarred open by Joanne's dad.

"What's going on in here?" he asks.

"Nothing Daddy," says Joanne. "We're just having fun."

"Well have some different kind of fun," he orders. Then he adds, "Play the phonograph and dance. The party will end in fifteen minutes."

He leaves. A quarter of an hour later so do we.

It hasn't been a bad night. It's brought me my first and only kiss from Marilyn.

Chapter 24

Hans

Around the time the Germans invaded Poland, Carolina Wren's former boyfriend, Hans Holder-- the one with brawn and no brains-- became Gram's third husband.

I suspect that Gram's first husband, my grandfather, wasn't the wonderful man that my mother has made him out to be. I think this because Gram's next two mates were so terrible that it's almost inconceivable her first could have been much better.

About the only thing good that could be said of Hans is that he isn't as malicious as Gram's previous husband, Warren LaGrange. This isn't because of his lack of trying. Hans is every bit as arrogant and mean as Warren. But he's also dumber. It's easy to evade his wrath by distracting him or by avoiding him. Only the latter would have worked with Warren.

Some people like to believe marriages are made in Heaven. I'm not one of them. I think the church does the Deity a disservice when it involves Him in any ceremony uniting a man and a woman. After all, even to a kid like me it's obvious that at least two- thirds of all marriages are mismatches. Moreover, how can anyone believe that God would take any part in approving the wedding of a wholesome, decent girl to a drunk or to a wife beater or to a child molester? It's equally sacrilegious to link Him with an All- American good guy being tied to a whining, cranky harpy? Since tragedies like these are forever happening, it should be clear that our Heavenly Father has washed His hands of marriage. Its dismal record of success suggests that if its governance is not in the control of the individuals involved then it's an institution ruled by luck or by Lucifer.

Anyway to get back to Gram and Hans. She wanted him. She got him. As the saying goes, about the only thing worse that she could have gotten was smallpox. Hans was a born Nazi. Until the Third Reich declared war on us, he openly boasted of being one.

He stands about six feet tall and weighs a lean and powerful two hundred pounds. His friends have nicknamed him, Muscles. Not only is this a fit description of his body but also of his mind. He loves to impress people with his strength. He can rip a telephone book in half with one tear. He can do the same with a deck of cards. His favorite stunt is to stand in front of a mirror and strap a leather belt around his chest. Then he'll take a deep breath. As his chest expands, the belt snaps apart and is ruined. Then Hans smiles at his image and beats his chest like Tarzan.

At meetings of the German-American Bund, Hans served as a sergeant at arms. When he wore his high boots and his brown shirt sporting a swastika arm band, he looked a lot like Rudolph Hess. Gram declared that when dressed in this outfit, Hans was smashing. My dad said, "Yes, smashing heads and trampling on decency."

Hans never was able to hold a job for long. When I first met him in 1938 he was employed as a lifeguard. Between then and the day that he was drafted in the fall of '43, he worked successively as a taxi driver, a security guard, a ticket taker at the Kenmore movie theater, a delivery truck driver for Mission Soda, an amusement park worker at Steeplechase, a Bungalow Bar ice cream driver, a moving-van worker, and a ditch digger for Evergreen Cemetary. He often served too as an apartment house superintendent so that he and Gram could live rent free.

Anyone with a work record like this might be presumed to be a jack of all trades. Hans, however, was merely a jackass at all trades. As a handy man, he was worse than worthless. Whenever he tried to fix anything, he'd generally ruin it completely. Once on a Friday evening before we could stop him, he tried to fix a leak in our bathroom sink.

Needless to say, until the plumber came on Monday, my dad and he had to use the bathtub faucet to shave.

Not only couldn't he hold a job for six months but also he never was able to stay in one place very long as a super. Anytime he succeeded at making repairs or fixing things, it was by accident. Usually after a few months of enduring his foul-ups, the manager of the apartment house would tire of listening to the complaints of the tenants and he'd fire Hans and hire someone equally worthless as his replacement. Whenever that would happen, Gram and Hans would move in with us. If within a month Hans couldn't find another building owner foolish or trusting enough to hire him, my mother would find one for him.

In late January or early February of 1943 my Dad gets bumped out of his job in the Ticket Receiver's office in New York's Pennsylvania Station. To continue working for the railroad he has to bump one of the two clerks in the system with less seniority than him. One works in Harrisburg; the other, in Washington. My Dad lets the fellow in Pennsylvania stay put. He takes the job in Union Station in Washington.

Because Dad will now be away six days in every week, Hans and Gram move in with us. While Mother works the swing shift at the Sperry Gyroscope Corporation, it's the duty of Hans and Gram to take care of Matt and me. Our grandmother does her part well. She keeps the house clean and makes our dinners. Every night on each of our plates there are two ample sized meat balls and a helping of boiled potatoes still in their jackets. The supper's only variety comes with the vegetable. If on Monday we get corn then on Tuesday we eat string beans. Wednesday it's carrots and on Thursday, peas. Then Gram starts another cycle with corn on Friday. On days when Mother is off or when Dad comes home, we may be served something exotic like chicken paprikash, spaghetti or chow mein for supper.

I think Gram's meals make for a very satisfactory diet. I'm not a gourmet when it comes to food. The fancier the dish, the less I like it.

Any dinner of meat and potatoes suits me fine. As for the vegetable, unless it's corn on the cob, I'd just as soon skip it.

When Hans moves in with us, he tells our neighbors that our house is his and that out of the goodness of his heart he's letting Mother, Matt and me stay on with him and Gram as guests. Of course this is nonsense. Yet, a lot of people believe him.

My jobs around the house are to tend to the furnace, to put out the ashes and the garbage, to go to the store, and to set and to clear the dining room table. My brother's duties are to sweep the walk and to dust the furniture. In addition Matt and I have to keep our room clean. Lastly, on Mondays, Wednesdays and Fridays I dry the dinner dishes. On Tuesdays and Thursdays it's Matt's turn.

Things at home run pretty well but I miss my dad. He works evenings in Washington. On his day off, Tuesday, he doesn't arrive home in Brooklyn till five in the afternoon. At nine on the following morning he has to leave us to return to Washington.

Sometime in April, Mother begins going out at night with her boss, Tom Gibbs. He's a nice guy but I would have preferred it if I had never had to meet him. Sometimes in front of everyone, he and mother kiss. Neither Matt nor I are comfortable with this. Nor is Tom. Yet Mother says it's okay and tells us that it's not in her nature to hide things from her sons. She adds that she knows we wouldn't tell our dad about this for we're not blabbermouths.

In February of '43 Hans is out of work but is collecting unemployment. He has plenty of time on his hands. One day he and Herman, a friend of his from the Bund, bring a small truck load of lumber into our backyard.

"What's the wood for?" asks Matt.

"I'm going to build a Pigeon Coop and you and Gus are going to help me."

After two weeks of incompetent construction the coop keels over and collapses for the third and last time. Hans decides that's enough.

He abandons the project and decides to use the garage as the coop. Herman cuts a nine inch square hole into side of the garage and around it he builds a tiny one way entry cage edged with a ledge. Then Hans purchases three pigeons and pushes them though the entry cage into the garage where water, feed and a rectangular array of pigeon spaces have been provided for them.

The next morning before I go to school Hans and I go out to check on the birds. When I open the garage doors to allow us to enter, the pigeons escape and fly off never to return.

Hans is mad. So he slams my left ear with a stinging slap for letting the pigeons escape. He calls this boxing my ear. It hurts. It hurts plenty. When he tells me that boxing ears is a time honored German custom, I get some insight into why Beethoven went deaf and why every twenty five years the Krauts made war on the world.

Soon Hans buys more birds and after keeping them cooped up for a week, he lets them fly. They circle around above our yard. After a while I guess they get tired. About half of them return to the garage within a few minutes. The rest land on the roof of the house of the neighbor behind us. There quite a few of them relieve themselves. One by one over the next hour they return to the garage.

Before Hans begins keeping pigeons I assume the birds all have identical markings and that only a fellow pigeon can tell one from another. Most pigeons that you see in the park or at Borough Hall do look alike. But people who breed pigeons know there are several varieties of them and that they come with distinctive markings. A flight can be orange or brown or any other color but always it has long white feathers at its wing tips. It looks nothing like a teega which bears little resemblance to a homer.

When Hans begins keeping pigeons, he has dreams of making money by breeding them. He buys in the first week about thirty birds to start the flock. He has had flights in a variety of colors and teegas galore.

People who are familiar with the behavior of ducks know that although white feathered ducks and colorful mallards may share the same pond, they naturally segregate and do not indulge in cross-breeding. Pigeons aren't like this. They're sexual democrats.

When Hans first gets the birds, he expects the males to mount the females immediately. But weeks go by and not an egg appears, Because I also am wondering why the mating isn't occurring, I go to the school library and read a small book on pigeons. It says the birds are monogamous. It also says they have breeding seasons.

When I tell Hans this, he says the book is full of s--- and that I'm an idiot to believe a word of it. "What my pigeons need is a red hot whore-bird to wiggle her tail feathers and get the boys aroused." So the following day he purchases what he believes to be such a bird. I guess she wiggles well or it just happens that it's time for the pigeons to come into season. In no time eggs begin appearing in the nesting sites.

When the eggs hatch the little chicks are as ugly as sin. Because they've not as yet developed feathers we can't tell what species of pigeon each is. Hans is sure that because he's a Nazi, his birds will be Nazis too and will mate only with their kind. However, it soon becomes obvious that the flock has never heard of the Nuremberg Laws. Either that or the birds opt to pay racism no heed. Hardly any pigeon mates with its own kind. So instead of producing saleable animals, Hans has crossbreeds.

Crossbreeds are not prized at all. They're called rats and no serious pigeon breeder would want one even if you offered it to him free for nothing.

Instead of attributing the fault for his raising a generation of rats to himself, Hans has decided it's been the doing of the damned Jew who had sold him the whore-bird. If that pigeon hadn't wiggled her hind feathers so seductively, she wouldn't have gotten the poor males so worked up that they lost their sense of racial pride and succumbed to their fowl urges to rape any female in sight. “Always,” Hans concludes, “in every screw-up if you look hard enough, you can find the insidious hand of a Jew.”

In addition to raising pigeons Hans decides to grow a victory garden. He will do this in the nine by twelve plot of earth next to the garage in our yard. One day late in March he brings home seeds for corn, string beans, carrots, lettuce, tomatoes and radishes. Because this interests Matt and me, he sets aside a small portion of the plot for us to tend to as a garden of our own.

Printed on every seed package are directions for planting. As usual Hans ignores them. German-Americans, he assures us, are born with a natural sense for farming. So he has us help him cut rows in the dirt and plant the seeds about two inches deep. Then we cover the seeds with earth and water them.

That night I pray that the pigeons will not eat the planted seeds and destroy the garden. God must have heard me. The garden stays unmolested.

When I awake the next morning I’m not naive enough to expect every plant to be full grown. I know that farming takes time. I do hope, however, to see a few shoots popping up somewhere. Instead everything is still under ground.

Because Matt and I read the directions on the seed packages, we decide to grow only two kinds of plants in the plot that Hans had set aside for us. Our choices are tomatoes and radishes.

We plant the tomatoes because we both agree this is the vegetable we both like best. Neither of us cares for radishes but we decide to grow them anyway. We’re anxious to test our skills at farming and know from reading the printing on the seed packages that radishes are the fastest growers of the plants on hand.

When we tell Mother of this, she says we’ve made excellent choices. Then she adds that while she and everyone else thinks of tomatoes as vegetables, they are, strictly speaking, fruits. I can’t believe this so I look it up. Surely enough, Mother's right. Although it's hard to believe, a tomato is a berry.

Because farming takes so long to get results, I never can get too interested in it. What I want from the plants is action as in Jack and the Bean Stalk. What I get instead is stationary boredom. About the only thing that I can imagine to be wearier than waiting for plants to grow is waiting for services to end in church on the first Sunday of the month.

Eventually, the garden grows. First come the radishes. In the weeks that follow the other vegetables arrive too. Last of all to mature is the corn. Fortunately, the tomatoes and other plants do not have to grow in its shadow. Unwittingly, Hans has planted the corn in its rightful place alongside the north fence of our yard.

Usually when the plants are sprouting, we can't tell what they are. Neither Hans, my brother nor I have had the foresight to mark the rows with stakes identifying the vegetables sown within them.

We don't discover we have carrots until Hans goes to weed the garden and yanks them up as such.

All things considered our victory garden is a success. It doesn't do a thing to overthrow Hitler's legions. It does, however, give me a liking for radishes.

One Friday night about a week before Hans has to report for induction into the Army, he and Gram call me into their room. As they sit me down, they tell me it's time for them to try to have an adult conversation with me.

Their words please me. I sense they're doing me an honor.

"Do you know what an adult conversation is?" asks Hans.

Reluctantly I admit I don't.

"What would you guess an adult conversation might be?" questions Gram.

"Well, since I often hear grown-ups arguing about money, maybe adult conversations are about money. On the other hand what I never hear them talk about is sex, so maybe it's about that."

They smile at this answer. Then Hans says, "What makes an adult conversation an adult conversation isn't the topic. Adults can talk about anything. What separates it from kids' talk and small talk is the intelligence given to it. Do you follow me?"

"I do," I answer.

"Good. Your grandmother and I are now going to try to have an adult conversation with you about the war."

That really gets my attention.

"Do you know who started this war? Do you know what it's all about?" asks Hans.

I answer, "The Japs started it when they bombed Pearl Harbor. They want to rule over East Asia and the Pacific."

"That part is right. But I was thinking about Europe."

"Oh," I volunteer, "that began when Hitler invaded Poland. His aim has been to rule the world. He declared war on us."

"The facts are right. The interpretation is wrong," he says and adds, "The Jews are behind this war. They're Bolsheviks. They're in control of Russia. They want to destroy America and take away everyone's property and rights. They want to enslave Christians."

I've not heard this before. "Then why are we their allies?" I ask.

"That's the sixty four dollar question. We are Russia's ally but we shouldn't be. It's all the fault of the wealthy Jewish capitalists who have Roosevelt's ear and run Great Britain."

Now I'm really confused. If the Jews are rich capitalists controlling Great Britain and the United States why would they be Bolsheviks seeking to destroy everything they've already got? It's a question I dare not to ask. I know its answer will involve more double talk. I don't have a need to hear that. Hans has me mixed up enough as is.

He and Gram talk on saying Hitler is a good guy who never wanted war with England or America. But when the British wouldn't let him fight the evil Bolsheviks, he has no choice but to declare war on England and France to save the world.

It's a self contradictory and absurd argument that I want no part of. So I keep silent and make sure I never contradict them. I feel that if I would, he'd box my ears. At all costs I want to avoid that.

After an hour Hans has talked himself out. Although Gram has been silent most of the time, she had done a lot of Humm-humming to show she supports his words.

It's evident now that the adult conversation is over. I thank them for it. I go to my room and turn in.

The next day when I come back from lugging customers' groceries at the A&P, Hans and Gram are enthusiastically raving about what a brilliant kid I am and how intelligently I carried on an adult conversation with them.

I'm surprised by this but also quite pleased. Being praised is nice even if I don't deserve it for in the talk with Hans and Gram I had been more of a bystander than a participant. I resolve that if ever again I get stuck in a similar pow-wow, I'll repeat my muteness. It can only add to my reputation as a conversationalist.

Chapter 25

Toughest Kid on the Block

At the end of June in '43, Gundar Eilenberg moved off of our block. That in and of itself wasn't of much interest since Gunny wasn't the kind of a kid anyone notices. He was a born loner. He never played in the trees in the war games that I had organized. Because he had poor vision and miserable hand and eye coordination, he seldom participated in baseball, punch ball, slap ball, stick ball or stoop ball. As a kid he had only one asset: his strength.

He was as strong as an ox. This enabled him to throw a ball at least one and a half times as far as any of the rest of us. That should have been impressive. However, his aim was lousy. Always he threw high and wide of his target. So in games no one wanted him as a team mate. Yet no one would ever tell him this. That was because in fighting he could lick any kid in the neighborhood.

His toughness, I'll admit, was impressive. As much so as the thickness of the glasses he wore. But as Gunny seldom hung out with us and never bothered to throw his weight around, we accepted his dominance as we did the weather. Like rain or sunshine his ability to beat us senseless was a fact of life. We had no choice but to contend with it. Yet as there wasn't a thing we could do about it, we mostly ignored it. He went his way and we went ours.

In May of '43 the motion picture Gentleman Jim plays in our neighborhood theater, the Avenue D. Everyone who sees the movie admires Errol Flynn and the fancy foot work he displays as the boxer, James J. Corbett. Ward Bond portraying the brawler, John L. Sullivan, can't touch him. As Errol bobs, weaves, dances, feints and darts around in the ring, he's as hard to hit as a Bob Feller fast ball.

Most of the kids in the neighborhood are captivated by the film. None more than me. Errol Flynn is my hero. Whatever his role whether it be Robin Hood fighting injustice or the Sea Hawk battling for freedom or General Custer dying with his boots on, he always keeps his poise and calmly faces his enemies with bravery and defiance. Not even Tyrone Power, a great swashbuckler in his own right, can match Errol in his ability to rally men and to lead them to overcome adversity. He, alone, has been born to play the lead in Gentleman Jim.

After watching this great picture it's only natural that we kids would be in a rush to hold our own matches. While most of us don't own boxing gloves, it doesn't matter. A few kids do. As only two pairs of gloves are needed for a bout, we're set and ready to go.

We measure and chalk off a fifteen by fifteen foot boxing ring on the street. Of course, our ring is without ropes. Even if we had enough rope to mark the boundaries, we couldn't use it. We'd have had to waste too much time lowering it to let cars pass.

As it's almost dinner time when we chose to do this, we decide to begin play after supper. We'll hold two round matches of one minute per round for the little squirts and three round matches of two minutes per round for bigger kids like me.

While eating, some of the kids must have been telling their parents of our plans. When we come back out some of my playmates' fathers and other grown-ups are taking part in our play as judges, timers and spectators. This makes for lots of excitement.

Unfortunately what happens next doesn't please me.

Gunny chooses to take part in the matches. Worse yet, the grown-ups decide on the pairings for the bouts. Because I'm the block's second toughest kid, they give me the toughest, Eilenberg, as my opponent.

Suddenly I realize I don't give a hoot for Errol Flynn or boxing. Gunny is half a head taller than me and at least twenty pounds heavier. If I were to get in the ring with him, he'd surely pound the blazes out of me.

I speak up and say if it's all right with everyone, I'll just be a spectator.

It's not all right.

Some of the kids begin calling me "chicken" and "coward." I'd gladly have stood for this. However, Marilyn happens to come by.

I can't let her see how yellow I am. So I concoct a lie. I say, "All right, I'll be happy to fight. I'm not yellow. I just don't want to take advantage of Gunny. He won't have his glasses on.

"Thanks, Gus," says Gunny with sarcasm, "but I won't need glasses to hold my own."

As the preliminary matches get underway, I offer up a prayer to God for immediate rain. I beg him to unloose a two hour thunderstorm. If that's out of the question, I'll gladly settle for a hurricane or a tornado. Anything disastrous will do provided it washes out the bouts.

God, of course, turns His deaf ear to my prayer. As usual He has plans of His own and feels no need for advice or consultation.

He goes, as usual, His own way.

I ask you, what would it have cost Him to allow a little cloud to burst over Brooklyn? Hell, as miracles go, rain's trivial. If the Almighty in His wisdom would choose at this moment to spare India twenty minutes of a monsoon and divert the storm to my neighborhood, everyone everywhere would be pleased.

God, however, decides to choose that moment to give the Devil his due. Throughout the evening the sky over Brooklyn stays as cloudless and clear as the Sahara's.

My worry, fear and misery proceed to grow.

The first bout lasts only one round. It's stopped when Marilyn's little brother Bobby takes a jab to the nose and starts to cry.

Matthew wins the next match. Its outcome leads him to jump up and down with excitement. I'm really proud of him until he says, "Gus, I did my part. Hooray for us Sterns. Now you can do the same with Gunny."

He's lucky so many others are around. Otherwise, I'd have decked him right then and there for his insolent idiocy.

Over the next half of an hour my anguish grows to heights higher than Everest. I'm becoming a portrait of woe and despair. My fear is overwhelming. It's a force with a presence that I can feel. It's breathing terror down my back and turning my spine to jelly.

When the time comes for me to put on the gloves, my panic oddly enough becomes mixed with relief. I know that in ten minutes, regardless of how black and blue the beating will leave me, it will be over.

As my gloves are being laced up, I concentrate on recalling the advice that I'd been given in the two boxing lessons that I had taken several months ago in the Flatbush Boys Club: "Crouch, move and always keep your mitts, especially the left, up at head level to protect yourself."

That's good, professional advice. So as not to forget it, I keep repeating it. Even when the ref, Mr. Bloom, calls Gunny and me to the center of the ring to tell us to fight fair, I'm not hearing anything he says. I'm only listening to what I'm repeating over and over inside my head: "Crouch, move and always keep my mitts, especially the left, up at head level to protect myself."

A whistle blows and the fight is under way. Gunny charges at me. He winds up and swings a round house right. I bob back and evade the blow. Then he charges again and misses again. As he flies past I counter punch with a light left. It's hardly more than a love tap but it excites the crowd.

"He moves like Gentleman Jim," someone says.

Now although I'm totally focused on Gunny, I'm surprised at the clearness of my mind and at my ability to take in everything that is going on around me. I'm buoyed by the fact that everyone is rooting for me.

Gunny comes at me again. He swings and misses. He resumes the charge. Repeatedly, I dance out of his way and counter punch as he goes by. The fight proceeds in this manner like a ritual.

Gunny as the saying goes telegraphs every punch he throws as if he's in the employ of Western Union. He keeps trying to deliver a knockout blow. I dance, bob and weave to stay never at home to receive his message.

Throughout that round and during all of the next he continues to charge and to swing wildly at me. He never manages to land a solid punch. A few times, he does whack the hell out of my arms. Those blows hurt. Yet their sting and their force are as nothing compared with the hurt and the damage they'd have done to me, if any had hit my head or body.

When the third round begins, Gunny's energy is spent. He comes at me in a slow charge, swings wildly and misses as usual. He tries again. He misses again. He's panting to catch his breath. I move in and hit him with two left jabs to his chest. When he lowers his arms to protect his body, I unloaded the only solid punch I throw in the whole fight. I hit him as hard as I can right in the kisser with a right cross. It lands with effect.

Immediately his nose starts to bleed. It doesn't trickle. It plops. Splotches of blood spill onto the street.

The fight is stopped. Mr. Bloom raises up my right arm and declares me the winner by a technical knockout.

I don't jump up and down to celebrate. I feel no glee. I'm more surprised and confused than elated by the turn of events. Miraculously, the ordeal has ended a minute and a half earlier than I had anticipated. I'm tired but unhurt. I've survived.

As far as I'm concerned, my victory has been accidental. I'm pleased that the fight is over and that I remain free of injury and pain.

People slap me on the back and congratulate me. I don't care.

Rather than glory I feel relief. I go over to Gunny. He's leaning against a tree. He has his head tilted back and holds a handkerchief up to his nose. It's badly stained and soiled with blood.

I say, "Good fight, Gunny. I was lucky."

"Damned right you were," he concurs.

"In a street fight you'd have killed me," I admit. "It was only the Marquis of Queensbury Rules and you're not being able to see well without glasses that allowed me to survive. In a real brawl a boxer like me doesn't stand a chance against a slugger like you."

His tilted head nods in agreement.

"I'm sorry I bloodied your nose. It looks bad. I hope it doesn't hurt."

"What hurts is my pride more than my nose," he says and adds, "I'm still the toughest kid on the block."

"Hey," I second, "you won't get an argument on that from me."

I then ask him to shake hands.

He takes my hand and gives me a smile. Then he adds a hug with his left arm. It half crushes me to death. I realize that while he's being a good sport, he's also delivering a message. It reads "Don't let this day go to your head. If you mess with me again, I'll squeeze you like an accordion and pound you like a drum."

The fights are over. Mr. Bloom is inviting everyone, even those who have not been in a bout, to walk with him up to the candy store on Avenue D and there be treated to an ice cream cone. His offer is being accepted without exception.

I look around for Marilyn. She's nowhere to be seen. She must have left during my bout with Gunny.

Suddenly I don't feel like celebrating.

I thank Mr. Bloom for his offer but beg off and go home.

Up in my room, I lie on my bed and try to make sense out of the events of the evening.

I had been almost paralyzed by my fear. Although I never overcame the dread that I'd felt, I had lived with it. In battle to my surprise I had excelled and had triumphed. Yet my victory was hollow and incapable of duplication. I had fought bravely but had done so only to mask my cowardice. At heart I was still yellow. All the courage that I had shown was merely evidence of my being inwardly too yellow to allow others, especially Marilyn, to see me as I truly am.

I grow tired. My reflections are leading nowhere. They seem to be as useless as they are depressing. I put them aside. I close my eyes and fall off to sleep.

In the weeks that follow the fights, I see that on the block I've gained in prestige. Half of the kids think that I've replaced Gunny as the toughest kid. I know that's nonsense but I don't advertise it.

Surprisingly Gunny because he's a little less feared becomes a little more popular. Of course, that doesn't last long. As soon as school lets out he and his family move.

All in all, Gunny's departure is not a good thing. Why?

Because now, to no one's benefit, I become unquestionably the toughest kid on the block.

On Park Place where I had played when we lived on Schnectady Avenue this kind of supremacy never could have happened. Because about forty kids, not counting girls, lived on the street, no one was the toughest. We lacked a static gang. Every boy had as playmates at least a dozen fellows within two years of himself in age. So everyone on the street in a fight could beat or be beaten by someone else. Consequently, the concept of there being a toughest kid was beyond our conception. At school, however, where our classes kept us in groups with everyone approximately of the same age, we did have such a thing as the toughest kid in class.

On Linden Boulevard, it was clear that Frankie was the best fighter and Kevin was next. Then I think came me. But who cared? We all knew that first is best and last is the rest.

My surprising tenure as the toughest kid on East 48th Street exposed my dark side. As long as Gunny was around the thought of throwing my weight around never occurred to me. Aside from the perpetual bullying I gave to my brother, I had never been one to allow my arrogance to reign unchecked.

Now as the undisputed boss of the block, I grow a swelled head. I stop suggesting to others what games we ought to play. I tell them. If there's any disagreement, I end it with a punch. I become a pint sized Hitler. I treat my playmates as badly as the Nazis do Jews or as Southerners do the Coloreds. If in playing ball I'm out by a step, I declare myself safe. Then I stare down everyone into agreement. In order to win in every game and in every activity, I never hesitate to cheat. Moreover, if a kid has in his possession something I want, I intimidate him into giving it to me as a gift. In short, I've become a mean, vicious bastard.

After a while no one plays with me. It gets so that when I set foot outside to play, doors slam as everyone heads inside to get away from me. Everyone flees from me and seeks the safety of his home. This bothers me. I realize what I've become, a bully.

I want my reign to end. I want to reform and to make amends. But I can't. It's too late. No one will come near me to hear my apology.

Soon on the sidewalk pictures are being drawn in chalk of a dopey looking character named Gus the Bully. Messages are also being written saying things like Gus stinks and I hate Gus.

Even though I know every piece of the vilification is justified, I decide not to take any more of it. So I write my own message at three different places on the sidewalk in order to be sure everyone will read it. I write Heaven help anyone who draws or writes bad stuff about me and I sign it Gus.

The next day in defiance of my message Bobby Maclaurin, Marilyn's little brother, comes down the block and on the street in front of my house he begins to draw a Gus the Bully dopey drawing. I come outside as he's doing this. Although he sees me, he keeps right on sketching.

I tell him, "Bobby, beat it."

He ignores me and chants, "Gus is a bully. A bully is Gus. Gus is a barrel of slimy, sick pus."

Defiance that brazen, I reason, has to be punished. I have given him and everyone else fair warning not to belittle me. If I were to let him get away with this, my name and my image would be mud forever more. I've no alternative. To preserve the little respect I still have left, I have to sock him. So I do so.

I feel miserable as I hit him.

He cries and flees home.

I knew this wouldn't score any points for me with his sister. But I also know that women despise weakness and surely I'd be despised by her and everyone else if I didn't live up to the words I had written on the sidewalk.

About a week later as I'm headed to the store, old man Maclaurin sees me pass by his house. He comes outside and as I'm crossing Foster Avenue, he calls to me and tells me to wait. I do this.

"You're Gus, aren't you?"

"Yes, sir."

"You're the neighborhood bully, aren't you?"

I don't answer.

"You're the kid who hit my boy, Bobby?"

Knowing that there's no way to deny this, I draw myself to attention and answer him as bravely and as manly as George Washington would have. "Yes, sir. That was me."

"You have the arrogant gall to answer like that."

I don't understand what he means by this. I suppose I'm giving him a puzzled look. Then because he's Marilyn's dad and I want to impress him, I explain, "I'm not being arrogant. I'm being honest."

That does nothing to appease him.

"How would you like it if someone bigger than you, hit you?" he asks.

"I wouldn't like it," I reply and add, "but if I went out of my way to provoke trouble by slandering someone, I wouldn't bellyache about the consequences."

Up swiftly from his side comes his open hand. It lands with a stinging slap on my face. I look at him. He's red with rage.

Since my being honest and forthright has failed to impress him, I say nothing.

"How did you like that?" he rants. It's not a question. It's a statement promising worse to come if I were to answer it.

I say nothing.

"From this moment on, none of my children will have a thing to do with you and you'll not have a thing to do with them. Do you understand?"

I say nothing. I just look in his eyes.

He turns around and walks away.

Chapter 26
The Babylon Captivity

By the rivers of Kingsport, there we sat down, yea we wept when we remembered Brooklyn.

Psalm 137, Verse l--updated.

In August of '43 in the middle of one of their Tuesday fights, my parents pause long enough to give Matt and me money to take in a movie. We figure the argument involves us. Otherwise we'd never be sent to a show without asking.

When we return home a truce is in place. Nonetheless, the air is tense. I feel that if I utter a word the old lady will sock me. I go quietly with Matt to our room.

"She's on the warpath," he says.

"No kidding," I answer.

"We'd better not bother her."

"Impossible," I reply, "as soon as she sees I'm breathing she'll use it as an excuse to slam me."

At dinner Mother fills four plates at the stove. She brings Dad's and hers to the dining room table. She orders me to bring Matt's and mine.

I put my brother's plate before him. Then to avoid her I circle the long way around to my seat.

We begin eating.

"Must you make so much noise?" she scolds.

"Excuse me," I answer more as a plea than as an apology.

Outside of swallowing I haven't made a sound.

I put some potato on my fork and carefully lift it into my mouth. Because I know she's watching me, I stare straight ahead.

I keep my mouth closed and avoid chewing.

"Well," she says venomously.

"Well, what?" asks Dad in exasperation.

"Well when is he going to stop his shenanigans with his food and swallow?"

As she speaks I see her attention is no longer focused on me. I swallow. Then the eyes of both my parents zero in on me.

"Swallow," says Dad.

"I did," I reply.

"This is ridiculous," says Mother.

"It sure is," Dad agrees and adds, "now let's eat in peace."

Mother's thin lips grow tighter. She looks at me with hate.

I don't dare to budge.

"Eat," she orders.

"I'm not hungry," I lie. "May I be excused?"

"No you may not," she replies. Then she asks, "What's wrong with the food?"

"Nothing. I'm just not hungry."

"Go to your room," Dad orders.

I get up and leave.

Three minutes later Matthew comes upstairs and goes directly to the bathroom. He's crying.

A minute later he comes into our room. He's still crying. From the top of his head to middle of his chest he has been splattered with food. He holds a wash cloth in his hand. Not too successfully he has been trying to clean himself with it. As he's too small to see into the bathroom mirror, he's missed most of the mess.

I walk him back into the john and help him to get clean. He tells me that after I left the table, Mother had started in on him.

Then Daddy ordered her to cut it out. So she picked up her plate and fired it at the old man. Because the dish slipped or because her aim was as cockeyed as any other female's, she missed Dad only to score a bull's-eye on Matt.

We go back to our room and close the door. Their argument is continuing. A couple of hours later we turn out the light and go to sleep.

In the morning while Matt and I are in the kitchen helping ourselves to corn flakes, Mother comes in and tells us Dad will join us in a few minutes. She adds that they'll have a joint announcement of some importance to make to us.

Matt listens with obvious puzzlement and wonder. I try to look concerned. Inside, however, I don't give a damn. I've lived through plenty of these scenes before.

In a while Dad comes down. He, as she, is wearing a robe. We boys are dressed and ready to run.

"Are you going to tell them or am I?" she asks.

He frowns at her. Then he tells her to sit down. He looks at us. He seems about to say something but pauses instead. He looks at her. Then he says, "we'll take this up some other time."

"Oh, no we won't," interrupts the old lady, "we'll do it now."

"Later," he insists.

With defiance she ignores the old man and announces, "You boys are going to go live in Tennessee with my Aunt Alice and Uncle Doug. You'll leave in a couple of weeks."

"Boys, go to your room," says Dad.

He hasn't looked at us. His eyes are on her. He's madder'n hell.

"No, stay," she says.

It's obvious, she's frightened.

We hesitate.

"Leave," he orders.

"He's going to beat me," she says.

"Goddamned right," he assures her.

"Don't hit her," I plead.

He looks at me.

"Don't," I beg.

"Don't worry, my children," says Mother, "I'll survive."

She's off again on one of her Sarah Bernhardt routines.

I hate her.

If the fellow threatening to pound the life out of her had been anyone but my Dad, I'd have cheered him on. But because it's him I can't. I love him. I'm afraid he'll hurt or kill her. Then the state would lock him up for life or give him the chair. They'd do that. The cops, the courts, the whole rotten system would gang up against him.

Matthew is crying. Mother goes and hugs him and tells him not to fear for her.

Suddenly, the whole scene seems insane and surreal to me. Dad never has hit anyone. He wouldn't have threatened to do so now if she hadn't been asking for it. I sense that she wants him to slug her. I watch and wait. I have no idea of what's going to happen next but I feel sure that whatever it is, it will be bizarre.

A look of exasperated resignation rises on the old man's face. He turns and leaves the room.

Twice more that day Mother restates the news that we'll soon be sent to Tennessee. The way she describes it she makes it seem like we'll be headed to Heaven. Matt gets enthused. He can't wait to leave.

I don't like the idea. Not one bit. I would tolerate the threat of having a white hot poker driven up my butt better than the thought of being sent seven hundred miles away from Marilyn. But because I know my feelings count for nothing, I say nothing. Instead I nod on cue. I know that to the old lady, Matt and I are mannequins, or more accurately, props. When she emotes as she's doing now, her real audience is herself.

That morning when Daddy leaves for work, I walk him to the bus. I tell him I don't want to go to Tennessee.

"I know," he says, "but there's nothing I can do about it. Your mother and I are breaking up."

"Well why can't I stay with you?"

"It wouldn't work," he says.

"I wouldn't cost much," I plead. "I can get a paper route as soon as I'm twelve. I could almost pay for my upkeep."

He smiles and says money has nothing to do with it. It's the legal custom in America for custody of the children always to go to the Mother.

"But she doesn't want us. She's sending us to Tennessee."

"She doesn't want me to have you. And that's all that counts. The court would never allow me to keep you kids. In divorce cases the woman always wins. Moreover, as I once lost a job because I was an agitator for the union, there isn't a judge alive who wouldn't be prejudiced against me in any of his rulings. So it's better not to go hopelessly into debt wasting money on lawyers in a losing cause. What little I have, I want to go to you, not to attorneys."

A couple of weeks later Daddy obtains trip passes for Matt and me. We will go by coach over the Pennsylvania Railroad from New York to Washington. After that we will go by Pullman over the Southern Railway to Bristol, a city half in Virginia and half in Tennessee. Kingsport, our destination, is just a twenty mile bus ride beyond Bristol.

When we leave on the last Friday in August, it's hot in New York. We're sweating under that heavy and oppressive heat you only find in Manhattan. Everyone of my blood relatives in Brooklyn except Gram comes to Penn Station to see us off. Everyone's nerves are frazzled. Dad and Mother aren't talking. Mom and Pop are. They're arguing as they try to outdo each other in showing attention to Matt and me. Each pins a ten dollar bill inside my pants pocket.

The terminal itself is packed. There must be five hundred people in the huge 7th Avenue waiting room and a couple of thousand more in the giant glass concourse. Half of the travelers are servicemen. The place is alive with movement and emotion.

Overhead the Public Address announcements can barely be heard over the continuing hubbub of the crowd.

Two pigeons in flight suddenly appear. They circle above and finding no place to land, they fly up to the rafters to roost peacefully out of sight. To them everything below must seem no more interesting than the traffic of ants.

I feel sad and very frightened. Matthew feels worse. He's bawling. When the announcement comes that boarding for our train is now underway, we are re-hugged and re-kissed good-bye by everyone except our parents. They accompany us downstairs to see us to our places on the train. When we're seated, Dad has me recite to him once more the directions of what I'm to do when we arrive in Washington and what I should do in case a foul-up occurs. I spell out everything in detail correctly. Then he tells Mother this won't work. She answers that it has to because it will only be worse when we'd go through it all over again tomorrow. He tells her he'll see her then. He's going to go now with Matt and me as far as Washington.

"Have it your own way," she says.

She kisses Matt good-bye and even gives me a peck. I'm too stunned to return it. It's the first and only time in my memory since her stay in the hospital in 1941 that she's kissed me.

She leaves.

Matthew cries some more. Not me. I feel good. I feel safe. Dad is with us. Nothing in the world could be better than that.

The train pulls out of the station. Matt sits on one side of the old man while I'm on the other by the window. When the conductor comes through he says "hi" to Dad. He doesn't bother to look at Dad's wallet pass and he refuses even to take up our trip passes. He's letting us keep them in case we ever need them to do the trip again.

No one talks much. The ride to Washington will take five hours.

That would have seemed half way to eternity without the presence of my Dad. I lean against him. He puts his arm around me. The clicking of the wheels, the rocking of the car and the touch of my Dad make me feel warm, cozy and good but also sad and drowsy. I want the ride to last forever.

The next thing I know we're pulling into Union Terminal in Washington. I've been asleep since Newark. As we leave the train we're met by the railroad aide who has come to meet us. Dad thanks her and invites her to join us for dinner. But the lady declines. She has just gone on duty. We thank her again. She says it was no trouble. She wishes us a pleasant journey onwards. Then she smiles and leaves.

I tell Dad that Mother has made more than enough sandwiches for us and that we ought to eat them or they'll go bad. He turns to Matt and asks if that would be okay with him. The kid says sure but first he has to take a leak. He isn't the only one. So we attend to this first and then go and get drinks and take a seat on one of the long benches in the waiting room. There we eat our ham-baloney sandwiches and count up how many servicemen are in the station. Most are soldiers but if you count all of the foreign uniforms and add them to the marines, sailors and coast guardsmen, the G.I.s are in the minority

Because we have some time to kill Dad takes us outside onto the street. The sun is almost down. Directly across from us about a quarter of a mile away is the Capitol building. Dad suggests we walk around it.

The structure is very long. Alongside its wide front entrance steps on the side nearest to the station there's a statue of a woman being axed by an indian. As we walk Dad tells us stories about the Congress. He says it's a wonderful institution even though many of the people in it are awful. By the time we get around to the back of the building the sun has set. In the dim twilight an obelisk can be seen. It's the Washington Monument. I'm not impressed by it. It's one hundred and fifty feet shorter than the Trylon at the 1939-1940 World's Fair and it has no perisphere beside it. Far off in the west at the end of a long, long lawn which begins at the capitol is the Lincoln Memorial.

As we finish our walk and re-enter Union Station, Dad asks us how we like Washington. Matt answers, "It's okay but I'd rather be in Brooklyn."

"Who wouldn't?" I agree.

When we board the Southern Railway Pullman Car we are as nervous as we had been in New York. Dad identifies himself to the porter, a negro named George, and tells him that Matt and I will be traveling with him to Bristol. He shakes hands with us and says it will be his pleasure to accompany us to our destination. He adds that we don't have a thing to worry about. He'll personally see to it that we'll enjoy the trip and be delivered safe and sound to our relatives in Bristol.

My brother and I have an upper and lower birth. Matt says he wants to sleep in the same one as me. I balk at that. I say I don't want to get peed on. That embarrasses him. He's about to cry.

Dad asks me to let him sleep with me as a special favor to him. Before I can say no, George intervenes. He assures me pee is no problem: it's a known fact that bed wetters never wet in lower berths.

I sort of think that's a lie. But I can't be sure. In truth I don't want to be alone in the strange bed. So I decide to believe him. I say I'll share my berth provided George will agree to wake Matthew up in the middle of the night and sees that he leaks. He gives the matter a moment of thought. Then he says okay.

We change into our pajamas and bathrobes in the john. George puts our bags away while Dad sits and talks with us. The old man makes me promise not only to write to him at least twice a week but also to keep a diary. I'm not to worry if I miss some days. The important thing is to keep writing. I also have to promise not to alter or to destroy any entry after I've ended it. He gives me a dollar so that I can buy stamps and stationery. Lastly he hands me his fountain pen.

Then he starts to give Matt a pep talk too. But the train is set to roll. So he makes him a quick present of the mechanical pencil which matches my pen. He kisses us both and in thanking George for agreeing to watch over us, he slips him some dollars. Then he leaves.

The train pulls out.

Matt is weeping. George comes and tells him not to cry but to smile. We're going on a great adventure. The next time we'll see our Dad, we'll have all kinds of interesting and wonderful things to tell him of the people, the places and the events that we'll have seen and encountered.

As we turn in and I button up the curtain fronting our berth, I realize George is right. I can look backwards and cry or I can look ahead to Tennessee and to the great day in the distance when we'll all be reunited.

I lean against my brother as we settle into the small but ample space allotted to us. He clutches his pencil and I, my pen. I think of the events of the day. A mishmash of visions and fantasies float by. The images of my folks merge with those of the thousands of servicemen I've seen since sun up. The whole of America's military seems to become one with my family. I feel a kinship with everyone in uniform. Like Matt and me most of the servicemen are riding away from home. Many of them will never return. Compared with these heroic fellows we have it easy. We aren't going off to war. We're only going to Tennessee.

As I drift off to sleep I realize that though sad, this has been a great and memorable day--a day filled with love and a day when I've discovered how good it is to have a brother.

When our train reaches Bristol it's a half of an hour late. George is helping us carry our baggage out onto the platform. We look up and down the station. No Aunt Alice. No Uncle Doug.

I'm on the threshold of panic. Suddenly I hear a voice reminiscent of Alice's calling "Wellington, Mackenzie, Wellington, Mackenzie."

I look and see the calling is coming from a lady in a big straw hat which is flapping and half covering her face. She's rushing towards us. She has the right build and voice to be our aunt but obviously isn't. I look around behind me to see who Wellington Mackenzie is.

There's no one else in sight except George, the conductor and Matt.

I turn back. As the woman gets closer, I think she sure looks like Aunt Alice. I take a hesitant step towards her. Matthew bolts for her and she for him.

"Aunt Alice," he shouts.

"Yes, Mackenzie, yes," she calls.

I'm set to run for her too but George calls, "Master Gus, your baggage."

"Oh, thanks George," I say and step back to get it.

As Alice reaches us the conductor is hollering, "All aboard." and signaling to the engineer to pull out. George steps back onto the train. I don't have time to introduce him to Alice. I shout and wave, "Good-bye, George."

He answers, "Good-bye boys. Pleasant adventures."

"Thank you, porter," says Alice.

He smiles and tips his cap to her as the train lunges forward. I sense I'll never see him again. I start to feel sad but Alice interrupts by asking, "How was the trip?"

We start filling her in on everything.On the drive to Kingsport with Doug, we keep it up and what we omit, we tell them afterwards when we reach home. Meanwhile they brief us on Tennessee and explain some sights we pass.

What I notice first is that Bristol looks a lot like Brooklyn around Flatlands. However, it ends quickly. In no time we're out of the city and into the country. There the land is hilly but not in the way I expect. The hills aren't shaped like cones but like giant pup tents which can go on for long distances. They're covered with trees.

I'm wondering where are the mountains. I keep an eye peeled

looking for a snow covered Alp or a peak like in the movies at the start of a Paramount picture. All I see, however, are these long tree covered hills and farms which are pitiful in comparison with those I've seen in Ontario. A few have horses while almost all have cattle. Doug says here and there we might see a few sheep. I look for them but I never see one.

Then I remember reading in Geography class that the Ural Mountains are only about 500 feet high. I begin to suspect the same might be true of the Appalachians. So I ask, "Are these hills, the mountains?"

"No, they're just hills," Doug replies.

"Will we see a mountain?"

"Certainly," says Alice, "Kingsport has a magnificent one just outside of town. It's called Bay's Mountain."

We pass through a town called Blountville. It lasts about three blocks.

"Is Kingsport bigger than Blountville?" I ask.

"Much," answers Alice, "it's like Bristol but nicer."

"Good," I say. Then I ask if Kingsport has streetlights, telephone poles and electricity."

She laughs and replies, "Of course, Wellington."

"Alice," I say, "this may sound stupid but I think you've forgotten who we are. He's Matthew and I'm Gus."

"He was Matthew and you were Gregory," she corrects. "Now that you're coming to live with me, you're both entitled to more elegant names. So from this day on you, Matthew, are Mackenzie and you, Gregory, are Wellington."

"Are you still our aunt Alice?" asks Mackenzie.

"For now, yes," she replies.

After this everyone grows quiet, especially me. I'm frightened. I wonder if her mind has become unbalanced. Fiddling with our names isn't a good sign. Her suggestion that hers too may change definitely implies insanity. I suspect that her personality has become split. But into what? That's a dark mystery which I wish neither to penetrate nor to solve.

Alice and Doug are rich. They don't think so. But the facts prove otherwise. They not only have a car, a telephone and a piano but also their modern home has three bedrooms and two bathrooms. The giant one upstairs is complete with everything. The one downstairs has neither a tub nor a shower. Their yard is spacious and well gardened. Altogether their house and grounds are as impressive as those of anyone I know in Brooklyn.

As it's common knowledge that Tennessee is teeming with morons like the characters in Lil' Abner and Snuffy Smith, I ask Alice as we're unpacking if she will take us around to see the hillbillies.

She laughs and says, "Maybe up in the hidden hollows of Virginia or Kentucky hillbillies can be found. None, however, have homes in Kingsport."

Then I ask, "You do have lots of colored people here?"

"No, we have very few," she answers.

I now know my brother and I are in trouble. Our parents have placed us into the hands of a lunatic whose contact with reality is questionable. I'm afraid to hear another word from her. She's hopelessly nuts. I just pray she isn't dangerous too.

In the following weeks I find out that everything Alice has said is true. The local men don't have beards and none carries a rifle. While some of the farmers come into town dressed in bib overalls, not one walks bare footed. Nor are the women smoking pipes or wearing boots like Mammy Yokum. Moreover, the percentage of colored people in Kingsport is way less than Brooklyn's. Even Alice's view of her being middle class is reasonably true for although her place would have been a palace in Flatbush, in this town it's merely a very nice upper middle class home.

I soon see that Southerners, especially in Appalachia, have a lot in common with Brooklyners. We've all been slandered and cast with false images and accents. Neither movies nor radio nor newspapers nor books has much respect for the truth about people.

Matthew, or rather Mackenzie, and I are both excited and pleased when Alice gives us each a separate room. Back in Brooklyn, only an only child lives this high. On Schnectady Avenue and Park Palace half of the kids sleep two or three together every night in the same bed. So having our own rooms really makes us feel special. It's like we've risen up in the world to become somebodies. The trouble is, we have. We're now Wellington and Mackenzie. Inside, however, I still feel like I'm the same old Gus and I figure with my brother, it's the same.

At dinner that first night Doug also keeps slipping and calling us Gus and Matt. Alice, ever alert, constantly corrects him. She also announces that on Monday we'll all go shopping and she'll buy us whole new wardrobes.

"Gee thanks," I say hoping she'll get me a baseball uniform.

"Yeah thanks," echoes Mackenzie.

She tells us we'll have to go to church tomorrow.

"It's still summer," I say, "Matt and I"

"Mackenzie," she corrects.

"Mackenzie and I are Episcopalians and Episcopalians don't have Sunday School in the summer."

"Up north it's true that neither Public School nor Sunday School begins until well into September. But here in Tennessee the calendar is advanced. The Public School has already started. I'm sure the same is true of Sunday School. I'll call afterwards and confirm this. However, Wellington, whether or not there is a Sunday School, you and Mackenzie will accompany us to church. We will expect you to do this regularly. As for your being Episcopalians, I can assure you that no one holds higher regard for that faith than I. You see, I, too, am an Episcopalian. But here in Kingsport, we'll attend the Presbyterian Church. It's quite similar to the Episcopal but a little more influential."

I'm getting very provoked. She's changed our names and now she's doing the same with our religion. I wonder what will go next. She's a self-assured woman possessing the will and manners of a cat. There was plenty of purring when we pleased her. When we don't, she unsheathes just enough claw to keep us disinclined to cross her. She puts me in mind of someone--my mother.

The next day when we stroll up the walk at the Presbyterian Church, I glance back over my shoulder and get a glimpse of part of downtown Kingsport. I see a clean, wide boulevard. Its name is Broad Street and because it has stores galore and two movie theaters, it reminds me of Flatbush Avenue. A few busy blocks to the south, it ends at the Clinchfield Railroad Station. Beyond that but off to the right is a magnificent Mountain. It isn't ice capped but in its own way it's every bit as impressive as an Alp.

Inside the Presbyterian church the pews have cushions and there's no knee railings for praying. At first this upsets me. As an Episcopalian I have always knelt and said a prayer before taking a seat in the sanctuary. It's impossible to do this now and not look like a fool. So remembering the adage, when it Rome do as the Romans do, I copy the behavior of the Presbyterians. I just sit there like an early moviegoer waiting for the show to start.

Episcopalians kneel to pray, stand to praise and sit for everything else. My Dad says we do a lot of spiritual gymnastics.

Presbyterians, I decide that morning, have a more civilized approach to religion. Kneeling is hell on old people. It should have been abandoned years ago. How it ever got into Christianity is a mystery that needs unraveling. I don't think Jesus as a Jew ever knelt to pray. I'm pretty certain that like his kin in the synagogues of today he prayed standing up and kept thrusting his pelvis back and forth like a degenerate shepherd copulating with a sheep. I suppose because conversing with God in this posture does seem obnoxious, disgusting and sacrilegious, the early fathers in the church dropped this style of praying and replaced it with kneeling. If so, if in the old days they could decide to improve things this way, I see no reason why we shouldn't do the same today. So taking everything into consideration, I'm in accord with the Presbyterians. Screw kneeling. Let's all get cushions on the seats and pray in comfort. Then maybe Christianity will cease being a religion of, by and for the hard-asses. It could become instead the all embracing and caring faith that its Founder always intended it to be.

After church, Doug and Alice take us on a sight seeing tour down Broad Street. Because one of Doug's passions is history, he tells us a lot about Kingsport. It's a planned, industrial community built only a generation ago by the Clinchfield Railroad. Not only Broad Street but also every other main thoroughfare in town is wide. A block long store in the center of the city is owned by a very important man named J. Fred Johnson. Although a city manager backed up by the Board of Mayor and Aldermen are the nominal leaders of the community, everyone knows the real head man in Kingsport is Mr. Johnson.

Like General Eisenhower he has enormous authority and never seems to abuse it. He cares for the welfare of the people and sees to it that businesses which treat labor unfairly are run out of town. Doug says if we were living in the 18th Century instead of the twentieth, we'd refer to him as a benevolent despot.

When we get down to the railroad station the view of Bays Mountain really becomes impressive. It's only about a mile away. On it bears, deer and snakes live. Since everything in Kingsport seems to be planned, I ask Doug whether the animals are native to the mountain or whether they've been shipped in by design.

He laughs and answers that the animals have always been here.

After the tour we go to dinner at the Kingsport Inn. My brother and I are allowed to make our selections from the menu. I pick out hamburger steak, potatoes, green beans, milk spiced with coffee and apple pie. Mackenzie, of course, chooses the same. While we're eating a lady friend of Alice's stops at the table to say "hi." Immediately,

Mackenzie and I rise up from our seats and wait to be introduced. Doug also stands up. The woman's name is Mrs. Barrow. She lives close to us and has stopped by to welcome us to Tennessee and to invite us to come by later in the afternoon to meet and to play with her granddaughter, Sarah.

Before I can decline, Alice thanks her for stopping by and accepts the invitation on our behalf. Mrs. Barrow compliments Mackenzie and me on our gentlemanly manners. Then her husband, who has been standing by the door waiting to depart, loudly clears his throat. "I must dash. I'll see you later," she says and leaves.

As she leaves we utter the usual formalities: "It was nice meeting you. I look forward to seeing you again." We add, "Good-bye" and sit down.

"I'm pleased," says Alice, "The Barrows are very important people and it was a sign of good breeding when you boys stood up. Doug and I are quite proud of you."

"Thank you," I reply.

"Thank you," echoes Mackenzie.

I decide to wait and finish my dessert before telling Alice that I never play with girls. I've sized up the situation. Our great-aunt lives life on the cover of the Saturday Evening Post. My brother and I don't. We're neither Norman Rockwell's urchins nor Little Lord Fauntleroys as portrayed by that sissy, Freddie Bartholomew. The sooner my aunt gets her head out of the clouds and comes back down to earth, the better off we'll all be.

When we finish eating, I summon up the courage to confront her. She cuts me off as I begin to speak. She announces that she has to retire to the Powder Room. Doug is ordered to pay the check.

As we leave the table I wonder whether Doug is anything more than an ornamental extension of Alice. As a quiet, kind, good-natured fellow he seems to have a genuine fondness for Matt and me. I wonder, however, how much of this is traceable to us and how much to our relieving him of his wife's attention.

Back at the house, Alice draws up a list of our chores. She's a stickler for neatness. She gives us enough work to do to keep us reasonably busy. I'm to be responsible for cleaning my room, tending the furnace, sweeping the walk, setting and clearing the table, and going to the store. I'm pleased she doesn't make me wash or dry dishes. On Saturday I'm to help in the yard for two hours by cutting grass or raking leaves. All things considered this is fair and reasonable except for one silly rule: after leaking she insists that both Matt and I put the toilet seat back down.

When she finishes giving us the rules, I tell her that I will try faithfully to obey them. I also tell her that as I'm not in the habit of playing with girls, I'd just as soon skip going over to Mrs. Barrow's this afternoon.

"Nonsense," she replies, "girls are fun. It's time you outgrew your childish failings. I'll take you over to the Barrow's now. We'll walk. It's less than a ten minute walk from here."

"But,"

"Wellington, there'll be no buts about this. We're going."

We go.

Once again I've been steamrollered.

Mrs. Barrow's granddaughter is everything I expected: a real pain in the ass. Although she's the same age as me, she's taller by two to three inches. Because she can look down on me, she thinks she's better and smarter. She asks me if I like Roy Acuff. I tell her I haven't as yet met him. She laughs and says I'm precious. I hate her.

Matt tells her she's pretty. She thanks him for that and asks us how we like Tennessee. We answer that it's okay but we miss Brooklyn.

She tells us she has just been to New York and has seen Oklahoma.

When I ask her if she saw a dust storm and Indians while out west, she laughs and says, "Silly, Oklahoma is a musical play on Broadway."

All afternoon she keeps flaunting her sophistication and making me feel like a jerk. Finally I call her Sarah Smarty Pants. That doesn't seem to bother her at all. So I sulk. In turn, she ignores me and talks with Mackenzie.

When we come home we have a light supper. Afterwards I go up to my room and write letters. Then I put an entry into my diary describing what I think of Sarah. That makes my day.

As Monday is Labor Day we spend the better part of it meeting neighbors and doing some sightseeing. On Tuesday in the morning Alice takes us to a clothing store. She has us each fitted for a new suit, a blue blazer and two pairs of slacks. She also buys each of us a fedora, a belt, some ties and a new pair of shoes. My brother and I now have more Sunday clothes than any kids we ever knew or heard of.

If Alice has faults, a lack of generosity isn't one of them.

After lunch she walks us over to our new school. When she goes to register us, the clerk asks her for our records. Alice says they're in New York because the policy of the New York City Board of Education is not to release records to private individuals but to mail them directly to the concerned schools. The clerk then asks us our names. Alice answers that that is a problem. She says we'd been Gregory and Matthew Stern but as we're soon to be officially adopted by her, she prefers to have us enrolled as Wellington Churchill Jones and Mackenzie Aloysius Jones. The clerk is confused. She goes and gets the Principal. He knows Alice. He tells the clerk to list us by our new names. She does. After asking us what grades we're in, the Principal, himself, brings us to our new classes.

The news that I'm being adopted comes as quite a shock. It explains a lot of things. I now know Alice isn't nuts. I'm glad about this. Overall, however, I still feel bad. I feel abandoned.

Lots of people think that school in the south is easy. I have to say that's a myth. School in Tennessee is every bit as hard as in New York.

One of the things that surprises me when I join the class is everyone's last name. Each sounds phony. Each seems as though it has been made up as in a novel or as in a movie. The roll goes "Allen, Anderson, Barker, Boone, Caldwell, Cox, Davis, etc." Up north it's something like "Abramowitz, Antonelli, Bolyai, Borkowski, Di Stefano, Epstein, etc." It's not just the last names which are different. Rachel, Becky, Sarah, Benjamin and Samuel--Old Testament names which in New York would be associated only with Jews-are here normal and common. What's even odder is that in all the time that I live in Kingsport, I get to meet only one girl named Mary.

A second thing about the school that I can't help but notice is that everyone is white and protestant. The lack of coloreds is no accident. All of the negroes in town--and there aren't many of them--go to their own school.

People think that southerners, without exception, are prejudiced. Regarding religion this is nonsense.

Not once in all the time that I spend in Tennessee does anyone ask me what church I attend. Not once do I ever see or hear of anyone being ridiculed, snubbed or beaten because of his faith. Conversations about religion just never come up unless you run into a Jesus Jumping Fundamentalist who wants to save you. He can be annoying. Yet always you know his intentions are decent. He wants to do you a favor. He'd be the last individual who'd ever do you harm.

Racial prejudice is another matter. It's right out in the open. In many places in Tennessee you can read signs saying, "No niggers or dogs allowed."

In Kingsport, colored people unquestionably are second class citizens. Still, the races do seem to be friendlier and kinder to each other in the South than up North. In New York everyone is so deceitful that when anyone not of your race smiles at you and agrees with you, you get the uneasy feeling that he resents you.

Anyway to get back to important things: I check out the girls in class that first day to see if there's one who could replace Marilyn as my secret love. There isn't. Smarty pants Sarah is the prettiest of the lot. On average the girls in Kingsport have it all over the ones in New York in looks. That, however, means nothing for as everyone with 20-20 vision knows, New York has the ugliest women in the world.

After a few days letters from home begin arriving. My Dad has moved out. He's living in an efficiency apartment downtown on Montague Street.

He's notified the Draft Board of this and has been reclassified from 3A to 1A. He expects to be drafted.

Mother writes saying she misses us and tells us to be good. Pop writes that Brooklyn isn't the same without us. He includes a dollar for each of us in the envelope. Everyone's letter has lots of questions: How do we like school, Tennessee, the food, etc.? We know they do this to give us ideas to write about.

Mom even calls us long distance. She speaks for a half of an hour. It must cost her a fortune. She says she'll telephone us on every other Saturday at 11a.m.

Life with Alice and Doug soon settles into a predictable routine. We don't see much of Doug except at dinner and weekends. Often he has to go back to work at night and sometimes he's sent out of town on company business for a week or two. Whether or not he's around, Alice is always in charge at home. At first, I see my aunt as a tyrant. When, however, I remember my history lessons about Catherine the Great, I decide Alice has to be either a disciple of the Czarina or her living embodiment. She's a benevolent despot. She's determined to do her very best for the people in her charge. When my Dad refuses to allow her to adopt us, I can't help but think of Matt and me as her serfs. She can't own us but she can control us. On the whole she's kind. She never hits us. Nor is she given to hugging or to kissing us. She treats us as she dresses us--like prep schoolers. She'd have made a great headmistress.

Naturally, the kids in Tennessee make fun of my accent. In turn, I make fun of theirs. I tell them that I speak English.

"Not lack uhs," they answer. We argue over who sounds the most like radio and movie stars. "For Christ's sake," I say, "Eddie Cantor, Fred Allen, Jack Armstrong, Humphrey Bogart, James Cagney, Barbara Stanwyck, Susan Hayward, Gene Tierney--they all talk like me. They answer "Next to no one sounds like you, not Lum and Abner, not Roy Acuff, not Gary Cooper, not Gene Autry, not Dinah Shore and definitely not any announcer or singer on radio." As I tune into their local stations, I realize they have a point. Very few of the programs here are the same as in New York. The non-network music is awful. The singing, if possible, is worse.

According to Doug, the movies in town are censored. In theaters throughout the South, motion pictures have to conform to local tastes. I can't figure out why: Hollywood hasn't ever made a film in which the Confederates have been villains.

Going to the store is another thing I find to be a little disconcerting. Few of the items for sale bear any of the brand names I've always assumed to be universal. There are no Bond, Wonder or Tastee breads. Nor are there Sealtest, Breakstone or Borden dairy products. Not only don't they have Philadelphia Cream Cheese but they also never heard of it. Aside from the A&P, Woolworth's and the gas stations, none of the franchises are familiar. If a Krug, Dugan or Pilgrim Laundry truck would come down a Kingsport block, I'd whistle, cheer and do a back flip.

It's also strange to live in a place with neither immigrants nor immigrant culture. Up in New York we have the Irish working as cops, transit workers and saloon keepers. The Italians toil as barbers, cobblers and pizza makers. The Chinese run laundries and restaurants. The Germans excel as bakers and delicatessen operators. The Negroes are janitors and shoe shine men. The Jews labor in the garment trade and operate as small business merchants in a whole variety of marginally profitable enterprises such as dairies, stationery stores and second hand shops. When you stop to think about all of this, it does seem as if God has created all the foreign nations in order to provide Brooklyn with experts in everything. The South is culturally deprived. No doubt about it. It lacks pizza, chow mein, hard rolls, crumb buns, major league baseball and tabloid newspapers. However, I have to confess it isn't all one sided. Yankees who die without ever having eaten country ham biscuits and hot cornbread haven't really lived. Perhaps the best thing of all about life below the Mason-Dixon line is manners--Tennesseans have some. People aren't pushy and rude like New Yorkers. No one hustles you. Nearly everyone is friendly and nice, even to Negroes.

Overall, I think, compared to Brooklyn life in Kingsport is dull. Southerners don't tell jokes much. When they do, they take forever to get to the point. Even worse, their humor is corny. People in Kingsport smile a lot and are gracious and good natured. In Flatbush they're grim and given to griping but they laugh a lot.

Gossip is another obvious difference between the cultures. In Kingsport everyone knows everything about everyone else. Half of the time it seems they're all cousins. Everyone knows the local news before it makes tomorrow's paper. Gossip at the Southern table is as common as biscuits and gravy. Much of it is vicious too.

When a neighboring teenaged girl was sent east on a scholarship to a private school in Richmond, all I heard for a week was speculation about who it was who had knocked her up.

In my letters to my Dad I write of these things. He writes back telling me I'm very perceptive but that I should exercise a little reserve and not rush to harsh judgments. Gossip, he suspects, is a small town trait and probably has nothing to do with geography. He says that the first time I was brought to Canada to visit my mother's folks, one of my diapers was hung outside to dry on a clothes line just before lunch. That afternoon throughout the tiny community of Parkhill the phones rang off the hook. Before the dishes of the evening meal were washed and returned to their places in the cupboards, the news of my arrival had become old hat.

Dad writes that he's pleased with me for noticing things like humor and gossip. He says it shows I have a keen and inquisitive mind.

I write back that I wish I did have a keen mind but the truth is that when you start living in a strange place, you can't help noticing the strangeness. Intelligence and intellect haven't got a thing to do with it.

He, himself, learns this first hand. A week after he's drafted in November, he and every soldier in his company can testify with authority that the Army is weirder even than Brooklyn and Tennessee combined.

Chapter 27
Place

The favorite word of my Aunt Alice is place. Half of the problems of the world she can and will trace to people either not knowing or not keeping their place. In Kingsport her way of thinking is rather common. She shares with Adolf Hitler and her peers in the country club a ladder of social, racial and religious values which enables her to determine the worth of people. At the top, of course, stand well-to-do white protestants like herself; at the bottom are Negroes, criminals and Canucks.

If she had not put the Hungarians on the same rung as the Mediterranean Catholics, I think I'd have bought into her system. It isn't inflexible and unfair like the Nazi's. Up and down movement between the levels is possible. Nothing stops her from plunging a low life Baptist to the bottom. Nor does anything deter her from raising the great Jewish composer, Jerome Kern, up almost to the same level as a Methodist.

Among Alice's lady friends, everyone draws her status from her husband's job. Wives of senior level executives have more prestige than those of middle level. Wives of physicians stand higher than wives of pharmacists. Women who work for a living are inferior to those who do only voluntary service.

Alice, of course, occupies a position less than an inch from the top. Only not being native to the area and lacking eligibility for the D.A.R. keeps her from being Kingsport's social queen. Among the men in town the caste system also operates but it is far less formal. With the kids I meet, it carries lots of weight. I suspect too that it influences the way we're graded at school.

In my classes as I noted earlier there's very little difference in the level of work required in Kingsport and in Brooklyn. If anything, I find Tennessee to be maybe a little harder. We don't have as many bright students as up North, perhaps, because we don't have any Jews. We don't have as many dumb ones either, probably because we don't have coloreds or Catholics. The teachers are much friendlier and nicer than in New York. They seem to care about what happens to us after school as well as during it. There is some favoring, I think, of the richer kids. I benefit from it. Yet there's also great understanding and sympathy for the poorer ones. This is understandable for when you live here a while you discover how very often people are related.

For six or seven generations the region had been isolated. The few families on hand had either to intermarry or to die out. This wasn't exactly a Hobson's choice. On average the Tennesseans were and are far better looking than New Yorkers. So even if they could have picked their mates from elsewhere, very few would have.

School in Kingsport is two weeks underway when I arrive. As a seventh grader, I'm in a class where we have different teachers for different subjects. We move as a unit from room to room and in each we take the same seats as in our homeroom.

On my first day at school because I'm wearing my suit, I expect to be dressed more formally than my classmates. I figure, however, on the second day when I'll be without a jacket, I'll look normal in a white shirt and tie. I discover otherwise. Very few of my classmates wear ties. Since neither the teachers nor my classmates make a big deal out of this, I take it for granted that nearly everyone in town is a Bolshevik.

Although I'm normally quiet and shy among strangers, I'm even more so in this odd situation. I'm many hundreds of miles from my true home. I'm in no hurry to make friends--or enemies.

At lunch time in the schoolyard on the second day Sarah comes over and says "hi." I'm grateful that she has written off my surliness. I return the "hi." She then introduces me to several of her girlfriends.

They want to know where I've gotten the strange name, Wellington. I think of telling them my real name but I figure Gregory would sound just as foreign. Fortunately, Sarah intervenes and tells them that England's greatest soldier, the Duke of Wellington, is an ancestor of mine and that I've been named after him. She also volunteers the information that my nickname is Gus.

"Guh-hus," drawls one of the girls, "Why Guh-hus?"

I look at her. She really is cute. And the way she says my name really gets to me. It sounds so-oh sex-see.

I can't think of a way to get Gus out of Wellington so I say, "With a name like Wellington, I needed a nickname. It was too late to get Humphrey since a fellow named Bogart had already grabbed it, so I had to settle for Gus."

Everyone smiles or laughs.

I decide to turn the talk away from me and ask them how they got their names. I have a reason other than inquisitiveness for doing this.

I had been so nervous when Sarah introduced us, I hadn't paid enough attention to what she was saying. I had heard but I hadn't learned everyone's name.

Now I desperately want to make amends. But before I can do so, the bell rings and ends our conversation.

As we return to class I mull over what has gone on during this meeting with Sarah and her friends. It seems logical to assume that on Sunday while I had been sulking, Sarah must have found out from Matthew that Gus was my nickname. He must have slipped up on calling me Wellington. God knows, that's understandable. I still haven't gotten him down as Mackenzie.

When Sarah tosses into the conversation that stuff about the Duke of Wellington, I have no difficulty in recognizing Alice as the source of her misinformation. It gets me to thinking that Hitler must have taken a page out of my great aunt's book when he wrote in Mein Kampf that to lie well you must tell whoppers.

His reasoning was that no small fib ever succeeds because it's ordinary and commonplace.

A great falsehood, however, lasts and is regarded as unquestionably true because it's too preposterous not to be believed.

Aunt Alice and my Dad's mother are a lot alike in the way they tell tall tales. However, there's a major difference between them. Mom never believes her own whoppers to be true. Alice always does.

At the end of that second day of school as our class leaves the building the inevitable happens. A hand reaches out and grabs my arm. "Hey, Wellington, you want to fye-yett?"

It takes me a moment to realize I'm being challenged.

"What I'd like to do is play baseball. Do you guys play that here?"

"Air you serious?" questions the fellow who has accosted me.

Again it takes me a couple of seconds to understand him. "Where do you play?" I ask.

"Ah pitch."

"I mean where's the ball field?"

"Here in the school yard or on a neighborhood lot. But this is football season. Baseball is over."

"Not where I come from."

"Where is this place that you come from where they play baseball during football season?" asks one of the two kids who stand close by and are obviously with him.

"America." I answer and ask in return, "What kind of a place is this where you play football during baseball season?"

"America. You don't sound like you root for the Vols?"

"I root only for the Brooklyn Dodgers and the Boston Red Sox."

"Don't you like U.T.?"

Never having heard of Hugh Tee, I answer, "I don't have anything against him. Is he on the Vols?"

They start laughing.

"Look," I say ignoring the laughter of the three Bolsheviks, "if you want to play baseball today, I'll go home and get my mitt and join you. I'm a pretty good first baseman."

"Air you a lefty?" asks the kid who has grabbed me.

By now I realize air is are. I answer immediately, "Yeah, are you?"

He answers, "Yes."

"Great. Then I'm your friend. Us southpaws have to stick together."

"So you don't want to fight?"

"Not with a fellow lefty. Not with you. I figure you could lick me. And if you did, we might not get along. I wouldn't want that."

"You're yellow," he says. His friends echo his words.

I know now there's no getting out of this. Appeasement has failed me just as it failed Neville Chamberlain. He's made up his mind to beat me up. He isn't going to back off until he does. If he whips me easily, one by one his friends will follow. The situation, as Jimmy Durante would put it, is precarious. I decide there's no point in stalling. If we go at it quickly before the school grounds clear, there's a chance a teacher or another kid's parent will break us up. So I say, "You want a fight. You've got one."

As he squares off to box, I charge into him. I guess I take him by surprise because he loses his balance and falls. I land on top of him. Then all of a sudden, rage overcomes me. All the anguish and all the misery I feel in being uprooted from my home, in being deprived of my identity and religion and in being pushed around by this playground thug surges through me as hot hate. I swing at him with all my might and keep at it until I've bloodied his nose. Then I grab his ears as though they're the handles of a loving cup and I pound and bounce his head three of four times on the ground. Simultaneously I'm screaming at him every foul word I know. Suddenly I see his eyes roll up. He's passed out.

As I get to my feet, I'm still shaking with rage. I bark at his friends and the small crowd that had gathered, "Get the f--- away from me and call a doctor. And remember," I add as I pick up my books, "it was he who started this. If any of you forget who was bullying who, I'll find out about it. And when I'm through with you," I say as I point to the seemingly lifeless form on the ground, "you'll envy him."

I walk away and after taking about twenty steps I begin jogging and soon find myself in a run. I don't believe I'm doing this because I'm scared, which indeed I am, but because I'm so charged with adrenalin that it's impossible to do less. A block later I slow down. At home, at Alice's, I go up to my room and change.

I know I'm in trouble. Soon the cops will be around to arrest me. In Tennessee I don't know whether I'll get the chair, be hung or face a firing squad. It all seems so incredible. In a hundred normal fights in succession that bully would have beaten me a hundred times. On the sole occasion in which I'll ever triumph as an underdog, I'm worse off than if I had lost and been pulverized. I realize too late now that I should have let the son of a bitch win.

I get out my money and count it. Twenty three dollars and sixty two cents. That just might be enough to make it back to Brooklyn. But how? The cops will be at the bus and train stations. I'm doomed. There's no escape.

I decide to wait it out and save my money for a lawyer. If there's any justice in Tennessee, I'll get off on self-defense.

I know I shouldn't have pounded his head on the ground but I didn't know it while I was doing it.

I hadn't meant to kill him. It was an accident. There was nothing pre-meditated.

Manslaughter is the only charge they can fairly pin on me.

Suddenly, I realize I don't even know the name of the kid I've killed. I feel sorry for him but I also feel hatred.

He started this. He brought his death on himself.

I begin to think of his family. They'd be screaming and wanting revenge. Everyone will see me as an outsider, a Brooklyn thug, a punk renegade from the Dead End kids. I'll probably be lynched by a mob. I've seen that often enough in the movies to know that lynching is synonymous with Southern justice.

I decide I'd better write a record of what had occurred in my diary. It could be, after I was captured and killed, the only way people could ever learn the truth about what had happened.

I sit down and begin writing. When Alice calls me to dinner, I come down and eat. Immediately afterwards I return to my room and continue the entry. Matt comes in to see me but I send him away. I keep writing. It's the first time I ever put something down on paper worth reading.

Up until then everything I wrote in letters or in a diary went something like "I ate breakfast. I went to school. I came home and played. I ate dinner. I listened to the radio." This one began "Today I killed a kid. I didn't mean to..." I then recorded my feelings, my thoughts and my memories of the day. I wrote eight pages. I was a little redundant--I still have this fault--but for the first time I was writing pretty much the way I write in these memoirs.

As the evening drags on I can't understand what it is that can be delaying the arrival of the Police. My nerves are frazzled. I go and take a shower. Then I sprawl on the bed and wait. The next thing I know, I'm awaking and it's morning.

At breakfast, I'm withdrawn and wrapped up in my worries. Alice looks at me and asks, "Why are you so sullen?"

I apologize for not having heard what she'd said and ask her to repeat her words. When she does, I manage to keep my composure and say, "Alice, I just want you to know that I'm grateful for all you've done for Matthew and me."

"Thank you, my dear," she says with a pleasant smile. Then she adds, "Please remember your brother's name is now Mackenzie.

"Yes ma'am."

I feel like faking illness to avoid going to school. If staying home could postpone the inevitability of my fate, I'd have done so. Since it can't, I abandon the notion.

When I get to the school there are lots of kids arriving. Standing by the door is the bully I beat up and his same two friends.

I hadn't killed him.

The immediate joy this brings me is instantly replaced by fear. Obviously, he's waiting to get even. I decide to speak first.

"I'm glad you're okay. I'm sorry I lost my temper."

He doesn't say anything. Nor do his friends.

"I think there's a high probability you suffered a concussion. I had one once myself. That can be dangerous. If you can stay out of fights for a month, you should come out of this okay."

His response as that of his friends is continued silence.

"If you guys do play baseball, I'd like to be your first baseman," I continue as though we were still having yesterday's conversation.

"I play first," says one of the two friends.

Because of his tone I take his statement to be a challenge. "Are you a lefty?" I ask.

"No."

"Then unless you've the grace of a gazelle and the coordination of a cat, your best isn't good enough," I say. "You catch pick-offs on the wrong side and you have to turn around to throw to any position on the diamond."

"You think you're pretty good, don't you?" asserts the bully.

"I'm too small to hit with power but I always make contact. Nobody strikes me out. As a runner I'm average. Only as a fielder am I first rate. Anything I can touch, I catch."

"Baseball's out of season," says the bully.

"Maybe so in Tennessee but in the rest of America, everyone's waiting for the World Series."

"We aren't hicks. We know that."

"Good. I wasn't saying you guy were hicks. I was just trying to make the point that until the World Series ends, baseball is still in season."

"Do you play football?" asks the kid who has no business playing first base.

"I'm not allowed to," I reply, "I've had a bone disease called osteomyelitis. It could come back and cripple me if I got injured playing rough tackle."

"Is that like rheumatism?" he asks.

"Hey we'd better shove off. School's about to start," says the kid who had been silent up till now.

"My friends call me Gus," I say.

"I'm Bobby," returns the bully and pointing he adds, "this is Eddie and that's Fred."

"Hi," I say.

"Hi," they answer and from that day on we're inseparable as friends.

Chapter 28

Amy

On the day Sarah had introduced me to her friends I had looked around our classroom to spot the cute little blonde who needed two syllables to say Gus. When I didn't see her, I was disappointed. I thought of asking Sarah about her. Then I realized that wouldn't be a good idea. Sarah was no dummy. She would immediately see through this and would spread the word that I was sweet on her friend. I'd sooner die than have to contend with that.

Sometimes the Hand of God is not above giving us a shove in the direction we desire but hesitate to go. Without my encouragement, Sarah approaches me a day or two after she's introduced me to her friends and asks how I like them.

I reply, "They all seem to be very nice."

"Do any strike you as being more interesting or nicer than the others?"

I sense I'm treading in a mine field. I pause and think how would a ladies' man like my uncle Ernie handle this question. That isn't a useful notion. He'd have said that each was magnificent in her own individual way. A tactful answer, no doubt, but quite unsatisfactory as it would encourage Sarah to continue to pump me for more detail.

I decide to change the subject. To get in her good graces I say, "Sarah, I'm afraid I wasn't very nice to you last Sunday when Matt and I came over to your Grandmother's place to visit you. I apologize for being surly and for calling you Smarty Pants."

"Why that's very nice of you Wellington. I accept your apology."

"All of my friends call me Gus. I wish you would too."

"Why, thank you, Wellington. I mean Gus. Does this mean we're friends?"

"I guess so," I answer and add, "but nothing more. I never get crushes on girls taller than me no matter how beautiful they are."

"Why Gus, you're very sweet. You're not at all like a Yankee. I must say I agree with you. Every woman should have a lover she can look up to."

Figuring the conversation is over I say, "It's been nice talking to you."

"Wait," she says as I back away, "you've never answered my question. What do you think of my friends?"

"They're all nice. Now, I've got to go play with Bobby, Eddie and Fred. See ya'."

"Did you like Amy?" she calls.

I'm just a few steps short of reaching the fellows when I smile and drawl out my answer, "Of koh-whas." Then seeing her smile, I turn and join my friends.

"What was that all about?" asks Eddie.

"Who knows?" I reply, "She was asking me about her friends."

"She asked if you like Amy?"

"Look," I reply, "the other day she introduced me to four or five girls all at once. When I meet that many people, I don't get anyone's name right. How good are you in remembering, four or five names for a bunch of strange faces? All that I saw was that they were girls and they had accents."

"They don't have accents. You do."

"You're right."

"You don't remember which one was Amy?"

"The only girls whose names I know are ones who've been called on in class. I haven't heard anyone named Amy being called on."

"Amy Holden isn't in our class," says Bobby.

"What does she look like?" I ask.

"She's short and blonde."

"Would she pass in a crowd if you gave her a shove?" I ask.

"What?"

"Is she pretty?"

As Bobby starts to answer, the bell rings. It drowns out his voice and prevents me from hearing him. It doesn't matter. I can read his face. It tells me "yay-uhs."

On Saturday in the afternoon as I'm mowing the lawn, Amy happens to be riding by on her bike. She circles around and calls out in her drawl, "Gus, do you remember me?"

God, she's cute.

I stop mowing and say, "Hi, Amy."

"You do remember."

"Of course, do you live near here?"

"Over in White City?"

"Where's that?"

"By the school."

"That's Kingsport," I say with bewilderment.

"Of course, White City is just the name of a development in Kingsport. I live on Yadkin Street."

"Why is it called White City?"

"Because when all the homes were being built and sold there, a clause was put into each deed saying the house always had to be painted white. No other color is allowed except for shutters."

She pauses and adds, "You'll have to come by and see this."

I'm amazed at how easy it is to talk one on one to a pretty Tennessee girl.

Up north I never had trouble carrying on a conversation with a member of the opposite sex if she was ugly. If she was pretty, I'd become nervous and tongue-tied. No conversation between Marilyn and me ever lasted longer than half of a paragraph unless a third person was present. Such an onlooker was for me a lifesaving distraction.

Otherwise my beloved's gaze could fix itself on me and cause me to tremble, then fade and melt like wax in the sun.

I ask Amy about her bike. It's a blue Columbia with size 20 wheels. She tells me it had been given to her a couple of years ago. She's now hoping to get a new one at Christmas.

She asks me if I like movies. I tell her everyone does except maybe for a few religious nuts who believe that the pictures are the work of Satan. Amy says there are some people like this in Kingsport but not many. Most of the crazy fundamentalists live back in the hills or down in the hollows. There when they aren't denouncing films, they're jumping for Jesus or taking up the serpent.

I tell her I've heard about Holy Rollers but what's this stuff about taking up the serpent. She answers that in the back woods there are churches where people drink poison and fondle venomous snakes. She claims it's a part of their religious services. It's supposed to demonstrate their faith in the Bible and their trust in God.

Even though I know she's pulling my leg, I smile. It takes talent to invent a cock and bull story like that. And it requires first class acting to tell it with a straight face. Clearly, Amy is interesting and playful as well as lovely.

Matt, or rather Mackenzie, comes out to tell me to hurry up and finish the mowing.

I introduce him to Amy.

As might be expected he tells her she's beautiful. That goes over big with her. Like Sarah, she thinks he's precious. I can't tell whether he's stupid or just a born lady's man.

I tell Amy I enjoyed talking with her but now I have to get back to the mowing.

Instead of answering my good-bye with a so long, she rides off saying, "Talk to you later."

I begin having fantasies about Amy. I still have plenty about Marilyn too. Just because my sweetheart is out of sight doesn't put her out of mind. It's more like the other adage 'Absence makes the heart grow fonder--for somebody else.'

A few weeks pass. One day in the schoolyard Amy and Sarah approach me. Amy asks if I'm good at arithmetic.

"If you don't give me problems of adding a lot of numbers, I guess I can hold my own," I answer.

"Are you good at working word problems?"

"Nobody but Sarah's good at working word problems but if they're not too involved, I can usually handle them."

Sarah smiles.

"Would you help me do some word problems in my homework?" asks Amy.

I feel embarrassed and a little out of my league. In a left handed way I show this by saying, "When you can get help from a pro likeSarah, why seek assistance from an amateur like me?"

Sarah breaks in, "We've tried that. The trouble is that while I can do the problems, I don't know how to help her do them."

Then Amy says, "I really need your help Gus. I don't want to get an A."

I can't believe my ears. What's wrong with getting an A? Hell, there are kids everywhere who'd die to get one.

Then with that drawl of hers I realize I haven't heard her through. She isn't saying she doesn't want an A but that she doesn't want an aigh-yeff.

An F means failing. Of course, she doesn't want that. So I agree to help her beginning that afternoon. But when we get to her house, we find that her mother has hired a brilliant high school sophomore as a tutor for her. He'll be dropping by at six-thirty in the evening to start her first help session.

I leave White City with disappointment and head home. A score of fantasies of kissing her every time she gets a problem right, and of consoling her with a hug whenever she doesn't, vanishes. I don't realize it then but my chance of a deepening relationship with Amy has peaked. From that evening on her heart throbs only for her tutor.

I have no other romantic mishaps while in Kingsport. After a while it doesn't even hurt to be around Amy. I realize that although biologically she's becoming a woman while I remain a boy, she is and will always be too immature for me.

God, as usual, has intervened in my life at the right time. He has helped to keep me true to Marilyn. She, after all, is in a class with Sarah when it comes to beauty, intelligence and charm.

Chapter 29
D-Day

Every American remembers where he was and what he was doing when he learned that Pearl Harbor had been bombed. The same should be true of D-Day but to me the initial news of the allied landings in France doesn't seem to be extraordinary. After all, in North Africa, Sicily and Italy as well as in islands throughout the Pacific we've built ourselves a record of successful invasions. Moreover, we've just taken Rome. The Axis has only three major capitols. After years of struggle we've managed at last to capture one. To me that seems to be far more memorable than another invasion.

While starting a new front in France doesn't initially impress me, I get over my ignorance in a hurry. As soon as I hear on the evening news a rebroadcast of General Eisenhower, himself, announcing the invasion, I know it's a big deal.

Like most Americans I had never heard Ike's voice. However, I had seen countless photos of him. As he was almost as bald as Winston Churchill, he was clearly not Hollywood's image of a leader. When we invaded North Africa, my Dad suspected Ike was placed in command only because his last name was Germanic. Until Hitler declared war on us, more German-Americans were probably pro-Axis than pro-Allies. Dad suspected that to insure the allegiance of this potential fifth column in America, President Roosevelt had politically promoted the German-Americans Chester Nimitz, Carl Spaatz and Dwight Eisenhower to their positions of military prominence. If so, America was fortunate. Each of these great men proved himself to be worthy of his post.

What surprises me most about Ike is his voice. In my opinion it doesn't match his face.

I don't know exactly who or what I expect General Eisenhower to sound like. I only know that I find his face and voice to be incongruous. Something similar to this has happened to me before with radio stars.

When I saw my first Jack Benny movie, I think I spent as much time staring in disbelief at the on screen imposter with Benny's voice as I did watching the movie. There seemed to be no way the great comedian could in any way resemble the middle aged fellow playing the scenes portrayed before me.

Similarly, but in reverse, I think that General Eisenhower's announcement of the Normandy landings could not possibly have been pronounced by the highly photogenic and familiar fellow I know and revere as Ike. But of course, the words are his. Moreover, if he thinks the Normandy landings are momentous then there can be no doubt in my mind nor in anyone else's that they are. Whether in right voice or wrong, Ike as the supreme commander has uttered the last and defining word.

More than with the war, my mind at this time is occupied with thoughts of returning to Brooklyn. I want to go home. Still I do have reservations about leaving Kingsport. I have been happy living the life of a rich kid. I've liked never having to fear being hit. I've enjoyed having my own room. It has pleased me that whenever I've come home from school Alice has been there. She has shown great interest in what has happened everyday to Mackenzie and me. I appreciate that. I also have found swell friends among the kids in Tennessee and I love the fact that as Protestants few of them sniffed me for my religion like the Catholics and Jews do in New York. While it will be good to see my family and to be able to take in a ball game at Ebbets Field, I know that nowadays the Dodgers are lousy and that since Hans, Ernie and my dad are in the service, Pop will be the only man around. Moreover, instead of being bossed by one domineering but organized woman in Alice, I'll be at the mercy of a martinet in Mother and of two scatterbrains in Gram and Gwen.

I look forward to regaining my identity and being called Gus. I've had enough of Wellington Churchill Jones. If ever again there pops into my head the fantasy of wishing that my name or parents were different, it will be a sure sign that I either have grown senile or have developed a brain tumor.

Chapter 30

Homecoming

Because Doug will be going to Washington on business for the Eastman Corporation, he has asked Matt and me to postpone our trip home for a few days in order to enable him to accompany us as far as the Capitol. We're happy to do so. We appreciate the company.

He has no trouble booking new Pullman berths for us on the Southern to Washington. From there we still shall have to switch trains and ride coach class on the Pennsy.

It's sad when we say good-bye to Alice. Mackenzie as usual cries. So does Alice.

In Bristol the train arrives on time and we board it and go straight to bed. In the morning about an hour before we arrive in the Capitol we're in the diner having breakfast. During our table talk I mention to Doug that it's a shame we aren't living in the twenty first century. By then long distance travel will be by air. Instead of a trip from Bristol to New York taking sixteen hours by rail it will be accomplished in three by plane.

He replies that we should thank God we aren't living in the eighteenth century when Tennessee was being settled. In those days a trip like ours would take two months.

I guess I must have looked at him with doubt and disbelief for he smiles at me and repeats his assertion. Then he adds, "Remember there were no roads. There were no bridges. There were just trails between communities. Inns and restaurants were only to be found in or near cities. If it got cold you froze or built a fire. If it rained, you got wet."

He then tells us of a trip from Greeneville, Tennessee to Princeton,

New Jersey that Hezikiah Balch, the founder of Tusculum College, took around 1790.

Balch was a Presbyterian minister who went North on horseback to seek funds to start his school. Everyday he would travel about a dozen miles. Everything he needed for the trip he packed on his horse or carried on his back.

"Even if the only thing he ate was beans, wouldn't it be an unbearable burden on his horse to carry a two months supply of these?" I say with disbelief.

He smiles and replies, "Of course it would have. However, the good Reverend didn't travel with all the food he would consume. Every time he reached a new community, he would bring news from the places he had just visited. So people were pleased to receive him. They were especially delighted since he was a preacher. A century and a half ago religious figures were highly regarded and were viewed as entertainers as well as educated men. Everyone would pile into church to hear a talk or a sermon from any preacher who was passing through town. The locals who put him up for the night felt honored to act as his host. It made them the envy of their neighbors."

"The Reverend Balch was a great man. People must have loved him," says Matt.

"He was a great man. Many people did love and admire him. But greatness, admiration and love can inspire envy and hate. Hezikiah Balch faced this problem. A rival Presbyterian minister and college founder, the Reverend Samuel Doak, hated him. He thought Hezikiah's form of Presbyterianism was too liberal, kind and forgiving. He viewed it as a threat to the traditional doctrines and practices of their faith.

"One day the two men chanced to come upon one another as they were crossing a muddy street in Greeneville. A board had been laid atop the ground to enable the walkers to keep their boots clean and dry. When Samuel Doak looked up and saw his rival approaching, he said in an angry voice. 'Step aside. I won't make way for a scoundrel.'

"'I will.' said Hezikiah, 'please pass.'"

When we stop laughing I say, "that's a good story but I think it's apocryphal. I've heard it on radio on Jack Benny's Show. Or maybe it was Edgar Bergen's."

"It probably is apocryphal and as a joke I don't doubt that it predates the Pyramids. Nonetheless, the story as I've told it is on record in the Tusculum Library."

"Why is it that people like Hezikiah Balch and Samuel Doak who are so alike are so often enemies?" I ask.

"Who knows?" he replies and adds, "It just seems to be the way of the world."

In Washington, after seeing Matt and me aboard the train to New York, Doug leaves. Even though he's an in-law I know I'll miss him. The saying that 'blood is thicker than water' has its limits. It should never be construed to mean that the world of kind, friendly, decent and caring people aren't as indispensable to us as our relatives.

At Penn Station we're met by Mother and Gram. It's good they're both here for Matt and I come back with about twice the luggage we had when we left. Without the both of them we could never have managed to carry everything from the terminal to the subway station two blocks away under the Empire State building.

When we arrive in Brooklyn we find that Gram, Gwen and Mother have just moved into a five room apartment on the fifth floor of a building on Foster Avenue and East 21st St. Matt and I are to share one of the bedrooms. The same is true for Mother and Gram. Gwen has been given a room of her own but everyone knows that will not last long. She's starting her ninth month of pregnancy.

In the living room hanging as a decoration on the window is a military service banner. It bears three blue stars. It strikes me as silly. Since our apartment doesn't face the street, it can only inform the birds and squirrels that three men from our home are in uniform. The absurdity of this pleases me. I resent displaying a star for my Dad. I think it's out of place. When I tell Matt this, he says maybe Dad's star is there for us.

I tell him he's nuts. Yet a while later as I lay in bed and review the events of the day, I reflect about what he's said and I realize he's right. It's obvious that I've become far too embittered by the breakup of my parent's marriage to be able to think straight.

Chapter 31
P.S. 152

As soon as I return to Brooklyn, thoughts of Marilyn sweep over me. Of course, during my ten months in Tennessee, not a day has passed during which my mind was not captured by images of her. However, these daydreams have been lackadaisical. Now that there's a chance that any day I can run into her, my musing about her grows to overwhelming proportions and takes on a renewed urgency.

I know I've outgrown my crush on Shirley Temple. But my feelings of love have not dissipated. Instead I think I've undergone what psychologists call a transference of affection. I now shower all of my passion for Shirley into the storm of feelings which overwhelm me for Marilyn.

Even though by hitting my beloved's little brother and by being slammed with a slap by her Dad, I had left Brooklyn on terrible terms, I sense that in time Marilyn will forgive me. We will meet again and marry. God will see to it. He knows of the intense love and desire I have for her. He'll fix it so that the future will re-unite us.

I know that our moving onto Foster Avenue will have drawbacks. The loss of a private bedroom will be but one of them. Yet, things aren't going to be all bad. Mostly, in fact, I expect them to be good. By not returning to East 48th Street, I no longer have to be seen, feared and avoided as the "Bully of the Block." I can lose a fight and say "Good Riddance" to my reputation. I can live again in Flatbush as a happy kid.

So when I have my first chance to meet new playmates around the corner on East 21st Street, I waste no time in getting down to business. "Hey guys," I say to four fellows who look to be about my age, "I'm a new kid on the block. My name's Gus. Gus Stern. I'm looking to make friends, to be a member of your gang." Then swallowing hard and doing my best to mask my fear, I add, "I'm also looking for a fight. So who's ever the toughest, put up your dukes and let's go."

I wait.

No one moves. No one speaks. Instead they look at me as though I am nuts.

What in blazes, I wonder, is the matter with them? Don't they realize how scared I am?

"Well?" I challenge. "Are you all pansies?"

If my words seem menacing, my tone isn't. I'm asking a question more than issuing a call to battle.

I wait for an answer. All I hear is silence. No one even budges.

Rats, I think, this isn't working. Maybe I'm being too forward, too aggressive. Maybe they think I'm a roughneck. Maybe they're afraid.

Fear begins to swell within me. Fear--not of fighting and of being beaten but of not fighting and of not being beaten. My life on Foster Avenue is threatening to become a repeat of every misery that I endured on East 48th Street. Only this time, it will be worse for here there'll be no Marilyn.

I'm growing desperate. I've put myself in a dire fix. I need to find a way out. But how?

"Look," I say, "In a fight I think you can see that I can hold up my end. I imagine that the same goes for you. So maybe none of us needs to prove anything. Maybe, we can take it for granted that we're all tough and can take it. So if it's okay with you, let's forget about fighting. What do you say we behave like college guys or like marines in the movies and become pals by just shaking hands."

"You're not from around here, are you?" asks the smallest of them.

"I'm from East 48th Street," I answer.

"You sure talk funny for someone from Brooklyn."

"Oh, that's because I just spent almost a year in Tennessee. I guess

I picked up some of their accent. Down there everyone thought my Brooklyn dialect sounded strange."

"Will you be going back to Tennessee?"

"Not if I can help it. Tennessee is nice but I prefer Brooklyn."

"Of course, who wouldn't?" says one of the others.

"What did you say your name was?" asks the smallest of them.

"Gus," I answer.

"Do you live at 2015?" he questions.

"What?"

He points at my apartment house. "Do you live in that building, 2015 Foster Avenue?"

"Yeah. I live in apartment 5E?"

"Are you rich?"

"You sure ask a lot of questions. And I still don't know who you or your friends are?"

"I'm Charlie Cardano. Want to shake hands and be friends?"

"Okay," I answer.

We shake hands. Then I do the same with the others. One says his name is Eddie McClintock. I ask if he wouldn't mind if I call him Mac instead of Eddie. He answers that he wouldn't mind at all. In fact, getting called Mac would please him. It's his Dad's nickname.

On meeting the other two, I know by their looks that they're brothers. They say their names are Jimmy and Johnny Bernoulli. I assume Johnny to be a year or so older than Jimmy. A couple of weeks later I learn I'm wrong. They're fraternal twins. Jimmy is the elder. In fact, he insists with a smile that he's a year older than Johnny because he was born at five to twelve on New Year's Eve, 1930 and his brother didn't arrive until five after twelve on the following day in the following year. Johnny doesn't appreciate the humor in that. I soon learn that he's always competing with Jimmy and always losing. As Jimmy puts it, "Only in ignorance and in ugliness can my brother top me."

Of course, at this first meeting none of us is at ease. A lot is going on besides talk. We're taking the measure of one another. We do quite a bit of what grown-ups call verbal sparring. We keep it up for half of an hour. Then it grows dark. We leave and go home.

In the weeks that follow, I begin to like living on Foster Avenue. Although a Catholic church is across the street from our apartment, the neighborhood itself is protestant. I love that. For the first time in Brooklyn I'm living mostly among people who don't appear to give a hoot about religion or ancestry. Instead, they act as though tolerance, politeness and decency is normal.

My new school, P.S. 152, on Glenwood Road, is hard. We're faced all day with different teachers for different subjects. The place has a tradition of scholarship. It's located only a block or two away from both Brooklyn College and the newly built Midwood High School. In this setting, our teachers seek extra hard to stuff so much knowledge into us that we'll never be able to flunk in any future school we go to. They work us to death. During tests they watch us like hawks. Cheating is rare. Maybe this is because a better class of kids live here than in other parts of Brooklyn. Maybe, however, it's because getting away with it is so difficult.

Unlike other schools which give you grades based on 100% in every subject, P.S. 152 has what they called the 150 point system. You have to get 105 points to pass and to be promoted. Some subjects, the hard ones, like Mathematics and English Composition are weighted to be worth twenty-five or thirty points. Some others are fifteens; some, tens. A few such as Art, Music and Shop go for five. In all courses the standards are high. If you can get 120 points or more on your report card, you make the honor role. Only about 10% of the kids get this.

On my report card at the close of the first six weeks, I have 107 points. That means I'm passing, but only barely so. As usual I haven't been bothering to do uncollected homework. When we're given assignments in one subject to turn in, I do them during class in another. I learned a lot of Math during English and a lot of Geography during Music.

Real homework, the kind that you have to do at home, I never do. I figure the Board of Education is entitled to own my body between eight and three. After that, my time is my own and I'm not surrendering a second of it.

Despite my homework style, I am paying attention in class. The fear of losing three more points haunts me. To do so means being left back and wasting half of a year of my life. It would also label me as a failure. I dread that more than I do the failing.

One of the five point subjects which we're required to take is Poetry/Grammar. Our class has it for the last hour on Wednesdays and Fridays. During the first six weeks the course has been all poetry. I get a three in it.

I think I deserve a five but I get punished because the teacher, Mrs. Merdearsch, is a prig who doesn't realize that ass is an inoffensive epithet coined by Victorians to avoid saying arse, the offensive, four letter word in our language. When I try to explain this to her, she'll not listen to me. So because she's stupid and stubborn, she fails me for using a proper word in a required twelve line poem that we've had to create about an animal. The poem follows:

The Porcupine
by Gregory Stern

The porcupine's no friend of mine
I dare not stroke him on his spine.
Indeed I'd sooner gargle glass
Than pat this critter on his ass
For of all mammals he's the kind
Who'd stab your palm with his behind.
So go and buy an asp or rat

If you must have a pet to pat
For one porc's worse, I guarantee ya'.
Than sixty sips of diarrhea.
In sum mankind, rejoice, we're minus
A porcupine's behind behind us.

At the start of the second marking period we switch teachers as the course becomes and stays grammar. At first I'm delighted by the change. Until I enter this class I've never heard of grammar. When I do, I figure it has something to do with problems facing old ladies. Boy, am I wrong.

Miss Fontenelle teaches the subject. She's a frozen-faced, fifty year old spinster. Charlie Cardano claims she missed her calling by not giving birth to Hitler. He says she has made our little piece of Brooklyn into Dachau. I'm not sure what that means but as it sounds impressive, I agree. Later when I find out that Dachau is a concentration camp, I really agree. Fontenelle is frightening. Everyone dreads her. At school on any bathroom wall you can read the writing, "Better to die and dwell in Hell than take a class with Fontenelle."

For the first week in Grammar, Miss Fontenelle has us memorize the definitions of the parts of speech. On Wednesday she begins by telling us, "A noun is the name of a person, place or thing." Then she asks, "Class, what is a noun?"

In unison we answer, "A noun is the name of a person, place or thing."

"Again class, what is a noun?"

"A noun is the name of a person, place or thing."

Next she goes along row by row asking us individually, "What is a noun?" When she gets to Charlie he answers, "It's a person, place or thing."

In silence for the longest ten seconds in history, she glares at him. Then with measured words she says quietly but firmly, "I am going to ask two more children to define a noun for me. You will listen to them. Then I shall call on you again. If you do not tell me the exact, letter perfect, correct answer, you and everyone else in this class will remain at 3 o'clock in this room to write 100 times, 'A noun is the name of a person, place or thing.'"

She resumes her questioning. When she gets back to Charlie, everyone is relieved and thankful to hear him say, "A noun is the name of a person, place or thing."

We finish the day learning the definition of the adjective. On Friday, our lesson is the pronoun and the verb. On the following Wednesday it's the adverb and the preposition. Two days later we end the parts of speech with the conjunction and the interjection. Miss Fontenelle congratulates us on our memorization. Then she tells us we will have a test next Wednesday. It will deal with identifying the parts of speech.

Cardano raises his hand.

"Yes, Charles?" she asks.

"Is identifying the parts of speech the same thing as telling you the definitions."

"No Charles, it is not? Identifying the parts of speech means knowing what parts of speech particular words are. Perhaps, you can illustrate this by giving us an example of a verb. Cite for us please a word which denotes action, being or state of being."

For a long while Charlie says nothing. Just about everybody else would do the same. We know the definitions but not a one of us, I think, knows what they mean.

At last Charlie speaks up and says, "Electricity."

In an instant it comes to me that he's right. Electricity, after all, has to denote action and being because in the Frankenstein movies electricity is what brings the monster to life.

As I turn my head to face Charlie to let him know, I admire his brilliance, Miss Fontenelle erupts with anger. She declares, "Charles

Cardano, if you are not an impertinent idiot, you are an imbecile. Electricity is a noun."

I have no idea of what impertinent means. I figure that in her exasperation she has tried to say permanent and has botched it. I wonder how she could call electricity a noun when clearly it does denote action. Moreover, it has nothing to do with the name of a person, it can't be the name of a place and since it doesn't occupy space and have weight, it isn't the name of a thing.

I feel bad for Charlie. He's neither an idiot nor an imbecile. He's one of the few in class who in math can do word problems.

Moreover, on his last report card, he had gotten 118. That put him only two points shy of making the Honor Roll.

Miss Fontenelle asks if any others of us can cite an example of a verb.

No one answers. If anyone can cite a verb, he doesn't. Only an idiot or an imbecile would take the chance of replying and being belittled?

As the bell to end class is about to ring, Miss Fontenelle informs us in her cold, calculating tone that come Wednesday on our first grammar test we will be asked to provide an example for each part of speech. Should anyone prove himself to be incapable of doing this, he will be kept back. He will remain in 7A until he dies or until the Military sees fit to draft him.

The bell rings. Grammar ends. My weekend begins. Although Miss Fontenelle has placed a sword of Damocles above our heads, I give it no thought. Why worry about her test when Wednesday is a long way off? In the interim anything may happen. With luck Miss Fontenelle could catch her heel in a subway grating, break her leg and be hospitalized for months. Better yet, she could have a heart attack and die. If that were to happen, I wonder what new rhyme about her would we be reading on the bathroom walls.

I have no memory of what I did over that November weekend. Indoors, I'm sure I read the paper and listened on radio to the war news. Almost certainly, I must have written a letter to my Dad who had just been transferred to the 106th Infantry Division. I suppose that if the weather was okay I played outdoor games such as ring-a-levio or stickball. If it rained my mother would have ordered me to take my brother to the movies. Even if money was tight she would have done that just to get herself a few hours of peace and quiet.

Those are some of the things I don't remember doing that weekend. What I do remember doing was not doing grammar.

"Sufficient unto the day is the evil thereof," are the words of a wise man who knew what He was talking about. At school on Monday and Tuesday I endure evil enough in just getting through classes. I give no thought to Wednesday. It's out there waiting for me but I succeed in keeping it out of my mind.

As burying his head in the sand can't save the ostrich from a charging lion, my ignoring of Wednesday does nothing to ward it off. It arrives. When it does, it fills me with panic. All morning, I keep hoping and praying that God as the Angel of Death will visit P.S. 152 and kill Miss Fontenelle. He doesn't. When I come home for lunch, I make up my mind to play hookey in the afternoon.

I don't.

Finally, the clock strikes two. Our class arrives in Miss Fontenelle's room. Doomsday has arrived.

Miss Fontenelle passes out paper for the test. We write our headings, look up and wait for the exam to begin.

Miss Fontenelle announces the first question. "Write a sentence with a noun in it. Underline the noun."

Although I'm filled with fright, I manage to keep my wits. This one I can get. I write, Electricity is not a verb

I look up and around. Next to me sits Zelda Tarski, 148 on her last report card, the smartest kid in school. By accident I happen to see her paper. Well maybe not quite by accident. On it she has written, 'I am wearing a blouse.'

I ask myself, why did she underline blouse?

Suddenly it comes to me. Her blouse is something she has on. It's a thing. So in the sentence she has underlined it. She hasn't underlined her real blouse but rather, a word which is the name for it. The word, blouse, is the name of a thing. So naturally it's a noun. It fits the definition.

Miss Fontenelle orders us to skip a line. Then she tells us to write a sentence with an adjective in it and to underline it.

I glance again at Zelda's paper. She's writing, 'My blouse is red.'

Why red, I wonder. Then it comes to me. Red is describing the noun, blouse. So being nobody's fool I write, My shirt is white.

Well, to make a long story short, throughout the remainder of the test, I keep glancing at Zelda's answers. As I do, the revelation continues. I'm not merely copying cleverly. I'm learning grammar and understanding it. So when we get to the interjection at the end of the test, I really outdo Zelda. She writes, 'Golly, I've lost my gloves!'

I counter with, "Jesus H. Christ, the cat needs more sand in the cat box!"

Needless to say, Miss Fontenelle never knows I've cheated. If she had caught me at it, I think I'd have denied doing so. That would have been one lie, I could have gotten away with. When it comes to knowing and understanding the parts of speech, I'm a second Albert Einstein.

Chapter 32

Death

By the time I entered the world and drew my first breath all but two of my great grandparents had given up the ghost. Neither of these survivors hung around long. The first to depart was Pop's mother. I called her Grandma. She passed away in 1937. I remember her as a kind, gray-haired, roly-poly lady who always greeted me with a cookie. I liked her a lot but she did have one fault: whenever she went to the bathroom she seemed to stay in it forever. Once when she was using the john, I had to do number one. I told Pop. He urged me to hold on. I did. Soon, however, my need became pressing and painful. I let him know my control was near its end. He said he understood and asked me to hold on just a little while longer. I did. Then I told him, I had no choice. I was about to leak on the carpet when he took me into the kitchen, turned on the water and hoisted me up to the sink. I peed furiously. As I relieved myself he pleaded with me not to tell Grandma. That surprised me. I couldn't imagine Pop being afraid of anyone, especially not of a nice, little old lady like Grandma.

As he scoured the sink with cleanser, he saw my fly was still open. He pantomimed buttoning his own and whispered "Button up."

"Okay," I said as I complied.

He brought his forefinger up to his mouth and signaled shush.

I laughed.

He finished cleaning the sink and we headed for the living room.

Then my memory fades.

My other great grandparent was Gram's mother. Although I visited her in Ontario shortly after my birth and again when I was three, I have no recollection of her. I do remember isolated details of the second Canadian trip but these had nothing to do with her. Mainly they were about eating green apples and suffering the runs.

Many stories have been told to me by my cousins in Ontario about Great-grandma's psychic talents. During the Battle of the Somme in World War I, she announced to the family that Ernie, her eldest son had just been killed. Two weeks later this was confirmed when the telegram from the government arrived.

Great-grandma was famous for sending a daughter or granddaughter into town to meet relatives coming to pay her a surprise visit on the afternoon train. Not always did they arrive. My dad jokingly said that Great-grandma has predicted seven of my mother's last three visits to her. Three weeks before she died, however, she did predict with accuracy the date of her death in 1940.

While all of this stuff about Great-grandma being psychic fascinates grown-ups, it never has held my interest half as much as the story of how during her childhood she lost the hearing in one of her ears. A bumble bee flew into it. The insect somehow managed to crawl into the canal leading to Great-grandma's ear drum and stung her. Already in terror, she now began suffering unendurable pain. As she screamed and cried, her mother held her still and tried to dislodge the bee. It wouldn't budge. So with a darning needle she stabbed it and then crunched it out piece by piece. When she was through, Great-grandma's ear drum was punctured. No one was ever quite sure whether this was due to the bumble bee or to Great-great-grandma's understandable misuse of the darning needle.

The departures of these ancestral ladies are the only contacts I have with death until Mom dies. Her passing in September of 1944 makes a strong impression on me.

Although Mom had been ill for a long time, I hardly had noticed it. She had breast cancer. About a year before her death the disease began to spread through her body and gave her an immense amount of pain. Since her nose didn't run and she never coughed or sneezed,

I thought her discomfort was troublesome but not lethal. Obviously, I was wrong.

Mom was fifty four when she died.

To me fifty four is old. If you check the statistics on the backs of baseball cards you can see that the physical skills of everyone over the age of thirty three rapidly run downhill. Mother thinks that's why both Jesus and her father died at thirty three. It's the age when any normal man is at his best. Only judges, generals and presidents can excel when they get past it. That's because wisdom is gained mainly through experience and that comes only with time. Once anyone reaches sixty he knows he's got one foot in the grave. After that about the only thing he can look forward to other than death is rheumatism or senility.

Ernie says Mom's cancer probably began many years before he detected it. He believes she might be alive today if she had told him of the tumor when she first became aware of it. It should have been removed or treated with radiation and cured.

Ernie's convinced Mom died because of her Victorian mentality. She regarded her breasts as untouchable to anyone but herself, Pop and her children during their infancy. Even to have her heart or lungs checked, she insisted on being the one to hold the stethoscope to her chest.

About the time when Matt and I went to live in Tennessee Ernie discovered his mother was seriously sick. He forced her to go the hospital for an examination. The x-rays of her mammary glands confirmed his worst fear. Despite all the treatment she was then given, her fate had been sealed.

Throughout her final year Mom's condition grew slowly but progressively worse. Her illness put me in mind of Normandy where the Allied attack never backed up an inch but advanced so slowly that it seemed the war might go on long enough for me to be in it. Finally, however, Mom's system like the German Army could no longer contain its adversary. Overnight everything collapsed. The struggle became a rout. During the same weeks that we freed France, Mom lost in rapid succession her voice, her sight, her hearing and her life. She died on the 12th of September 1944.

Ten days before Mom's death, I'm told that her end will come within two weeks. I'm shocked. I have watched her deterioration but I've assumed it's reversible. After all, Ernie is a great physician. I figure he can fix anything. Hasn't he been first in his class and hasn't he been told by just about every member of the faculty at the Long Island College of Medicine that no brighter student than he has ever attended their school?

When Mom dies, I'm at home. Mother asks me if I want to attend the funeral and the reception. I answer, "yes."

The wake is held at Kennedy's Chapel on the corner of Rogers and Church. Simultaneously, New York endures two days of rain as a hurricane sweeps by. Ernie and my Dad who are both on leave have to be at the Funeral Home almost continually to act as the official greeters. When Mother and I pay the funeral home our first visit, we enter into a foyer and sign a booklet called a Book of Remembrance. Everyone puts his name in it to show he has come and paid his last respects. After I add my John Hancock we go through a doorway on the left into a large room set up with folding chairs. Opposite the door and high on the wall is a huge cross and under it is the coffin bearing Mom's remains. A prie-dieu has been set up in front of the casket for those who want to kneel and pray. Flowers are everywhere.

As we walk up to the coffin I look at the dozen or so people who are already seated. I see Gwen and Gram. I start to wave but Mother nudges me to keep looking ahead and to be solemn.

At the coffin Mother says, "Doesn't she look beautiful?" It's less a question than a statement which I realize demands my agreement.

I peer at the corpse. It doesn't look at all like Mom. It appears to be a giant doll made up to resemble her. I suspect that my grandmother's body has become lost and that this mannequin is serving as a substitute until it can be recovered. It's robed in a long white dress edged with gold embroidering. A small but elegant corsage adorns its waist.

Mother says, "Aren't you going to kneel and pray?"

This is the second command thrown at me as a question. I kneel to comply. I wonder what I should pray. For half of a minute I kneel there like a moron unable to decide. The Lord's Prayer seems out of place. It doesn't refer to death or to the afterlife. The Hail Mary of the Catholics has the right stuff but I don't know it. The Apostle's Creed might work but it's too long. Finally I say to myself to hell with all of this. In silence I rattle off the grace, "God is great. God is good. Let us thank Him for our food. Amen."

I rise feeling like a jackass. Mother, oddly enough, seems pleased and compliments me for an appropriate display of reverence. We then walk over to the chairs and sit down by Gram and Gwen.

The conversation of the women begins with "They did a wonderful job of making her up, didn't they?" and slides directly into "How did you get here?" and "Isn't that Mrs. X entering. My how's she's aged which reminds me…" From that point on everything they say is their usual table talk.

I'm getting bored. In fact I'm past getting. Then Pop walks in. I watch him go to the coffin. He makes the sign of the cross and kneels to pray. Then when he rises he turns and walks our way.

I smile at him. He winks and pats me on the head. Then he says "Hi" to everyone and begins flirting with Gram. She tells him he's a terrible rip, but she loves it. Then he invites everyone to join him in a trip to the tavern across the street for a little libation.

The women decline. I ask please to be allowed to join him. Mother says no because I'd only be a pest. Pop tells her that's impossible for anyone blessed enough to bear the name of Gregory Ulysses Stern is by definition handsome, charming and entertaining company. He then re-extends his invitation but I alone join him.

On our way out we're joined by my dad. In the bar I drink a coke while Pop and the old man each have a shot. Pop makes a toast, "To Mom, may she rest in peace."

We clink glasses as Pop adds, "She looked pretty good."

"That's because her mouth was closed," says Dad.

Pop smiles and comments, "She always meant well." Then switching subjects he asks Dad, "How's Ernie taking it?"

"Badly, but it's a blessing. Her death is the best thing that could happen to him. He hasn't as yet had a decent relationship with a woman because of her. She's made of him a textbook model of Freud's Oedipus Complex."

"I don't know what in hell you're talking about but I'll drink to it anyway," says Pop. Then he orders another round of drinks for all of us.

Dad declines. He has to say hello to a couple of other people and get back across the street.

After he leaves Pop asks, "Well, young fellow me lad, are you able to handle this business of death?"

"Of course," I answer.

"The sight of a dead body doesn't bother you?"

"A little," I reply and add, "What bothers me most is the corpse not looking like Mom."

"The dead always do look different. You'll get used to it."

"I guess so but I hope I won't have to get experience at it for a long time."

"Hear, hear," says Pop as he downs his second shot.

"The oddest thing," I go on, "was sitting back and watching her in the coffin. The further away from her I got, the more she looked like herself. I also had the strange feeling that if I said to her, 'Start breathing and get up,' she'd have done it."

"Why didn't you say that?" he questions.

"I thought about it but decided not to because I was afraid she'd do it."

"Do what?"

"Why start breathing, get up and walk around. We couldn't have that. It would have upset the whole order of things. It would never do for a twelve year old to have the power of God."

"So you let her stay dead to preserve the natural order of things," he says with a smile.

"I knew that any command that I'd have given her wouldn't have mattered. She was dead. Nothing could change that. But still, I didn't want to take a chance on doing so."

He laughs and wants to order me another coke. But I've not as yet touched the second one standing before me on the table. So he backs himself up.

I go off to take a leak.

The john in this tavern has gigantic porcelain urinals. They tower over me and protrude outward to give a fellow a lot of privacy. I feel dwarfed. It's like peeing in the Parthenon.

When I come back out Ernie is entering the bar. He takes the same seat next to me in the booth as had my Dad. Pop looks at him and speaks up with his customary greeting, "Well, young fellow me lad, how's it going?"

"Okay, Pop," he answers and adds, "But I don't think Greg's handling it too well."

"How's that?" asks Pop.

"I don't quite know. It's hard to put your finger on it. He's dispirited. But six months from now he'll probably be in the best shape of his life. Mom sort of stunted him. It was all unintentional but it wasn't good. In psychiatric terms, he's been suffering a classic case of the Oedipus Complex."

Pop doesn't bat an eye. Nor do I. He merely says, "Interesting." Then he orders a shot for Ernie and a final one for himself. I finish my coke with them as Pop offers another toast to Mom. Then we recross the street and rejoin the mourners.

Dr. Wilson is present. After a few minutes he gets up and leads us all through a small service which he reads from the Book of Common Prayer. Then everyone files past the coffin and leaves.

A small group of out of town relatives and friends come home with us. When we get there Mother thanks our neighbors for watching Matt. She then sends my brother and me to bed.

On the following day, I don't go back to the wake. But on the day of the funeral I ride in the first limousine with Ernie and my family. I'm told Pop isn't able to join us because he has an urgent business deal at work. I don't question that. It's what everyone always says whenever Pop's been cockeyed drunk and unable to handle his hangover.

At Evergreen Cemetery the coffin containing Mom is delivered sealed inside a long rectangular box. It's placed over the open grave. Everyone stands with a flower in his hand while Dr. Wilson reads a final service. Then we all return to the cars we've left parked nearby.

In the months that follow I have quite a few dreams about Mom. I miss her. I feel sorry that I hadn't shown more concern for her at her funeral. But she knew I loved her and that I think is far more important than whether I said and did the correct things at her funeral.

Chapter 33

War and Change

Although Mother has signed a lease to remain for one year in the apartment on Foster Avenue, our stay there lasts less than six months.

Before Matt and I return from Tennessee only one kid, a sophomore at St. Francis Prep., lives in the building. He's Francis X. O'Malley and, believe it or not, he really calls himself Francis instead of Frank. Right away this tells me that he's weird. At first I figure he's a Giant fan but when he snubs me when I say hello to him as we ride up the elevator, I know he's something worse. I never see him out on the street playing games or talking to people. More than half of the fellows in our gang on East 21st Street don't even know that he's in the neighborhood. He's as faceless to them as the driver of a passing car.

Whenever anything goes wrong in the Foster Avenue building the landlord's agent, Mrs. Ott, always puts the blame for it on Matt or me. If the elevator stops functioning at eleven in the morning on a school day, she'll insist that this has to have been caused by us. She'll concoct a lie saying the trouble is traceable to our having pushed two or three different floor buttons simultaneously when we left for school at eight o'clock. One rainy day when she, herself, manages to skid and to fall on a wet spot inside the lobby by the front entrance, she claims my brother and I are responsible for her plight. She insists we left a slippery puddle in her path when we neglected to wipe the wet soles of our shoes on the door mat. These and similar mishaps are always found by her to owe their origin to misdoings by the Stern boys.

At first whenever complaints about us are brought to Mother, she believes them. It doesn't matter how much Matt or I protest our innocence, she regards us as guilty and punishes us accordingly. After a few months of this, however, she comes to her senses and surprises everyone by boldly standing up to Mrs. Ott. She tells the old battle axe to stop acting as if the building is an adjunct of the Third Reich. No longer will unfair accusations against Matt and me be tolerated. We're no longer to be blamed and held responsible for every failing in the building.

Mother indicates that before the arrival of her sons the elevator had gone on the fritz, hall lights had burned out and people had endured slipping and tripping accidents in the building. Not once, however, has any of these unfortunate incidents been attributed to Francis. Instead, they've been accepted as natural. So in the future, Mother tells Mrs. Ott, when mishaps arise, they are to be handled in the same manner as of old unless there's clear and convincing evidence that Matt or I have been involved.

I have never heard Mother speak up to an outsider as forcefully and as forthrightly as this. Of course, inside our home she has never been one to hesitate to say her piece. But with strangers and acquaintances it has always been her way to act docilely and deferentially. To see her now stand tall both surprises and pleases me. Yet, I can't help but wonder what has brought this about. For a while like Constable Bumble in Oliver Twist I put her change in character down to the increase in the amount of meat in our diet. Later, however, I realize it probably is a byproduct of her job. Women who are going out into the world to work are acquiring more than money with their paychecks. The income is also adding to their personal sense of independence, self worth and power.

Of course this confrontation creates ill will and enmity between Mrs. Ott and us. So to everyone's benefit and satisfaction, an agreement is made to allow us to vacate our lease.

On the first of December 1944, Mother, Matt and I move with Gram and Gwen into a one family house at 1 Martense Court.

After Mom's funeral both Dad and Ernie return to duty.

My uncle stays stationed at the Presidio in San Francisco until January of 1945. Then he's shipped out to Hawaii. After about a week in Oahu, he's sent to Tarawa in the Gilbert Islands. There he sits out the remainder of the war and an ensuing year of peace. However, neither he nor we ever know while the war continues that he won't be sent into a combat zone.

When reports in February of 1945 come to us of our Navy's assault on Iwo Jima, everyone in the family fears Ernie is taking part in it. When April brings news of our landings on Okinawa, our fright resurfaces. Throughout that spring as we review the accounts of the Kamikaze attacks on our fleet and of the fanatical fighting occurring on the island, we stay braced for the worst. Our dread continues as we await the invasion of Japan's home islands. We anticipate enormous casualties and pray Ernie will not be one of them.

No one has any doubt that the Japs will fight to their last man. After all the horrible atrocities they've committed, they probably reckon that they have no choice to do otherwise.

I've heard some people say President Truman's decision to drop the atomic bombs on Japan was wrong. I can't understand their reasoning. Without such nuclear blows to nudge Hirohito to surrender, the Japanese would never have capitulated. They are asked to do so during the conference held by the allies in Potsdam during July. With contemptuous silence, they spurn this offer. They are belligerent fanatics intent on success or suicide. Since they won't yield and since the civilized world cannot tolerate their subjugation of East Asia and the Pacific, our President's choices are reduced to terrorizing them atomically into submission or to destroying them conventionally one by one. If Harry Truman had opted for the ladder course, not only would the Japanese have just about vanished as a race but they'd also have taken with them another million of our servicemen.

When I see newsreels of the destruction visited upon the Japanese,

I can't help but feel sorry for them. Yet with malice towards all and charity for none, they've sent their servicemen out to savage the world. To those whom they subjugated they've been as cruel as Cossacks and as pitiless as Pizarro. Every terrible thing that has happened to Japan their nation has earned and has deserved ten times over. When you look at the Rising Sun's record of torture, of rape and of murder, and when you witness the Japanese depraved indifference to the plight and suffering of all whom their military victimized, you have to be a saint not to spit at them. What Churchill said of the Hun that "he's either at your throat or at your feet" goes double for these people. I don't trust them.

I never shall. I suspect that in twenty years they'll be attacking us again.

As Ernie goes west to do his part in the Eastern War, my Dad returns to Camp Blanding. As soon as he arrives there, he has to turn around and come north again and join the 106th Infantry Division which is shipping out to England. About a month later the unit is in France. It then goes into the line in the Ardennes. This is expected to be a quiet sector of the front. With winter setting in, everyone looks forward to some peace and quiet before the return of better weather. Then our soldiers will begin their final assault on the Reich.

In life, as the poet says, "The best laid schemes o' mice an' men gang aft a-gley an' lea'e us nought but grief an'pain for promis'd joy."

Truer words have never been spoken. Whether judged from the perspective of the Allies or of the Axis, the events that winter are disastrous. In mid-December a half of a million German soldiers race behind their Panzer divisions and steamroller over our forces in the Ardennes. On the first day of the battle they overwhelm my Dad's unit and for the next two weeks they advance westward almost to the Meuse River. Their goal is to cross it and to swing North to take Antwerp. This would separate the British and American Armies. Were this to occur, Hitler believes the English will sue for peace rather than endure another year of war and a possible second Dunkirk. Of course, the German thrust fails. The ultimate victory in the Battle of the Bulge goes to us. Yet it comes only after six weeks of bitter combat with an enormous cost in casualties.

When battles are reported on the radio or described in newspapers, the details are never current. The events being depicted are relayed to us anywhere from a day to a week late. Of course, the mail from the front is even slower. So right into January we continue to get letters from my dad. And it isn't until after New Year's that the telegram comes telling us that Dad is missing in action. Shortly thereafter his letters stop. The last one we get from him is dated December 12th. Two days earlier we've received one he'd written on the 14th.

Although I've been anticipating bad news, I keep hoping it won't arrive. I almost become optimistic as the days pass and nothing untoward reaches us.

After the telegram comes and after the letters stop, I persist for a while in believing that my Dad is safe. By April, however, I'm beginning to give up that illusion. Although I know that there's still an outside chance that my Dad has not been killed but merely captured, I don't hold much hope in this. I know from the news reports of the massacre at Malmedy that the German soldiers have been machine gunning unarmed American prisoners of war as readily and as callously as they've been murdering Jews.

My Dad is dead. Although I don't want to admit it, I know it's true. So I go about my daily life in much the same outward manner as always. Inwardly, however, I'm fluctuating between rage and despair.

At school I sit and look at my teachers as though I'm giving them my full concentration. They probably believe I'm hanging on their every word. In reality, I'm so wrapped up in my anger that I hear nothing. To me their mouths move mutely like those of fish in a tank. I watch them and think: Who cares about this pointless knowledge? Who cares that your sum of six ridiculous five-digit numbers is 382,466? I care only that my Dad is dead.

As I'd sit there I see before me looming like a double exposure the scene in the class and the vision of my Dad's mutilated corpse lying in the snow somewhere on the frozen soil of Europe. Never again, I realize, will I or anyone else be able to see and to talk with him. Never again will we hear his soothing voice or feel the warmth of his comforting touch.

I guess I go through those days in 1945 behaving like a zombie. I suppose everyone in grief does the same.

Chapter 34
St. Joseph the Carpenter

It is a good thing that I'm so busy during the first half of 1945. I need to keep occupied. It isn't healthy to dwell upon thoughts of my Dad. His death I lay at my mother's feet. If she hadn't been screwing around, he would never have moved out and gotten drafted.

Most of my friends aren't friendly with their fathers. In fact, if they weren't related and were meeting each other for the first time, few would have a thing to do with one another. I think that's how I would be with my mother. I'd regard her as a beautiful but cold woman whose mere touch could turn water into ice. In turn, she'd look at me as someone not worth her notice. Even as contemporaries I doubt whether we'd have five words to say to one another.

One evening I walk by a store where a boy my age is helping his Dad change the display in the window. The two of them have been working a while and will be continuing to do so for another hour or two.

I envy the kid.

I sense he has been roped into the job. Surely he's wishing to be any place but where he is. Yet I also know that as he gets involved in what he's doing, he'll begin to fantasize. He'll imagine a tomorrow teeming with shoppers. His attractive display will catch their eyes. None will be able to resist it. Its magnetism will draw people into the store in droves and bring his Dad a day of record sales.

Then reason interrupts and destroys his fantasy. After all, the kid has been through this before. He knows tomorrow will not be noticeably different from today or any other day.

I'm pained by the narrowness of his concern. I know that he's missing the moment. Its wonder, its beauty and its bliss is eluding him. Yet, I still envy the kid. He's with his Dad. And the wonder, beauty and bliss of this will eventually be sensed and appreciated by him in retrospect.

I think of a touching print that I've seen. It's entitled St. Joseph the Carpenter. It's by de La Tour. In the painting young Jesus holds a candle. It illuminates His face, casts light upon the closeness and the laboring of His dad and leaves the rest of the scene barely discernable in shadow.

For me it is a picture of great poignancy. It inspires within me feelings of warmth and overwhelming sadness. It makes my eyes smart. I restrain my tears.

My Dad had been my best friend. He hadn't been like other kids' fathers. He never played at being God. Nor was he Hollywood's image of a parent, a pain in the ass know-it-all who's at his best when condescending like Judge Hardy to listen to the silly ravings of his simpleminded son. My mother bought into that image. So too did others. But my Dad, never. He didn't play roles, at least, not with Matt and me. He was always real.

Although it has been a German bullet or bomb that has killed him, I see my mother as having triggered it. I hate her.

I can barely mask the feelings of antipathy that I have towards her. To hide my hostility, I do what I always do when I don't want to be involved with someone. I behave politely. I've always used politeness to maintain my privacy and to keep an insurmountable and unbreachable wall of distance between myself and those whose company I disdain.

Chapter 35

Flatbush Boys' Club

When we move to 1 Martense Court, the first thing I do is rejoin the Flatbush Boys' Club. This time, however, I take the physical myself. If I were the only one being tested for a hernia, I'd find the examination embarrassing and frightening. However, as I'm just one of fifty fellows being told to turn his head and cough, I breeze through the ordeal as if it were nothing.

Often, something like the Boys' Club physical, which initially can terrify the wits out of me, proves to be nothing troublesome when I'm able to come back and face it at a later date.

I remember the first time I went to Ebbet's Field.

My dad wants us to sit in the second tier. Because I lack the courage to walk with him up the unscreened ramp to the upper level, he's forced to sit with me in the lower grandstand. A year later when I return to see my second big league ball game, I charge up the ramp and hardly give it a thought.

When you're little, one year can make a difference in allowing you to face things and to behave like a man.

As I now am once again in the Boys' Club I run into some of the fellows from the old neighborhood on Linden Boulevard. Although they have been good friends, I feel neither a need nor a desire to keep their company. I just gravitate naturally to hanging around with the kids from my new block.

My time in Tennessee has enabled me to sharpen my skills as a baseball player. But in Brooklyn this is a useless gain. Hardball in Flatbush is almost as foreign as soccer. This is so because to find a field on which to play we have to travel to the Parade Grounds edging Prospect Park. To me every one of these trips seems to be well worth the trouble. We have a lot of fun on the diamond. Our teams are made up mostly of kids my age. However, there are always a few fathers on hand. They spice up our line-ups with power. Every time we play, the games are close. It's exciting stuff. The only trouble is not enough of us are dedicated to playing the sport two or more evenings in a row.

At the Boy's Club the big noise is basketball. Because I haven't played it much and because the kids from the parochial school keep at it regularly, I'm outclassed in the gym. Of course, the longer I now play with the fellows the better I get. Nonetheless, I never become good enough to start on the 100 lb. team. Whenever I can manage it, I practice by playing three-on- three pick up games in the Holy Cross schoolyard. There I learn much and improve my game considerably. But being well coordinated and having good anticipation on half court games is never going to enable me to become a full court first stringer at the F.B.C. I'm too short and too slow to guard the truly talented kids. I do, however, get to be our team's sixth man. That may not sound like much but as we're always in contention for the league championship, I think I could be a starter on just about every one of the teams we face.

The best thing about making the 100 lb. team is playing at Madison Square Garden. Between the halves of the college double headers, two Boys' Club teams take the floor and play their hearts out to entertain the spectators. Always when I play there, the arena is full. Always at least 18,000 fans watch us.

The first time I go to Madison Square Garden, I warm the bench. The next time, the coach puts me in for a half. I only touch the ball twice and do nothing spectacular. I don't even get to take a shot.

The third time that I go to the Garden, I come there determined to sink a basket. What I want above all is to hear announced over the Public Address System the immortal words, "Field Goal by Stern." I feel that if I sink a bucket, I can die happy. My life will have peaked and I'll have had my moment of glory.

On that third visit, I again remain on the bench with the other scrubs all through our first half. Because the court is at least 24 feet longer and 10 feet wider than our home court, three trips up and down court wears everyone out. When the college teams come out to retake the floor, our score is tied at 8 to 8.

Between the halves of the second college game, the coach puts me in. As soon as I touch the ball, I heave up a set shot from twenty feet out and miss.

I glance at the coach. He doesn't seem upset.

As the other team advances the ball up court I anticipate a pass and made a neat interception. Breaking immediately with me for our basket is my best friend and team mate, Ron Linxweiler. As there is but one man for the two of us to beat, I flip Linx the ball on what I assume will be a give and go with me doing the scoring. This isn't part of my pal's scenario. He's dying to hear "Field Goal by Linxweiler." So he keeps the ball. Our opponent guards him and leaves me free for a lay up. It doesn't matter.

Linx shoots. He misses. We lose the rebound and the opposition goes down court and scores.

We're down by four points and the coach has the first stringers up and set to come in on the first whistle. It's now or never time for me to seek my glory. On a poor pass we lose the ball but recover it on an errant throw by an opponent. Then lo and behold I'm open and a pass comes to me. I aim my shot to go over the front rim but my toss is wide and off target. Then a miracle occurs. The ball hits the backboard and banks in for a bucket. I'm standing atop seventh heaven. I wait for the glorious P.A. Announcement.

The horn blows for the substitutions. Then the announcement comes: "Field goal by Linxweiler."

For a moment I'm stunned. Then I run to the desk and shout "Stern.

My name's Stern. I scored the basket. Linxweiler wasn't involved. I'm Stern. I made the bucket."

"Sorry," says the announcer.

The coach and my teammates on the bench are laughing. To them the P.A. man's screw up is a riot.

The game resumes. No correction is made. Life goes on. And my moment of glory passes with 18,000 cheers for Linxweiler.

I'm heartbroken. I'm angry at the announcer, furious with the big wigs who hired him and embittered with God. There's no way this should have happened. By rights I should be entitled to a thousand dollars in compensation. But I know better than to hold my breath to wait to collect it.

At the Boys' Club, I get involved in many activities other than basketball. There's a contest going on to determine the club's Boy of the Year for each of the different age categories. I'm enrolled in the one for Intermediates (ages 11 to 13.) We're given points for taking part in different activities. For example when I make the 100 lb. basketball team, I'm awarded twenty five points. When I win the checkers tournament, I get 20 points, the runner up receives 10 and all others are given 5 for participating.

The library holds the most contests. Every Monday and every Thursday in the evening they run one. In each of these ten points is awarded to the winner and two given to each loser. The procedure followed by the librarian, Mrs. Lie, is to read a question and wait for someone to call out the right answer. Whoever manages over an hour and a half to answer the most questions correctly earns the highest score and is declared the night's winner. Often Mrs. Lie embellishes the contest by awarding as a gift to the winner any book he wants from the shelves. Because I desire to acquire a full set of Pee Wee Harris books, I enter her contests religiously. And invariably, I win. She'll ask things like "Who wrote The Vicar of Wakefield?" or "Where is Patagonia?"

With most kids she could have asked these questions in Greek and they'd have done no worse. Fortunately, because my mind always has been a storehouse for useless information, I get more of the answers than all the other kids combined.

After about a month it becomes clear that either Warren Wilson or I will be the eventual winner among the Intermediates. He's a go-getter. No matter how many points I gain by winning the contests in the Library, he gets just as many by scoring big in the afternoon activities. Because I'm delivering newspapers then, I have to pass these up. For several months the two of us have been running neck and neck. Then in February I get sick for a week. This puts me so far behind him in points, I decide to throw in the towel and forget about the contest. Besides, I've already won all of the books in the Pee Wee Harris series. That leaves me with a diminished incentive to push on. I quit going to the Library and play basketball instead.

Around the time the Allies reach the Rhine, the Director of the Club calls some of us kids into his office. Matt and I are among them. He tells us we're the winners in our age brackets for the Flatbush Boys' Club Boy of the Year Award.

"Sir," I say, "there must be a mistake. Warren Wilson and I are both Intermediates. If you've been using the contest points to figure out who deserves to be the Boy of the Year, I don't belong here."

"Yes you do, Gus. You're the Intermediate in the Flatbush Boys' Club who's to be our Boy of the Year. Because Warren led everyone, everywhere, in all the Boys' Club in the city in contest points, he's being honored as New York City's Boy of the Year. As he'll be given a special prize of a one hundred dollar war bond, he'll be ineligible for the local award. So as his runner-up you've won it. Since Matthew also was first among the Midgets, you two will probably be the only brothers in Brooklyn to be named simultaneously as Boys of the Year in a Boys' Club."

That makes me feel pretty good. I'm proud of Matt as well as of myself. I feel even better when I learn that each of us is to be awarded a royal blue baseball jacket. On the front on one side it will bear the emblem of the Flatbush Boys' Club. On the other, it will have the individual's name stitched in.

The Director ends his conference with us saying we will be presented with our awards at the Annual Dinner for the Sponsors of the Boys' Clubs on the 12th of April in the Main Ballroom of the Hotel St. George. If all goes well, there will be an orchestra in attendance and plenty of booze for the old rich people present. As they get tipsy, they undoubtedly will tell us stories of what their lives were like when they were children. We're advised to listen respectfully. Then if the evening follows the pattern of the past, these swells would be patting us on our backs and stuffing quarters and even dollars into our pockets while telling us that as long as America can keep producing kids like us, we'll always be a great nation.

When we leave the Director, I'm looking forward to the awards ceremony. It promises to be Christmas in April.

Eighth grade at my new school, P.S. 246, is proving to be a snap. We seldom learn anything new. We just review over and over everything we've been taught in the first seven grades.

One day my mother asks why I never do homework. When I tell her I do it in class, she insists that I stop doing so and pay attention to the teacher. When I protest, Gwen comes to my rescue. She says she too never was taught anything in the eighth grade as everything was review.

Gwen insists that education in the U.S.A. could be shortened by two years and become far more effective than it is at present. She says we're taught new material in grades one through five. Then in grade six to offset the criticism broadcast by the Junior High teachers that the kids can't read, write or do arithmetic, the teachers stop introducing new material and concentrate instead on reviewing the old stuff. All that this does, however, is to send the slow kid a message that paying attention and learning aren't important. Whatever he misses now, he'll be taught again later. Gwen insists that such repetition bores the bright kids and tells them school is a place where you send your mind to give it a vacation.

She then adds that because High School teachers complain about the incompetence of the kids coming out of the elementary schools, the eighth grade curriculum repeats the material covered in grades one through seven.

Although I know she is right, I'm glad no one in education listens to her or shares her view. I like not having anything new to learn. I also think the mind is as entitled as the body to rest and relaxation. Taking vacations from learning is in my opinion a good thing and deserves to be continued. Accordingly, I ask God in my prayers to see to it that at the university level the professors have plenty of complaints about the ignorance of their incoming freshmen. If so, I know I'll then be able to look forward during my last year in high school to another pleasant interlude from learning.

On April 12th, I pay Linx a buck to cover my paper route. Then Matt and I ride the subway to Borough Hall and walked the half mile or so up to the Hotel St. George. We both have been there before with Ernie who used to love to swim in the hotel's famous salt water pool.

It's a little after half past five when we enter the hotel lobby. We're early. The ballroom won't be open for a while. We take seats on separate high backed wooden chairs and wait. We both have visions of rich tycoons stuffing our pockets with money. Surely this is going to be a night I'll always remember.

After a while Matt decides to take a leak. I tell him to ask at the main desk where the john is and then go there on his own. I will save his seat.

In the lobby a little commotion is obviously going on at the main desk. There everyone seems to be agitated and murmuring. I pay them no mind. I figure someone has been charged too much on his bill and is making a dignified stink about it. People in ritzy places like the Hotel St. George have been known to do this.

Soon Matt returns. He looks excited and a little distraught. I figure he couldn't find the john and was coming to ask me for help.

I'm wrong.

"Have you heard?" he asks.

"Have I heard what?" I reply.

"Have you heard that President Roosevelt just died?"

"Where did you hear a rumor like that?"

"In the Men's Room."

"It figures," I reply as I motion to him to reclaim his seat.

"It's no rumor," he insists. "Everyone's saying it."

"It's an April fool's joke and it's eleven days late. Sit down and grow up. It's my turn to go the john. Watch my seat."

In the latrine as I leak I overhear the same rumor being discussed by the colored attendant and some grownups. So after buttoning up and washing, I go to the front desk to ask if they know anything about the President's dying. Before I have a chance to open my mouth, I see people gathered by a radio. I eavesdrop with them. The announcer is saying Mr. Roosevelt has succumbed to a stroke earlier that afternoon while he was on vacation in Warm Springs, Georgia.

I go back to my seat and apologize to Matt.

A half of an hour later as we take our seats in the ballroom the festive occasion to which we had looked forward has been forgotten. No orchestra plays. No one gets up and dances. Over two hundred people just sit in their seats and stare at each other. A pall of gloom hangs over us. It has enshrouded everyone in misery and despair.

A minister says grace. Waiters bring the food in and the meal begins.

In alternate places at our table the four F.B.C. Boys of the Year are seated. Between us are the director, Mrs. Lie and two coaches.

"This place is too solemn. We need to smile and laugh," says Matt.

Then looking slowly around the table he continues, "Will someone like my brother kindly favor us with a fart?"

The two coaches, the other boys and I laugh. Mrs. Lie manages to contain a smile. The director scowls. He tells Matt to act his age.

Matt answers, "I am acting my age. I'm a nine year old."

"Cut it out and be quiet. You're drawing attention to us. We don't want people to regard us, the representatives of Flatbush, as unpatriotic, insensitive clods."

We eat in silence. At the other tables everyone does the same. Long faces remain the uniform of the evening not only at our table but at everyone's.

The meal closes with tiny cups of coffee called demitasses. They have the consistency and flavor of sludge. After they're served some bald headed big wig from Borough Hall gets up and makes a 15 minute speech comparing the President to Moses. He claims that both had been great leaders as each had guided his people through terrible trials and tribulations. He assures us that each had brought his following from darkness and despair up to the glorious light of the promised land. He closes noting that both died a month or so short of victory.

Everyone applauds.

I utter a silent prayer to God. I call upon Him to bring on a band and end the wake. The President deserves a New Orleans style funeral. Let's have music and dancing. Let's concentrate on the good things he gave us. Rather than mourn his death let's celebrate his life. Let's give everyone something to smile, to cheer and to be happy about. Let's uncork the champagne. Let's loosen up. Let's have people tell us stories of their youth. Let's put them in the mood to plug up the pockets of the Boys of the Year with money.

As usual God turns his deaf ear to my plea.

The evening drags on in solemn silence. Everyone stays mired in misery. Some I think enjoy this. I'm not one of them.

At 9:30 Matt and I are on the subway headed home. Neither of us has picked up even a penny at the affair. Although we're unhappy and disappointed with the turn of events, we know we'd been through an evening we'll always remember.

Just before I fall asleep that night I think of President Harry Truman. I wonder if he and the men in the Cabinet and in the Congress are sitting around and moping with long faces like everyone in Brooklyn. I hope not. We have two wars to win. Our leaders and our countrymen need to stay focused on these and to leave the mourning of the old President to his widow and to his bereaved family. That, I think, is the best way to honor this great man whom we've lost.

Chapter 36
Therapy

When I get off the trolley it's barely past two thirty. My appointment with our minister, Dr. Wilson, isn't until three. I walk the two long blocks down to the church. With every step towards it my nervousness grows.

On reaching St. Charles' I enter it at the side door leading to the minister's downstairs office. I don't need eyes to know where I am. Upstairs in the church the too sweet smell of incense is, as usual, overpowering. Down here it becomes tolerable as it mixes with the aroma of the lemon oil on the furniture and forms the familiar odor that I'll always link with Sunday School.

I walk down the small hall to the minister's office. It's closed. I take a deep breath and give the door three light knocks. I wait. After a few seconds I rap again. I've been hoping for no answer so that I can turn around and head home with a clear conscience. Suddenly one room away, a door opens. A lady whom I've never seen walks out. She looks at me and says, "You must be Gregory."

I nod.

"I'm Mrs. Dudley," she continues. "Dr. Wilson is still visiting patients at the hospital. We expect him back shortly. Won't you come in and have a seat while you wait for him?"

"If it's okay, I'd rather walk around the block until he comes."

"Fine, if he arrives before you return, I'll tell him that."

Out on the street there are plenty of parked cars but little traffic. As I stroll along my nervousness shrinks. I know, however, that it will build again on the way back.

It is ridiculous for me to be here. My mother has to have been out of her mind to have arranged this meeting. While her opinion that I'm not taking my Dad's probable death well is true, it still doesn't give her grounds to make me see the minister or force him to see me.

I can't imagine him having a heart to heart talk with me about the Flatbush Boy's Club, P.S. 246 or the Dodgers. If he tries to swing the conversation his way to slip me one of his sermons about salvation or sin, well all I can say is, it isn't going to work.

I try to put the minister out of my mind. I concentrate on better stuff. I think about Marilyn. I want her to come riding down the block on her bike. Using telepathic thoughts which I've learned about on a mystery program on radio, I try to contact her. I give this my all. It doesn't work.

When I've circled the block I check in with Mrs. Dudley. The minister still is away. I re-walk the block twice before he arrives.

"Have a seat, Gus," he says as we enter his office. "Your mother tells me, you're doing fine at school."

"I'm doing okay," I agree and sit down.

He's dressed in his usual black suit. As he sits in the seat behind his desk, he's framed by the window behind him. Its light surrounds his head and gives it an aura. It has a chilling effect. He looks like Saint Count Dracula.

"You're squinting," he says.

"It's the light from the window. It's bright."

"My daughter used to tell me whenever she sat where you are at this time of day that she couldn't tell whom I looked more like: the Savior or Satan."

"I think you could pass for both too."

"It's a little stuffy in this place, don't you agree?"

I nod yes.

"Let's go for a walk," he says. As we don our coats he adds, "If I had my life to live over, I'm not sure I'd be a minister."

"It must be boring to be a minister," I say. "I'd hate it. But if you weren't one, what would you be?"

"What do you think I could be?"

"I don't know," I answer as we go outdoors, "maybe you could get a job as a public address announcer at Ebbets Field or Madison Square Garden."

"You think so?" he asks.

"Well, now that I think of it, they're rather hard jobs to get. Maybe, too hard. But I think you could make it as a barker at Coney Island."

"That's interesting," he says with a smile. "What kind of job do you hope to get when you're older?"

"I don't know yet. I've given it some thought but I can't decide. I'd like to be a Dodger but if I can't, maybe I'll become a printer like my grandfather or a mathematician or a scientist like Albert Einstein."

"You like arithmetic?"

"Not really. But it doesn't matter. My uncle, Ernie, says to be good at math you only have to be good at logic. Knowing the basic operations of adding, subtracting, multiplying and dividing is to a mathematician what spelling is to a writer. It's nice but it's not necessary to be good at it."

"I know what you mean. In college I took a minor in mathematics."

"Then what made you decide to become a minister?"

"Obstinacy and ignorance. I thought the world could be made better by my preaching. But like a lion's roar in the desert, the message I voice is seldom heard. When it is, it more often repels than attracts the listener."

"I think you have a great voice. That's why I said that you should have been a barker. I think you're living in the wrong age. People today just don't like to be preached at.

"My Uncle Doug once told me that in the days before radio and movies, a good sermon was a good show. People used to come to a service to be entertained. But nowadays, church is no more fun than a visit to the dentist."

"If you're going to have healthy teeth," he counters, "the visit to the dentist is necessary, isn't it?"

"I guess so. But still a guy doesn't have to like it."

We wander over to Eastern Parkway. It's a nice, warm Saturday and the traffic which is light because of rationing seems extra light. Every time a subway train passes beneath the street, I can hear its rumble.

"What kind of math do you like? he asks.

"I'm not sure. Geometry, I guess. I don't know much about proofs but I do know how to calculate areas and volumes." '

"Do you know the Pythagorean Theorem?"

"In a right triangle the sum of the squares of the sides is equal to the square of the hypotenuse."

"Very good."

"Ernie, my uncle, taught me that. He also showed me a picture proof of it. He told me about Pythagoras and other famous mathematicians. He even told me the theorem appears to be older than Pythagoras but his discovery of it was like Columbus's discovery of America. Others may have reached it earlier but until he found it the world didn't change."

"Do you know anything about the circle?"

"We covered it in class. It's circumference is pi times the diameter and its area is pi times the square of the radius. It has 360 degrees."

"Do you know why it has 360?"

"My teacher said probably it should be three hundred and sixty five or six. Then it would have had the same number of days as it takes for the earth to circle the sun. But as those numbers are not easily divisible, the mathematicians settled on 360."

"Three hundred and sixty is indeed a very divisible number."

"It kind of makes me think God screwed up."

"How so?" he asks.

"Well, if he had made the year three hundred and sixty days, a week could be changed to six days and there then would be sixty weeks in a year. That would mean each season could last exactly fifteen weeks and every year the same date would occur on the same day of the week."

"Did you just figure that out?"

"No I did it while I was in school."

"Oh, I see. It was part of a lesson."

No, I just figured it out on my own. I did it while the teacher was talking about something else."

"If you were doing this instead of listening, you must have missed out on the material being taught."

"I don't think so. I think you've forgotten how school operates. Any day half of each lesson repeats what was taught the day before. Then the last half is new stuff. So if you only come to school every other day, you won't miss out on anything."

"There's a lot of repetition."

"Always."

"In Latin there's a great proverb about repetition."

"I know. You're going to say, 'Repetition is the mother of learning.' My dad always quoted that. But I think repetition is the mother of boredom."

"Some repetitions are fun."

"I can't think of one."

"What about repetitions away from school?"

"You mean things we do in play?"

"That's part of it."

"Well in stick ball things like swinging aren't predictable. You can swing and miss. You can swing and hit. So when you come up to bat you're not really repeating. You're discovering. Same thing with going to the movies. You can call it repetition but still it's different. I wouldn't pay to see the same picture again. I did that a couple of times and it was boring. Not as boring as school but not much better than it either."

"What about music? Do you like to hear your favorite songs replayed?"

"I sure do."

"And what about treats--do you tire of ice cream?"

"I guess you're right. Some repetitions are great."

"I think you're right too. Predictable repetitions are seldom as much fun as ones with variations."

I've got to admit I was pleased when he said that. It has made me feel good to be walking and talking with him. He isn't writing me off as unimportant the way most adults do.

"A year is a kind of repetition, isn't it?" he goes on. "We get the same four seasons in the same order. Yet every year is different."

"I suppose so," I say.

"I think you know so. You like baseball and you know that even though the Dodgers every year are the same old Dodgers, they're still different. Rookies come up; veterans go down. Some players have improved years; others, worse. The team is rather like a tree which every spring grows new leaves and changes even though it remains the same old tree in the same old place.

"Our lives are a lot like the lives of the Dodgers and the tree. Every day we rise and go about our business in much the same manner as we did yesterday and as we will do tomorrow. We eat our three squares. We share in the troubles and joys of our families. We retire and awake at the customary hours. These repetitions give continuity to our lives. They provide us with constants, reassuring constants, into which we can root ourselves and hold fast when we're buffeted by the winds of erosion, misfortune and change. The cycles of repetition whether they be daily, monthly, yearly or generational are gracious gifts. They remind us that nature is logical and generally predictable."

He pauses in thought. Then he looks at me and smiles as he asks, "Do you follow me, Gus?"

I don't want to hurt his feelings so I lie a little and say, "I guess so."

A big grin spreads across his friendly face. "I'm sounding like I'm in the pulpit, huh?"

"A little," I agree.

"A little more than a lot," he suggests.

"Well," I return, "let's just say a lot more than a little."

He laughs and puts his great arm out and draws me to his side with a fatherly hug. "Your Dad would be proud of that line. He likes to play on words with me."

"With everyone," I add.

"What do you say we engage in one of my favorite repetitions? Let me treat you to some ice cream."

That's an offer I'm not about to turn down.

We cross over to a candy store around the corner. When I order a strawberry cone with chocolate sprinkles, he calls it a splendid choice and gets the same for himself.

Back on the street we begin retracing our steps and talking about baseball. Neither of us holds out much hope for the Dodgers.

"Backing Brooklyn," he says, "is like being against prohibition. It's the right but losing choice."

He asks me if I knew how to calculate batting and earned run averages. I tell him I've known how to do that stuff for years. He asks me if I've ever played "Interesting Numbers."

I have to admit I haven't. In fact, I tell him, I've never heard of it.

"Well, that's not surprising because I'm just now making the game up. We'll work it this way. I'll give you a number, say twenty, and you'll tell me it's interesting because in baseball it refers to..."

"How many games a good pitcher wins in a season."

"Right, now let me see. Three hundred."

"A good batting average."

"One hundred."

I'm stumped for a second or two. Then in a flash it comes. "The number of wins the best teams shoot for in a season."

"You're really good," he says. "Let me try you on some really tough ones. Fifty six."

"Joe DiMaggio's hitting streak."

"Five hundred and eleven."

"Cy Young's total wins."

I really take to this game. I'm a born whiz at it. We play for a couple of blocks and I get every question right. Then he has to stop because I've exhausted his supply of interesting numbers.

He asks me if I think there are numbers away from baseball which are interesting.

"Number seventy-seven in football," I say.

"Red Grange," he states with a smile and adds, "but I'm thinking of numbers not attached to anything. I'm seeking numbers which in and of themselves are interesting. For example, we could say four is an interesting number because it is the smallest number which is the sum of two different odd positive numbers, one and three. We could say, but we wouldn't want to say, four is interesting because most animals walk on four legs or because there are four bases in baseball. Do you follow?"

"I think I do. Twenty-one is interesting because mathematically it is the sum of one, two, three, four, five and six, and not because non-mathematically that's how old you have to be to vote."

"You've got it," he says.

Then he tells me an interesting story of a mathematician in England who went to see another mathematician in a hospital. To get there he took a taxi whose registration number was 1729.

Because he thought this was a dull, uninteresting number he hoped it would not be an unfavorable omen about the health of his friend. At the hospital he told his bed-ridden colleague of this. Without hesitation the sick mathematician remarked that 1729 was a fascinating number. He pointed out that it was the smallest number which was the sum of two cubes in two different ways:

$10^3 + 9^3 = 1729$
$1^3 + 12^3 = 1729.$

That's a nifty story. I tell Dr. Wilson that my visit with him this afternoon will never be forgotten because it now will be impossible for me not to remember 1729 as the most interesting of seemingly uninteresting numbers.

When I get that sentence out, he says I'd never have to worry about being employed because anyone, who can double talk as well as I just had, will always have a job awaiting him in Washington.

Dr. Wilson then says, "Maybe 365 and 366 are numbers similar to 1729. With a little patience, imagination and investigation they may indeed prove worthy rivals of 360, a number which no one would call uninteresting. Nonetheless, 360, I think you'll agree, has its drawbacks. Let us suppose God had made the year to be 360 days long. Then all of the things you indicated would be true. Every date and every holiday would forever be on the same day of the week. That's monotonous. That's also terrible. If you were born on a Wednesday, you'd never be off on your birthday. 360 seems to be a great number to describe something incapable of change but this virtue is also a failing. 360 lacks the fullness to allow for the variations that we meet in life. In the course of a day or a week or a year, we don't just go around in repetitive ruts. We have ups and downs. The cycles of our lives are spun on a spiral. We age and evolve and advance towards death no matter how constant our adherence is to life's repetitions. So maybe it's a good thing not to have a 360 day year. Maybe it's nice to be able to make February shorter than May. With 365 or 366 we get these things. We get repetition but also the salvation of change."

"I see your point," I say.

"Gus," he continues, "Popes, princes and presidents set up calendars. If they all agreed to institute a five day week to get

73 weeks evenly into the year, they couldn't pull it off. Every

fourth year they'd have to squeeze in that three hundred and sixty sixth day for the leap year. Wouldn't they?"

"They would," I agree.

"So perhaps, 365 and 366 may have virtues which 360 lacks."

He looks at me and waits for me to nod. I'm not ready to.

"What's the trouble?" he asks.

"I think the things you said are true. My question is why 365 and 366 instead of 359 or 361. If God has something up His sleeve and knows what He's doing, 365 and 366 would have to be interesting in some stronger way than just not being 360. They each would have to have hidden greatness like 1729."

"Maybe, they do," he says.

Without my noticing it we've arrived back at the church.

"I'll tell you what," he goes on, "why don't we both agree to do some checking of these numbers. Maybe they do have mathematically interesting properties. And then again, maybe they don't. Let's meet next week at this same time and place, and compare our findings. What do you say?"

"Great. But aren't you forgetting that I came here today to get lectured at. Maybe, you'd better do that now."

"I think we'll skip it," he says. "I'm too involved with these ideas you've given me to concentrate on lecturing. Besides, I think you've heard my voice enough today. So if you don't mind, we'll skip the formal meeting. Is that agreeable with you?"

"Sure," I say with relief.

"Good. Now if your mother asks you about our visit today, tell her the truth. Say we got involved in interesting things and we just never had time to get to the uninteresting ones."

"Okay," I agree.

"And remember to play around with 365 and 366. I suspect they have hidden mathematical virtues like 1729. I think you're just the right fellow to uncover them."

"I'll give them my best," I promise.

"I know you will. Until next week then. God bless you."

"Thanks. Until next week. And, oh yes, thanks for the cone, for the game 'interesting numbers' and for a swell time just talking. God bless you too."

Over the next few months, except for the two times when he has to be out of town and the one time he's called away for an emergency. Dr. Wilson continues to meet weekly with me on Saturday afternoons. Although we talk about lots of things, he seldom brings up religion. Nor does he bore me with stuff about being good. I'm sure he knows that I already know everything there is to be said about it.

Most of the time I spend with him is taken up with walking and talking. Our conversations never have set topics. Whatever comes into our minds we speak about and if nothing comes up we just stroll around and enjoy the day. I never once feel like I have to force the exchange. Nor, do I think, does he. Once we spend several hours on his back porch repairing, replacing and sanding floor planks. We can't discuss much. When you get busy like that the talk stays mainly on giving directions and asking for help.

Oddly enough that's one of the times we do talk religion. We also chant and sing as we labor. Dr. Wilson says that's an old trick devised by sailors to help relieve the drudgery of work. He does most of the sawing and drilling but he sees to it that I have a hand in doing everything too.

As I'm setting a plank down into place I catch my finger between it and another board. I suffer immediate pain and before I know it, I've shouted, "Ouch, God damn it!" When I realize what I've said and who I've said it before, I pull the injured finger out of my mouth and utter, "Sorry."

Dr. Wilson smiles and asks, "Do you think that when Jesus was helping Joseph with his carpentry, he ever squeezed a finger between two planks and cried out, "Ouch, God damn it?"

"I suppose not," I answer. Boy am I embarrassed.

"I wonder," he says. "What makes you think He didn't swear?"

"Are you kidding? Everyone knows Jesus was perfect. He couldn't possibly have screwed up and hurt himself. Even if the impossible happened and He did, He wouldn't have known how to say what I shouldn't have said because He didn't know English. And finally, He wouldn't swear because He'd never lose His temper."

"The reasoning is sound, Gus. There is, however, one problem."

"What's that?"

"At the Temple Jesus, the man, did get mad. He got very mad. He threw the moneychangers out."

"I hadn't thought of that. Wow, you're right."

"If Jesus as an adult could lose His temper, I see no reason why He could not lose it as a boy. I'm certain too that He had accidents like tripping and falling, bumping into things or even accidentally squeezing his finger between two planks. He couldn't very well be a perfect boy, if He didn't go through the experiences, feelings and thoughts common to every boy."

"I guess you're right," I admit.

"I'll bet that more than once Jesus let go with something equivalent to 'Ouch, God damn it' in Aramaic."

"Do you really think so?" I ask.

"Of course. Moreover, neither His earthly father nor His heavenly Father would have found His swearing to be unforgivable. When it comes to easing pain an appropriate expletive often is more effective than morphine."

"You're saying that to make me feel better. And it helps. But still I broke the commandment. I'm in for it."

"Technically, Gus, you're right. But in the spirit of Christianity, I'm sure you're already pardoned. After all, the Lord isn't a Philadelphia lawyer concerned with punishing us over technicalities. He's an understanding, kind and gracious judge. He'll forgive you. After all, that's His business."

"What's His business?"

"Forgiving. God is the J. P. Morgan of the forgiving business."

With amazed disbelief I look at him and say, "Let me get this straight. God's the J. P. Morgan of the forgiving business and the Third Commandment is a mere technicality?"

"Don't be a wise guy!" he says. Then he looks at me for a moment and breaks into laughter.

To back up a bit I really wow him at our second meeting when I prove conclusively that his theory that 365 and 366 are interesting numbers is true.

I had found 365 to be the sum of two squares two different ways and to be the sum of three squares at least four different ways. These findings enabled me to formulate the interesting equality:

$$10^2 + 11^2 + 12^2 = 13^2 + 14^2$$

As for 366, I discovered it to be the sum of successive squares from eight to eleven. But what excited me most about this number was that I could write it as the sum of six sixes with exponents in the following manner:

$$366 = 6^3 + 6^2 + 6^2 + 6^2 + 6^2 + 6^1$$

The praise that Dr. Wilson showers on me for this math warms me with pride. He's especially taken with my run of successive squares to total 365 on both the left hand and right sides of the equation above. It makes him suspect this is a special case of a more general relationship that begins with $3^2 + 4^2 = 5^2$.

At our third meeting he shows me that his suspicion was true. He devises the relationship:

$$(2k^2 + k)^2 + (2k^2 + k + 1)^2 + \ldots + (2k^2 + 2k)^2 =$$
$$(2k^2 + 2k + 1)^2 + \ldots + (2k^2 + 3k)^2 \; k = 1, 2, 3 \ldots$$

I think these equations are in their simplicity as elegant as jewels.

I had found one diamond and from it he had gathered in a whole field of precious gems.

I'm amazed. I ask him how he came up with the system. He answers a little trial and error at the start. As soon as a pattern emerges, apply a little algebra and the general equation follows with ease. He goes through this in detail with me. There's only one trouble: what's simple to him is way too complex for me. He thinks he's teaching me how to develop a few formulas. The lesson that I'm learning, however, is that my pace in mathematics will never be more than a crawl until I master algebra.

My ignorance has left me feeling disheartened. I have no trouble plugging in values for k to see how his algebraic equation works. That, indeed, is simple. But coming up with all those algebraic expressions in his equation seems way beyond me.

For a day or two afterwards I mope around avoiding math. I guess I feel like a fellow who telephones for his first date and gets rejected. He never wants to ask a girl out again. But after a while the pain of rejection diminishes and the same urge that propelled him initially to disaster propels him to try again. So it is with me in my need to pursue math. No discouragement can defeat my natural love for the subject. That week during the day at school I flunk arithmetic tests demanding that I add correctly six numbers of six digits apiece. In the evening at home, I play around with more interesting mathematics and develop the following system which is close to Dr. Wilson's in style but light years behind it in elegance:

$$4^2 + 5^2 = 1^2 + 2^2 + 6^2$$
$$7^2 + 8^2 = 2^2 + 3^2 + 10^2$$
$$10^2 + 11^2 = 3^2 + 4^2 + 14^2$$

I can see the pattern. I know that the next line has to be $13^2 + 14^2 = 4^2 + 5^2 + 18^2$. I also see that on the right hand side of these equations I can characterize the first term as the square of k and the second as the square of (k+1). The third term on the right is beyond me. On the left hand side I see the vertical columns advance by threes. I know this probably means that somewhere in the formulas for both left side terms the figure 3 has to appear. But I can't figure out how.

I think I know what St. Paul on his way to Damascus felt for while I'm riding the trolley to get to my third meeting with the minister, I, too, experience a revelation.

I hadn't been thinking about anything in particular. I certainly wasn't thinking about math. Then all of a sudden KAPOW!!! I was hit with the thought that in my system of equations the initial base term on the left is the three times table plus one.

Like Archimedes jumping out of his bathtub shouting Eureka, I cry out "Hot damn, I've got it." For instantly it is clear to me that the formula for the system is as follows:

$$(3k + 1)^2 + (3k + 2)^2 = k^2 + (k + 1)^2 + (4k + 2)^2.\ k=1, 2, 3\ldots$$

At church when I scribble down this equation and inform Dr. Wilson of my revelation, he smiles. I tell him in a scolding tone, "This is no laughing matter."

He can't contain a smile as he replies, "I understand. I really do."

"All those hours," I tell him, "all those frustrating hours of struggling and getting nowhere. They were wiped out in a flash. Suddenly and without effort, from out of nowhere the formula was before me. If I knew miracles were this easy to obtain and were open to duplication, I'd do nothing in life but ride the Nostrand Avenue trolley."

I had spoken these words with seriousness. As he began to laugh I realized how comical I sounded. I laughed too.

Then suddenly another revelation hits me. "Miracles are laughing matters," I say to him, "miracles are the greatest of all laughing matters."

Chapter 37

Changes at Home

Shortly after the death of President Roosevelt, my mother leaves the Sperry Gyroscope Corporation to take a job as a technician in the X-Ray department of St. John's Episcopal Hospital. For her this isn't an overnight decision. It's a carefully thought out deed.

By the end of August of '44 it has become clear to Mother and to everyone else except some die hard Nazis and Japs that the Allies are going to win the war. Thanks to General Patton's Third Army our forces have bolted out of Normandy and in the space of a few weeks have managed to free almost all of France.

In October in the Pacific we successfully invade and soon recapture the Philippines.

In November from the Marianas our B-29 bombers begin flying daily bombing raids over Japan.

The inevitable defeat of the Axis seems imminent.

Not everyone in the U.S.A. is overjoyed with this. Plenty of Americans are prospering. Many do not look forward to peace. For them it seems to augur a return to hard times.

In mid-September of '44 during Mom's funeral Mother tells Ernie that she's fearful of being axed at Sperry's. She foresees that as soon as the end of the war becomes certain, the big contracts given by the government to the defense industries will end. Lots of workers are going to be laid off. At her plant those who were the last hired shall be the first fired. Spelled out these are the w-o-m-e-n. Mother realizes that even if she survives the seniority cuts at the corporation, she'll still be canned in order to make work available to returning servicemen.

She doesn't need glasses to read the writing on the wall. It tells her the time has come to find work in an occupation immune to economic change and not prejudiced against members of her sex. Employment as an x-ray technician seems capable of providing her with the job security she seeks. So she asks Ernie to use his influence to help her find such work.

Of course, my uncle immediately applies himself to the task. He calls around and finds from his contacts that he can get Mother hired right away at the Kings County Hospital. He also discovers that in a few months an opening will develop at St. John's. As he knows this would be by far the better of the two jobs, he tells her to be patient and to await its offer.

Naturally, Mother follows his advice. She applies for the position at St. John's. As a church going Episcopalian bearing recommendations from Ernie and our minister, Dr. Wilson, she's a shoe-in. Moreover, since the Bishop knows her and likes her, she would be hired with or without her excellent references.

Mother's change of jobs does not please me.

As long as she has stayed on the swing shift at Sperry's, I have been able to avoid her.

Now that she begins working from eight to five, she comes home for dinner and is around all evening. Even on the nights when she's on call, relief for me from her company is sparse.

As often as not I clear out after dinner and go to the Boys' Club. But I have to be back home by eight thirty. Only on special occasions such as when I participate in a scheduled activity at the Boys' Club, am I allowed to return home at a later hour.

Sometimes she tries to engage me in conversation. She'll ask about school, my paper route or the Boys' Club. I always answer her questions politely but curtly. However much she tries to draw me out, I never find myself having anything to say. So after three or four dissatisfying minutes of interrogation, the tension between us becomes unbearable but always more so for her than for me. I ask to be excused. If she refuses to grant me this, I neither frown nor smirk. I listen to her with well-mannered patience. But at my next opportunity, I ask again to be excused.

To an outsider observing my behavior, I suspect I look like a surly brat doing his damnedest to be intentionally offensive and disrespectful to his mother. The truth, however, is the exact opposite. I'm bending over backwards not to be discourteous.

What in the Name of Heaven am I supposed to say to her? She and I have never had a relationship that wasn't strained. I can count on the fingers of one hand the full number of times that she has ever uttered a kind word to me. From the cradle onwards the most generous things I ever heard from her were commands, questions and neutral comments such as "Take out the garbage," "Did you bank thefurnace?" "Bring me my pocketbook," "Good, you finished dusting. Now go to the store," "If you're ready to apologize, you may come out from the corner," "Haven't you done yet what I asked?" "Here's twenty cents, take your brother with you to the movies."

Some kids tell me they feel warmth when they hear their mother's voice. I've never sensed anything in it but dread.

So what am I now to say to her? Am I to feed her a line worthy of a romance novel, "Mother dear, forgive me. I've been an ungrateful son. While you have faithfully executed the maternal burdens and duties laid upon you by society and the state, I've been a self-centered slob. For not tossing me hungry and bare-assed out into the cold, I bless you. Never again shall you receive from me indifference and disfavor. You'll have only my unbounded admiration, love and respect."

On a mouth full of vomit like that, I'd have choked to death.

Other than chromosomes she and I have nothing in common except discomfort in one another's company. To her I remain what I've always been: an annoyance and a burden. I'm the cross that an inconsiderate God has given her to lug like the rock of Sisyphus up to the top of Golgotha. For my part, I accept her as an oppression that I have to abide because I have no option to do otherwise.

What good can an honest conversation do us? What good can come out of her parading forth her feelings or to my confessing to having absolutely none for her. To give voice to truth would only have served to make things worse.

I feel no desire to provoke her or to hurt her. My reticence is merely my way of trying to safeguard the tiny, tenuous touch of civility that barely operates between us.

Chapter 38

The Eagle

In February of '45 while the Big Three talk strategy at Yalta, I begin my job as a newspaper boy. I go to work for the Brooklyn Eagle. I'm given a route on Ocean Avenue extending from Church Avenue to Cortelyou Road. There most of my customers are Jews. I'm happy about that. I know from carting groceries that Jews are reliable tippers.

Delivering newspapers is a decent job. It's sole drawback is that my stops are far apart inside apartment houses. Because of this and the insistence on service by the customers, I seldom finish my run in less than an hour. I would like to wing my Eagles down the halls in the general direction of the subscribers' doors. Instead, I have to place the papers on their doormats. Often to save time I avoid elevators if it's necessary to ring for them. I spend lots of energy racing up and down stairways and hurrying through halls. This unintended exercise keeps me in good shape. Still, about halfway through the route, I generally quit rushing. Time, I discover, is to my dragging ass less precious than rest.

For a week's supply of papers we carriers charge each customer a quarter and pay the Eagle nineteen cents. As my route has around sixty-five stops, my earnings with tips averages about six dollars. I should make more but often people owing me money move and leave me stranded with their bills. Invariably these chiselers are Irish. It's also true that my best tippers are Irish. There's no overlap--the swindlers are always the same ones who never tip.

My boss is a fat, thirty year old fairy named Roger Cauchy. Because he affects a lisp and fakes a French accent, he introduces himself to newly hired carriers as Me-stair Woe-zhay Coh-shee. Realizing that no one, not even a Frog, can make sense out of his slurred garbling, he hands his listener his business card as he speaks. This merely adds to the confusion. Anyone who reads the card tends to call him Mr. Cawkey or Mr. Cow-chee. We boys have dubbed him with dozens of unflattering nicknames. To his face, however, most of us call him Mr. Cauchy or Boss.

I can't stand Cauchy. Nor he, me. Our enmity, however, has nothing to do with his sexual perversion. On meeting, we just draw an instant dislike for each other.

It isn't often that such an irrational hate takes hold of me. Whenever it does, I fight it. The battle, however, is generally futile. Always at the very moment I'm sensing my unexplainable and insane dislike for someone, he's simultaneously being flooded with the same distaste for me. Only once out of the seven or eight times that this has happened to me have I found my feelings to be unjustified. That one instance occurs with Sammy Schwartz in the fifth grade. He turns out to be an okay kid. Just before we move away from P.S. 181, I tell him of the revulsion I felt for him at our first meeting and how pleased I've been to find that my feelings were uncalled for. He laughs and says I wasn't alone in experiencing such insanity and that it was all he could do not to let his ill will towards me win out.

I've noticed too that my feelings can work the other way too. Every best friend, I've ever had, I've taken to immediately. When I tell Ernie of this, he smiles and says it's probably not uncommon for most friendships like most romances to begin in an instant. He says that a physicist named de Broglie has shown that all forms of matter have distinct vibrations. Consequently, it's not unreasonable to suspect that among people some will vibrate in harmony and some, in disharmony. Emotions, according to my uncle, may have a basis in biology that only the heart and not the mind can fathom.

On the first two days that I work as a newspaper carrier, Cauchy short-counts me. Each time when I do my run of sixty two customers,

I come up three papers short. I have to go and buy street copies from a candy store and return to the route to complete it. It makes me ripping mad. The first day, I assume the boss has made an honest mistake. After the second I know better. From then on, I check the count and go out of my way to embarrass him whenever he tries to rob me.

Our delivery office is located in a store on Church Avenue near Bedford. It's just a door or two down from the remedial public school which is filled with protestant morons and parochial school drop outs and delinquents. Slim Finn, from the old neighborhood, finishes up his education there. Cauchy calls our office, Le Quartier General. One of the newsboys looks that up in a French-English Dictionary. It just means Headquarters. It's one big room with a john closeted in the rear. The furniture consists of the manager's desk and chair and two long tables on which we boys perch while we wait for the Eagle truck with the papers to arrive.

My fellow carriers are generally eighth graders and high school freshmen. Most are nice guys but as such, there's nothing noteworthy, interesting or memorable about them. Fortunately for these memoirs, there are two exceptions: John Jack Bourbaki and Jack John Bourbaki. They're twins enrolled as sophomores in the honors program for Arista students at Erasmus Hall High School.

Upon hearing their preposterous names and being told they're mathematical prodigies, I assume them to be of Hungarian descent. Indeed, they are.

Except for one twin being right handed and the other left, they are the spit and image of each other. If the cowlicks on their scalps had not forced John Jack to part his hair on the right and Jack John to part his on the left, no one--not even their mother--could tell them apart. When I meet Mrs. Bourbaki, I'm surprised by her thick French accent and amused by her penchant of calling neither son by name. She merely says "twin" and whichever boy she happens to be looking at knows it's he who should answer.

Once I ask them how they've come by their names. They laugh. Then between them they tell me the following story which I'm sure is untrue. Nonetheless, I've never quite been able to disbelieve it.

"The hard times of the Depression had hit Europe before America," says John Jack. "So our Dad decided to emigrate to America. After a two year wait and the payment of appropriate bribes he was given the green light by the U.S. government to enter America. On his way from Hungary, he stopped over in Paris to put the touch on relatives who had been living there since the end of the first World War as emigres. There Papa met Mama. Soon they were married and we were conceived. Then after borrowing even more heavily from our cousins and uncles, our parents managed after months of payments of more appropriate bribes to obtain permission for her as a French citizen to emigrate to America."

"Our family name was Bolyai," breaks in Jack John. "Our parents were Magda and Zoltan Bolyai."

"Please brother," says John Jack, "at the appropriate time and for the appropriate bribe, I'll allow you to interrupt and carry on with the tale."

Whipping out a dollar and placing it in John Jack's hand, Jack John says, "Now is the appropriate time. May I have the floor."

"Absolutely, carry on," yields John Jack while pocketing the cash.

"Just before our folks landed at Ellis Island, Mama went into labor. But somehow she managed to hold off giving birth until she was off the ship. Otherwise we could have been Norwegians.

"When Papa learned he had a son, he named me Miklos, after his brother. A few minutes later, Mama who never does things in half measure, doubled her output and gave birth to my twin, Janos."

"Everything my lying brother has said is true," interjects John Jack returning the dollar, "except that I was first and he arrived as a mere afterthought."

"Butterfly s---! But I'll let it pass, brother, the floor is now yours."

With a deferential salaam, John Jack says, "The proud parents of the two new American citizens now were returned to processing. Neither had trouble passing the physical exam. Each was as fit as a fiddle. Where they ran into a problem was at the registration desk. There their names were changed."

"I don't understand," I say, "I know that people often assume new names when they come to America. But I always thought it was through choice. How could anyone get away with changing a person's name against his will?"

He smiles and might have answered, had his brother not re-slipped him the buck and taken up the cudgel saying, "With ease. It's done all the time. Remember immigrants aren't aware of our Constitution. They know nothing about rights and everything about wrongs. As newcomers they're frightened. Many have been refugees or exiles living always on the margin of oppression. They're intimidated. America, to them, is a strange land where people speak in a strange tongue. Although many of these immigrants are literate, half write in an alphabet as undecipherable to us as ours is to them. The Ellis Island forms printed in English make no sense to a Hungarian. As far as a Magyar is concerned, everything written not in his native tongue is Greek.

"The first Americans the immigrants see at Ellis Island are uniformed officers. They're intimidating. They look, smell and behave like cops. The other non-uniformed personnel resemble Gestapo agents. As a consequence the poor, the tired and the huddled masses yearning to be free get herded and pushed about like docile cattle. When at last, they exit Ellis Island and enter the real America they have to be just as shocked by the outcome as the Jew who on his arrival in Auschwitz receives a real soap and water shower."

It's now the other twin's turn. The buck has been passed and the tale is continued by John Jack. He assumes the officious pose of a bureaucratic clerk and in a voice of rising anger he orders, "You, the

Hunyak with the bitch and twin bastards! Step forward and give us your name. Step forward. Name! Name, goddamnit!"

"Zoltan Bolyai," said Jack John getting into the act.

"Well, Sultan Bullseye, your name won't do. We'll give you a new one and make a real American of you. Joe Baldwin. That's a good name. That's what we'll call you Joe."

"Excuse please, sir. You get wrong my name. Zoltan Bolyai, sir, is whom I am."

"Look Baldwin, you'd better face facts. Americans aren't going to learn Hungarian. Hungarians are going to learn English. So Joe Baldwin's your name."

"Zhoe?"

"Yes, Joe."

"Excuse me more sir, Zhoe I can say. Ballvan, I cannot. Have you please a name easier to say."

"How about his?" said John Jack pointing as though there's a real person standing at his side. How about the last name Bourbaki?"

"Bourbaki, hokay. Bourbaki is good American name, yes?"

"It's perfect. And now your wife's name?"

"Magda."

"Magda Bourbaki, okay, I like it. And the babies?"

"Miklos and Janos."

"Hold it, hold on Joe and think. No one here can say those names. They're unAmerican. You don't want to brand your kids as dumb Hunkies for all of their lives. Give them American names. Now,tell me, are the infants boys, girls or half of each?"

"Boys."

"Well then give the boys American names like John or Jack or Joe. What do you say to John Jack Bourbaki and Jack John Bourbaki?"

"Thank you, sir."

"One last thing, Joe. Are you Catholic?"

"What?"

"Catholic. You know, the religion of rosary beads, fishes and nuns," says John Jack making the sign of the cross in imitation of the Immigration Officer whom he was impersonating.

"Oh, Catholique. Yes. Yes. We are Catholique."

"Well, then get the little bastards re-baptized. Remember Joe, John Jack and Jack John.

"Welcome to America."

I wait for them to continue but apparently the story is finished.

Both brothers looked sad and serious.

For a long time nothing is said. Then Jack John looks at me like he's about to cry and says, "Sad, isn't it?

For a moment I'm tongue-tied. They stare at me with serious concern. I look back at both just as seriously and answer, "Butterfly s---."

Everyone loves the twins. They're bright, handsome, good-natured, quick witted, irreverent and crazy. They delight in practical jokes and in sowing confusion: once when we're still in the getting acquainted stage, I guess wrongly that I'm talking to John Jack and ask by name for the whereabouts of his bother.

"Hey, I'm right here talking to you," he answers. "if its John Jack you want, he's in the jack, johning off."

Cauchy has the hots for the twins. He has no idea which is which and he doesn't care. All he wants in this life is to bugger one while being buggered by the other. The fact that he'll never know which twin is the bugger and which the buggeree only makes the fantasy more appealing and thrilling for him.

The twins enjoy tormenting the old fairy. Everyday they play crossfire while urinating in the office john. Cauchy always stops whatever he's doing to join in. Indeed, as soon as the fellows set a foot in the door, he's asking if they need to pee. One always answers yes while the other says no. Five minutes later he'll ask again and get the same result. More often than not the brother who earlier said yes is the one now saying no.

Soon the delivery truck with the papers arrives. Cauchy begins counting and distributing our copies of the Eagle to us. When all but one or two carriers has been attended to, the twins heed the call of nature and head for the john. Not wanting to miss out on the ritual, Cauchy drops what he's doing and races to the toilet too. As the three of them leak simultaneously they aim their urine to intercept each other's arc. When two streams cross paths, the pissers holler "crossfire." If all three flows collide, the twins bark and howl like wild dogs. That breaks the rest of us up and makes our boss's day.

Sometimes while everyone's focus is directed on the john, I'll finish packing my delivery bag. On the way out of the office, I'll go over to the stack of uncounted papers and swipe a few. A third of these copies I keep for myself for street sales. The rest I leave down the block in a doorway for the twins.

We don't swindle from Cauchy everyday. We do it just often enough to keep Cauchy believing that it's either the Main Office or the drivers of the delivery trucks who are short counting him. Since the twins are always the last carriers to receive their papers, they're the ones whom Cauchy has to provide with money to buy replacement copies.

There's a reason why I don't leave all of the stolen Eagles in the doorway and seek later to collect my share of the loot from the twins. Because in the original packing of the papers some get shredded or torn, the Main Office usually throws in three or four extra copies in their deliveries to the District Managers. So if I steal six, Cauchy really only has to lay out money for two or three. To profit from the thievery, we have to sell a few papers on the street.

I never clip papers from the old fag just to get an extra nickel or two. I rob him on principle. I do it to crunch his cubes and to get back at him royally for having swindled me on the first two days that I had shown up for work.

I have mixed feelings about having Cauchy as a boss. If the Paper would can him, I'd cheer. Yet at the same time I want him around. Much as I like the Bourbakis, I don't trust them. They're fun and great company but their humor is often sadistic. As long as a target as inviting as Cauchy is on hand, he stays the butt of their practical jokes and the rest of us can breathe safely. If ever we were to lose the old fag, there's no telling who'd be their new target. I would not want it to be me.

Among the less endearing and somewhat surprising traits possessed by Cauchy are his prejudices. He hates Jews and detests colored people. Now there's nothing unusual in that. In a queer, however, this attitude is rare and uncommon. Fags are usually accepting of other people's flaws. After all if you're as abnormal as a fellow without a nose, you can't very well ridicule someone with pimples. Nevertheless, Cauchy could, would and did defame the least of Christ's brethren.

Although our turnover in carriers is high and although every week at least one kid from the minorities applies for work, Cauchy never once during my stay hires a non-Christian or a negro.

On my third day of work, I make a point of checking the count of the number of papers he gives me. I won't move them off the table until I'm sure all sixty two are there.

"What zuh true bell, Stern?"

"No trouble. I'm just checking the count."

"Zare are sixty two pay pairs. Don't you trust me?"

"I trust you, Mr. Cauchy. I just don't trust your arithmetic. You obviously have learned to count at the public school around the corner. There are only 59 papers here. That's three shy of 62."

"Let me see," he demands. It's clear that my irreverent wise crack about him being educated at the remedial school has zinged him. He recounts the papers and begrudgingly hands me three more copies.

"You're not Catholique?" he utters.

I can't tell whether this is a statement or a question.

"I'm not Catholic. I'm a Christian. A real Christian--I'm a Protestant."

"You behave like a Zhew. I sink maybe you are a closet Zhew."

"If I were," I answer bussing my lips, "we'd be kissing cousins. Which Temple do you attend?"

"I am no Zhew."

"Then prove it by never short counting me on my papers again."

If at that moment a coon or a kike had come through the door seeking to be a carrier, I think the fag would have struck a blow for equal rights for all Americans and have fired me to hire him. In that proud moment, he would have overcome his prejudice.

I wouldn't have been happy about this but I wouldn't have grieved. I could always make a buck carting groceries at the A&P.

Cauchy used to go queering in Greenwich Village on Friday evenings. If on the next morning he showed up at work wearing the rag, we knew he had spent an unsuccessful night trying to get blown, buggered, jerked-off or molested. He'd snap at us and insist on silence. Maybe for half of a minute we'd comply. But sooner or later we'd crush his cubes.

Once, for example, the silence that follows his outburst is broken by one of the twins firing off a fart. When the laughter dies, Cauchy barks, "Okay,you've had your fun. Now knock eet off." Of course, not even ten seconds passes before a new barrage thunders forth. Then all morning long the salvos continue as everyone who has wind to pass does so and keeps the rest of us in stitches and tears with laughter.

We get our papers around 10 a.m. on Saturdays. However, we have to be in the office a half of an hour earlier to pay our bills. On his desk Cauchy unrolls a huge tally sheet. On it he records the daily counts of our papers and the amount of money each of us owes for the week.

One Saturday in mid-May before collecting our money he makes a speech. He tells us the Eagle will be holding a subscription contest during the first ten days in June. If during this period a carrier manages to obtain five or more new subscriptions, he'll get to go on a free trip on the fourth of July to Philadelphia. There he'll visit Independence Hall and see the Liberty Bell. Best of all he'll be taken to a double header at Shibe Park. Moreover, for getting the five subscriptions, he'll get five dollars spending money. As a further bonus the Paper will shell out an extra three bills for every new customer a boy can get beyond the first five.

"Big deal," pipes up one of the fellows, "I ain't had five new subscriptions in five months. Fat chance any of us has got of winning."

"You never can tell. You might get lewkee," Cauchy continues, "anyway if you get any new subscriptions between now and Zhune, don't turn them een till then. Give yourself a shance to ween."

Then he begins to call us one by one in alphabetical order to come over and pay our bills.

When he calls Jack John Bourbaki, each twin looks at the other as though neither is he.

Cauchy snaps, "Knock eet off. Today eet does not mattair who ees who. You both have the same number of pay-pairs thees week so you both have the same beal: twelve thirty-five."

Jack John comes forward and pays. While doing so, he glances into Cauchy's lunch bag. It has been serving as a weight to keep the tally sheet in place. The kid asks, "What are we having for lunch?"

"I'm eating schicken. Your mothair can tell you what you're having." Then turning to the other twin he says, "Your beal is also twelve thir..."

He never gets to finish the sentence for Jack John simultaneously had been announcing, "Chicken. That's a Jew food."

"Zhew food. Nevhair," says Cauchy.

"Your secret is out," returns the twin. With a grin he adds, "You devil. Here everyone's been so suckered in by your posturing as a fairy that we've all overlooked the obvious. You're a Jew."

"You're crayzee," he counters.

"Not me. You're the one who's crazy, but crazy like a fox. I see now what you've been up to."

"Stop thees now. I don't like eet."

"Of course you don't. The chicken gave you away. You're secret is out. You're unmasked at last. You're a Jew who just fakes at being a fag. Fags are pro-Jew, pro-Negro and pro every other un-Americanism."

"You're insane. Everyone eats schicken. Zhews, Catholiques, Protestants--they all eat schicken."

"True but Jews never eat the wings. They only eat the best cuts. The wings they leave for their colored maids."

"Ha," says Cauchy. He fumbles around in his lunch bag and comes out with a chicken wing. Then peeling back the roasted skin, he begins nibbling on the meat. Finally he swallows. Then in a voice bristling with righteous indignation he asks, "Now what have you to say?"

"I'll be damned," replies the twin, "I never thought I live to see the day when a Jew would violate his dietary code and eat food fit only for niggers."

We roar with laughter.

John Jack smiles playfully. It looks to me as if he's just starting in on his ball breaking. But seeing all the hate that fills Cauchy's face, he backs off. It's the sensible thing to do.

Later when we have our papers packed and are leaving for our routes, I tell the twins that I thought Cauchy's speech about holding onto subscriptions until the Contest time in June is good advice. I add that it surprises me and strikes me as out of character for him to be looking out for our interests.

John Jack smiles and says , "For a bright guy. My fellow Hunyak, you're a real asshole. If there's a contest for us, there's also one for him. If he can deliver in June his quota of subscriptions, the Eagle probably has promised him fifty bucks, a blow job from the Ballet Russe and three free feels of Elliot Roosevelt's ass."

Just before Memorial Day the twins break some sad news to us. Their parents have been offered jobs with an international organization designed to care for people made homeless by the war. Their family is leaving for Europe on the twentieth of June. The boys ask Cauchy to get them a letter from the Eagle guaranteeing them payment by the 16th of June of any bonus money they earn in the contest.

Cauchy said this isn't necessary. The paper won't go for it. They won't change their way of doing business just to please a couple of kids off the street.

The twins threaten right then and there to quit.

Not wanting to deliver the papers himself, Cauchy says there is another alternative.

"What?" asks Jack John.

"I'll guarantee it," replies Cauchy.

"In writing?"

"In writing."

"1 don't trust, you."

"Trust me," says Cauchy.

"Then read this and sign it," says Jack John whipping out and handing him a legal form that says 'Contract' at the top.

Naturally this frightens our boss. He refuses to sign it.

"Then give me back that form and take this other one to your Boss and get him to sign it on behalf of the Eagle."

They continue to haggle as I leave to deliver my papers.

The haggling between Cauchy and the twins goes on for a few days. No one signs any forms but somehow the matter is resolved. I think the Circulation Manager of the paper tells the boys and their dad that in view of their impending departure for Europe, all monies due the kids will be paid to them by the Paper by Saturday, the 16th of June at the latest.

I share Cauchy's view that the twins have raised a ruckus just to break his chops. Hell, between them they probably won't get ten new customers. So it has to be "much ado about nothing."

Cauchy tells the boys he's glad they're leaving. He calls them perpetual pains in the ass and stupid smart-alecks. Then he tops off his tirade uttering the cliche,"If you air zo smart, how come you air not reesh?"

John Jack cracks a smile and says, "Patience, Cauchy, patience. Give us time. We're only fourteen."

His brother interrupts saying, "Anyway, you've got the question backwards. You should be asking the rich why they're not smart. Only an imbecile would say to Einstein, 'If you're so smart why aren't you rich.'"

"I'd say eet to him," says Cauchy defiantly.

"Thanks for proving my point," replies John Jack.

His brother breaks back in saying, "Let me tell you about Thales, a mathematician in ancient Greece. He was asked the same question. He replied that there was no talent to making money. To prove his point, he went about cornering the market on wine presses. Then when the grapes ripened, everyone had to come to him to make wine or lose his crop. He charged a high price and became the richest man in the world. But he considered himself to be first, last and always a mathematician."

Cauchy rejoins, "If what you say ees true, eet happened centuries ago. No mathematician could do zat in zuh twentieth century. None have zuh brains."

Jack John counters by asking, "Ever hear of J. P. Morgan, the millionaire?"

"Everybody has heard of him," replies our boss.

"Well check him out. He was a mathematician. He studied at Gottingen, the greatest mathematical school in history. They wanted to keep him there on the faculty."

"Baloney, I don't believe you."

"Whether or not you do, it's still true."

"Everyone knows zuh two of you are mathematical wizards but personally I sink you'd rather be rich."

"We'll make our fortunes," says John Jack, "and we won't abandon mathematics. You'll see."

A day or two before the circulation contest ends, most of the guys have turned in only one or two new subscriptions. In our office, except for the twins, I'm high man with six. All over Brooklyn it's much the same. One or two kids in each district makes the quota. Most aren't even close.

Our office has the distinction of leading all others in acquiring new subscribers. In fact we not only lead each office individually but also we lead them all collectively. This is because each twin has enlisted over two hundred new customers.

When after the first day of canvassing each twin turns in about forty completely filled out subscription cards, Cauchy flies off the handle. He dresses the Bourbakis down saying there's nothing funny about phoniness. The contest is serious business.

Then he throws the cards back at them.

For a few seconds the brothers just glance at him. Then in a low calm voice Jack John says, "The subscriptions are real. Go check them out. And if ever again you take it into your pea sized brain to throw money away, throw away you own and not ours."

"Cut zuh bull," replies the fag.

Jack John turns to his brother and announces, "We don't have to take this s---. Let's call his boss."

"Zuh cards are phonies," says Cauchy.

"Some of the subscribers have telephone numbers. Call them. They'll verify their subscriptions."

Cauchy looks at the boys. Then he picks up the cards and sorts them into two piles: those with phones and those without.

He takes five from the stack with phones and goes across the street to call them.

In twenty minutes he returns smiling. The subscribers are for real.

Because Saturday, the sixteenth of June, is the last day of work for the Bourbakis, the brass at the Eagle informs Cauchy they'll be at our office that morning with certified checks to pay the boys the amounts due them. They also plan to hold an ice cream and cake going away party for the twins. We're told to look nice as there will be a camera man and a reporter on hand to cover the event as a story for publication.

On the day before the big occasion the twins ask Cauchy to let them pay their bills then instead of on Saturday. They advise him that with the ceremonies going on, it might be easy to fail to collect their money. They could be half way across the Atlantic before anyone would notice or remember details as small as their non-payments.

"I'd notice. I'd notice immediately," says Cauchy.

"But maybe not immediately enough. And if we had to pay to exchange currencies to pay you, rest assured we'd dock it from your bill."

"You have a point," he says as he finishes counting out the 287 papers for Jack John's route. He gets out his keys, goes to his desk and from the bottom drawer he lifts out the metal strong box in which he keeps his cash.

Cauchy opens it on the desk. It contains no cash but it does have a couple of wire cutters, a few pencils, a Waterman's ink bottle and some envelopes and paper. From another drawer he gets out his tally sheet. As piles of newspapers are on his desk, he moves to one of the long tables to review the tally sheet. There he calculates the bills for the twins. Jack John's owes $54.53 and John Jack's, $55.48. Both turn in the correct amounts, mostly in singles and fives. Everyone except Jack John watches as Cauchy counts the money. The twin goes and picks up the strong box. As he brings it to the table, it looks to me like he slips something into it. Because this doesn't make ssense, I write off what I think I've seen as an optical illusion and ignore it.

Cauchy is almost done counting the money. John Jack is begging him to hurry. He needs to leak and he wants Cauchy to take part in this, their last "crossfire." Jack John meanwhile sets the strong box down just to the right of the boss's elbow.

"Hurry," says John Jack.

"I am," says Cauchy.

Finally, realizing that the money count is right, the boss stashes the cash in the box. He closes it lock tight. Then he puts it away in the bottom desk drawer and hurries to join the twins in their last official Crossfire.

The next morning most of us are at the Eagle office when the Brass--Messrs. Lewis and Randall--arrive. They're accompanied by a reporter and a photographer and to celebrate the occasion they bring us cake and ice cream as well as napkins, paper plates and wooden spoons and forks. Half of the cake has icing in the design of a bald eagle. The other half contains the message:

Bon Voyage Bourbakis.

Soon the twins arrive. We give them a cheer: "2-4-6-8, who do we appreciate?" and sing two songs: "For he's a jolly good fellow," and "We hate to see you go."

Mr. Randall then takes the floor. He congratulates the twins on their remarkable drive in bringing into the Eagle family more new subscribers than all of the other news boys combined. He says it's obvious that two such enterprising fellows are going to enjoy successful careers as adults. Then he presents them with certified checks for enormous amounts of money and asks them what they're going to do with all that cash.

Irreverent to the end, Jack John says, "We're going to use the money to erect a statue of a pigeon in a park in Nice, France. Once it has been installed we hope everyday to see a general on horseback ride up to it and dismount and defecate on it."

Then shifting the topic the twin continues, "I want to be serious for a moment. I want everyone, especially Mr. Lewis and Mr. Randall to know that our remarkable feat of enlisting so many subscribers could not have been accomplished without the advice, counsel and help of our manager, Mr. Cauchy. To him we owe everything."

Cauchy is beaming. He speaks out thanking the lads and says it has been his pleasure to be their guide.

With the end of this ceremony, we finish off our ice cream and cake. The twins pose for pictures. There's a group one with all of us delivery boys and several others of the twins with Mr. Lewis, Mr. Randall and Cauchy.

Then it's time to attend to business.

Cauchy gets out his tally sheet and opens his strong box. He calls Leo Cardano over to pay his bill of eleven dollars and forty cents.

Leo hands him the cash. Cauchy puts it into the strong box with his left hand as he checks off the payment on the tally sheet with his right. In depositing the money on top of the cash already in the box from yesterday, Cauchy nudges some of the contents. This inadvertently exposes a small vial which catches Leo's attention.

"Holy S---!" says Leo, "Cauchy is a kike."

Everything stops. Everyone's eyes but Leo's are on Leo. His eyes are on the vial. He points to it and says, "It's a foreskin."

We figure he's kidding around, doing something like this to let the Bourbaki boys know their custom of crushing the old fag's cubes will continue as a lasting tradition.

Cauchy lifts the vial out to examine it. It has a label on it showing letters from the Hebrew alphabet. The label also contains some writing in script.

Cauchy puts the vial back in the box but Leo quickly lifts it back out. He begins reading the label as Cauchy reaches out desperately to try to get his property back: "R. Cauchy, Mazeltoff--Rabbi S. Cohen."

Then Leo holds the vial up to the light. There in a colorless solution is a piece of flesh. It has to be a foreskin.

Cauchy goes to grab the vial and says, "Okay which of you deed thees?"

Everybody laughs.

Leo hands the vial to Mr. Lewis. He examines it for a second or two and says, "Jesus Christ, I thought I had seen everything."

Then he adds in disgust, "What am I doing, holding a filthy thing like this?" He returns the vial to Cauchy.

Everyone is speechless.

"Eet's some kind of meestake," says Cauchy, "I have a foreskin."

"We know. We can see it in the bottle," says Leo.

The laughter that follows this goes on for a while.

Mr. Lewis and Mr. Randall say they have to get back to the Paper. They leave.

Cauchy shifts between despair, rage and resignation.

The papers come. We demand that he get on with the business of collecting our money and counting out our copies of the Eagle. We have better things to do that to sit around and listen to him deny the undeniable.

As I leave with my papers, the twins leave too. They walk with me down the block to the corner of Flatbush and Church.

"Before I say 'so long' to you guys, how about telling me where you got the foreskin?"

"What do you mean?" asks Jack John.

"Don't bulls--- me. I saw you put that vial in his box yesterday just before you did your crossfire routine."

Both brothers smile.

"Come on," I press, "Where did you get the foreskin?"

"It isn't a foreskin," says John Jack. "It's a piece of skin from a chicken neck turned inside out. We put it into the vial and poured some rubbing alcohol over it. The label we got from a kid in class with us at Erasmus. The hardest part of the job was trying to figure out how to spell mazeltoff.

"You really are geniuses. Where on earth did you get such idea?"

"Only God can answer that," says Jack John, "the plan just came to me in a flash when Cauchy ate the chicken wing to prove he wasn't a Jew."

At the corner we say, "Good-bye." John Jack adds, "We'll send you a card from France. Who knows, Gus, but that our paths will cross again. Meanwhile don't forget us.

"Are you kidding? Every time I see a butterfly, every time I see a chicken neck, every time I hear of a circumcision, I'll think of you two."

We shake hands and part.

A few days later the six new kids, who have taken over delivery of the five hundred papers that have been on the routes of the twins, begin coming in with hundreds of cancelled subscriptions. To determine the cause of this the Eagle sends out representatives from the Circulation Department to determine the reasons for such widespread customer dissatisfaction. This investigation is a senseless waste of time and money. The cause of the cancellations is evident to anyone who will listen to the new newsboys. Everyday they tell why their customers are dropping the paper. It's because during the contest the twins were soliciting new business by offering people a dollar to sign a subscription pledge to take delivery of the Eagle for three weeks.

The boys pointed out to the potential subscriber that it would only cost him 75 cents to take the paper for this period. So with the free dollar he could tip the carrier a nickel each week and still come out a dime ahead for the three weeks of free delivery of the newspaper.

For every dollar the twins gave away to new customers they got back three as a bonus in the contest at the Eagle.

When Mr. Lewis learns of this he's furious. He comes down to our office and in front of all of us boys he chews out Cauchy's ass. He reminds the fag that the twins had given him full credit for their soliciting techniques. He adds that he can't imagine where Cauchy had come by the brazen gall to have gloated before his bosses and his newsboys about his part in the deception.

Our manager tries to get a word in edgewise but it's to no avail. Mr. Lewis calls him a conniving kike and a homosexual thief. He finishes by giving him his two weeks notice.

"How can you call a Nazi like Cauchy a kike?" I ask.

"Shut up kid," says Mr. Lewis, "besides what makes you think he's not one."

"I think he's too stupid to be one," I answer.

As the fellows laugh, I add, "Everyone knows they've got more brains than the rest of us."

Mr. Lewis looks at me. He's about to say something. Then he changes his mind and leaves.

A few days later Mr. Lewis must have calmed down. He allows Cauchy to keep his job. No one knows why he has relented. I like to believe the twins had a hand in this. After all, what better practical-joke could the guys play on the old fag than to have him maintain his miserable job.

Chapter 39

Facts of Life

With the end of the war in Europe, I wait everyday for a telegram or a letter to come bringing us news of Dad. Reports on the radio and in newspapers tell of captured American servicemen being liberated in every occupied zone including Russian controlled Czechoslovakia. These accounts have given hope to me throughout April and May. By June, however, my despair returns. I know that the next and last thing we'll ever hear about Dad from the government will be an official notice declaring him to be dead.

Pop has trouble too coping with this. I can't tell whether he's drinking more than usual. I just notice that now when he's three sheets into the wind he's no longer the happy drunk we all knew. Now he's morose and melancholy.

Except for the booze I guess I'm a pint-sized edition of my grandfather. I stay sullen. I want to see every German on the planet rounded up and shipped in an overcrowded cattle car to a concentration camp. There, I pray, he'll be tormented, beaten, humiliated, starved and gassed to death. As a final retribution and fitting insult, I think the Allies should turn over all of the Reich to the surviving Jews and Gypsies for a homeland.

Imagining this is for me a gratifying daydream. Even though the notion is nuts and would be something I'd never allow to happen if I were God, I still delight in musing about it. I envision a special punishment for all of the soldiers in the Wehrmacht who have murdered captured Allied soldiers. I picture these Nazis running naked through a mile long gauntlet. From each side Negroes, Jews and Gypsies are casting onto the fleeing bastards small porous bags of s---. When the splattered

Krauts finish this ordeal, they are allowed to wash up--not, however, with soap and hot water but only with syphilitic whores' piss.

Usually when a fantasy this absurd captivates me, it hangs around and dominates my thoughts for months. I'll keep augmenting and embellishing it but seldom will I change its essentials. It's very much like what goes on in my mind when I'm in love. I'll daydream about my girlfriend a hundred times a day but at least ninety six of those times I'll just be doing re-runs on a few basic fantasies. When a new love enters my life, images of her displace and replace the thoughts I've had of my former flame. Except for this change of leading lady the new fantasies which I develop are much like the old. Surprisingly, I never find the repetition to be boring. My daydreams are a lot like musical recordings. They provide delight and pleasure no matter how many times they're played.

Some experts would have us believe daydreams are, at best, wastes of time and at worst, signs of insanity. It's my opinion that listening to such experts is a waste of time and a sign of insanity. Daydreams are gifts from God. They relieve us of boredom. They brighten our day. They give harmless vent to our hate. They help us to survive disappointment and misfortune. Without them who among us would be normal?

One evening around the first of July as Gram, Gwen and Matt are leaving to go to the movies. I ask to join them. I'm told that's out of the question. When I question why, Gram replies that I have to stay home in order to have a conversation with Mother. She says that it's for this reason that they're now leaving.

I can't believe my ears.

Certainly Mother has long ago sensed that I can't stand to be alone with her. Why is she now trying to force a confrontation? She knows me well enough to realize that this will be a waste of time and a futile effort. I'll never acknowledge to her my true feelings. Nor would I ever concede that our relationship is abnormal. My behavior towards her will be polite, proper and cold. She'll talk. I'll listen. Nothing will change, nothing, that is, except my hate for her. That, because it lacks a limit, can always be doubled.

With the family gone, we go into the dining room. I sit down in my usual chair. Mother wanders into the kitchen for a moment and brings back a cup of coffee for herself and a glass of soda for me. After setting these down she takes her seat at the foot of the table.

"I must talk to you about something important," she says. It's obvious from her tone that she's not comfortable.

I wait for her to continue.

"This really is difficult for me," she confesses and pauses.

I squelch a desire to ask how in blazes can you think it's less so for me?

I'm envisioning the theatrics awaiting me. In the next hour I'll be subjected to the full Sarah Bernhardt treatment: the scenes of the self-sacrificing mother and the histrionics of the misunderstood martyr and the penitent saint.

"Because your father can't do this, the job falls to me. So let me begin by asking whether you've noticed any physiological changes happening to you, particularly with regard to the opposite sex?"

Surprise and confusion sweep over me. Whatever she is driving at is a mystery to me. So after a moment or two I answer, "Physiological changes, I'm not sure what these are. I guess I'm not sure what physiological means. Isn't it a synonym for physical? Do you mean bodily changes?"

"Yes. That's exactly what I mean."

"Well," I reply, "I was four feet eleven and three-quarters and under ninety pounds the last time I was measured. Do you think I might be a five footer now?"

"No, that's not what I mean. What I'm asking is," she says and pauses. Then she repeats "What I'm asking is," and pauses again. Finally on the third repetition she gets it out. "What I'm asking is have you noticed physiological changes occurring in your privates?"

This sure as hell isn't the conversation I've been anticipating.

"I haven't started to grow hair down there yet." I acknowledge.

"Are you getting erections?"

I look at her. Is this inquisitor the same woman I've known all of my life?

"Yes," I confess.

"When?" she prods.

"Jesus, Mother, some things are private."

"When?" she persists.

"Hell, I don't know," I answer in exasperation, "the damned thing is always coming up and for no apparent reason except maybe to embarrass me. It comes up a lot at school especially when the bell is about to ring and I have to stand up. It's also stiff in the morning before I leak."

"What I want to know is does it ejaculate?"

"Does it ejaculate?"

"Yes, does it ejaculate?"

"It pees yellow and the bubbles that foam on it, I think, is the scum that makes babies in women."

Now I guess it's her turn to be nonplussed.

She gets up from the table to get a warmer cup of coffee. I down my soda.

When she returns she says, "I guess all you've learned about sex and the facts of life has come from the street."

I nod yes and think, where else? Only girls are given information about sex by their parents. Boys are never told anything.

"The process by which babies are made is not quite what you've learned on the street. Males do not pee into their mates to have children. That's disgusting."

It sure is, I agree in silence.

"When people reach the physiological stage called puberty, they become adults. They're able then to make love. When they do, the man gets an erection. As he penetrates the woman, wonderful feelings fuse through him and his partner. When the feelings reach an unimaginably joyful climax, the man's body experiences a near seizure. He ejaculates. A white milky fluid passes out of his penis and flows into the woman. It is this fluid which contains his seed. Without it he cannot become a father and a woman cannot become pregnant."

Some of this is old hat but most of it is news hot off the press. "How can I tell if I've reached puberty?" I ask.

"This comes for a boy around the time he's thirteen. A girl goes through a similar change when she's eleven or twelve. In a girl the outward indications of her development are the enlargement of her breasts and the widening of her hips. In a boy the change is evident in the deepening of his voice and in the eventual growth of hair on his face. However it's the unseen parts which tell the story."

She really has my attention. "What unseen parts?" I prod, forgetting for the moment that she's my mother.

"You'll know when you've reached puberty by the dramatic new feeling that will overcome you when the milky fluid flows out of you. Believe me, you won't have to be told that it's not urine. You'll probably experience this during a nocturnal emission. Out on the street a nocturnal emission is called a wet dream."

She then goes into further detail about everything she has broached. She particularly emphasizes the power of the feelings that sweep through people not only while they engage in sex but also while they're contemplating it. And if what she tells me is true, sex and having sex must be about the only things adults ever think about.

After an hour or so, our discussion ends.

Twilight has arrived. As it's too dark to go out and play, I go upstairs and write of the conversation in my diary. As I do, I realize that while I still hate my mother, the enmity I feel is now perhaps only a fraction of what it has been.

Chapter 40
V-J Day

"Did you hear the news about the atomic bomb?" asks Linx.

I look at my friend and lie, "Who hasn't? It's really something, isn't it?"

"Do you think it's as powerful as they claim?"

"Must be or else why wouldn't they just call it a bigger blockbuster?"

From the look that now crosses his face I can see that somehow he has seen through my bluff. This annoys me. I'm tempted to do what I always do when I'm caught in a lie: admit to nothing and bluff on. But Linx is too great a friend to deceive. So with a smile and an obvious pretense at anger, I pony up and say, "Alright, you've got me. You know I've never heard of the atomic bomb. So what is it?"

"The President says it's a single bomb that can destroy a whole city. We dropped one on a place in Japan called Hiroshima. Now it no longer exists."

"Okay," I say, "For my lying I had that one coming. Now stop jerking me off. The atomic bomb. What is it?"

"Honest Gus, it's what I said. A single bomb that destroys a city."

I have to believe he's telling me the truth. Nonetheless, it doesn't make sense. No weapon can be this powerful. Surely, this is nothing more than a ploy devised by our military to enable the Japanese to save face and surrender.

Of course, there's nothing fictitious about the atomic bomb.

What was and is amazing to me is that if after Hiroshima the Japanese were willing to surrender, why didn't they do so at once. They answered President Truman's promise of a "reign of ruin" with the same contemptuous silence that they had given to the peace proposal he had tendered to them during the Potsdam Conference.

Two days after Hiroshima, the Russians jump into the battle and invade Manchuria. The Japs fight on. The day after this we give them Nagasaki. Apparently this gets their attention. Six days later their Emperor come to his senses and capitulates.

I have no idea of where I was or what I was doing when news came of the Japanese surrender. I do remember people making noise and trying to celebrate V-J Day as they had V-E Day. However, their joy seems forced and not spontaneous. For most Americans the defeat of Japan to end World War II is an anticlimax.

After the capitulation the newsreels bring home to everyone the barbarism of our enemy. The Japs have tortured, murdered and even beheaded thousands of their prisoners. Of those servicemen who survive the terrors of Japanese incarceration, few are more than walking skeletons.

Epilogue

Mother remarries in 1946 and we move that year to Freeport. Her husband, Mike Moran, is a nice guy who seldom is sober. He's works as a grocery clerk. Mother loves him because when he wears his blue serge suit and red tie, he reminds her of her dad. He always pays her compliments and plenty of attention, especially when he wants her to go out drinking with him. It's not the best marriage but I think it's going to last for no matter how self-destructive Mike is, he's still a better husband than was my dad.

Gwen and Randy live in a small brick Cape Cod house that they brought in New Hyde Park. They have a little girl, Laura, and another child due in April. He works for Republic Aviation.

Hans and Grandma are divorced. He got to whoring around with colored women while he was in the Army. After he gave Gram a double dose of the clap, she threw the Nazi bastard out.

She now works in a beauty parlor where everyone in the clientele looks and acts like a floozy.

Pop has married Margaret, the nice Irish lady with whom he's been cohabiting ever since Mom and he broke up fourteen years ago. They still live in Flatlands on Ryder Street.

Ernie has stayed in the military but has transferred to the Air Force. He's now a flight surgeon stationed in Laon, France.

Matt is in the 7th grade at Freeport Junior High. He loves living on Long Island.

Before we moved to Freeport, I spent a year as a freshman at Erasmus Hall High School. I hated that dump. I was put in a class where everyone's surname started with an S or T and we were all taking

Spanish. Because I never did homework, the language teacher referred to me as El Estupido. (I'll forego the pleasure of repeating what I called her.) The institution had an enrollment of 6,888 students. If half were coeds, 3,400 could have been winners in a Miss Ugly pageant.

Five months after I arrived in Freeport, I achieved puberty.

A physician might attribute the tardiness of my sexual development to my small stature, (I'm almost 5 ft. 3 in. tall and weigh over 100 lbs.). He'd be wrong. Had I stayed in Tennessee or moved sooner out to Freeport, the sight of so many wholesome and gorgeous girls would long ago have set fire to my gonads.

Since I'm now blest or plagued with an insistent and almost perpetual hard on, I'm inclined to believe the Lord did me a favor in leaving me for so long in Flatbush.

My relationship with my mother remains strained. I no longer blame her for the death of my dad. Hell, I don't even hold the Germans responsible for it: Americans showed the same complicity as everyone else in kowtowing to Hitler and in allowing World War II to occur. Like Christ, my dad and every other G.I. who fell in battle died for our sins and did so to save us.

In time things should work out between Mother and me. She's given up the notion that Matt and I can be molded into images of her father. She's 34 now. All of her girlhood myths have died or are dying. While I'm sure I'm a disappointment to her, she more or less accepts me as I am.

I think I'm beginning to understand that mothers are people too. Sooner or later, whether I like it or not, I suspect that I'll accept this as something more than a fact. But right now, I'm still too bitter, angry and unforgiving to allow her a right to exist on clay feet. Whether that's because I'm a teenager or because I'm too obstinate and too myopic to see things otherwise is for the moment an unanswerable question.

CPSIA information can be obtained at www.ICGtesting.com
Printed in the USA
BVOW04s0759230114

342730BV00002B/166/P

9 781478 70298